School Stories

This edition published in 1996 for
Parragon Book Service Limited
Units 13–17 Avonbridge Industrial Estate
Atlantic Road
Avonmouth, Bristol BS11 9QD
by Diamond Books
77–85 Fulham Palace Road
Hammersmith, London W6 8JB

First edition published 1992 for Parragon
Book Service Limited

Printed and bound by Caledonian International
Book Manufacturing Ltd, Glasgow

Conditions of Sale

Elinor M. Brent-Dyer

The School at the Chalet

Jo of the Chalet School

·PARRAGON·

Contents

The School at the Chalet

First published in a single volume in hardback in 1925 by
W & R Chambers Ltd.
First published in paperback in 1967 in Armada

CHAPTER ONE

Madge Decides

"If only I knew what to do with you girls!" said Dick in worried tones.

"Oh, you needn't worry about us!" replied Madge.

"Talk sense! I'm the only man there is in the family—except Great-Uncle William; and he's not much use!"

"Jolly well he isn't! Poor dear! He's all gout and crutches." And Madge threw back her head with a merry laugh.

"Well then! I ask you!"

She got up from her seat on the settee and walked across the room to her brother. "Dear old Dick! You really mustn't worry about Joey and me. We shall be all right!"

He lifted his fair boyish head to look at her. Not pretty in the strict sense of the word, yet Madge Bettany was good to look at. She was slight to the verge of thinness, with a well-poised head covered by a mop of curly dark brown hair. Her eyes were dark brown too—the colour of old brown sherry—and were shaded by long, upcurling, black lashes. Dark eyes and hair presupposed an olive complexion, but there, Madge had deserted the tradition of the Bettany women, and her skin showed the wonderful Saxon fairness of her mother's family. Her mouth was wide, but with well-cut lips, and her slender figure was as erect as a young poplar. There was enough likeness between her and Dick, despite the disparity of colouring, to proclaim them unmistakably brother and sister. Now she slipped a hand through his arm as she announced, "I've got a plan all ready for us."

"Let's hear it," he commanded.

"Well, the best thing is to go over all the possibilities."

7

"Oh, for Heaven's sake, don't make a long story of it!" he implored.

"All right. But I want you to see my point, so——"

"That means it's something you think I shan't approve of," he said shrewdly. "Well, get on and let's hear the worst."

"You see," began his sister, balancing herself on her toes, "whatever happens, Joey and I must keep together. We are all agreed on that point. But—there's no money; or, at any rate, very little. You can't keep us on your pay; that's quite out of the question! So last night, I thought and thought after I had gone to bed; and, honestly, I think my plan's the only one possible."

"Oh, for Heaven's sake, cut all that!" groaned her brother. "What do you want to do?"

"Start a school," was the sufficiently startling reply.

"Start a school!!" He stared at her. "My good girl, that sort of thing requires capital—which we haven't got."

"Yes, I know that as well as you do!" retorted his sister. "At least, it does in England. But I wasn't thinking of England."

"My dear girl, it's an awful undertaking to run a school. And you look such a kid! Who on earth would have you as Head? And anyway, you haven't told me yet where you want your blessed school!" he protested. "You don't suggest coming out with me to India and starting there, do you?"

"No, of course not. Though, if there hadn't been Jo to consider, I might have done it. But we couldn't keep her there; and I won't leave her in England. So what I've thought of is this. D'you remember that little lake in the Austrian Tyrol where we spent the summer five years ago —Tiernsee?"

"Rather! Topping little place, right up in the mountains, 'bout an hour's train run from Innsbruck, wasn't it? You went up in a mountain railway from some rummy little town or other—I forget its name!"

"Spärtz," supplied his sister. "Yes, that's the place. It was gorgeous air up there; and you could live for next to nothing."

"Is that where you mean to have your school?"

8

She nodded. "Yes. There was a big chalet there which would be topping. It was not too far from the lake; fairly near the steamer, and yet it was away from the paths. I shouldn't want a large number, not at first at any rate—about twelve at most, and counting Joey. I should want girls from twelve to fourteen or fifteen. I would teach English subjects; Mademoiselle La Pâttre would come with us, and she would take the French and German—and the sewing too. Music we could get in Innsbruck."

She stopped and looked at Dick somewhat doubtfully at this juncture. A frown was robbing his face of half its boyishness. He knew very well that Madge had set her heart on this project, and that he had neither the strength of will nor the authority to turn her from her purpose. They were twins, and all their lives long she had been the one to plan for them both. If she had determined to start this school, nothing he could say or do could prevent her. Their only relatives besides Great-Uncle William, before mentioned, were two aunts, both married, and both with large families and small means.

"It's no use appealing to the aunts," she said. "Just consider how we are situated. We are orphans, with a sister twelve years younger than ourselves to be responsible for. Our guardian got his affairs into a frantic muddle, and then conveniently—for him! —died, leaving us to face the music. You're in the Forests, and your furlough is up in three weeks' time; Joey is delicate and shouldn't live in a wet climate; and between us we seem to have some fairly decent furniture, this house, and six thousand pounds in East India Stock at four per cent.—or something over two hundred pounds a year."

"Forty over," interjected Dick.

"We can't live on that in England," she went on, unheeding the interruption. "Even if I did get a post in a school, it would mean school-fees for Jo. But we could manage in Austria. It's healthy—Tiernsee, and it's a new idea. I know of one child I could have for the asking—Grizel Cochrane; and we'd have to advertise for the others. I don't see why we shouldn't make it pay in time."

"What about apparatus?" suggested Dick. "You'd want desks, and books, and so on, I suppose?"

"Get them in Innsbruck. My suggestion is that we sell most of the things here, keeping only what we absolutely need, and buy out there. I went over the chalet while we were there, Dick. A fortnight ago I wrote to Frau Pfeifen. Her answer came this morning. I wanted to know if the chalet was vacant, and, if it was not, if there was any other place she could recommend. It is vacant, and she thinks the owner-manager of the Kron Prinz Karl—that big hotel not far from the boat-landing—would let me have it all right."

"I wouldn't have agreed to the idea if you had consulted me," he replied. "As it is, I suppose I must say 'yes'. You'll do as you like, whether I agree or not. I know that! But you've got to promise me one thing."

"I'll see," returned his sister, cautiously. "What is it?"

"That you'll cable me at once if anything goes wrong, and that you'll write at least once a week—oftener if you can."

"All right. I agree to that. Now will you go and fetch Joey, and we'll tell her. I know she's a bit anxious about what's going to happen, but I couldn't say anything till I'd discussed it with you first of all. She's upstairs reading."

"Jo reads entirely too much," he grumbled as he went to the door. "That's one thing I hope you'll alter a little."

"She'll have plenty to take her out of doors," replied his sister serenely. "She really needs other companions. Call her, old thing."

His yell of "Joey!" resounded through the house a second later, and was answered by a shriek of "Coming!" There was the sound of flying footsteps, a thud in the hall, and then Joey, or, to give her her proper name, Josephine, fell rather than ran into the room.

Anything less like Madge and Dick it would have been hard to imagine. Her cropped black hair was so straight as almost to be described as lank, her big black eyes made the intense whiteness of her face even more startling than it need have been, and her cheeks and temples were hollow with continual ill-health. Like her brother and sister, she had been born in India; but, unlike them, had come home at the early age of seven months. The frail baby who had never known her mother or father had thriven in the soft

10

Cornish air of their home till she was four years old. Then a neglected cold had brought on an attack of pleuro-pneumonia, from which she had barely struggled back to life. Since then, her health had been a constant worry to those who had charge of her. What made things still more difficult was the fact that Miss Joey possessed at least five times as much spirit as strength, and fretted continually at the restrictions they were obliged to enforce. The exertion of her flight downstairs brought on a bad fit of coughing, and until it was over, and she was lying back on the settee, whiter than ever with exhaustion, there was no thought of telling her the news.

"I say, old lady," Dick began, "you mustn't sprint about like that!"

Jo lifted her eyes to his. "I'm sick of 'don't!'" she remarked. "Why did you call me, Dick? Anything settled about us yet?"

"I suppose so," he growled. "But just listen to me for a minute. I'm sorry you're sick of 'don't', but I think you might have a little more consideration for Madge. You know how she worries when you cough."

"Sorry, old thing!" Jo sent up a little smile at her sister. "I was so anxious to hear, I forgot about not dashing round. What are we going to do? I can see it's all fixed."

"Yes, it's fixed," replied Madge. "It's my own idea, and I hope you'll like it."

"Well, what is it?"

"Madge is going to run a school."

"Madge run a school!" Jo sat bolt upright. "*No!* She's much too young!"

"I'm twenty-four——" began Madge heatedly, when Dick interrupted her.

"You listen to me, my kid. Remember Tiernsee?"

"Rather!"

"Well, you're going there. Madge will open the school in that big chalet not far from the lake. Mademoiselle La Pâttre will come with you to look after you both, and help with the school."

"What a simply ripping idea! When are we going? Before you do, Dick? Who are the pupils?"

"Don't be silly! Of course you can't go yet! There's this

11

house and furniture to see about, and Madge will have to buy her paraphernalia in Innsbruck——"

"Dick," Madge interrupted, "I don't think there'll be much trouble about selling the house. You know, the Corah Mine people want a place for their managers to live in, and it's within quite decent distance of the mine. Don't you think they might buy it?"

"Good idea! Yes, I should think they might. It's the sort of place they want, of course. I'll take a stroll up to old Everson and get him to see it through. Since we're all going, the sooner we get the business over and quit the better."

"I'll go and see the Cochranes," decided Madge. "I know they'll be thankful to get rid of poor little Grizel. What fees shall I ask, Dick? D'you think £360 a year would be too much?"

"Sounds rather a lot," said Dick dubiously.

"It's only what most decent schools charge. I've got some prospectuses to see."

"Well, I'll get along and see old Everson while you interview the Cochranes. What are you going to do, Joey? It's too wet for you to go out," said Dick.

"I'm going back to finish *Quentin Durward*," returned Jo firmly. "You'll take all our books, won't you, Madge?"

"Most of them, anyway. But you needn't start to pack them yet. This is only March, and we shan't be going till next month at earliest."

Jo returned to her little bedroom, where a blazing fire relieved the gloom of the rainy day, and her well-beloved books awaited her.

"Best thing in the world for her," observed Dick when she had gone. "Well, I'm off to settle old Everson."

"Insist on his doing things at once, Dick. I want to get off and be settled before the summer visitors arrive at Tiernsee. He'll want us to play round till September if I know anything about lawyers, and it makes no difference really, because I've made up my mind to go. Mademoiselle will be thankful to get away from England too."

"You're sure it's all right about her coming?"

"Yes. I spoke to her a week ago, and she said if you consented, she would come."

12

"Righto! Well, so-long! Hope you get the Grizel kid!"
And with this, Dick turned and left the room, while Madge
ran upstairs to get her raincoat and hat, before she, too,
ventured out into the hurricane of wind and rain with
which March had arrived that year, to seek her first pupil
for the Chalet School.

CHAPTER TWO

Grizel

SEATED AT the old schoolroom piano, Grizel Cochrane was
diligently practising scales and exercises. She had no real
love of music; but her father insisted that she must learn;
and since she must learn, then, also, she must practise. Her
stepmother, whom Grizel hated with all the intensity of her
childish soul, had decreed that, although this was her last
day at home, the dreary hour of scales and exercises must
be done as usual.

"Thank goodness, I shall be away from all this after tomorrow," she thought. "I love Miss Bettany, and Jo is a
dear. I'm glad I'm going away from England—glad I'm
leaving them! They don't want me, and I can't endure
them!" Tears pricked at the back of her eyes at this thought,
but she resolutely drove them back. At fourteen and a half
Grizel Cochrane had realised she was decidedly an un-
wanted member of the Cochrane family. Her mother had
died when she was five. After her death, Mr. Cochrane
had sent the child to his mother's, and led a bachelor life
for the next five years. On Grizel's tenth birthday he had
married again, most unaccountably, without informing
his second wife of the fact that he had a daughter. That
she discovered when they reached home after the honey-
moon, to find Grizel awaiting them on the steps. At first,
Mrs. Cochrane insisted that the child must go to boarding-

school. Her husband calmly replied that one reason for his second marriage was that he wanted Grizel under his own roof. He also pointed out that if she were sent away at once people would talk. She desired that less than anything, so she gave way. Grizel went daily to a big high school in the neighbourhood, and, nominally at any rate, received the same care and attention as any of her friends. But life at her grandmother's had spoilt her in many ways, and before long she and her stepmother were at daggers drawn with each other. Mr. Cochrane, never a particularly loving parent, refused to interfere. By slow degrees the wilful, high-spirited child gradually became a frightened, nervous creature, who did as she was bidden with a painful readiness.

Later, she became the excuse for many "scenes", and on the day when Madge Bettany set off in the wind and rain to secure her for the Chalet School, Mr. Cochrane had at last given way, and agreed to send her away. Then the great question had been "where?" To them, considering the point, had come Madge, and with her a complete solution of the problem. It was satisfactory from all points of view. Grizel's father realised that if she were sent away with such an old friend as Madge Bettany, it would give rise to no gossip in the little town, which was beginning to conjecture at the causes for her loss of spirit. Mrs. Cochrane rejoiced in the fact that it would be sheer absurdity for her to make the long journey from Innsbruck to Cornwall for any holidays but the summer holidays. Grizel herself only wanted to get right away from her present surroundings, and Madge went home thrilling to the fact that she had gained her first pupil.

For the next fortnight or so everyone had been kept busy. Grizel found herself condemned to sitting and sewing name-tapes on to new stockings and gloves and handkerchiefs, as well as having to endure various "tryings-on". At any other time she would have resented all this intensely. Now it was, for her, just part of the joy of going away. Madge had been unable to say, at first, when they would go; but Dick, having applied for and received a month's longer furlough, bustled their old solicitor to such an extent, that the middle of April found them with house

14

and furniture sold, boxes packed, and everything ready. What was more, the Chalet School had two other pupils in prospect. Mademoiselle was bringing a little cousin, Simone Lecoutier, from Paris, and a business friend of Mr. Cochrane's, an American, had been fired with enthusiasm over the school, and had written asking Miss Bettany if she could find room for his twelve-year-old Evadne next term.

To Grizel it seemed almost impossible that it could be she who, on the morrow, would be taken up to London by her father, unusually indulgent, and there given over to Miss Bettany's charge. Madge and Jo had left their old home early in the previous week, in order to pay farewell visits to such relatives as remained to them.

"It's too good to be true!" thought Grizel ecstatically; "and that's ten o'clock, thank goodness!"

She finished off the scale of A flat melodic minor in grand style, and then shut down the lid of the piano with a bang. She had heard her stepmother go out a few minutes previously, so she ran down to the kitchen, where the cook, who adored her, and spoilt her when it was possible, welcomed her with a wide smile, and made haste to proffer a rock bun.

"Just out of the oven, Miss Grizel, love," she said.

Grizel accepted it, and, sitting on the table, munched it with good appetite.

"This time tomorrow I shan't be here," she said, when it was disposed of.

"No, lovey. It'll be the train this time tomorrow," replied the good woman in her soft, sing-song voice.

"And then Paris next day—and then Innsbruck next week!" Grizel spoke exultingly. "Oh, Cookie! I'm so thrilled, I'm so thrilled, I can't keep still!"

"Eh, it's a lot you'll be seeing, Miss Grizel. And you'll write to Cookie and tell her all about the grand sights in them furrin cities, won't you?"

"Of course I will, Cookie dear! I'll write to you as often as I can." And Grizel jumped down from her perch and, flinging her arms round Cook's neck, gave her a hearty hug. "I'll write to you every week if I can."

"There's a love! And—Miss Grizel, dearie, I was over

to Bodmin last night, and I got this for you to remember your Cookie by."

"Oh, Cookie! How dear and kind of you! Whatever can it be?"

Grizel took the narrow parcel, feeling its shape with childish curiosity before she opened it. A little scream of ecstasy broke from her as she realised what it was—a beautiful Waterman fountain pen.

"Oh, Cook! And I've always wanted one ever so!"

The tears stood in her grey eyes as she carefully examined it. Cook, looking down at the small flushed face, felt rewarded for her long tramp of the night before. and for the sacrifice of a new spring hat, which had been necessary to buy the pen.

"I've nothing to give you," said Grizel, sudden sadness in her tones.

"You'll be giving me your news, lovey—maybe a picture-postcard or two! That's all I'll be wanting from you. Now you'd better go, Miss Grizel. The mistress only went down to the butcher's, and she won't like it if she finds you here."

Grizel nodded. With a final hug and a kiss, she turned and ran upstairs to her own little room, cuddling her new possession. Some paper lay on the little dressing-table. and she "tried" the pen on it. Cook had had it filled ready. and it was a beauty- -neither too fine nor too broad. She wrote her name with a flourish several times, and then, hearing Mrs. Cochrane's step on the stairs, tucked it away into her attaché case, and screwed up the bits of paper. thrusting them into her pocket just in time. When her stepmother entered the room she was standing gazing out of the window, and whistling softly. Mrs. Cochrane frowned at her.

"Grizel! I have told you before that I will not allow whistling! Kindly obey me! As long as you are under this roof you will do as I tell you!"

Grizel obeyed. The disciplining of the past three years had taught her the value of unquestioning obedience, if it had taught her nothing else.

"You had better put on your outdoor things and come with me," went on her stepmother. "You ought to say good-bye to the Rector and Miss Fareham; and I have to

16

go to the Rectory. Hurry up now, and brush your hair, and be downstairs in ten minutes' time."

She left the room, and Grizel did as she was bidden; but all the time that she was putting on the new blue travelling coat, and changing into her outdoor shoes, she was murmuring softly to herself, "Only today left! Only just today! Tomorrow will soon be here now."

Walking demurely at her stepmother's side, she went down the garden-path, which was already bordered with wallflowers and tulips, gaily a-nod in the spring breeze, and out into the street, where they met two of the girls from her old school.

"You will want to say 'good-bye' to your friends," said Mrs. Cochrane graciously—she was always gracious in public. "I will wait for you at the Rectory; but don't be long, as there are still one or two things I want to do."

She passed on, and Grizel was left with them.

"It's tomorrow you go, Grizel, isn't it?" said the elder of the two, a pretty fair child of fourteen, Rosalie Dene by name. "Aren't you sorry to leave home?"

Hitherto Grizel's pride had kept her from making any revelations about home matters. Now, somehow, it didn't seem to matter. She would not come home for more than a year, for she was to stay with the Bettanys all the summer.

"Sorry?" she said fervently. "I'm not sorry; I'm glad— glad, I tell you!"

"Grizel!" gasped Rosalie. "Glad to leave home and go right away!"

"'Tisn't like your home," replied Grizel sombrely. "You've a mother!"

"Well, but you have Mrs. Cochrane, and I'm sure she's awfully sweet to you."

"Yes, when there's anyone there to see it," replied Grizel recklessly.

The two schoolgirls stood in horrified silence. They didn't know what to say.

Grizel broke the spell. She held out her hand.

"I must be going," she said briefly. "Good-bye. Write to me sometimes."

"Good-bye," said Rosalie flatly. "Of course I'll write if you will."

"I'll send you some postcards," responded Grizel. "Good-bye, Mary!"

Mary, the other child, mumbled something in farewell, and then Grizel ran off, leaving them still staring after her.

"Well!" ejaculated Rosalie at last. "Did you ever?"

"Never!" replied Mary with finality. "I didn't think Grizel Cochrane was like that!"

"I wonder what mother will say," said Rosalie thoughtfully.

What Mrs. Dene actually said when she heard her daughter's story was, "Poor little dear! I hope she will be happy in Austria, then."

Meanwhile, Grizel hurried to the Rectory, where her stepmother was waiting for her, and took leave of the Rector and his sister, both of whom were fond of her. They had farewell gifts for her too, in the shape of a new Kipling and a big box of chocolates, and she said "good-bye" to them with real regret. They had always been kind to her.

After the Rectory visit, Mrs. Cochrane took her into the town to do some shopping, and it seemed to the little girl that never before had they met so many acquaintances in one morning. Everyone was very kind, and wished her good luck and a pleasant journey. One or two told her that they envied her her visit to foreign countries, and most people begged for postcards. Grizel promised them to all and sundry, and all the time her heart was beating madly with delight to think that this was the last time for many a long month that she would be here. Then they went home to lunch, and after it was over, her stepmother dismissed her to the moors, where she ran about like a wild thing till the little silver watch on her wrist warned her that it was nearly tea-time, and she had better be turning homewards. Her father came in for tea, and brought with him a folding Brownie Kodak in a neat leather case with a strap to sling across her shoulders. The general atmosphere of kindness seemed to have infected even Mrs. Cochrane, and so that last evening passed off well. The next day Mr. Cochrane took her up to town, and gave her into Madge Bettany's charge at Victoria.

CHAPTER THREE

The Joys of Paris

"RIEN A DECLARER?"

"Rien à declarer!" replied Madge firmly, with one eye
on her two charges. The custom-house official grunted as
he chalked the mark on the three suitcases, which was all
the luggage they had with them, Mademoiselle La Pâttre
and Dick having gone out to Tiernsee early in the previous
week with the trunks and cases of books, ornaments and
pictures, which were all they were taking with them from
England. Experienced Joey promptly helped to fasten the
cases again, while Grizel, flushed and excited, gazed round
her, wonder in her big grey eyes. She had never been out
of England in her life before, so even the draughty,
prosaic *douane* of Boulogne, where everyone had to go in
queue with their cases, was invested with a certain pleasure
glamour for her. The hoarse voices of the *douaniers,* the
clamour of their fellow-passengers, the unusual trains with
their funny, high engines, and little steps up into the
carriages, were all fresh and new to her. Madge cast an
amused glance at her absorbed face as they settled down in
their second-class carriage. The only other occupant was a
little fat man in a loud check suit. He was mopping his
face with a white handkerchief adorned with scarlet spots.

"Eh, it's 'ot," he said, his accent at once betraying him
for a Yorkshire man. " 'Ot for this time o' t'year it is."

Madge was always interested in people, so instead of
snubbing the good-hearted little man's advances with frosty
good breeding, she answered him pleasantly. He had had
little education, as was evident, but he felt a kindly, if
curious, interest in the trio in his carriage, and when, a
little later, they produced sandwiches and milk, he van-

ished, to return with some magnificent gooseberries, which he begged them to share with him. Again, Grizel looked for the icily polite snub her stepmother would have given him. Madge only thanked him for his kindness with the direct simplicity which was so much a part of her charm, and offered him sandwiches in return.

Over their meal they became quite friendly, and, before they reached Paris, he had found out that she proposed running a school in the Tyrol. He commended the scheme, and offered to try to find her pupils among his customers— he was a wool manufacturer from Bradford, as it turned out. They were quite sorry to say "good-bye" to him when they reached Paris; but he was going on to Lyons that night, and they were to spend the next two or three days in the gayest city in the world. It was five o'clock—or seventeen, if you cared to take French time—by the time they had arrived, and both Jo and Grizel were tired, so Madge made no attempt to do anything that night. They went to their hotel, a quiet one, not far from the Madeleine, and after having arranged for the remainder of the week, they were shown to their rooms, where *thé à l'Anglais* was sent up. They all woke early next morning, and after *petit déjeuner* of coffee and rolls, prepared to go out. Naturally, since they were so near, the Madeleine was their first objective. Jo had seen it before, but she was perfectly willing to visit the great church which Napoleon had begun as a "Temple of Glory". and which he was destined never to finish. Grizel looked at it with wonder in her face.

"Somehow, I didn't think Napoleon was a religious man," she observed thoughtfully. "Whatever made him want to build a church?"

"He wasn't; and he didn't," explained Madge. "I forget what his idea was, but it certainly wasn't the idea of the average man. But then he wasn't an average man, of course! Anyway, it's rather a wonderful thing, isn't it? Not to be compared with Notre Dame, of course!"

"Is he buried here?" asked Grizel.

"No, in the Invalides," replied Jo, who was an enthusiastic admirer of the great Emperor.

"Well, I think we've seen everything here, so we may as well go to the Champs-Elysées," said Madge. "We'll take a bus there. Then we'll go up it a little way, and get another bus to the Pont Alexandre. From there, it's easy to get to the Invalides. We'll have *déjeuner*, and after that, we go to the Louvre by the Métro."

"And the opera tonight," supplemented Joey. "Oh, topping! "

Madge nodded. Mr. Cochrane had given her an additional cheque, with the request that she would take Grizel about as much as possible. He was not a devoted father, but some strange feeling of regret that he meant so little to his only child had prompted him to do this.

"Children always enjoy that sort of thing better when someone of their own age is with them," he had said. "Please include Miss Joey in the party."

"Are we really going to the opera?" asked Grizel incredulously.

"Yes. It's *La Bohême* tonight. I don't know how much of it you'll understand, but the music is lovely," replied Madge, as they boarded a bus. "Look out of the window, Grizel. We're coming to the Place de la Concorde, where the guillotine stood during the Reign of Terror."

Joey, the insatiable reader, murmured softly, "Sydney Carton!" But Grizel's knowledge of the French Revolution was confined to that gained from the *Scarlet Pimpernel* stories, and when, as they reached the famous space, the younger girl softly quoted the closing sentences from *A Tale of Two Cities*, she paid no heed. The Champs-Elysées pleased her far more with their bustle and life. Madge chuckled softly to herself as she walked between them. The outlook of the two children was so totally different. Joey always saw Paris through a rose-mist of history and legend; Grizel, now that her first wonder was over, so obviously took all that side of it for granted; and devoted herself to its life and people.

After Les Invalides, they had *déjeuner* at one of the many restaurants, and then took the Métro to the Louvre. The opera was an entire success. True, neither of the girls understood much of the story, but the exquisite music appealed to both, and even matter-of-fact Grizel felt a lump come into her throat when Mimi died. The next day was

21

devoted to a trip up the river to St. Cloud and Sèvres, which pleased Miss Cochrane far more than the Louvre.

"I like to see things done," she explained to Joey. "Of course, pictures and statues are all right, but they're not half so interesting as seeing people do things now. And I think St. Cloud is awfully jolly! I wish we'd been able to go up the Eiffel Tower, though."

"You've done quite enough for today," declared Madge, with an anxious eye on Joey's white face. "Tomorrow we'll go out to Versailles, and then on Monday we must be getting on."

On the next day they went to Versailles, and spent long, happy hours wandering about that magnificent extravagance of Louis XIV. The gardens filled them with admiration, and Grizel thrilled at seeing the Hall of Mirrors, where the Peace Treaty had ended the Great War. From there, they went on to the Trianons, with their dainty artificiality, where poor Marie Antoinette and her court ladies had played at being milkmaids and shepherdesses clad in flowered silks, while, less than twenty miles away, the Paris mob was beginning to cry aloud for bread. The whole place was peopled with gay, exquisite ghosts for both Madge and Jo, and even Grizel became infected by them, and half expected to see some hooped and powdered lady, with raised fan and brilliant eyes, beckon to her from behind one of the statues. Madge was wise enough to take them back early, after they had seen the famous fountains playing, and the next day was spent in visiting Notre Dame and looking at the shops.

Grizel was anxious to buy nearly everything she saw, but Madge kept a tight rein on her. She would only allow her to change a little of her money into francs, and then she insisted that choice must be carefully made. Finally, at the Louvre a lace collar was chosen for Cook; several postcards were bought and sent off; then, at Jo's suggestion, they went to the Luxembourg Gardens, which lay bathed in April sunshine. Grizel was deeply interested in the French children who romped about there, carefully watched by mothers and nurses. The *carrousel*, with its lions and elephants, and gay little hurdy-gurdy, took her fancy completely, and she insisted on having several 'goes,' rather to the amusement of Jo, who strayed off to the fountain, where sailing bare-legged and crop-haired small boys were sailing their boats to a general chorus of, 'Quel est beau!' 'Ah, mon Dieu!' 'C'est bien que possible!' 'Voleur! 'C'est le mien!' And, more than once, 'Fermes le bec, toi!'

Here Madge and Grizel found her when they came a little later, haranguing two small, bewildered-looking boys in a polyglot mixture of French and English.

Grizel laughed, "Oh, Joey, I think it's lovely! I caught the ring five times, and the man said it was superb!"

"Well, now let's have *déjeuner*," suggested Madge. "I'm hungry, if you aren't."

Déjeuner over, they strolled along to the Champs-Elysées, and joined in the merry throng round "Guignol", which is a French version of Punch and Judy. Tea they had at a *pâtisserie*, where Grizel rejoiced once more in the delightful custom which ordains that each customer shall take a plate and fork to the counter and help himself to delicious sandwiches and cakes before settling down.

"So much more sensible than English shops," she said. "They always bring the things you don't want——"

"Like horrid spongy cakes with butter-icing!" chimed in Jo. "I loathe them! Now éclairs, I could go on eating for ever!"

"And beautifully sick you would be," said Madge firmly. "No, you don't, Joey, my child! Remember, our train leaves at nine. Finished? Le comptoir, s'il vous plaît." This last to the pretty waitress who stood near. After that, they returned to their hotel to pack up and have dinner, and half-past eight saw them at the Gare de l'Est, climbing into the Paris-Wien train express.

"Here start our Austrian adventures," observed Jo, as she curled herself up comfortably in a corner. "You can't count Paris!"

"Can't you? I do!" replied Grizel. "It's all been absolutely thrilling, so far!"

"Go to sleep and don't talk," ordered Miss Bettany. "We shall be in Switzerland, I hope, when you wake tomorrow."

"Switzerland?" Grizel sat bolt upright in her excitement.

"Yes; we reach Basle about six in the morning. Now, be quiet! "

And she refused to say another word or to let them talk, so they subsided, and before long all three were fast asleep, while the great train hurled onwards through the darkness.

CHAPTER FOUR

Austria at Last!

IT WAS HALF-PAST SEVEN on the Wednesday evening when the Vienna express slackened speed before entering the Innsbruck Station. By this time Grizel was weary of the train, while Jo's tongue had long ceased wagging, and she lay in her corner of the carriage gazing dreamily out at the darkening landscape.

"We're only an hour late," observed Madge, as she collected their belongings together. "We've missed the last train of the mountain railway, so we'll have to go to an hotel somewhere for the night."

"I shan't be sorry," replied Grizel decidedly. "Will Mr. Bettany meet us, or shall we have to fish for ourselves?"

"Dick will meet us all right," said Jo, rousing herself up to answer this question. "Where shall we put up, Madge—at the Europe?"

"I suppose so," replied her sister. "Or there's the Kreide, only it's farther away."

"I hope it's somewhere near," returned Jo wearily. "I should like to have a bath and go to bed! Hello, we're slackening!"

"There's Dick!" exclaimed Madge, as she hung out of the window. But Dick had seen her, and was already running along by the side of the carriage, shouting a cheery greeting to them.

"Shove the cases through the window!" he called, as the train stopped. "Bustle the kids out! I've got a porter here! Rooms booked at the Europe!"

Dick was an experienced traveller, and both he and Madge spoke German fluently, so they were soon past the barrier and out into the big square, where carriages intended for two horses, but drawn by one only, were waiting for hire, while the coachmen, picturesque enough figures in their short open jackets, full shirts, and little green Tyrolese hats with the inevitable feather at the back, leaned up against the wheels, shouting chaff to each other, or smoking their long china-bowled pipes. Beyond, they could see the great snow-capped mountains towering up in all sides, while round them thronged tow-headed, grey-eyed children, begging for *Krönen* with a persistence which suddenly died away as Dick addressed them with a ready flow of language.

"Awful little beggars!" he said as they dispersed. "They're nearly as bad as the natives at Port Said. Tired, Grizel? Here's our hotel; nice and handy for the station, you see!"

"Is everything all right at the Chalet?" asked Madge, as they entered the big hotel. "Has Mademoiselle's cousin arrived? I've got another pupil—an American called Evadne Lannis. She's coming in September."

"Good for you," replied her brother. "Yes, everything's all right, and the kid—Simone, her name is—arrived Friday of last week. Mademoiselle stayed down here till today, and sent up the things by rail. I got the place scrubbed out, and dear old Frau Pfeifen came along, and her eldest girl, and we've got it quite ship-shape. There's a big room they had built on for a *Speisesaal*, and we've turned that into a classroom. I knocked up some shelves, and we've got the books up. Two little rooms we've given to you and Mademoiselle, and a huge loft affair we've put the kids' beds in. It holds eight easily, so you'd better buck up and get four

25

more. There's a landing-stage just opposite, and the water's quite shallow. Old Braun at the Kron Prinz Karl says you can bathe from there in the summer. Now I'll get your keys, and then you can go and beautify yourselves while I order some food for you. Come down to the *Speisesaal* when you are ready."

"What's a *Speisesaal*?" asked Grizel, as they went up in the lift.

"It's German for dining-room," explained Madge. "Here we are! Now buck up, you two, and make yourselves tidy, and then come and tap at my door."

They hastened joyously, and in a marvellously short time they were ready.

Then they went down to the *Speisesaal*, where they found Dick and a delightful meal awaiting them, together with a most obsequious waiter.

"Nothing really exciting," said Dick. "Only *Kalbsbraten*—all right, Grizel! That's German for roast veal! and *Kartoffeln*, otherwise spuds, and *Apfelntorte*, which isn't apple-tart, although it sounds like it."

"What is it, then?" Grizel wanted to know.

"Sort of cake with cooked apples on it," said Jo swiftly. "Oh, it is nice to have the funny things again! I think foreign food is much more interesting than English! Must we really go to bed after supper? I don't want to in the least."

"It'll be nine o'clock before you're settled," retorted her brother. "You can trot round Innsbruck tomorrow if you're so keen! It won't run away in the night, you know."

"When do we go up to Tiernsee?" asked Grizel.

"Not till the half-past seven train tomorrow evening," replied Madge. "There are one or two things I want to get, and you really must see a little of Innsbruck while you are here. We will go to the Ferdinandeum Museum and the Hof Kirche, and you must see the old house with the golden roof."

"Is it really gold?" asked Grizel in awestruck tones.

"Oh dear no! And it is really just the roof of the balcony to a window. But it's very famous, and you ought to see it."

"Then there's the Mariatheresien Strasse with its swagger shops," chimed in Dick, "and the great Triumphal Arch. And you must go down and have a look at the Inn. You'll have plenty to do tomorrow, I can assure you. I'll go up during the morning, Madge, and take the cases, then you and the kids can come on later."

Everyone agreed to this programme, and Jo and Grizel went off to bed quite happily, while their elders took a stroll up to the little station, where the electric railway, which is known as the Stubai Bahn, begins.

"You ought to take the kids up here some day," observed Dick.

"Some day," agreed Madge; "but do remember that I'm here to start a school in the first place!"

"Geography," he said shortly, with a twinkle in his eye. "You might make a week-end expedition of it in the summer and take them to the edges of the Stubai Glacier. You could get rooms in Fulpmes, and the Stubai valley is lovely."

"I know," said Madge, sighing. "It all is! But oh, Dick! Supposing it isn't a success! Supposing I fail!"

"Tosh!" he said easily. "You won't fail! You've too much grit for that. Other people might; but you'll go on! Buck up, old thing!"

"But I'm so young," she said—"only twenty-four, Dick!"

He gave her arm a reassuring squeeze.

"You'll pull through all right! Keep your hair on, old girl! We'd better be getting back now. You're tired, and ought to be in bed."

"Yes, I am," acknowledged Madge. "Oh, Dick, I shall be so thankful to get to our own house! I must say it sounds attractive. What is little Simone like?"

"Didn't see much of her," he replied. "She struck me as jolly quiet. Very dark, of course; not a bit pretty like that Grizel kid."

"Yes, Grizel will be lovely when she's grown up," said his sister. "I should think she's clever, too. Oh, Dick, she and Jo were too funny for anything in Paris! Joey was dreaming it all into history, and Grizel is so absolutely matter of fact. She simply couldn't understand Joey and her dream-pictures."

"Jolly good job," said Dick austerely. "Jo dreams far too much."

"Well, she hasn't had much chance to do anything else," replied Madge. "Perhaps Grizel and Simone, and Evadne when she comes, will make her different."

"Oh, she'll be better in the mountains," was his answer. "Half the trouble has been her health. She's better already, I think, even though she's tired."

"It can rain at Tiernsee," Madge reminded him.

"I know that. But she'll have companions of her own age. And don't you worry, my chicken! Everything's going grandly! "

With this assurance the subject was dropped, and presently they reached the hotel, and Madge retired to bed.

The next day was spent in shopping and sight-seeing. Dick left them early in the day, and went up to Tiernsee with the cases and the rugs, while the three girls explored the city to their hearts' content. Grizel, quick to learn, was already picking up phrases in German, and she took the greatest delight in practising them. Jo, whose German had been fluent in the past, found it coming back to her, even as her French had begun to do in Paris. She instructed her friend as they went about, and eventually poured so much information into her, that it was small wonder that Grizel became muddled. The result was a mistake that the Bettanys remembered against her for long enough.

Madge had decided to take both children to have their hair shampooed before going up to the lake. She remembered, from their last sojourn in the Tyrol, a very good hairdresser's shop in the Museum Strasse, and thither she took them. The hairdresser had a little English, but not much. When the shampooing was over, he asked them whether the final rinsing should be of hot or cold water. The German for "hot water" is *"heisses Wasser"*. Jo came through the ordeal all right, demanding a lukewarm rinsing for the last. Not so Grizel. She forgot what the German for "cold" was, but remembered, as she imagined, the word for "hot". The temptation to exhibit her knowledge of his language was too great to be resisted, and she reduced the man to horrified silence, and the Bettany girls to helpless laughter, by boldly demanding "*heiliges Wasser*".

It was the expression of outrage on Herr Alphen's face as much as anything that rendered it impossible for Madge to do anything but choke wildly; while he himself, a most devout Catholic, decided that this was only one more example of the madness of the English. It struck him as profane in the extreme that anyone should demand to have her hair rinsed with holy water. Still, doubtless these poor creatures knew no better. With a resigned expression and outspread hands, he carefully explained that it was impossible to give her what she asked. He assured her, however, that he would put some of his very best toilet preparations into what was used if she would only say whether she would have it hot or cold, or, like the other Fräulein, lukewarm.

Of all this harangue, which was poured forth at top speed, Grizel understood not one word. Finally Madge, choking back her laughter with great difficulty, came to the rescue, and the shampoo was finished.

"But I don't see what there was to giggle at," observed Grizel to Joey when they had finally left the shop. "And why did that man get so fussy when I asked for hot rinsing water? Did he think I should catch cold after it? I wanted a cold rinse, as a matter of fact, but I couldn't remember the word for it, so I asked for hot."

"That's just what you didn't do," Joey informed her solemnly. "You've shocked poor Herr Alphen most horribly, and I'm not surprised! I only wonder he finished you at all! "

"But why? What did I do?" demanded the bewildered Grizel.

"Oh, you only asked for a final rinsing of holy water! And he a Catholic—at least I suppose so! "

"But I only said what you told me," protested Grizel.

"They're rather alike in sound," admitted Joey. "The beginnings are the same anyhow. I wonder if he's got over it yet?"

At first, Grizel was inclined to accuse her friend of pulling her leg, but when she finally realised that the mistake was her own, she cheerfully joined in the laugh against herself.

"Well, anyhow, that's one thing I shan't forget," she said, as they made their way to the station. "I couldn't if I tried after that!"

"I don't believe you could," agreed Jo—Madge was buying their tickets to Spärtz. "If you'd insisted, I wonder if he would have tried to get some for you! They're awfully obliging here, you know. Hullo, Madge! Got them all right? Doesn't it feel grand to count in hundreds and thousands?"

"No, rather a nuisance," replied her sister. "Now come along. Our train is over here. Have you got those books safe, Joey?"

The journey from Innsbruck to Spärtz is of no particular interest, but the little mountain railway, which carries you up to a height of three thousand feet and more above the sea-level, is something to remember. Higher and higher they climbed, now and then stopping at a tiny wayside station, till at last they reached the great Alp, or rather Alm, as they are called in the Tyrol, and there before them, dark, beautiful, and clear as a mirror, spread the Tiernsee, with its three tiny hamlets and two little villages round its shores, and towering round on all sides the mighty limestone crags and peaks of the mountains.

The railway terminus is known as Seespitz, and here the steamer was waiting for the passengers. Dick was there too, ready to help with the parcels.

"It's a jolly walk round the lake," he said, "but tonight I think we'll take the steamer. It's about a quarter of a mile nearer from the Briesau landing-stage than it is from here, and I know you're all tired."

The little steamer waited ten minutes, then her whistle blew, and off she went—first to Buchau at the opposite side of the lake, and then to Briesau, where they were welcomed by good Frau Pfeifen, who almost wept for joy at beholding Madge and Joey once more. From the landing-stage to the Chalet was a good ten minutes' walk, and then they saw the welcoming lights, and heard Mademoiselle's warm French greeting. They were at the Chalet School at last.

CHAPTER FIVE

The Chalet School Opens

BY DEGREES they settled down in the Chalet. The end of April found them ready to begin work. The huge room, which had been built to accommodate eighty people at meals, had been partitioned off into two good-sized class-rooms. A third next to them had been made of a small room which had been used as a lounge. Another one, on the opposite side of the door, had been turned into a sitting-room, sacred to Madge and Mademoiselle. There were no carpets on the floors, but they were brought to a fine polish with beeswax and hard rubbing. The furniture, with the exception of the schoolroom appointments, was all old. There was but little as yet; Miss Bettany intended buying here and there, and having it as good as might be. In the long kitchen at the back of the house Marie Pfeifen reigned, with a younger sister and a cousin to help her, while Brother Hans cleaned shoes and knives, and attended to the huge porcelain stoves which warmed the place throughout.

Dick Bettany's furlough was up on 29th April, and he had to say "good-bye" to them, before getting the Paris express, since he intended joining the boat at Marseilles. Actual schoolwork would start on the following Monday, and Madge was very thrilled over that, for, in addition to Joey, Grizel, and Simone, she had four day-pupils whose parents lived round about. So they would begin with a very fair number.

Joey and Grizel were just as thrilled as she was. Simone, though quite nice, was very shy and quiet.

So, when Monday came, they were all agog to meet the strangers.

School began at nine-thirty, when a little body of school-girls were to be seen coming along the lake road, carrying books and chattering.

"There they are!" cried Joey from her vantage-point at the window. Then a minute later, in amazed tones, she added, "I thought Madge—my sister, I mean—said there were only four!"

"So she did," replied Grizel, joining her.

"Well, there's six there anyhow, and one's quite a tiny one!"

"Let's go down and meet them," suggested Grizel.

"Good scheme! Come along, Simone!"

"Hello!" she said, holding out her hand in welcome, "I'm Jo Bettany, and I know you are coming to the Chalet School. Do tell me your names, won't you? And why, there's six of you, when we only expected four."

One, who was obviously the eldest, came forward and took Jo's hand.

"How do you do?" she said in careful English. "You are Fräulein Bettany's sister, are you not? I am Gisela Marani, and these are Gertrud Steinbrücke, Bernhilda and Frieda Mensch, Bette Rincini, and my younger sister Maria."

"These are Grizel Cochrane and Simone Lecoutier," said Joey.

The two Maranis and Bette Rincini were slight, graceful girls; Gisela and Maria very dark; Bette, brown, with wavy brown hair, brown eyes, and a warm brown skin. Gertrud was brown-haired, grey-eyed, and very pretty, and the two Mensches were of the fair German type. They were all between the ages of twelve and sixteen, with the exception of Maria, who was obviously not more than nine. Seeing Jo's eyes fasten on her small sister, Gisela apologetically explained her presence amongst them, and also Gertrud's.

"Mamma thought that perhaps Fräulein—ah, but you say 'Mees', do you not?—Bettany would be so kind as to permit Maria to come also. She is younger than we are, but it would be dull for her at home, and she is clever. And Frau Steinbrücke has long wanted to send Gertrud to an English school, so she is with us, and her mother will come herself to explain."

"Well, come in and take your things off," said Joey, wondering to herself how Madge would take it. "This way in. This is our cloakroom. Have you brought slippers to change? Righto! We shan't do much in the way of lessons today, you know! Just get to know what we know, and about books, and so on. You're the oldest, aren't you, Gisela?"

"Yes, I have sixteen years," replied Gisela, "and Bernhilda is next."

Bernhilda smiled at Joey, but she was obviously too shy to say anything just at present. She and Frieda rather reminded Joey of two dolls with their fair hair, blue eyes, and rosy faces. She knew, because Madge had told her, that Bernhilda was fifteen and Frieda twelve. Bette looked about fourteen and a half, and Gertrud was evidently much the same age. When they had all changed, she led them into the first of the big schoolrooms, whither Grizel and Simone had already gone.

"Now we're all here," she said. "Shall we sit down? I expect my sister and Mademoiselle will be here presently."

They sorted themselves out, Gisela, Gertrud, and Bernhilda taking three desks at the back, while Bette, Grizel, and herself sat in the next row, and Frieda, Simone, and little Maria occupied the front row. There was a minute's silence. Then came the sound of light, swift footsteps, and a moment later Madge entered the room, head well up, although her heart was beating rather quickly. She welcomed them all with a pretty, shy dignity, listened to Gisela's explanation of Gertrud and Maria, and assured her she was very pleased to have them, and then turned her attention to the business of the day.

Prayers were followed by the working of some exam. questions by all the girls, so that she might have some idea as to how to arrange them. As all lessons, save French and German, were to be taken in English, she found the foreign girls worked rather more slowly than would otherwise have been the case, and little Maria did nothing at all. The arithmetic was not done in the ways to which she was accustomed, and there were many quaint turns of speech in the short English compositions; but, on the other hand, both Joey and Grizel rather came to grief over the French, while Simone's German was dreadful, and Grizel's worse. Finally, after much consideration, she decided to work all of them, save Simone, Maria, and Frieda, together in English subjects. Maria, Joey, Grizel, and Bette would form one French class, while the others would make another; and for German, Grizel and Simone would have to be specially coached. It was also obvious that she must get another assistant as soon as possible. "We are growing quickly," she mused. "I only hope it continues."

At twelve o'clock she finished work for the morning, and bidding the Tyroleans to bring some sewing for the afternoon, dismissed them for two hours, during which she saw that the children had their dinner, insisted on Jo's practising for an hour, and, finally, entertained Frau Steinbrücke, a stout, cheery lady, who informed her that all Tiernsee was talking about her, and who prophesied that, in the summer at least, she would have quite a large number of pupils.

At half-past two punctually all the girls were settled in their places again, each with some sewing, and Mademoiselle took charge. Here, both Jo and Grizel came off badly, since both hated their needles, and even little Maria was more expert than they were.

Grizel mused, "I wonder who will be appointed Head Girl?—the first Head Girl of the Chalet School!"

"Ah, yes; I have read of the Head Girl in your English school-stories," replied Gisela pleasantly. "And also Prefects."

"Yes. I know Miss Bettany means to have this exactly like an English school, so I expect we shall have them too." Then she began to giggle. "Rather weird to have Prefects when there are only nine of us!"

"But soon there will be more," observed Bette Rincini,

who up till then had worked in silence on Gisela's other side. "Mamma said at *Mittagessen*——"

" 'Dinner'," corrected Gisela.

"Ah, yes, dinner—that already many of our friends are talking about us, and she makes no doubt that many more girls will come."

"How jolly!" commented Grizel. "I like a big school. Do you have big schools in Innsbruck?"

"But yes. The public schools are very large. I did not go to them; Gisela and Maria and I had a *Mamsell*. But our *Mamsell* has gone away to be married, so Mamma is very pleased for me to come here."

"Bernhilda and Frieda went to the public school," observed Gisela, "but they, too, are pleased to leave it. My father says that the English schools are deficient in education, but they give girls a more healthy life, and Herr Mensch agrees with him. There are others, too, who think the same, so, as Bette has said, we shall, without doubt, soon become a large school."

"But our schools aren't deficient in education!" said Grizel, firing up. "You get a jolly good education at the High Schools!"

"But you have such a short period in school," returned Bette. "You work for no more than five or six hours. Now we begin at eight o'clock in the morning and work till twelve. Then we begin again at thirteen and go on for another four hours."

"How ghastly!" said Grizel sincerely. "Almost as bad as Germany!"

"But in Germany, so my cousin Amalie has told me, they work even harder than that. And they have no games as you have."

"Well, we certainly shan't work like that," replied Grizel decidedly. "I'm sure Miss Bettany would never hear of it!"

"No; she is English," agreed Gisela.

At four o'clock the command came to fold up the work, and then the six day-girls got ready for their walk home. The Maranis and Gertrud lived at Torteswald, a small village about twenty minutes' walk from Seespitz, and the Mensches were at Seespitz Gasthaus for the summer, while Bette had to go all the way to Buchau. As it was a fine day, she meant to walk instead of taking the steamer, and Grizel and Jo volunteered to accompany them to the Seespitz landing—Simone had disappeared as soon as they were dismissed, and they could not find her, though Joey ran, calling, through the house.

It was a delightful walk, and they found each other very friendly, although shy Frieda only smiled and scarcely spoke at all. Gisela, Bette, and Gertrud were anxious to find out all they could about English schools, and they asked many questions.

They chattered on about school topics till they reached the Seespitz Gasthaus, where Bernhilda and Frieda said "good-bye" to them.

"Will you, perhaps, come and eat an English tea with us on Saturday?" asked Bernhilda, just before they parted. "Mamma would be so pleased if you would come; and Simone also."

"Thank you, we'd love it," replied Joey.

"Our first invite," she said gleefully to Grizel as they trotted back to the Chalet. "Well, what do you think of them all?"

"I like them," returned Grizel with fervour. "Gisela's a dear, isn't she? Do you think Miss Bettany will make her Head Girl?"

"Oh, I expect so; she's the eldest. I say, there's Simone! Hullo, Simone! Why didn't you come with us?"

"I went for a little promenade," replied Simone.

"Well, why didn't you promenade with us?" demanded Grizel. "There's no need for you to go off by yourself like that!"

"You had enough," returned Simone.

"Oh, tosh!" declared Joey in friendly fashion. "You mustn't go raking off by yourself. There's only us three boarders at present, and we must stick together!"

Simone looked wistfully at them, but made no remark, and as they had reached the Chalet, the conversation dropped.

CHAPTER SIX

Joey Gives a Promise

BY SATURDAY it was quite obvious that the Chalet School would have to enlarge both its premises and its staff. It had started actual work with nine pupils. In five days' time these had swelled to seventeen, two of them being English girls whose parents wanted to go to Norway, and were not anxious to take their children on such a tiresome journey. So, as Joey said, there were two more boarders straight off.

Amy and Margia Stevens were nice little people of eight and eleven, who had spent most of their short lives in travelling, since their father was Foreign Correspondent to one of the great London dailies. Margia, the elder child, was a motherly person, who adored her small sister; Amy was a dainty, fairylike little creature, who thought Margia was all that was wonderful.

"It really is time they mixed with other girls," said Mrs. Stevens, as she sat talking to Madge and Mademoiselle; "but until this year, Amy has been so delicate, I did not like to leave her anywhere, and it was out of the question for Margia to go alone. We must go to Bergen, but I did not want to send them to a convent school. When we heard of you, it seemed quite providential."

Bette Rincini's cousins came from Innsbruck to live at Buchau with their uncle and aunt for the summer months, and it was taken quite as a matter of course that they should come with her. Then two sisters came from Scholastika at the other end of the lake, and two small children came from the Kron Prinz Karl, where they were staying with their parents.

"It is awfully thrilling!" said Joey to Madge on the Saturday morning as she sat curled up on her sister's bed. "I didn't think schools grew as quickly!"

"They don't generally," replied Madge. "It just happens that we've made a lucky pitch. Joey, is Simone Lecoutier happy? She's such a quiet little thing, and those eyes of hers look naturally tragic. Are you and Grizel kind to her? I hope you don't go off together and leave her alone?"

"Do you really think we'd be so mean?" demanded Joey, righteously indignant. "Why, we haul her along wherever we go when we can find her! But sh 's so weird! Soon as ever lessons are over, she slides off by herself, and where she gets to is more than I can say."

Madge let the subject drop, and suggested instead that Joey had better go to her own quarters.

Joey left the room and went downstairs to the big dining-room, where Marie was just putting a big dish of honey on the table. Simone was there already, looking, as she usually did, almost painfully tidy in her blue and white checked frock and long black pigtails. The Chalet School uniform was to be a short brown tunic with shantung top, but so far, Joey and Grizel were its only members to have them, although the others were getting them made, and Simone's, at any rate, would be ready by Monday.

Her sister's question had aroused fresh interest in the little French girl in Joey, and she regarded the younger child gravely as she saluted her with the pretty Tyrolean greeting, "Grüss Gott!"

"Bon jour," said Simone soberly. She was rather white, and her eyes looked as though she had been crying.

"Why don't you give me 'God's greeting'?" asked Joey laughingly. "I think it's such a nice thing to say to anyone." She came closer. "Simone, why have you been howling? Aren't you happy?"

"I am ver' 'appee, zank you," replied Simone with dignity.

"Then you don't look it," retorted Jo in her most downright manner. "If you're happy, why don't you chirk up a bit?"

Simone lifted tragic dark eyes to her face, but anything she might have said was lost, for Grizel came running in at that moment, followed in more stately fashion by Mademoiselle, and Simone promptly became muter than any oyster.

As a matter of fact, all that was wrong with her was that she was dreadfully homesick. She had never been away from her mother before in her life, and wanted her badly. She slipped off again as soon as breakfast was over, while the other two were chatting. Jo missed her presently as she went off, quite cheerfully, to what was, for the moment, known as the Junior form-room.

"Slipped off again!" she thought. "Simone! Si-mo-one!" She raised her voice in a long melodious call, but no Simone answered it. "Si-i-i-mo-one! Where are you? Simone!"

No response came, so she dashed upstairs—in complete defiance to rules—to see if the small girl had taken refuge in the dormitory. But when she pulled aside the pale yellow cubicle curtains, she found the cubicle quite empty. A hasty rush through all the living-rooms helped her no further, for Simone was not there. Marie, when questioned, declared she had not seen the young lady since breakfast, and she was sure she was with neither Mademoiselle nor Fräulein Bettany, for they had gone off to Spärtz half an hour before. Jo wandered out into the warm sunshine, and turned to gaze at the Bärenkopf, a mountain which greatly took her fancy, although they had not climbed it yet, since it was considered dangerous, at any rate for amateurs.

"I'll have a shot at that some day," she thought, as she looked at the bold, rugged outlines. Then she gave an exclamation, for among the trees which clustered at the foot of the slope of the Bärenbad, another mountain, she had caught a flash of the blue and white frock which Simone wore.

"So that's where she goes!" she thought as she raced across the flower-besprinkled grass which lay between her and the woods. She soon reached them, but by that time Simone had disappeared, and although Joey shouted again and again, there was no answer. Finally, just as she decided to give up the hunt and return home, she stumbled over the root of a large tree, and went headlong on to a

39

nest of old leaves, and there was Simone, sobbing as if her heart would break.

"Simone! What's up? Don't cry like that, old thing! Aren't you well?"

At the first sound of her voice Simone had half sprung up, then she collapsed again into the little huddle she had been when Jo found her.

"Is anything up?" asked the latter again, as she made a valiant effort to pull the other child into her arms. "Tell me, Simone, old thing!"

"I want my mother!" sobbed Simone in French, so that it was all Joey could do to make it out. "I want my mother and my home!"

"You poor kid!" Simone was exactly ten weeks younger than Joey, but for the present the English girl felt very maternal towards her. "You poor kid! There, don't cry, old dear! You'll be all right soon!"

Simone stretched out a hot, sticky hand and grabbed Joey's.

"I am so lonelee!" she sobbed. "You and Grizel are such friends!"

"I say, we didn't mean to make you feel out of it," replied Joey, whose conscience was very busily at work. "Honour bright, we didn't!"

"You are of the same nationality," went on Simone, who, once she had started to make confidences, evidently meant to go on. "You live in the same town, and know each other well, and me, I am only one. And now there will be two more, and I shall still be only one."

"Simone," Joey said. "I'm awfully sorry Grizel and I have been such beasts. I quite see we have been beasts, even though we didn't mean it! Now I want you to mop up—here's a hankie! —and come back with me, and we'll start again. I'm sure Grizel will see it, and we'll all be pally together."

But this was not what Simone wanted. Truth to tell, she had conceived a violent affection for Jo, and Grizel, with her vivid prettiness and more obvious qualities, repelled her. So she sobbed on, while Joey sat, nearly distracted, and not knowing what to do.

"Simone, I do wish you'd stop!" she said finally. "Do

stop crying, old thing! I'll do anything I can for you; honest, I will!"

Simone made a big effort. "Will you be—my friend?" she choked out.

"Of course I will! I am! We both are!"

"No; I mean—my *amie intime*! Oh, Jo, if you only would, I think I should be happier! Grizel makes friends with everyone. Gisela Marani loves her, and so does Bette Rincini! I don't want her; I want only you!"

Jo promptly hugged the younger girl, and said "Righto! we'll be pals. And now, do mop up, there's a gem!"

"You will be my *amie intime*?" persisted Simone, even as she scrubbed her eyes hard with Joey's handkerchief. "You will relate to me all your secrets, and walk with me?"

"Yes, as long as it doesn't interfere with other people," responded Joey. "I can't tell you other people's affairs, Simone! And look here, you mustn't come rushing off by yourself. It might come on a thunderstorm or anything, and we shouldn't know where you were. At least, I should now, but the others wouldn't, and it might worry them."

"I will p—romise to do it no more," replied Simone soberly.

Simone accepted the hand Joey stretched out to her, and got on to her feet.

"You're all leaves; you'd better let me brush you down!" said Jo. "You'll have to change before we go over to the Mensches this afternoon; you can't go in that frock now! It looks as though you'd slept in it!"

They went slowly down the slope, and crossed the grass to the Chalet, where they were met at the door by Grizel, who had just finished her practice.

"Hello!" she said. "I've just finished. What shall we do?"

"I'm going to practise," replied Jo. "I haven't touched the keys yet!"

"Not practised? But you went when I did!"

"Well, I changed my mind. I've been out with Simone, so I've got to do it now instead; and she's got to change her frock. Come on, Simone!" And Joey vanished into the house, leaving Grizel looking after her in startled fashion.

Simone followed her, and Grizel was left alone to

wonder, first, what on earth the French child had been crying about; second, why Joey had left her practice till this hour. She could come to no satisfactory conclusion, so she gave it up, and wandered off to the landing-stage to see if any visitors were coming, as the steamer was just crossing from Buchau. She was rewarded for her interest by seeing a party, unmistakably English, leave the boat, and, giving their luggage in charge of the porter, make for the Tyroler Hof, one of the largest hotels in Briesau. What interested her most was the fact that, besides a lady and gentleman who looked very bored, there was also a girl of about her own age.

"I wonder if they are staying long?" she thought to herself, as she turned and went back to the Chalet to see if the other two were ready to come out. "P'r'aps it'll be another pupil for the Chalet School. Oh, I do hope so!"

CHAPTER SEVEN

The Tiernjoch

"SOME NEW PEOPLE came this morning," said Grizel.

They were all five—Joey, Simone, Bernhilda, Frieda, and herself—gathering flowers in the stretch of meadow that lies between Seespitz and Torteswald. The flowers in the Tyrol are wonderful, and now, in mid-May, the place was a veritable fairyland. Even Grizel and Joey, fresh from Cornwall, where the wealth of bloom is almost as rich as it is in Devon, were thrilled with the riches at their feet, and gathered armfuls of gentian, anemone, hepaticæ, heartsease, narcissi, and daisies, which they would later arrange in the bowls and jars at the Chalet.

There had been a good deal of chatter about school affairs—or rather, Joey and Grizel had done the chattering, and the others had put in an occasional word. Now Grizel changed the conversation.

"Some new people came this morning."

"How interesting!" said Bernhilda politely. "Were they English?"

"They looked like it," replied Grizel. "There were three of them—father, mother, and a girl about fourteen, I should think."

"Perhaps another pupil for the Chalet School," suggested the elder girl, glancing at her watch as she spoke. "I think, if you do not mind, that we had better return now, as we shall have tea at——"

"Four o'clock!" put in Joey. "You told us the time before, Bernhilda, and it is so muddling when you talk of sixteen o'clock."

Bernhilda laughed. She was a rather sedate, well-mannered girl, and Miss Bettany had already decided to appoint her as Second Prefect. Gisela was to be Head Girl, and Bette and Gertrud would be subs. Madge would have preferred an English girl as head, but Grizel was too irresponsible, and Joey too childish for her to dream of it.

Bernhilda now led the way to the *Gasthaus*, her arm slipped through Grizel's, while the other three followed, Joey keeping up a lively flow of conversation, to which shy Frieda only responded by smiles. Simone had remained glued to her side the whole afternoon, and it was beginning to dawn on Joey that she might have undertaken a friendship which was to prove rather tiresome on occasion.

In this order they reached the hotel, where kindly Frau Mensch was awaiting them with tea, accompanied by great platefuls of delicious-looking little cakes which, Joey knew, must have come from Innsbruck, since such things were unprocurable in the lake villages. She welcomed them cheerily, and soon they were all sitting round the table, while their hostess inquired, "Thee mit Citron oder mit Rhum?"

With a sudden shock Joey realised that she was being asked whether she would have tea with lemon in it or rum. She hated the one, and had no idea of taking the other, so she was not very sure what to do. Luckily, Bernhilda came to the rescue.

"Oh, Mamma," she said. "I think Joey and Grizel prefer *Thee mit Milch*—do you not?" turning to them.

"Yes, if you please," replied Joey promptly.

Frau Mensch smiled kindly. "Of course, if that is what you desire, my children. Kellnerin," she called to the waitress, "bitte, Milch!"

The milk was brought and the tea was made, the Mensches taking it in the same way, though Frieda evidently disliked it. Towards the end of the meal Herr Mensch appeared. He was a big, jolly man, with fair hair and grey eyes, and, since he was in one of the big banks in Innsbruck, his English was much more fluent than his wife's. His children obviously adored him, and he sat down, pulling Frieda on to his knee with a loud and hearty kiss.

"What hast thou done today, Mädchen?"

"I have studied my lessons for Monday," replied Frieda seriously, "and I have helped our guests to gather flowers."

"Such glorious flowers! " put in Joey eagerly. "I do think Tiernsee is lovely! "

"Thou lovest it already, Fräulein?" He looked pleased. "It is my home—where I was born. I fished yonder"—he pointed at the blue lake waters—"many a day ere I was thine age. I climbed the Tiernjoch when I was but eleven, and brought my mother home some edelweiss. *Ei!* But my father was angry! I had gone in disobedience, you understand, and his stick was ready for me; but my mother begged me off, and there was no punishment that time." He broke into a great roar of laughter, and the girls joined with him.

"Why should you be punished for climbing the Tiernjoch?" asked Grizel curiously. "Which is it, Herr Mensch?"

"The Tiernjoch is dangerous for all but the most experienced climbers," he replied, "and the edelweiss grows only in one part, which is the most dangerous of all. Thou dost not know it, *mein Kind*? Come then, and I will show it to thee. We will walk to Buchau—canst thou walk so far? And Fräulein Joey, and the little one?— then we will go to Buchau, and from there I will name you the mountains, and all three shall see them."

They set off through the thick grass, listening eagerly

44

while Herr Mensch told them about the time when he was a boy here.

"We did not then think of the hundreds of tourists from all countries who would come and visit our little lake," he said. "And now we have even a school!"

"Papa, Grizel saw some English people come today," said Bernhilda. "They are at the Tyroler Hof, and there is a girl of our age. Perhaps she may come to the Chalet School."

"That would be very pleasant—another compatriot," he replied seriously. "Now see, my children, there is the Tiernjoch, that large one who lifts his head into the clouds. In front of him stands the Bernjoch, and that one, to the side, is the Mittelberge—all very difficult to climb. That one that seems to watch over Briesau—see how he bends protectingly!—is the Mondscheinspitze, quite easy to climb, and there is a hut on the Alm where one can obtain milk and butter and cheese. We will climb there some day if Fräulein Bettany will permit it. It is a walk up the valley, and then it is very pleasant on the mountain, with flowers growing, and butterflies so tame, they will not flutter when one approaches."

"How topping!" said Joey. "I should love that!"

"I want to climb the Tiernjoch," said Grizel suddenly. "I like difficult things!"

The kindly giant—he really was almost a giant!—looked down at her with a smile. "Na-na, mein Kind! A good Mädchen will wait till there is time for a whole day and a guide. That cannot be until the summer. Then, perhaps, it may be possible. But the little expedition up the Mondscheinspitze can be made on a Saturday, and we will take the herdsmen some tobacco, and drink of their milk, which is very rich with cream, and so come back. To climb the Tiernjoch one must start very early in the morning before the sun has risen, and climb for six—eight hours before one reaches the summit. But the Mondscheinspitze, that is a nice little climb."

Grizel said nothing further, but her lips set in obstinate lines, and Joey, looking at her, felt assured that it would take more than Herr Mensch's speech to make her change her mind.

"I wish we hadn't said anything about it," she thought to herself. "I know Grizel will think of nothing else now, and I shall have to spend half my time trying to persuade her not to!"

How heartily she was to wish this thing before the summer was over Joey did not then know—which was, perhaps, just as well. Now she turned her attention to Herr Mensch, who was pointing out the mountains behind them, and naming them: "Sonnenscheinspitze, Alpengluckjoch, Maria-Theresienspitze, Wolfkopf, Schneekoppen. But these are not such mountains," he went on, "as the Dolomites. Some day you will doubtless see those too."

"Papa took us there two years ago," observed Bernhilda. "We stayed in the *Gasthaus* at Primiero, and our cousins came too. It was very pleasant there, and they have many lovely flowers. You would like those, Grizel."

"Did you climb any of them?" asked Joey.

"Oh, no! The Dolomites are very difficult to climb," explained her young hostess. "But Papa and Onkel Paul used to go for days. Once or twice they took my brother with them——"

"Brother! I didn't know you had a brother!" interrupted Grizel, somewhat rudely, it must be admitted.

"Oh, yes; my brother is eighteen, nearly nineteen. He is at the University of Bonn," replied Bernhilda. "He will be a doctor some day, and perhaps I shall be his *Hausfrau* till he marries."

"Perhaps he won't," suggested Joey. "I know Dick, my brother, says he won't. He says the Deccan is no place for women, and he loves his work too well to give it up."

"Oh, I hope Gottfried will marry some day!" said his sister earnestly.

"We all hope that," said her father. "And now we must be returning, for there is quite a long walk, and the little one looks weary."

He reached out a big hand and pinched Simone's cheek as he spoke.

She blushed, and edged nearer to Joey, who felt suddenly cross with her. If Simone was going to be so idiotically shy, and stick to her like glue all day, Joey felt

46

things were going to be tiresome. And why, oh, why didn't she talk instead of standing there deathly silent?

"It's been awfully jolly of you to show us all these things, Herr Mensch," she said, with a surreptitious poke at Simone. "It makes it seem twice as nice to know the names of all the places; doesn't it, Simone?"

"Yes," replied Simone faintly.

"We are going up the Bärenbad Alpe some Saturday soon and have cream," went on Joey. "Marie—Marie Pfeifen, who does the work for us, says that it is awfully nice cream; and it's an easy climb, so we shall all be able to go, even the new little boarders. Did you know we were to have two new boarders on Monday, Bernhilda?"

"No, I had not heard of it," responded Bernhilda.

"Well, we are—Margia and Amy Stevens. Margia is eleven, and Amy is about the same age as Maria Marani. That makes five of us boarders, and p'r'aps we shall get some more."

Suddenly Grizel caught her arm. "Look!" she cried. "There are those people I told you about this morning that I saw going to the Tyroler Hof! See—coming this way!"

They all looked with interest at the trio who were walking in their direction—a tall, bronzed man, with erect, soldierly bearing; a small, slight woman, sallow of skin and fashionable of dress; and a schoolgirl of fifteen or thereabouts, whose most noticeable features were a pair of enormous dark eyes, and a long, fair pigtail swinging to her waist. She was walking slightly behind the others, and there was a sullen, unhappy look in her face. Just as the two parties met, the woman turned to her, saying sharply, "Juliet! Hold yourself up! Good gracious me, child, you look positively deformed! Put your shoulders back at once!"

The sharp, scolding tones brought back her stepmother to Grizel, and involuntarily she shivered. Joey, noticing, slipped an arm through hers with a little squeeze. The girl Juliet looked at them curiously as she passed them. She had made no effort to straighten herself, and Bernhilda commented on this when they were out of hearing.

"But how disobedient!" she remarked.

47

"I can tell you their name," said her father. "He is a Herr Captain of the Indian army—Captain Carrick. He came into the bank this morning to change some money."

"I don't think he looks kind," said Joey. "What a pretty name the girl has—Juliet! Don't you think so, Grizel?"

"I thought she looked dreadfully unhappy," replied Grizel. "And how funny to have fair hair with those dark eyes!"

"Do you think so?" asked Bernhilda. "There are a great number of people living in Wien who are like that. But as for unhappy, she did not do as she was told."

Herr Mensch approved of this. "The young should always obey," he said. "Is it not so, my little Frieda?"

Frieda, who would as soon have thought of flying as of disobeying her parents, said in her shy, soft voice, "Yes, Papa!"

Grizel made a little impatient movement, but Joey's hand on her arm checked any remarks she might have made, and they went on to the *Gasthaus*, talking about the mountains. The girls went in, and the three boarders got their flowers and said "good-bye" to Frau Mensch. She kissed them all, and told them to come back whenever they liked. Then, accompanied by Bernhilda and Frieda, they went out, to find Herr Mensch waiting for them at the boat-house.

"Come!" he said. "It is a long walk, and *die Kleine* looks tired! I will row you across to your own landing-stage. Bernhilda and Frieda, you may come too. Run, Frieda, and tell Mamma!"

Frieda ran quickly back, and presently returned, and they pushed off.

It was glorious on the lake. The day had been very warm for mid-May, but now, with the evening, had come a little cool breeze that ruffled the surface of the water into tiny ripples, and set the curly ends round Grizel's face dancing gaily.

They rowed out into the centre, and then Herr Mensch rested on his oars, and nodded towards the mountain he had named for them—Alpengluckjoch.

"Look!" he said, "Alpengluck tonight!"

48

They turned and looked. As they did so, they saw the grey limestone crags flush into rosy life with the reflected light from the setting sun. All along the westward side of the Tiernsee the peaks caught the glory: It reflected on the silver thread of a mountain cataract high up in the Sonnenscheinspitze, and even cast a faint glow over the lake. For five minutes the wonder lasted, then it began to fade, and Herr Mensch took up his oars again and rowed them in leisurely fashion to the Chalet landing-stage.

"It is beautiful!" said Joey in low tones. Her imaginative temperament had been fired by the loveliness of what she had just seen. "I have seen it once or twice from the windows, but never from the water before."

"Yes, it is a glory," replied Herr Mensch; "but it always brings bad weather with it. We shall have rain tomorrow."

He brought the boat up to the landing-stage as he spoke, and helped them out. Madge had seen them coming, and came running down the path to meet them. When the Mensches had gone and were beyond calling range, she turned to the three.

"Girls," she said, "I have news for you! We have another day-girl. She is an English girl, whose people are Anglo-Indians. They have just come to Tiernsee. When they heard of us, they came at once, and she starts on Monday. She is fifteen and a half, and has only been to school in the Hills. Her people are army people, and her name is——"

"Juliet Carrick!" burst out Grizel impatiently. "Oh, Miss Bettany, is it—is it? Do say it is!"

Madge looked at her in amazement. "Yes, it is," she answered; "but how do you know?"

They explained to her about the meeting near Buchau, and Grizel enlarged on the way Mrs. Carrick had spoken to the girl.

"I believe she's her stepmother!" she concluded.

"No," said Madge, "she isn't. Don't get wild ideas into your head, Grizel. If they only came to Tiernsee today, I expect they are tired, and that is why Mrs. Carrick scolded."

Grizel said nothing further, and Madge thought no more of it. But when Herr Mensch heard, he looked thoughtful.

"I hope things will go well with Fräulein Bettany," he said to his wife. "I did not like that man—I do not trust him."

And he resolved to advise Madge to write to her brother at the earliest opportunity, and see if any information could be gathered about these people who had come so suddenly.

However, when he spoke about it some days later, he found that she had done that very thing already.

"I know it seems mad to take anyone so abruptly," she said, "but they were so anxious, and—well—somehow he persuaded me. And they have paid a term's fees, of course, and if I find from my brother that she is not a desirable pupil, I can get rid of her quite easily by saying that we are full up. Anyhow, it is probably for this term only, as they expect to go to England in September; but they had heard of Tiernsee, and thought they would like to see it, so they broke their journey home."

And after that the good-natured Austrian felt he had nothing left to say for the present.

CHAPTER EIGHT

A First Prefects' Meeting

"Gisela!"

"Yes? Do you want me, Gertrud?"

"I should be glad if you would summon a Prefects meeting."

Gisela lifted a surprised and inquiring face to her friend.

"A meeting, Gertrud? Oh, but why? Nothing has gone wrong?"

"No," agreed Gertrud, "but I am afraid something will go wrong very soon."

In her earnestness, she forgot the school rule which said that, during school-hours, and save in French and German lessons, nothing but English was to be used, and dropped into her native tongue.

"Oh, Gertrud! You have forgotten," said Gisela reproachfully.

"I am sorry, Gisela! I was thinking about the meeting," apologised Gertrud. "Shall I enter my name in the Order Book?"

"No," said the Head Girl firmly. "It is not good for the Juniors that they see a Prefect's name there. You had better report yourself to Miss Maynard. And now, tell me, why do you wish this meeting?"

"There is mischief going on in the school," returned Gertrud, perching herself on her friend's desk. "It is partly that new girl, Juliet Carrick, but I think Grizel Cochrane is making it also."

"How tiresome!" Gisela knitted her black brows at this information.

During the seven weeks that she had been Head Girl, there had been no real difficulty to meet. This was partly because of the novelty of things to all the girls; but also her own personal character had a great deal to do with it. Miss Bettany had chosen wisely in choosing her as Head of the girls. Bernhilda made a very good second, and Bette and Gertrud were rapidly learning their duties as Subs, but the most reliable person was Gisela.

"Ready?" said Gertrud. "Then shall we call the others? They are by the landing-stage."

"Yes. Would you ask them to come to our room, Gertrud?" said Gisela. "I will await you there."

Three weeks previously, Madge Bettany, after a long discussion with Mademoiselle and Miss Maynard, who had been added to the staff as mathematics mistress, had given over to the Prefects a small room on the first floor for their own.

"Even if they have just four chairs in it, it will give them a feeling of being a little different from the rest of the school," she said.

Miss Maynard, herself a High School girl, had agreed, and the four delighted girls had, accordingly, that possession of which they had read so much in their English school-stories—a Prefects' room.

Miss Bettany had explained to them that, beyond chairs and a small table, she could give them no furniture yet; but they had promptly joined forces. While Gisela brought some pictures and a couple of bowls for flowers, Gertrud produced a set of bookshelves which she had induced her brother to make; Bernhilda contributed a pretty blue and white tablecloth and a fancy inkstand, and Bette presented a little clock and a bracket on which to place it. In one book Gertrud had read of the " Prefects' " notice board. Careful questioning had soon drawn from Joey all there was to know about this, and now a similar board hung over the bookshelves, with notices of various kinds on it, all written in Gisela's pointed Italian handwriting. The two big bowls were full of Alpen roses, and on this sunny afternoon it was as charming a girls' room as could be wished. The Head Girl pulled up the four chairs round the table, and seated herself at the head, paper and pencil before her. Presently there came the sound of footsteps on the stairs, and then the other three entered. Very smart and businesslike they looked in their school uniform, which every girl now wore as a matter of course. Gisela looked at them with approval. The most English of English Prefects could not have looked more orthodox, she thought.

"Gertrud tells me you wish a Prefects' meeting," began Bernhilda, as she took her seat on Gisela's right hand. "What is it that you wish to discuss with us?"

"It is Gertrud's idea," replied the Head Girl. "She thinks that things are going rather——"

"Wonky," supplemented Bette, as Gisela paused to search for the right word.

The Head Girl now made a little bow to her Sub, and continued:

"Apparently Gertrud fears that Grizel Cochrane and Juliet Carrick are about to cause trouble. Myself, I have noticed nothing."

"But I have," said Bette composedly. "I quite agree

with Gertrud, and I think Juliet Carrick is at the bottom of it"

"Why should you think that?" demanded Gisela.

"Because, until she came, Grizel Cochrane never rebelled against our authority. But now she is tiresome," replied Bette. "She is even rude."

"How so? She has not been rude to me as yet. How has she been rude to you?"

"I told her to go and put her shoes away," said Bette, "and she said it was sickening having fussy foreigners always at you."

"That was very rude," said Gisela slowly. "What did you do?"

"I said I was sorry she looked at it in that way," returned Bette, "but as I was a Sub-Prefect, and one of my duties was to see that the cloakroom was kept tidy, I was going to see that it was kept tidy."

"What did she say then?" queried Bernhilda with interest.

"Said I thought myself everybody," replied Bette. "I told her not to be impertinent, and saw that she put the shoes away, and that was all."

"I think it was sufficient," said Gisela quietly. "And you, Gertrud?"

"Talking after the silence-bell had been rung," said Gertrud. "I told her to be quiet, and she looked at Juliet and laughed."

"What did Juliet do? Laugh too?"

"Yes, and shrugged her shoulders. It is not good for the Juniors to see that in a girl as old as Grizel or Juliet."

"I don't think you need worry about the Juniors," said Bette. "Amy and Margia would never behave like that, and Maria is too fond of you, Gisela, to worry you that way. Nor would Suzanne and Yvette. Giovanna will be good, because she doesn't want a fuss with me, and I couldn't imagine either Frieda or Simone doing anything but keeping the rules. Joey, of course, will do as she's told, too. It really is only Grizel, and she wouldn't if Juliet didn't encourage her!"

"Well, I must make a punishment," said Gisela. "I am sorry, but Grizel must not be rude to the Prefects." She thought deeply for a minute. "I shall send for her and make her apologise to you, Bette, and you, Gertrud. Then I shall say she is to learn some German poetry in her play-hours. Yes, that is what I shall do! Will you fetch her, Bette?"

Bette got up and left the room, to return ten minutes later by herself.

"She refuses to come," she said briefly.

"Refuses to come?" There was consternation in Gisela's voice. "But did you tell her that the Prefects wanted her?"

"Yes," said Bette. "She just laughed, and said if we wanted her we could go to her; she wasn't coming to us!"

There was a silence. No one had foreseen that Grizel would go to quite such lengths as this, and they were uncertain how to deal with it. It was, had they but known it, the testing-point of the Prefect system in the Chalet School. Had they given way, or taken no notice of the English girl's defiance, it would have been "good-bye" to all hope of self-government. Luckily for the school, Gisela Marani was made of too fine stuff to throw up the game weakly. To her mind there was only one course to follow, and she followed it.

"I must report the matter to Miss Bettany," she said quietly. "Bette, will you come with me? She will want to hear what you have to say."

"Shall we wait till you come back?" asked Gertrud.

"Yes, I think it would be better, if you do not mind. We will make haste."

The two girls left the room, and went downstairs to the sitting-room.

Madge Bettany, enjoying a much-deserved rest, looked up with surprise when, in answer to her "Come in!" they entered, closing the door.

"Well," she said with a smile, "what is it that you want? Anything wrong, Gisela?"

"I have come to make a report to you," replied Gisela steadily.

Madge's face sobered. "To report a breach of rules? Must you, Gisela?"

All indecision had vanished from Gisela's mind now.

"Yes, I must," she answered firmly.

"Well, what is it then, dear? Sit down, both of you, and tell me."

They sat down, and then Gisela unfolded her story, looking every now and then to Bette for corroboration. Miss Bettany grew more and more serious as they progressed, and when, finally, they had finished, she sat for a minute or two without speaking. As a matter of fact, she had herself noticed a change in Grizel's manner of late. She realised, of course, that after four years of such rigorous training as the child had had, reaction must follow with the greater freedom; but she had not expected anything quite so bad as this. She had no desire to punish Grizel, but this sort of thing could not be allowed. As for Juliet, she sincerely hoped that September would see her far enough away from the Tiernsee.

"I will send for her," she said at length. "Where are you? In the Prefects' room? Very well, then! I will come back with you, and she shall come and apologise for her rudeness to you. I am sorry this has occurred, Gisela."

"I, too, am sorry," replied Gisela. "I wish it had not been necessary to trouble you with it, Madame."

"You were quite right to report it," returned her headmistress. "We cannot have this sort of thing occurring. Will you find a Junior, Bette, and send her for Grizel? Then I will follow you upstairs."

Thus dismissed, they left the room. In the passage they met Amy Stevens.

"Please tell Grizel Cochrane that Miss Bettany wants her in the Prefects' room at once," said Bette, while Gisela passed on in silence.

"Yes, Bette," said little Amy. "In the Prefects' room? All right."

She ran off, and Bette followed Gisela upstairs. They were greeted by a duet of "Well?" as they entered the room.

"Miss Bettany has sent for Grizel, and she is coming here herself," replied Gisela.

A minute later the headmistress appeared, looking sterner than they had ever seen her before. She had just taken her seat, when there was a tap at the door, and Grizel entered with an air of somewhat forced defiance.

55

Left to herself, she would never have behaved as she had done. But there was a certain weakness in Grizel's character, and she was easily led. Juliet Carrick was just the type of girl to exercise a good deal of influence over Grizel. In the first place, the child's generous pity had been aroused by what she had seen and heard of Juliet's family life. There was no doubt that Captain and Mrs. Carrick found their daughter a good deal of a nuisance, and the girl had a most unhappy time. Then again, Juliet had grown up in the class of Anglo-Indian society that considers the English the only nation worth mentioning, and her training in a Hill school, where nine-tenths of the girls were Eurasians who looked down on their native cousins with a bitter contempt, had helped to foster this feeling. She had sneered at "foreigner Prefects", asserting that they could not possibly act adequately. Grizel was feeling sore at what she considered Joey's extraordinary fancy for Simone Lecoutier—and all the time poor Joey would have given much to be rid of this friendship!—and she therefore followed Juliet's lead, with disastrous results to herself, and to others later on.

Madge wasted few words on her when she appeared.

"You have been rude to the Prefects, Grizel?" she asked.

A mumble was the only reply. Madge took it as meaning "yes".

"You will apologise at once," she said coldly. "I will allow no rudeness from you younger children to my Prefects. You had better understand that at once. Ask their pardon, and then do whatever they give you for punishment." There was a silence. "Come, Grizel!"

There was that in the headmistresses's voice which compelled Grizel to obedience.

Without raising her eyes, she muttered, "I'm sorry!"

Miss Bettany was wise enough to realise that it would be well to accept this. She waited till Gisela had accepted the apology, and had set the culprit a short German poem to learn. Then she said, "You may go, Grizel!" And when the child had dashed away, she left the room.

As for Grizel, she had rushed off to the pinewoods,

where she vowed, amidst her tears of shame and anger, that she would pay them all out for treating her in this way.

CHAPTER NINE

Simone's Exploit

IF ANY of the girls had been inclined to defy the Prefects, Miss Bettany's prompt action over Grizel Cochrane's behaviour had put an end to any such ideas. The school was rapidly settling down, and the twenty girls who made it up already felt a great pride in it. All the day-girls stayed for dinner now, arriving at the Chalet by half-past eight in the morning and staying till six o'clock in the evening. Lessons began at nine and went on till twelve, when there was a break for the midday meal. At two o'clock they started work again, and went on till four. Tea was at ten past four, and then, from five to six, the Seniors did preparation and the Juniors practised. Twice a week Herr Anserl came up from Spärtz and gave music lessons to the more advanced pupils, while the others learned with Mademoiselle. Miss Maynard taught mathematics and geography through the school, and Miss Bettany herself undertook the English subjects. French, German, and sewing were Mademoiselle's department, and she was form mistress of the Junior form. At present they had only the three forms—Senior, Middle, and Junior.

Two days after the Prefects' meeting, a long letter came from England from Mrs. Dene. Mr. Dene had been the senior curate of the Parish Church at home, but he had accepted a chaplaincy in the West Indies, and they were not anxious to take Rosalie there. Then Mrs. Dene had thought of the Chalet School at Tiernsee, and she wrote to ask if Rosalie might join them in September. If so, would Miss Bettany also have room for Rosalie's cousin, Mary Burnett?

Miss Bettany wrote back saying that she would be pleased to have them both.

The same day, an Italian lady whose acquaintance she had made came to make inquiries with regard to her little daughter. Signora di Ricci was a charming person, and she was obviously very anxious that Vanna should come. Madge knew Vanna, and liked her; so, with Evadne Lannis, there were four more pupils for the Chalet School.

Sitting on her desk in the Middle schoolroom, Joey Bettany proclaimed the news of the coming of two more English girls in the autumn.

"How old are they?" asked Margia Stevens.

"Rosalie's about fourteen and Mary's twelve," replied Joey.

"Oh! One for the Seniors and one for us," observed Frieda Mensch, who was beginning to get over her shyness. "That will be jolly!"

"Tophole!" agreed Joey. "We are spreading, aren't we? You'll love Mary, Frieda. She's such a dear, steady old thing! I'm glad she's coming!"

Simone, who was, as usual, glued to her side, changed colour at this, but for once Joey took no notice. Truth to tell, she was getting thoroughly tired of Simone's jealousy and all-in-all friendship, and there had already been more than one scene, when Simone had accused Jo of hurting her on purpose, and not liking her any more. The last time, unsentimental Jo had very nearly declared that she didn't; that she was fed-up with all these fusses! But Simone had melted into tears at the least harshness, and cried so piteously, that Joey hadn't the heart to do it. Now, unheeding of the little French girl at her side, she went on enthusiastically: "Mary was a form below me at the High School, but they lived near us, and we used to play together. We were in the same netball team too."

"And the other girl—Rosalie; is she, too, pleasant?" asked Frieda.

"Oh, yes, quite jolly!" replied Joey. "She's awfully pretty too, and jolly clever as well! Oh, bother! There's the five-to-nine bell, and I haven't got my books out! Mind, Simone!"

She brushed past Simone as she jumped down, and dashed to her locker to collect her possessions. The French child looked at her with big, mournful eyes, but Joey took no notice.

At lessons that morning Simone seemed unusually stupid. All her arithmetic was wrongly worked; her dictation was full of mistakes; and she knew not one word about history, although, as Joey well knew, she had thoroughly prepared it on the previous evening. As question after question passed the little girl, and she either did not answer at all, or else talked utter rubbish, Miss Bettany's brow grew blacker and blacker. She had just left the Seniors after a tussle with Grizel, who seemed to have taken leave of her senses lately, and she wondered whether that young lady's spirit of lawlessness were infecting Simone. Finally, she closed her book with an angry snap.

"Simone! Why have you not prepared your work? I am surprised at you! You must do this lesson over again at half-past four, and please never give me such disgraceful work again!"

Simone said nothing. She felt utterly miserable and unhappy, and only longed to fly away somewhere where she could cry her heart out. The others were looking at her with startled faces. It was so unlike Simone to have to be spoken to like this. Meanwhile the bell rang, and, under their Head's watchful eyes, they were forced to file out of the room in proper order. Nor were they able to speak until they had escaped with their glasses of lemonade into the open air.

Then Simone was discovered to have disappeared.

"What on earth can be the matter with her?" demanded Joey of a select group, composed of herself, Margia Stevens, Frieda Mensch, and Suzanne Mercier. "D'you think she's ill or anything?"

"She was all right at first," replied Margia. "She was talking like anything at breakfast, and she ate heaps!"

"But look here! She knew that history last night—I

know she did! And she never gets returned work! Why, she's top of the form every time!" protested Joey.

"Let's try and find her," proposed Margia. "If she isn't well, Miss Bettany ought to know. She might be going to have measles or anything."

At that moment the bell for the end of break went, so they had to return to their form-room and French composition. Simone did not put in an appearance; but then, as Joey said afterwards, they all thought that she must be poorly and have gone to tell the Head, who had sent her to bed. Mademoiselle herself did not miss the child. Simone was always so very quiet and inconspicuous, and naturally, she did not require nearly as much attention as the others. The last lesson was geometry with Miss Maynard, and as the little French girl's arithmetic was appallingly backward, it had been decided that, for the present, she should concentrate on that. When, however, she did not put in an appearance at *Mittagessen*, Miss Bettany promptly inquired where she was.

"In bed, I think," replied Joey with equal promptness.

The Head's black brows were drawn together in a frown of perplexity.

"Bed? But why? Who sent her? Isn't she well? Mademoiselle——"

"I know nothing," replied Mademoiselle. "I have not seen her since this morning."

"Nor I," replied Miss Maynard. "She came to my arithmetic lesson, of course, but she doesn't take geometry, and I haven't seen her since before recreation."

Miss Bettany got up, looking disturbed. "Joey, why do you think she has gone to bed? Did she tell you she felt poorly?"

"Oh, no." replied Joey. "Only, she got all her work wrong, and it isn't like her, so we thought she must be ill."

"Run upstairs and see if she is there."

Joey vanished, to come back a few minutes later looking flushed and startled.

"She isn't there, Madge," she said, using the forbidden Christian name in her earnestness. "There's no one there. But in her cubicle I found—this!" And she held up a long, thick plait of black hair.

A gasp sounded through the room. Madge, Mademoiselle, and Miss Maynard stood as if they were transfixed to the spot, while Joey Bettany stood holding that awful relic of Simone before their eyes.

As if someone had released a spring which was holding her, Mademoiselle leaped forward and snatched the plait from the trembling Joey.

"And where, then, is Simone?" she shrieked in her native tongue. "What has become of her?"

"Nothing very terrible can have happened, Mademoiselle," said Madge, coming forward hastily. "She must have done it for a joke or for mischief, and now is probably ashamed to show herself!"

Mademoiselle turned on Joey. "Josephine, you are the friend of Simone! Why has she done this thing?"

Joey shook her head helplessly. "I don't know, Mademoiselle—honest Injun, I don't! I'd have stopped her if I'd known."

Things certainly seemed at a deadlock. Amy had stopped crying, mainly because no one was taking any notice of her, and the rest just sat in stricken silence.

"Well," said Miss Bettany at length, "we had better try to find her. Miss Maynard, will you take the table while Mademoiselle and I go to search? Yes, Joey, what is it?"

"Oh, please, may I come too?" asked Joey breathlessly. "I've just remembered where she might be—in the pines. I can find it in a second."

"Very well," said her sister. "Mademoiselle and I will go through the house, and you can try this hidey-hole you say she has in the pine-woods. Put your hat on, though—the sun is very hot today."

Joey only waited long enough to snatch her hat from its peg in the cloakroom before dashing off to the pine-covered slopes at full speed. As she ran, her brain busied itself with the question of why Simone should have cut her hair, of which, as a matter of plain fact, she had been rather vain. She reached the hollow between the big roots, where she had found Simone before, but it was empty. There was no sign at all of the little French girl, and Joey's heart stood still for a moment. She had been so sure she would find Simone there. As she stood, wondering whatever she should do now, a little sob caught her ear. At once she swung round, and scrambled over the sticks and dead pine-needles in its direction. There, in a little heap, lay Simone, crying as even Joey had never seen her cry before. The ends of her hair where she had sawn off her plait stood up like little drakes' tails, an effect which would have made her friend giggle helplessly at any other time. Now, however, she only tumbled down beside her, flinging an arm round her, and hauling her up on to her knee.

"Simone! Oh, Simone! What is the matter with you?"

"Go away!" sobbed Simone, in her own language. "Go away, Joey!"

"No fear!" replied Joey. "I'm not going till you're ready to come with me. And anyhow, I want to know why you've chopped your wig like that. You once told me you wouldn't have your hair cut for anything. Why on earth did you do it?"

"I—I thought you would like it!" Simone choked out. "You have often laughed at me because my hair was long, and I thought if I cut it short you would love me, and not leave me when those new English girls come next term!"

"Well!" Joey sat back and gasped. "Of all the mad ideas!" she said, when she had got her breath back. "I don't care whether you wear your hair cropped like a convict or trailing round your feet like Lady Godiva! Really, Simone, you are a perfect idiot! And why did you rush off here like that? I nearly had a fit when I went to find you in your cubicle and found only your pigtail!"

"I look so terrible!" sobbed Simone. "And then I thought of what Cousin Elise would say, and how Miss Bettany would be angry and you and all the other girls would laugh, and so I ran away."

"Well, now you're coming back," said Joey firmly. "I don't know what Madge will say to you, or Mademoiselle! But you can't stay here for ever, and I want my dinner— I came out in the middle of it! As for laughing at you, I shan't; and I don't suppose the others will either. Now do stop howling and come on!"

At first Simone refused to budge, but finally Joey succeeded in getting her to come back with her, and they reached the Chalet, both of them feeling hot and tired.

After one glance at the French child's face, Miss Bettany packed her off to bed without one word of scolding; and when she had finally dragged the whole ridiculous story out of her sister, she sent that young lady up to her cubicle with strict instructions to go to sleep. Then she betook herself to Mademoiselle and unfolded the tale to her.

"In a way, it's just as well," she said, "for all that mass of hair was far too much for her in hot weather; but of course she had no business to cut it herself like that. You had better take her over to the Kron Prinz tomorrow and let the hairdresser there trim it. Now I must go to my class."

The next day Simone was taken to have her hair properly cut, and, much to her relief, the other girls said very little about the whole affair, although her cousin scolded her roundly. Altogether, Simone deeply regretted the fact that she had ever touched her hair—the more so, since Joey Bettany, instead of being impressed by what she had done, characterised the whole thing as "idiotic nonsense!"

CHAPTER TEN

The Cinema Actresses

IT WAS A MERCY, as Madge Bettany said, that for the next week or two everything went quite ordinarily. Grizel and Juliet gave the Prefects no further trouble; Simone ceased, for the moment to behave in a sentimental way; Amy Stevens gave up crying on the smallest provocation; and there was peace in the Chalet School. The only event of any note was an accident Bernhilda had with the red ink.

All the stationery was in one cupboard, the key of which Miss Maynard kept. Bernhilda had been appointed Stationery Prefect, and she went every Friday and gave out the new stationery as it was required. It was not a very heavy task as yet, since everyone had started with new books at the beginning of the term. Scribblers and little notebooks were what were mainly required, with a very occasional exercise-book, and Grizel Cochrane, in her capacity as ink monitress, came on Mondays for the week's supply.

On the Monday following Simone's exploit, Grizel came as usual with her ink-can. She found Bernhilda, who took her duties very seriously, engaged in tidying the top shelf of the cupboard. The Prefect, sitting on the top of the step-ladder, looked down at her Junior.

"Oh, Grizel, will you please take the ink?" she said. "I want to finish this before the bell rings! It is in the big jar at the bottom."

"All right, Bernhilda! Don't you worry; I'll get it all right," replied Grizel cheerfully. Juliet had been absent on the Thursday and Friday of the previous week, and had not yet turned up, so Grizel was a much nicer girl in consequence.

Having directed the Junior's attention to the big ink-jar, Bernhilda returned to her task, while Grizel uncorked the jar, and, carefully tilting it on one side, began to fill her can. Both were absorbed in their work. Grizel had very nearly finished, when Bernhilda gave a sudden shriek, and dived forward, nearly collapsing on to Grizel, who echoed her shriek. At the same time there was a crash as the large pint bottle of red ink fell heavily against the step-ladder, and smashed, sending a fountain of red ink in every direction. Bernhilda's tunic suffered, but the one who came off worst was Grizel, who was almost directly underneath. In her dive forward, the Prefect managed to catch the bottom portion of the bottle, and the rest fell clear of the Junior; but the ink deluged her—hair, frock, hands, even her legs were dripping with it.

The combined shrieks of the two drew the staff hastily to the spot. Mademoiselle, under the impression that there had been a fearful accident, rushed forward with a cry of "Where, then, is the injury?"

Miss Maynard and the headmistress, who had both realised almost at once what had occurred, were hard put to it to keep from laughing, although the latter promptly produced a handkerchief, and set to work to try to wipe off some of the ink. By this time Bernhilda had reached the ground, and was giving a somewhat incoherent account of what had occurred.

According to her story, she had turned some books round sharply, and had caught the ink-bottle with a corner. She had tried to catch it, but had not been in time to prevent its breaking. The rest they could see for themselves. Grizel, who had not been actually hurt, was furious.

"I'm all ink, and my tunic is ruined!" she said in choked accents.

"No, I don't think so," replied Miss Bettany gravely. "You must get out of it at once, of course, and Marie must wash it immediately. Then I think it will be all right. Luckily it's your cotton tunic. And you must go and get a bath. I'll come and wash your hair, and then you'll be all right by recreation. Don't look so distressed, Bernhilda. It was an accident, and you couldn't help it. But I advise you, for the future, to put all liquids on the floor of the cupboard."

When recreation came, a very clean and exceedingly indignant Grizel joined the others, secretly expecting to be well teased about her unexpected bath. Luckily for her, however, she found everyone buzzing with excitement over some news Juliet Carrick had brought that morning.

It appeared that a certain well-known firm of film producers had decided to use the Tiernsee as part of the setting for a film which should give *Life in the Austrian Tyrol*. It was one of a series of educational films that they were doing; and since it was not, of course, always possible to get the natives of the country to pose for them, they had sent the "principals" over from America. These six important people, together with the director, the camera man, and a business manager, were making the Tyroler Hof their headquarters for the time being. They were going to use all the villages and hamlets round the lake as settings, and also some of the Alms, where the cowherds lived during the summer in wooden huts, while the cows browsed contentedly on the sweet, short grass of the upland pastures. They intended to go beyond the lake and.

following the course of the little Tiern, take some of the hamlets and villages on its banks. Just why they should have hit on the Tiernsee was hard to say. Juliet was not occupied with that question. It was the whole idea which appealed to her, and she was full of it.

"They are going to the Ziller Thal after this," she chattered eagerly, "and Kufstein as well, before they go south to the Dolomites. They've done Innsbruck and the Stubai Thal and round about there, and Mr. Eades—that's the camera man—said they had some glorious close-ups of Hall and Spärtz. He was awfully interested in us, and I think they mean to ask Miss Bettany to let them take us. Isn't it thrilling?"

Miss Bettany, however, when approached on the subject by the said Mr. Eades and a Mr. Sindon, the business manager, refused to hear of it. She was icily courteous and absolutely decided. Nothing would induce her to reconsider the matter, and the two gentlemen left the Chalet, realising that, as one of them later expressed it to Juliet, "It was abso. N.G. Nix on the 'movies' stunt!"

Most of the girls cared very little either one way or the other, but Juliet herself, Grizel, and one or two of the more thoughtless ones were bitterly disappointed. They had already, in imagination, seen themselves on the screen. People all over Europe and the British Isles, at any rate, would know them, and now it was all spoilt by Miss Bettany's refusal.

"It's a shame!" cried Juliet, to a select gathering on the afternoon of the day on which she learned of her head-mistress's decision. "Why couldn't we be filmed? Big schools like Eton and Winchester are! But Miss Bettany always does that sort of thing! She's thoroughly narrow-minded!"

"No, she isn't!" returned Grizel, who had moments when she realised that her present behaviour was anything but what Madge had the right to expect of her. "It's different photographing boys at sports, and doing us here by the lake. Oh, I can't tell you how, but it is!" And from this position she refused to budge.

Juliet gave it up, for she was clever enough to realise that once Grizel had made up her mind to a thing, wild horses wouldn't move her. However, Anita Rincini, Sophie Hamel, and Suzanne Mercier were more easily swayed, and were soon persuaded into thinking that they had a grievance against Miss Bettany. The manager of the "movies" also felt he had a grievance. He had foreseen a glorious advertisement in the school. It was, so far as he knew, an entirely new idea, and the girls looked so fresh and dainty in their uniform, and the whole thing would have made an excellent foil to his continental scenes.

"If only I could get just one or two of your kids!" he said to Juliet. "It would be an easy matter to rig up a schoolroom scenario. And we could take you sculling, and swimming, and so on."

These words gave Juliet an idea. "Could you really do it?" she asked. "If I got some of the girls together in our uniform, could you really manage?"

"Of course I could!" he said impatiently. "Come to that, I suppose I could rig up something in the States when we get back."

"But it wouldn't be the same scenery," said Juliet earnestly.

"We could fake it near enough for the public," he replied.

"But it would be better with the same backgrounds, wouldn't it?" she asked.

"Of course it would! But that school-ma'am of yours won't even listen to the idea, so where's the good of talking about it?" he returned irritably.

"Supposing I were to get two or three of the others to come, couldn't you take us?" queried Juliet.

Mr. Sindon's face lit up at the idea. "I could manage it, of course," he said slowly. "When could you arrange for it? Because we are off next Friday, so it would have to be before then."

"Would Saturday do?"

"Yes, that would do very well. Saturday, then, at ten o'clock in the morning. Bring your swimming suits, and we'll get you in the water."

Juliet tackled her four satellites, and by dint of flattery, coaxing, and, in the case of Sophie Hamel, frank bullying, got them to agree to join her. As she had expected, Grizel was the hardest of them to capture. She gave in when Juliet had alternately scolded and pleaded with her for nearly half an hour, and agreed to be at Geisalm, a little hamlet a mile and a half up the lake shore, on Saturday morning. It would be an easy matter for her to be there; for, on Saturdays, they were left very much to themselves, Madge Bettany having a theory that it was better to trust girls than to watch them continually. They were not allowed to bathe or go boating unless a mistress was there; but otherwise no one interfered with them, and so far there had been no necessity for interference. Therefore, ten o'clock on Saturday morning found Grizel, in company with Juliet, scrambling along the narrow rocky path that leads from Briesau to Geisalm.

"Aren't you thrilled?" demanded Juliet, as they stopped to rest on the great "fan" of alluvial rock which marks the half-way between the two places. "I am! I've never acted for 'movies' before."

Grizel did not suppose Juliet had, and her conscience was beginning to wake up very thoroughly, which may have accounted for the vehemence with which she said, "Oh, rather! Awfully!"

Juliet shot a quick glance at her from her queer, dark eyes, but she said nothing beyond, "Well, we'd better be getting on!"

They went on their way—slowly and carefully, for at this part the path was not very wide, and went almost sheer down to the water, whose vivid blueness told how deep it was. At any other time Grizel would have enjoyed that scramble over the rocks, and the rapid run past the place where the mountain water dripped from a crag that overhung the path. She had enjoyed this very walk a score of times. But now she felt half angry and wholly unhappy, and I think that if it had not been for her fear of Juliet's mocking tongue, she would have turned back even then. So absorbed was she in her uneasiness, that she never noticed a broad-bottomed rowing boat with four people in it heading for Scholastika. Juliet, who, at the moment it passed, was gathering a bunch of purple scabious and white moon-daisies, did not notice it either.

The occupants of the boat glanced up, attracted by the

splash of brown against the green of the Alm which they had reached. Juliet they passed over, but as Joey Bettany's eyes lingered on the other gym-frocked figure, she gave a gasp.

"Herr Mensch!" she cried. "That's Grizel! Whatever is she doing here?"

Herr Mensch turned a placid face towards the place, but the two girls had vanished behind the clump of trees which protects the footpath from the lake at this point.

"So?" he said politely. "Then that is why we could not find her when we came to fetch you? But is it wrong for her to be here?"

"I'm sure my sister doesn't know about it," declared Joey. "She thought Grizel must have gone to buy apples from the old woman at Seespitz, 'cos she said so!"

Herr Mensch's fair, German-looking face became troubled.

"That is very wrong of das Mädchen," he said gravely. "Would you like us to land at Geisalm and take her into the boat?"

Joey thought rapidly for a moment. They had never been told that they were not to go to Geisalm by themselves, but she knew that Madge was always a little nervous about that path, especially the narrow bit of it.

"Yes, please! I think it would be better, if you don't mind!"

Without a word, the good-natured Austrian turned the boat towards the little green triangle with its big white *Gasthaus*, which forms Geisalm. A group of people were standing there talking together. Joey recognised the cinema folk, but still she didn't guess what was up until Bernhilda cried, "Why, there are Sophie and Anita. How strange for so many of the Chalet girls to meet here today!"

Then Joey understood.

"Oh!" she said, and her face, pale no longer, but tanned by the hot sunshine, flamed with sudden anger. "Oh! How can she, when Madge said not!"

"How can she do what?" asked Bernhilda, who was slow at grasping things. "And of whom are you speaking, Joey?"

"It's Grizel! Juliet's done it, of course! She's mad on them!" replied Joey incoherently. "Oh, Herr Mensch! Please stop them! Madge will be so angry, and it isn't fair when she said she wouldn't!"

Herr Mensch was quicker than his daughter. With a final pull he brought the boat neatly to the landing-stage and sprang out.

"Stay here!" he said curtly to the three girls with him, and then he strode off to the group by the *Gasthaus*.

Mr. Sindon was considerably surprised when he found himself confronted by an angry giant of a man, who requested to know, in very good English, if he intended taking photos that day. Something in the angry giant's voice warned him that he had better give an answer at once, and to the point, so he replied that he was. It was at this moment that Grizel and Juliet came upon them. Herr Mensch took not the slightest notice of the elder girl, but he turned to Grizel and, in tones which literally scared her, told her to go to the boat at once. With her he sent Anita and Sophie. Then he spoke to the paralysed Mr. Sindon.

"I am sorry, mein Herr, if in taking these young ladies away I am causing you any inconvenience, but they are here without the knowledge or permission of their parents and guardians. I wish you good-day!" And with this he turned and strode back to the boat, where Anita Rincinni, who happened to be the daughter of his own great friend, had dissolved into tears. Sophie looked scared, and Grizel was beginning to recover sufficiently to feel furiously angry at having been treated in this summary fashion. But Herr Mensch took no notice of her at all.

"How did you get here?" he asked the other two in their own language.

Sophie pointed to the light rowing-boat moored to the landing-stage. "We rowed across from Scholastika," she explained.

"I see," he said. "Well now, you will row back with me." Then he turned his attention to the English girl. "You will come with us," he said. "Get into the boat."

Grizel gave him one look—and obeyed. Sophie and Anita had already started. In a grim silence they pulled up the lake to Scholastika. Bernhilda and Frieda were too much afraid of their father's anger to speak.

At Scholastika, Herr Mensch grimly marched them before him, first to the Rincinis' villa, and then to the hotel where the Hamels were staying. While there, he rang up the Chalet, and told Madge that, as they had met Grizel, he was taking her with the others to Maria Kirche to see the famous church there, and they would all return in the afternoon. Then he went back to the girls, and sending Bernhilda and Joey on in front, took each a hand of Frieda and Grizel.

It was not a pleasant expedition. And when they returned in the afternoon, Herr Mensch had a long conversation with Miss Bettany, which ended in a more serious scolding for Grizel than she had ever known since she had left England. What hurt her more than anything was the knowledge that she was not to be trusted by herself—at any rate for the present. As for Juliet, Captain Carrick had made arrangements only that morning for her to be a boarder for the remainder of the term, as he and his wife were going to Munich to visit some friends, and did not want to take her with them. Miss Bettany resolved to keep a watchful eye on the new boarder.

CHAPTER ELEVEN

The Head's Birthday-party

"Joey! Are you busy, or may I come and talk to you?"

Joey Bettany raised her head with a start at the sound of the voice. Looking down from her perch on the fence which shut off the Alm of Briesau from the Geisalm path, she saw Gisela Marani standing beside her, book in hand, a very serious expression on her charming face.

"Hullo, Gisela! What's the trouble?" she said cheerfully.

"It is this book," explained Gisela, tapping it. "Will you come with me to the seat by the boat-landing? I wish to discuss it with you."

"Rather!" Joey slid down from her seat with great goodwill, and, slipping her arm through Gisela's, strolled along by her side.

"Look!" she said suddenly. "There's some new people from the Kron Prinz Karl. They came last night. Father and mother, and two girls and two boys, and a grown-up girl. Don't they look jolly?"

Gisela glanced idly in the direction in which Joey was pointing. Then her face suddenly changed, and her lips curved up in a smile of surprise and pleasure.

"Wanda!" she cried.

The elder girl, a slim, fair person of about fifteen, turned round at the sound of her voice. Then she uttered a little cry and ran towards them.

"Gisela!' she exclaimed.

The younger girl and a small boy of about seven looked up too, and in a minute they also were racing up to the little group.

Gisela embraced them all, while Joey stood on one side, feeling rather in the way. But the Austrian had no idea of leaving her out.

"Wanda—Marie—Wolfram—this is my English friend, Joey Bettany. I am now at her sister's school in the large chalet over there. Joey, these are Wanda and Marie von Eschenau, and their brother Wolfram. I was at school in Vienna with Wanda and Marie when we lived there."

Joey had never been a shy person; she had travelled about too much for that. So now she came forward and shook hands easily.

"Hullo! " she said. "Are these your holidays?"

The elder girl, whom Gisela had saluted as Wanda, smiled.

"But no; not holidays," she said, and her careful speech reminded Joey of the first few weeks of the Chalet School. "We have left our *lycée* and we are resting here until Mamma finds us one where we can be always—ah! you call it 'boarding-school', I remember."

"Oh, Wanda!" cried Gisela. "You must come to the Chalet School!"

"That would be very pleasant," said Wanda politely. "Listen! I hear Mamma calling. *Auf wiedersehen!* Goodbye, Fräulein Joey."

And she hurried off, followed by the other two.

"What *pretties*, Gisela!" said Joey enthusiastically. "What did you say their name was?"

"Von Eschenau," replied Gisela. "It would be very jolly if Wanda and Marie came to the Chalet School, for they are nice girls."

Gisela was, at the moment, much more engrossed in the book which she had been reading than in the arrival of her old friends, and as soon as they were comfortably established on one of the white seats by the landing-stage she began her discussion at once.

"Papa brought me this book two days ago," she said, exhibiting to Joey's interested eyes a girl's school-story with a gay paper jacket.

"*Denise of the Fourth*," read the English girl. "Who's it by? Muriel Bernardine Browne? Never heard of her! What's it like?"

"I find it interesting—in parts," replied Gisela, "though some of it seems to me impossible. But there are descriptions of two things which interest me very much, and I was wondering if we also could not have them.

"The two things are a magazine, first. In the school of this story, the girls had a most interesting magazine. It gives examples from it. See!" And she rapidly found the place, and gave it to Joey, who skimmed through the chapter with a widening grin on her face.

"It is amusing?" queried the Head Girl. "You find it funny?"

"It's a shriek," pronounced the critic. "But it's rather an idea. We ought to have a magazine. The only trial is, it will be so frightfully difficult to decide what language it will be in."

"But of course it will be in English," said Gisela. "We are an English school."

"It would be rather fun," mused Joey. "Who'd be editor? You, I suppose?"

Gisela shook her head. "Oh, no," she said earnestly. "I do not know enough about it. Perhaps Miss Maynard would do it."

"She might; but it ought really to be a girl. Well, go on! What's the other scheme you liked so awfully?"

"The Head's birthday," replied Gisela, turning over more pages. "See, Joey! In this they had a dance, and they gave the Head beautiful presents, and had a splendid time!"

Joey grinned. "I've never heard of a school where the girls gave the Head a slender gold chain on which was swung an exquisite pendant studded with diamonds! The most we ever rose to at the High was a really decent reading-lamp. But the holiday stunt is all right, and so is the dance. Madge's birthday does come this term, as it happens. I vote we ask her for the holiday, anyhow."

"But she must also have a gift," protested Gisela. "And flowers as well. What day is it, Joey? Soon?"

"It's July the fourth," replied Joey—"next Thursday. It would be a ripping scheme to go for an expedition somewhere, wouldn't it? Tell you what! We might go up the Mondscheinspitze and have a picnic there, and then come down and have the dance in the evening! Oh, gorgeous!"

"And the gift?" persisted the Head Girl. "We all admire and love Miss Bettany so much, we would wish to give her something."

"Oh, well, that's for you to decide!" returned Joey.

"But of course we will! You will want to give your own souvenir; we won't ask you to join unless you wish it. But I know the others will. What would Miss Bettany like?"

"Oh, any old thing! She'd like whatever you give her!"

"The flowers will be easy," pursued Gisela thoughtfully. "We have a garden, Bette has a garden, Anita and Giovanna have a garden, and so has Gertrud. We shall have roses, lilies, and marguerites."

"Let's go and ask the others," proposed Joey. "It's nearly time for prep. anyhow. You'll have to ask my sister for the holiday, you know, and you'll have to give whatever you do give her."

Gisela coloured faintly. She was rather inclined to be shy.

"In *Denise of the Fourth*, Mervyn, that's the Head Girl, asks them to cheer the headmistress," she said. "I should have to do that too?"

"Of course! What do you think? Here's Gertrud and Grizel coming. Let's tell them now, shall we?"

"Don't you think it would be better if we waited till everyone was together?" suggested Gisela diffidently. "And should I not ask the Prefects first?"

"Ye—yes, I suppose you should," conceded Joey reluctantly. "All right! You go and call a Prefects' meeting, and I'll go and see what Simone is up to. I haven't seen her since *Mittagessen*."

Joey skipped off, leaving Gisela to follow at a more stately rate, as befitted a Head Girl.

Simone greeted her friend with mournful eyes.

"I looked for you everywhere, Joey," she said reproachfully.

"Well, I was reading on the fence," responded Joey briskly. "Then Gisela came to talk to me about a new book she was reading. Oh, Simone, do you remember those people who came to the Kron Prinz Karl last night by the last boat? We've just met them; they're friends of Gisela's—come from Vienna, and they're here for a while. You remember the two pretty girls like fairy princesses? Their names are Wanda and Marie, and Gisela wants them to come to the Chalet School. What's the matter?" staring in undisguised amazement at Simone, who looked as if she were about to burst into tears. "Aren't you well?"

"Oh, Joey," said Simone pathetically, dropping into her own language in her agitation—"oh, Joey, don't have any more friends! Please, Joey, don't! You've got Grizel, and Gisela and Bette, and I've only got you! And now you want those two new girls that you don't know at all! Oh, Joey, don't be so selfish!"

Joey stood stockstill in her amazement.

"Selfish!" she repeated. "Selfish! It's you who are selfish! I've told you over and over again that I'm going to have all the friends I want, and it doesn't make one scrap of difference to my being pally with you! I don't mind *your* having other friends—I don't see why you don't! Margia would chum with you if you gave her half a chance, and she's a jolly nice kid! It's no use looking like that, Simone! It doesn't make one scrap of difference! If I like Wanda and Marie, I'm going to like them. If they do come to the Chalet and we want to be pally, I shall be!" Then she relented somewhat at the look of misery in Simone's great dark eyes, and slipped an arm round her shoulders, giving her a gentle little shake. "Do buck up, Simone, and be—be a man! You'd be twice as jolly if you only would! Look here! There's five minutes before the bell goes—I forgot my watch is fast—and there's just time to tell you what Gisela was talking to me about. Come along and let's go and sit by the boat-slip and I'll tell you about it. It's awfully thrilling!"

But although Simone allowed herself to be drawn towards the little wooden landing-stage beside the Chalet, the dumb wretchedness of her expression did not relax, and all the time that Joey was enlarging on Gisela's "topping" idea, she sat without making the slightest effort at cheering up. Finally, even happy-go-lucky Jo Bettany gave it up in despair. What could you do with a girl who refused to be interested in birthday-parties and sat looking like a chunk of solid misery?

Joey was thankful when the bell went, and she was able to go off to her own form-room, where there were plenty of people interested in all she had to say about the newcomers at the Kron Prinz Karl.

"It would be splendid for the school if they did come," said Anita Rincini. "I have heard Papa talk of Herr von Eschenau. They are very well born."

"What a silly reason!" said Grizel crushingly. "The real question is, Will they be all right in school? Are they good at games, for instance?"

"They will not know cricket," laughed Sophie Hamel, coming to the rescue, for Anita was too much squashed by Grizel's remark to say anything. "You will have to teach them that, Grizel. Two more, perhaps, for your team." For Grizel, who was keen on cricket, and had been a shining light of the Junior Eleven at her last school, had been appointed cricket captain, and was proving a very capable coach. Perhaps one reason for her success was that the other girls were all so keen on being an "English" school, that they took her criticisms and sarcasms in good part, and really tried to learn the game. As for the Juniors, they spent most of their free time in fielding practice. The games mistress at the High had been very insistent on the necessity for smart fielding, and Grizel, quite a good, steady bat, had nevertheless excelled in bowling, which naturally made her more determined to have good fielding than if it had been the other way round.

They had tennis, too, for most of the girls played it quite well, and Gisela Marani and Gertrud Steinbrücke were exceptionally good. However, there could be no doubt about it, cricket was the more popular game.

Now, in answer to Sophie's remark, Grizel spoke quite graciously.

"We shan't be playing cricket next term. I don't quite know what we shall play; do you, Joey?"

"Not an earthly!" returned Joey promptly. "I should think it'll be hockey, though. My sister was awfully good at it when she was at school. But isn't there heaps of snow here in the winter?"

"Oh, yes," said Anita readily. "The lake is frozen, too, and there is much skating."

"Girls! Why are you talking?" said Gertrud's voice at that moment. "You ought to be working! Sit down, please!"

They went to their seats, while Gertrud, who had come to take preparation, arranged her books to her liking on the mistress's table. Then there was silence while they got on with their preparation in the cool, quiet room.

As soon as the bell for tea went, Joey literally pitched her books into her locker, and fled along the passage to find Gisela. She wanted to know what Madge had said about the birthday-party. However, she had to possess her soul in patience, for the Head Girl was in the Prefects' room.

Luckily, those great people had decided to make all arrangements as soon as possible, and when their own tea, which they were allowed to have by themselves, was over, they came down to the *Speisesaal*, where the others were, and Gisela, blushing furiously, murmured a request to Miss Maynard, who was taking tea. Miss Maynard nodded, and got up at once.

"Yes, certainly, Gisela! We have just finished, so I will say 'Grace' and then leave them to you."

She said "Grace," and then went out of the room.

"Will you all please sit down," said Gisela, when the door was shut.

They all sat down, Joey squeezing her hands together in her excitement; for, of course, this must mean that Madge had agreed, and they would be able to go up the Mondscheinspitze, which she had been longing to do ever since Herr Mensch had told them about it.

Gisela was quite brief. She explained to them about the English custom of celebrating the Head's birthday, and told them that she and the Prefects had thought it would be a good plan to celebrate Miss Bettany's. Miss Bettany had no objection to their having the holiday, and, subject to the weather being fine, had agreed to their making an expedition up the Mondscheinspitze. If it was wet, they were to have a party in the Chalet.

"Miss Bettany has been very good to us," went on Gisela, "and I think you would all like to join to give her some souvenir of the first term of the Chalet School; would you not? So any who wish it may bring contributions to Bette Rincini or myself tomorrow, and on the Saturday we will go to Innsbruck and purchase something. And on Thursday, will those of you who can, please bring flowers, and come early, so that we may also give her a bouquet."

Then she ceased speaking, and waited. But the burst of enthusiasm which answered her told her that the idea was most popular, and, as Joey said later on, "That was that!"

CHAPTER TWELVE

Shopping—and a Meeting

SATURDAY PROVED to be a gloriously fine day. Joey and
Grizel in their short white tennis frocks, with bare brown
legs, looked delightfully cool, and the others in their brown
gym tunics regarded them enviously.

"You look so nice and fresh!" said Margia Stevens. "I
wish I was going into Innsbruck today!"

"You needn't," laughed Madge from the foot of the
table, where she was buttering Amy's roll for her. "It will
be stewing hot in Innsbruck today. Remember we're three
thousand feet above sea-level as it is, and there's a
delightful breeze from the lake; but there won't be a
breath of air down in the valley. What it will be like by
noon I can't think. Luckily, Gisela and Bette have enough
common sense to make you keep quiet then, or I wouldn't
let you go. Finished? Very well. You'd better run along
or you'll miss the train, and make the others miss it too.
Have you got plenty of money?"

"Heaps!" declared Joey. "Come on, Grizel. buck up!
Good-bye, everybody. Expect us when you see us!"

With this she danced out of the room, followed more
slowly by Grizel, and soon they were hurrying along by
the lake-path towards Seespitz and the mountain railway,
where Gisela and Bette awaited them impatiently, while
Fräulein Helfer, the Rincinis' *Mamsell*—or mother's help,
as we should call her in England—was already sitting in
the train.

"Come! You are very late!" cried the Head Girl. "I had
fear that we must await the next train, and Papa says that
it will be so hot in Innsbruck later on."

"Awfully sorry," returned Joey in unruffled tones. "I think our clocks must be wrong, because we thought we had oceans of time. Good-morning, Fräulein Helfer. Hope we haven't given you spasms! Isn't it a glorious day?"

Fräulein Helfer, who understood about half of this speech, bowed and smiled nervously.

"Joey, have you yet learned what it is Madame desires?" inquired Gisela presently, as the train puffed its way importantly down the mountain-side.

Joey shook her black head vigorously. "Not an idea. I think it'll be best if you just get what you think. Whatever it is, she'll be sure to like it, because you've given it. Hullo! Some people at Wachen! I say, what a crowd!"

"Summer visitors," said Bette. "Germans, most of them. That woman in the tartan dress comes from Berlin—I heard her say."

"What a size she is!" commented Grizel, as the lady in question lumbered into the car.

"What a tremendous way up we are! What would happen if anything broke, Gisela?" said Joey.

"I do not think it could happen," replied Gisela seriously. "I have never heard of it. But if it did, we should plunge over the side and on to the path to Spärtz, which lies down there."

"Wouldn't it be awful if the lake were suddenly to overflow? It would come down here like a mill-race, wouldn't it?"

"Joey! What horrid things you imagine!" protested Grizel.

Joey laughed, and stopped her imagining, to gaze at the lady from Berlin. She certainly was enormous—far fatter than Frau Mensch. She looked uncomfortably hot, too, in a dress of scarlet, green, and yellow tartan, with a little straw hat adorned with scarlet and green bows perched on the top of her head. Her yellow hair was scraped back off her wide face, making it seem larger than ever, and she stared in front of her with eyes like grey glass. Suddenly, as if attracted by Joey's interested regard, she glared at the small girl.

"Engländerin!" she snorted in guttural tones.

80

"Rather!" responded the irrepressible one. "And proud of it too!"

"Joey! Be quiet!" said Gisela firmly.

"Why should I? She spoke first!"

"It makes no matter. She is much, much older than you!"

Gisela had not intended her remarks to be overheard, but her voice was of the clear, carrying order, and the lady from Berlin not only heard, but understood.

"Schweine!" she said, and then heaved her bulk round, nearly upsetting her opposite neighbour, an inoffensive little Tyrolean who was going to market in Spärtz.

"Isn't she rude?" observed Joey. "All right, Gisela! I'm not going to say anything more. Did you say your father was going to meet us at Innsbruck?"

"Yes. Fräulein Helfer wishes to visit her parents, and Papa is going to be our escort. He will see us at the station, and will take us to the shops. Then we are going to have lunch at the Mariatheresien Restaurant, and afterwards we shall go for a drive along the Brenner Road, and go back by the last train. There is a *Gasthaus* up the Brenner where we can have coffee, and we will take cakes with us. Do you like it?"

"Topping! Isn't it, Grizel?"

"Rather!" said Grizel. "It's tophole of Herr Marani to do it! "

"I am so glad you are pleased!" said Gisela courteously. "Ah, we have arrived at Spärtz, and there is our train to Innsbruck on the other side of the platform! Come! We must hurry!"

But it was easier to say that than to do it. Frau Berlin, as Grizel had christened her, took her own time about getting out, and as she blocked the doorway, the girls had, perforce, to wait until she was well on to the platform.

"Come on! We shall miss the train if we don't buck up!" shouted Joey.

They nearly did miss it, for *Mamsell* was not accustomed to dashing from one train to another, and had it not been for Grizel and Gisela, who hauled her up the steps and into the carriage with little ceremony, she would have been left on the platform. As it was, she was gasping and scared.

"But never mind that; we've caught the train!" said Jo practically.

It was full, as it was the Wien-Paris train, so they had to content themselves in the corridor; however, it was only for a short time, and then they reached the outskirts of the capital of the Tyrol, where tall, flat houses faced them, with *plumeaux* hanging out to air from the open windows, while the hot valley air rushed to meet them as they whirled past.

"Here we are!" exclaimed Grizel, as the train drew up beside the busy platform. "And there's your father, Gisela. Let's get out! There's no horrid fat Frau Berlin to stop us this time!" As she spoke, she swung herself down on the platform, bumping into someone who was going heavily past. The someone turned and glared at her. Horrors! It was Frau Berlin herself! What would have happened it is hard to tell, for she had obviously heard and understood Grizel's indiscreet remarks. Luckily, at that moment Herr Marani came up, and quickly grasping what had occurred, he raised his hat, apologising courteously to the furious lady for the English child's clumsiness. Frau Berlin was not to be placated, but she rolled onwards, after directing a venomous glare at the impenitent Grizel.

"You must be more careful, my child," said Herr Marani, after he had assisted the others out of the carriage and through the barrier. "You might have hurt that lady very much indeed."

"I'm sorry," murmured Grizel untruthfully; while Gisela added, "Indeed, Papa, she was very rude as we came down, and called us *Schweine*."

"Hush, *mein Liebling*! I do not like to hear such words from thy lips," said her father, as they crossed the station square, which lay white and hot in the brilliant sunshine. "Let us talk of our errands instead. We need not think of an ill-bred Berliner, but only of what is pleasant to us all."

"There is a shop in the Museum Strasse where one can buy beautiful china," said Bette, as Gisela seemed to be reduced to silence by her father's gentle rebuke. "We had thought if we gave Madame a little coffee-service. We have collected enough money for a small one. Would she

82

like it, Joey? Or we can get her a necklace of carved ivory beads?"

"It's topping of you!" said Joey cordially. "She'd rather have the china, I believe. She doesn't care a great deal for jewellery."

"The coffee-service then, by all means," agreed Herr Marani. "I must go in here for two little moments to buy some cigars. Then we will go to the china shop and purchase the coffee-service."

"How shall we carry it home?" asked Grizel practically, as they waited for Herr Marani outside the shop.

"Gisela, is there anwhere where I can buy a picture of the Tiernsee? I think M—my sister would like that best," said Joey.

"Yes, of course! There is a very good shop in the Mariatheresien Strasse where they have pictures and photographs too. We can go there as we go to the restaurant."

Herr Marani came out of the shop at that moment, and taking Joey's hand, and with Bette on his other arm, said, "And now we are all ready for the important part of our holiday. Let us go to the shop." He turned off as he spoke down one of the side-streets that lead from the Landhaus Strasse to the Museum Strasse. "Now this is the shop where the china is sold. Let us go in and choose."

It was all very well to say it, but it was dreadfully difficult to decide among so much. There was one coffee-service bespattered with pink roses on a black ground, and another with a purple clematis pattern all over it, and they paused a long time before one in gold and black. However, they finally agreed on one with a blue and yellow design on a white ground, which had a quaintly foreign air to both Joey and Grizel, and Herr Marani told the woman in charge to pack it up and have it ready for them to take to the station when they should return from the Brenner drive. Then they left the shop, and turned out of the Museum Strasse into the Mariatheresien Strasse, which is a fine, wide street with very good modern shops. Whether you look down or up it, you see the mountains with which Innsbruck is ringed round. At the south end stands the triumphal arch and gate, and beyond them, the Herzog Friedrich Strasse, with its crowning glory of the *Goldenes Dachl* or "Golden Roof".

Grizel loved the great wide sweep of the more modern street; Joey preferred the history-steeped narrowness of the Emperor Frederick's day—and there you have the difference between the two girls. Herr Marani had discovered it long since, but it amused him to see it once again in their arguments about the two most famous thoroughfares of his beloved native city. However, time was getting on, so he hushed their arguments, and led them across the road to the shop on the opposite side of the street, where Joey soon succeeded in choosing a charming picture of the Tiernsee for her sister. Then they crossed once more, and entered the Mariatheresien Restaurant.

They did not pause in the crowded room which faces on to the street, but went right through to the Garden Room, where palms, a fountain, and creeper-hung trellises gave an open-air atmosphere which was very delightful. Electric fans whirling round kept the air fresh and cool, and they all sat down with sighs of relief. It really was boiling in the streets!

When she was comfortably settled, Joey looked round, and gave a little squeal.

"Gisela! Look! There's that horrid fat woman!"

Gisela, who was opposite her, promptly turned round, nearly overturning her chair as she did so, and saw, sitting a few yards away, their late enemy of the train. She had not seen them, for she was buried in a current number of the *Fliegende Blätter*, which is the German *Punch*, and she looked hotter than ever.

"Horrid old freak!" murmured Grizel. "Doesn't she look awful?"

"Like a scarlet hippopotamus!" suggested Joey. "If I were as fat as that I should go and drown myself."

Herr Marani, who had been discussing the menu with the waiter, turned at this moment, and caught the last speech of his youngest guest.

"Josephine!" he exclaimed in horror.

Joey had the grace to blush. "I know it's rude of me," she mumbled, "but—she is fat, isn't she, Herr Marani?"

"Hush, my child," he replied. "It is wrong to say such

things of one so much older. Now let us discuss our drive up the Brenner Road. I propose that we go to the Alte Post, where we can get coffee and rolls and butter. Perhaps we may be able to find a zither-player, and then you shall hear some of our mountain songs amidst the grandest scenery on earth. Then, when we have had coffee, and you have gathered your flowers, we will come down, and stop at the shops for our parcels, and then we must catch the train. You like that? Yes?"

"Oh, rather!" said Joey enthusiastically. "It's jolly good of you to give us such a ripping treat, Herr Marani."

He laughed. "I, too, like a little holiday. Here comes the soup."

Joey's eyes widened at the thought of soup on so hot a day, but when it came, she discovered that it was iced, and very delicious. From her seat she could see Fráu Berlin gobbling up soup also, with small regard for good manners. However, Herr Marani kept her attention occupied, and she soon forgot the fat lady. Frau Berlin, on the other hand, had just seen them, and she looked furious. In her indignation she allowed her temper to overcome her discretion, and she spat vehemently in their direction, just as the head waiter passed between them.

There was an instant uproar; for he, in the shock of the moment, stepped heavily backwards, almost upsetting Gisela, whose plate of soup went flying. Herr Marani sprang to his feet, and a couple of Italians who were lunching near joined in at once, pouring forth a flood of questions and exclamations, and, when the angry manager appeared on the scene, explanations of the whole affair. Several people who were sitting near stood up to see better what was happening. The author of all the disturbance snorted out something about *Verdammte Engländerinen*, and demanded her bill. Ten minutes later she had gone, everyone had sat down, the head waiter's feelings had been soothed by a gift of *Trinkgeld* from Herr Marani, and the manager had vanished, with only a very hazy idea of what had occurred, but convinced by everyone that the fault lay with Frau Berlin.

"I hope that is the last time we shall see her," said Gisela.

85

"She has been horrid all round!" declared Grizel with conviction. "But it was rather fun, wasn't it?"

"Yes, it was," agreed Bette; "but, like Gisela, I hope we shall see her no more."

However, they were destined to meet her again, though this they could not possibly know just then.

They finished their meal without further disturbance, and then Herr Marani took them back to the Station Square, where they got into one of the quaint open carriages which always amused the English girls so, and set off for their drive into the mountains.

CHAPTER THIRTEEN

At the Alte Post

"Oooh! Isn't this gorgeous?" Joey Bettany drew a long breath as she gazed round her at the mountains which rose on every side in majestic splendour, while below, the pine forests swept down to the valley, where the Inn went brawling past, hurrying down to join Father Danube. Herr Marani smiled kindly down at the little girl. Her enthusiasm pleased him, for like all Tyroleans, he loved his country devotedly.

"It is finer farther up," he said. "As we get higher and higher, we see the peaks at the other side; and if we go high enough, we can see the Stubai Glacier. We must take you there some day."

"If it's fine, we're going up the Mondscheinspitze on Madge's birthday, you know," said Joey eagerly.

"So? That is a pleasant little climb."

"I want to climb the Tiernjoch," put in Grizel. "I mean to some day, too!"

Now Grizel had said nothing about climbing the Tiernjoch lately, so Joey had imagined she had forgotten about her desire to make its ascent, and she was thoroughly dismayed at Grizel's remark.

"I wish Herr Mensch had never said anything about it!" she thought.

Herr Marani raised his eyebrows at Grizel's words. "The Tiernjoch? It is not a girl's climb. Best leave it alone —for the present at any rate," he said decisively.

"I mean to go," said Grizel stubbornly. "And I'm not a baby, Herr Marani."

"But will Madame permit it?" put in Gisela somewhat tactlessly. "It is, as Papa says, a very difficult climb—I have not done it yet! It would tire you, Grizel."

Grizel made no answer, but her mouth took its old obstinate lines, and Joey made haste to change the conversation.

Their kindly host pointed out to them a huge, white, barn-like building up the mountain-side.

"That is the Alte Post," he said. "We shall be there in half an hour now, and then we will have our coffee——"

"Papa!" Gisela interrupted him with a cry of dismay. "The cakes! We have forgotten the cakes! Now we shall only have rolls and butter."

"Gott in Himmel! But how thoughtless!" Herr Marani looked as perturbed as his daughter.

"Perhaps they will have *Kuchen* at the inn," suggested Bette, not very hopefully.

"And anyway, it doesn't matter," added Joey. "We can get cakes any day when we're in the town."

The big Austrian's face cleared at that. "That is true, *Bübchen*. You shall have cakes for Fräulein Bettany's birthday to make up for your disappointment today. My mother makes delicious honey and nut cakes, and I will ask her to make some for you."

"Oh, that would be ripping of you if you will," said Joey fervently.

"Topping!" agreed Grizel.

"Grandmamma makes wonderful cakes," said Gisela. "We all love them."

"Madge will be bucked!" murmured Madge's small sister. "She is going to have a jolly birthday!"

"It won't be a bit like English birthdays," observed Grizel. "Except the presents, of course, and the flowers!"

"And the birthday cake," added Joey. "She and Mademoiselle have made a huge one, all rich and plummy, with a threepenny and a button and a ring in."

"But why?" demanded Gisela. "I do not understand."

"Don't you? Why, whoever gets the threepenny will be rich, and the ring means marriage, and the button an old maid," explained Joey. "We always did at home; and candles round the cake too—as many candles as you are years old."

"Is Miss Bettany going to have candles?" queried Grizel with interest.

"I don't know; she didn't say. I expect she will, though. Oh, Herr Marani! Just look at those flowers! Can't we get out and gather some?"

"Best to wait till we return," he advised. "Then your flowers will be fresh to take home. We are almost there now. Just one more turn and we reach it."

"I say! Wouldn't it be awful if Frau Berlin were to be there?"

All the others turned to Grizel, who had made this charming suggestion.

"Goodness! I hope not!" This vigorously from Joey.

"What a dreadful idea, Grizel!" Thus Gisela.

While Herr Marani said decidedly, "Oh, I should not expect it!"

"Still she might be," persisted Grizel. "We've met her once already."

"Then, if she should indeed be there, I shall trust you to say nothing, do nothing that may upset her," said the Austrian gravely.

"Supposing she spits at us again?" suggested Joey. "She might!"

"Then you will remember that you are English, and an Englishwoman is not revengeful. Gisela and Bette, you must be careful of what you say. I do not wish a disturbance which might mean that we could not have our coffee at the *Gasthaus*."

"And here we are!" exclaimed Bette. "We will remember, Onkel."

Herr Marani gave orders about the coffee to a pretty dark-eyed girl who had come out on hearing the noise of the wheels.

"Coffee?" she said, in the low-German patois of the country. "Yes, I can give you coffee, very good, and bread-and-butter too."

"Have you any cakes?" asked Herr Marani.

She shook her head. "Na; Kuchen, nein! Aber Marmelade," she added good-naturedly, seeing the disappointment on the four girlish faces. "Marmelade ist sehr gut."

"We will have that, then," decided Herr Marani.

She nodded. "Im Speisesaal—fünf minuten." She held up the five fingers of her left hand to emphasise her remark, and then ran off.

"I always think it's so funny to call jam 'marmalade'," observed Grizel idly. "What a pretty girl, Herr Marani! But she looks quite Italian. Look! There are some more! What heaps of children!" as four or five tow-headed urchins came shyly round the corner of the house to stare wide-eyed at the visitors.

"All probably grandchildren of the innkeeper," said Gisela. "Sometimes three or four families will live together in a place like this. Papa, see! How near the mountains seem!"

"It is only seeming," said her father. "Look, Josephine! That is the way you came to Innsbruck. There is the line, over there, across the river. And now, our five minutes are up. Let us go and see if our coffee is ready."

Bette and Grizel ran on in front, bursting into the *Speisesaal*, only to draw up in amazed silence. There before them sat Frau Berlin, drinking coffee and eating bread at one of the tables!

She looked up as they entered, and her already purple face deepened in colour as she glared at them.

"My only aunt!" gasped Grizel, finding her voice at last.

Herr Marani was equally thunderstruck; but before anything else could be said, Frau Berlin heaved herself to her feet.

"I will *mit* English pig-dogs not eat!" she announced in thunderous tones.

"Well, we don't want to eat with you!" retorted Grizel before Gisela could stop her.

The woman glared at her in stupefied silence. Herr Marani put out a hand, and dragged the English child back with small ceremony.

"Be silent!" he said sternly. "Go outside, all four of you!"

However indulgent he might be in some ways, Gisela knew that her father insisted on obedience, so she hauled Grizel out into the open air, followed by Bette and Joey, who were half scared, half inclined to giggle.

"Grizel!" exclaimed the Head Girl when they were outside. "How could you speak so rudely! She has right to be annoyed now!"

"I'm not going to be called 'pig-dog' by any measly old German!" retorted Grizel.

Gisela threw out her hands with a little gesture of helplessness.

"You are an idiot, Grizel!" remarked Joey casually. "You're spoiling our fun by being so stupid! If you'd left it alone, she'd have been in the wrong; now it's us!"

"Well, you can let that fat old pig call you names if you like," flashed Grizel, "but I won't! You aren't a bit patriotic!"

"How dare you say that!" Joey was becoming heated now. "I'm as patriotic as you, but I've a little more common sense! If you'd held your tongue, she would have been in the wrong. But now you've been abominably rude and let us down! Patriotic! Huh! If that's your patriotism, I'm glad I don't possess any of it! A nice name she'll give all English girls now, thanks to you being 'patriotic'!" She stopped for sheer lack of breath, and Gisela promptly interfered.

"It is of no use to quarrel now. It is done, and it is a great pity, but it cannot be helped. Joey, will you come with me to gather some of those flowers? And Bette, perhaps you and Grizel will go the other way and see what you can find."

"Certainly," said Bette promptly. "Come along, Grizel!"

Grizel's quick passion had died by this time, and she was feeling rather ashamed of herself, so she meekly followed Bette; while Gisela, taking no notice of Joey's lowering expression, walked up the road, chatting easily about the flowers which grew in glorious splendour everywhere. By the time they returned to the *Gasthaus* in answer to Herr Marani's call, the storm had blown over, and they were able to enjoy the excellent coffee, *Butterbrod*, and *Pflaume Marmelade*, which the pretty girl of the inn laid before them on a table outside. She also produced some apples, and they made an excellent tea. Herr Marani was, apparently, quite undisturbed by his encounter with Frau Berlin, whom they could see in the *Speisesaal* thunderously drinking her coffee, with her enormous back ostentatiously turned towards them. However, Grizel was not to get off quite so lightly, for when the meal was over, and they were gathering flowers to take back to Tiernsee, their host called her to him.

"Mein Kindchen," he said gently, "another time, please do not be so violent in your patriotism. There is no real harm done this time, but it has not made our little expedition the pleasanter, and I do not think Miss Bettany would like it."

"No," agreed Grizel meekly. "I'm sorry I was so rude, Herr Marani."

"Then we will forget," he said cheerfully. "Come, I will get you some of those ferns for your bouquet, and then we must return, or we shall be too late to catch our train, and I am sure you do not want to walk up the mountain-road from Spärtz."

"Don't forget we must call for the picture and the china, Papa," said Gisela, as they were once more seated in the carriage, rattling down the mountain-side. "The others will wish to see what we have chosen."

"Of course," he said. "I can understand that."

"It's getting hotter, isn't it?" remarked Joey. "There was a lovely fresh breeze up by the Alte Post, but down here it's quite hot."

"That is because we are lower down," laughed Bette. "Onkel, did you see Herr Rittmeister von Eschenau yesterday? He had bought Wanda and Marie six books of English school-stories, all new. Wanda said she would lend them to us."

"Ah, that reminds me," said her uncle. "Josephine, Frau von Eschenau has told me that she wishes to send Wanda and Marie to the Chalet School. Do you think your sister will be able to have them for boarders?"

Joey's face flushed as she said joyfully, "Oh, how gorgeous! I like Wanda and Marie so much; don't you, Grizel? Yes, I'm sure she can have them. Oh, what splendacious news!"

"We are growing! We'll be a big school soon," said Grizel. "There are four more girls coming next term, and with Wanda and Marie, that will make us twenty-two, and there may be more yet!"

"Are we going to live at Tiernsee all the winter, Papa?" asked Gisela.

"Yes, I think so," he replied. "I shall spend the week with *Grossmutter* in town, and come for the Sunday. Herr Mensch is going to do the same; and Bette, I think you are to live with us."

Bette clapped her hands. "How delightful! Oh, Onkel Florian, I am so glad! It would have been so lonely in Innsbruck without you all!"

"Hasn't this been a day of happenings?" said Joey presently as they reached the town.

They retrieved their purchases and made for the station, where Herr Marani left them for a moment in order to buy a paper. As they stood in a little group waiting for him, Grizel suddenly uttered an exclamation. "Oh, see! Joey! Look! There is Captain Carrick over there!"

Her clear accents carried high above the other noises, and the man at whom she was pointing, in defiance of good manners, heard her, and turned. It was, indeed, Captain Carrick. Raising his soft hat, he came over to them.

"Well, girls! Fancy seeing you here! I found I had to run into Innsbruck to go to the bank. I have left Mrs. Carrick waiting for me in Munich. How is Juliet? She is not with you, I see."

"No; we came in to buy a birthday present for Miss Bettany," explained Grizel. "We are going back now."

"And so am I—going back to Munich. But your mention of Miss Bettany reminds me that I have a note for her from my wife—something about her summer frocks, I think. I wonder, Miss Joey, if you would mind taking it for me. I forgot to post it, and she will get it all the sooner."

"Oh, rather!" Joey took the note, and then the Captain bade them "good-bye" and strolled away.

"Joey, you look puzzled," said Bette. "What is it?"

"Nothing," said Joey briefly. "Here's Herr Marani."

They accomplished the rest of the journey without any further happening, and were met at Seespitz by Madge, Miss Maynard, Simone, Juliet, and the Stevens.

"We thought we'd stroll round to meet you," explained Madge. "What lovely flowers! For me? Oh, thank you, girls! "

"Madge, this is for you! " said Joey, producing the note. "It's from Captain Carrick. I saw him in Innsbruck, and he gave it to me to give to you, because he had forgotten to post it. He came in to go to the bank, and was going back to Munich tonight, he said."

Madge's black brows had been drawn together in a quick frown at the sound of the forbidden Christian name, but something in Joey's tone checked her. She glanced irresolutely at the note.

"Read it!" urged Joey. "Read it now, Madge!"

"Oh, yes, Miss Bettany, please read it!" echoed Juliet, who had gone suddenly white on hearing Joey's news. "Yes, read it!"

With a murmured word of excuse, Madge opened the envelope, and began to read, a little puzzled frown on her face. Suddenly she gave vent to an exclamation.

"Oh, how dreadful! What am I to do?"

CHAPTER FOURTEEN

Juliet, the Incubus

AT ONCE they all closed round her—all, that is, save Juliet.
She stood on the outside of the little circle, with white face
and eyes full of dread. None of them noticed her; they
were too much interested in Madge and the letter.

"What is it?" demanded Joey. "What's the letter say?"

Madge, reading the closely written words on the sheet
of thin, foreign paper, did not answer her, so Joey shook
her arm slightly.

"Madge, what is it?"

With an effort the elder girl pulled herself together, and
realised the startled little crowd of children round her.

"Never mind, Joey," she said sharply. "Miss Maynard,
will you take the girls home, please? Tell Mademoiselle I
shall be back presently. Herr Marani, I must have a man's
advice."

"Certainly, Fräulein. I shall be pleased to do anything
for you that I can. Will you not come back with us? It
is difficult to talk business here. Gisela, you may go to
Buchau with Bette, but make haste to return."

The various parties set off, Miss Maynard taking the
Chalet girls by the lake-road to Briesau, while Bette and
Gisela struck off across the water-meadows in the direction
of Buchau, on the opposite side of the lake, and Miss
Bettany and Herr Marani turned towards Torteswald.
No one even noticed that Juliet stayed where she had
dropped in the long grass in a little heap, shaking with
silent sobs.

Herr Marani left the subject of the letter severely alone
until they reached the Villa Hubertus, a pretty wooden
house just outside Torteswald. Arrived there, he put

Madge in a chair on the verandah, and disappeared indoors, to return presently with a cup of coffee, which he insisted on her drinking before they discussed any business whatsoever.

"You have had a shock," he said. "Drink the coffee, Fräulein."

Miss Bettany drank it, and felt better. He took the empty cup from her, placing it to one side, and then sat down beside her.

"And now, Fräulein, tell me what has troubled you in this letter."

For answer, Madge held it out to him. "Will you read it?" she said.

He took it from her, and read it slowly through.

"DEAR MISS BETTANY," Captain Carrick had written,— "Perhaps you will be surprised at what I am going to say. Possibly you will think and say very hard things about me. That is my misfortune. However, let me break to you at once the news that I am presenting you with my daughter Juliet. Circumstances over which I have no control force me to leave Europe at once with my wife. A sulky school-girl will only be an encumbrance to us, added to which I have very little money. At least you have been paid a term's fees, and I dare say you can make the girl useful to you, and repay yourself for her food and clothes in that way.

"If, in the future, I find myself able to afford to keep her again, I will send for her. Until you hear from me to this effect, she is in your hands and at your mercy.

"I regret that I am forced to these measures, but I see nothing else for it. Of course, if you like, you can send her to the nearest orphan asylum; but I have more faith in your goodness of heart. For your own convenience, I may as well tell you that neither my wife nor I have any relatives, so search for them will be as useless as search for us. Juliet can tell you that much herself.—Au revoir!
                                          "LINDLEY F. C. CARRICK."

Herr Marani swore deeply in German when he had finished reading this heartless letter. Then, realising that Madge could understand him, he apologised hastily.

"I crave your pardon, Fräulein. It is the callous impudence of this man! He is not worthy of the name of either 'man' or 'father'! That poor child, to be abandoned thus!"

At these words, a slight figure rose out of the bushes which came up to the edge of the verandah, and a sobbing voice said, "Miss Bettany! Oh, have they left me again?"

"Juliet!" cried her headmistress. "How did you come here?"

Herr Marani made three strides, and was off the verandah and beside the child in a moment. He gripped her by the arm and drew her in to Miss Bettany, who looked at the red-rimmed eyes in the white face with a softening glance.

"What did you mean by 'again'?" demanded the Austrian.

Juliet flung herself down on her knees by Madge's side.

"Oh, I was so afraid when they made me a boarder!" she sobbed. "They did it once before in the Hills; but that time the Head found them and made them take me back. Then we came here, and ever since he told me I was to be a boarder, I have been afraid they meant to leave me. In one way, I'd rather be with you, because you are kind to me. But oh, it's so dreadful to be thrown on people's charity!" she finished with a little dry sob.

Madge slipped an arm round her. "You poor kid!"

It was such a pitiful existence the child had shown her in that little gasping, sobbed-out speech! She was furious at the letter, but she could not vent her anger on the girl kneeling beside her.

"Don't cry, Juliet. We'll fix things up somehow. It's very hard luck on you."

With these few words she had won Juliet's passionate allegiance, though she was not to find that out till afterwards. Now she turned to her host.

"Herr Marani, I must think what to do. Perhaps you can help me. Meanwhile, Juliet ought to be at home—it's getting late. Here is Gisela coming. I just want to know if you can tell me whether it would be possible to get on to Captain Carrick's tracks. Could we wire them at Munich Station?"

Herr Marani shook his head. "I do not think he will have gone back to Munich. He is much more likely to have gone east to Wien, or else straight through to Paris. We can try, but I do not think it would be worth it. Take Juliet home now, and I will think what is best to do. Yes, that is the best plan."

"Thank you, Herr Marani. We will do as you say. Come, Juliet, it is supper-time now. Stop crying, child, and come along."

"You will permit me to row you across the lake?" said their host. "It is growing late, and the last steamer has gone."

Madge thanked him with her prettiest smile. She was, as a matter of fact, thankful to have him with them, for for he was right in saying that it was growing late. She had been out all day, and was feeling tired out with exertion and the shock Captain Carrick's letter had given her. So she fell in readily with the kind Austrian's suggestion, and even meekly accepted the loan of a huge shawl belonging to his wife when he brought it to her with the remark that her gown was thin and that, on the lake at any rate, it would be rather chilly now. Juliet was muffled up in a similar wrap, and then they set off down the quiet road over which the occasional chalets cast dark, gloomy shadows in the bright moonlight. Feeling the child beside her still quivering with an occasional sob, Madge slipped one hand from under her shawl, and clasped the thin fingers in a reassuring grip.

"It is very good of you, Herr Marani," she said, addressing her host. "Indeed, I think everyone is kind in Austria."

"Oh, *bitte sehr*," he said, glancing down at her with a smile. "We should be a rude people indeed if we were not grateful to the lady who is doing so much for our girls. And we are not Prussians, you know!"

"It's funny," said Madge slowly, "but the only discourtesies I have met with have been from Prussians. The Bavarians I know are all delightful, and as for the Tyrolese, I cannot say how much I like them. But the Prussians seem to be filled with a hatred as bitter and venomous as vitriol."

Herr Marani laughed. "We had a good example of that today. The little Grizel makes a worthy opponent."

"An opponent? Why, what do you mean? What on earth has Grizel been doing?" demanded Madge with a feeling of dismay.

"Oh, she was not really to blame," he replied. "It was a Frau Berliner who created most of the disturbance, and das Mädchen is patriotic—and hot-headed. Here is the boat, mein Fräulein. Will you sit in the stern, please, and steer?"

He helped them in, and pushed off from the land. When they were well away, he told them of Grizel's encounter with the fat lady of Berlin, describing it with a good deal of humour, and glossing over Grizel's behaviour as much as might be.

"Oh, dear! I'm afraid Grizel has been dreadfully rude," sighed the young headmistress. Then, with a sudden change, she began to laugh. "I should like to have seen it, all the same! I can just imagine it! She is a thorough little John Bull—the result, I suppose, of never having left her own country before. Joey, my little sister, is much more of a cosmopolitan. But then, she has travelled fairly widely."

"It was very funny," agreed Herr Marani with a reminiscent chuckle, as he drew up by the Chalet boat-landing. "No, thank you, Fräulein," as Madge invited him to come in for coffee. "I must return. My wife is away, and the children will be expecting me. Auf wiedersehen!"

"Auf wiedersehen," called Madge softly, as the boat shot out into the moonlight once more. Then she turned to Juliet. "Come, Juliet! It's appallingly late, and you ought to have been in bed an hour ago."

Juliet clung to her arm a moment, her face gleaming white in the dusk.

"Miss Bettany, you've been awfully good to me! I'm so sorry I was ever horrid to you! If you'll keep me, I'll do my level best to help you and—and not be a nuisance! I promise you I will!"

Madge looked down at her with a little smile. "I shouldn't turn you out even if we were in England, Juliet. Certainly not in a foreign land. Your father guessed rightly when he guessed that!"

Juliet looked at her with an expression in her eyes which made the elder girl exclaim sharply, "Juliet! What are you thinking?"

"I was thinking—oh, Miss Bettany, do you think they are really my father and mother? Do you think perhaps I am a foundling, and that's why?"

"Nonsense," replied her headmistress firmly. "That's all rubbish, my dear child. Of course they are your father and mother! Now come along in, and then you must have some hot milk and go to bed and to sleep. Come!"

She turned towards the house as she spoke, and Juliet, her mind set at rest on this point which had troubled her for long, followed obediently. At the door they were met by Mademoiselle, who was looking anxious.

"I had begun to have fears for you, *ma chérie*," said the little Frenchwoman as they entered. "It is so late, and Juliet will be so weary. Go straight upstairs to bed, *ma petite*, and I will bring thee a cup of warm milk. Go quietly, for all are now asleep."

"Yes, Juliet, go," said Madge. "Good-night, child! Sleep well, and don't worry!"

"Good-night, Miss Bettany," replied Juliet. "And— and thank you." She turned and vanished up the stairs, while Madge and Mademoiselle went on to their sitting-room.

"There is a cablegram, Marguérite," said Mademoiselle, as the English girl dropped limply into the nearest chair. "Drink this coffee, *ma mignonne*. Thou art weary."

"I'm completely done," replied Madge candidly, as she opened the cablegram.

She read it aloud. " 'Have nothing to do with Carrick. Writing.—DICK.' Oh, well, it's done now! Read this, Elise, and see what you think of it."

She tossed Captain Carrick's letter across to her friend, and then turned her attention to the coffee, eggs, and rolls Mademoiselle had provided for her.

Meanwhile, the Frenchwoman read the remarkable communication with many ejaculations, but of horror and surprise. When she had finished it, she turned back to the beginning and read it over again.

"But, *ma mie*," she cried in her own language, "it is villainy, this!"

"Villainy pure and simple," agreed Madge. "As for that poor child Juliet, what do you think she had got into her head? That she was a foundling, and that was why they had done it. Apparently it isn't the first time either. They did it once before in India, she says." And she repeated Juliet's pitiful story, while Mademoiselle uttered little cries of sympathy.

"Of course he is quite right," finished the girl soberly. "I shall most certainly keep her! But imagine the poor child's feelings! Of course it's a silly, morbid idea, and there is no foundation for it except this abominably callous treatment of her; still, that's what she was thinking."

"Oh, there can be no truth there," agreed Mademoiselle. "There is a most clear likeness to both parents. But, my Marguérite, have you thought that there will be now another mouth to fill and another body to clothe? Soon it will be winter—already it grows colder at nights—and she has no winter garments at all."

"Well, what do you propose I should do?" demanded Madge. "Follow the delightful suggestion he offers as an alternative to keeping her, and place her in an institution? You *know* you wouldn't hear of it! No, I shall keep her. Next term I shall let her help with the little ones, so that she need not feel under too great an obligation to us. She can do quite a lot without interfering with her own work, and as she will be the oldest of our boarders, it need surprise nobody. Now I vote that we go to bed. It's eleven o'clock, and I'm dead tired. What a blessing tomorrow is Sunday and we can take things easily!"

At the head of the stairs she turned before going to her own room.

"Don't let the others know about this," she said earnestly. "It would make it so dreadfully uncomfortable for Juliet. I will go and see her tomorrow early, and warn her to say nothing. *Bonne nuit*, Elise."

"Bonne nuit, ma mie. Le bon Dieu te garde," responded Mademoiselle.

Then they went to their own rooms, and presently darkness and silence reigned over the Chalet.

CHAPTER FIFTEEN

Sunday

THE BOARDERS of the Chalet School always declared that
Sunday was quite one of the best days of the week. To
begin with, they could stay in bed until nine o'clock if
they were so minded. Then, after their breakfast of coffee,
rolls, and honey, they all assembled in the meadow which
ran up from the lake edge to the pine wood, and Madge
read aloud to them for an hour. The Catholics generally
attended High Mass, but the service was held only once
in three weeks. After the reading, they were allowed to
wander about as they liked, so long as they kept within
call, and they were summoned to dinner at twelve o'clock.
In the afternoon, they generally took books and lay outside,
reading, or talking quietly, or sleeping; and in the evening
Madge took the English girls, and Mademoiselle the
Catholics, and they had quiet talks which never lasted
more than an hour. Then they were once more free to do
as they pleased until Marie's bell called them to supper
and bed.

On this particular Sunday, the first person to awaken
was Jo Bettany. She had a funny trick of opening her eyes
to their widest extent and then sitting bolt upright, wide
awake in an instant. This morning, as she sat up in her
little wooden bed, gazing straight out of the window, she
suddenly remembered Madge's expression as she had
read Captain Carrick's letter the night before, and her
hands clenched.

"If he's worried Madge, I—I'll take it out on Juliet!"
she thought. "I hate him—horrid man! Poor old Madge!

I wonder if I could wake her? What time is it?" She burrowed under the pillow and found her watch. Seven o'clock, and much too early to disturb anyone on a Sunday! Joey tucked it back and turned her attention to the book at the bedside, which Dick had presented to her just before he had departed for India. The sight of the green covers of the book recalled her brother's cablegram to her memory, and she began to wonder what news it had contained. Obviously it had been nothing serious, or her sister would have let her know before this.

At this point the sound of a light footstep aroused her, and, turning her head, she saw Madge come in, moving cautiously as she skirted the other beds. Her face lighted up as she met Joey's gaze.

"So you are awake!" she said in low tones. "I thought you might be. Fetch your things along to my room, and we'll dress and go out. I want to talk to you."

Joey slipped out of bed, clutched at her garments, and then tip-toed along to her sister's room. Miss Bettany was standing in front of the mirror brushing out her hair. She turned round as her small sister entered, and smiled involuntarily at the funny little figure in the yellow dressing-gown.

"You do look a fright, Jo!" she said in true sisterly fashion. "Now hurry up and get dressed. I had my tub before I came to fetch you, and I've filled it up again for you."

Joey deposited her clothes on the bed and departed.

Madge then left the bedroom to make a raid on the larder. When she came back, bearing two large chunks of currant cake, Jo was ready, and her bed had been stripped and the *plumeaux* hung over the balcony. The Bettanys were not demonstrative as a rule, preferring to show their affection by deeds rather than words, so Madge understood what that act was intended to convey, though all she said was, "Here, catch! That's all I could find. There isn't any milk either, so if you're thirsty, you'll have to drink water."

"Thanks awfully," said Jo, with her mouth full. "Ripping cake Marie makes, doesn't she? Are we going for a trot?"

"Just a short one. It's a glorious morning—going to be boiling later."

"I'm glad. I love hot weather," replied Joey, as she crept downstairs after her sister.

"Be quiet! You'll wake the whole house if you yell like that!" returned Madge, the headmistress completely merged in the elder sister.

Joey gave a subdued giggle, but moderated her tones at once. Madge, glancing at her, felt a throb of joy. The three months in a dry climate had already made a great difference to her. The cough had vanished, and the warm sun and clean mountain air had wiped out the unnatural pallor which her constant illnesses in England had produced. She was getting plumper, too, and her eyes were bright. Pretty she would never be, not even with the elusive prettiness of her elder sister, but she had lost her goblin-like appearance.

"You look pounds better," decided Miss Bettany. "Tiernsee suits you."

"Rather!" agreed Jo. "Suits you too, old thing! You're a bit more freckly, of course, but I'm not sure it isn't an improvement."

"Freckly! You little horror! " exclaimed her sister. "It's a mercy the girls don't hear you! And that reminds me, Joey, you really must try to remember not to use my Christian name before them. You did it again last night. Yes, I know it was because you were excited; but you mustn't do it, even if you are thrilled about something."

"Awfully sorry," murmured Joey. Then she slipped her hand through Madge's arm. "Madge, what was in the cablegram from India?"

"Business," replied Madge briefly. She turned and looked at her small sister thoughtfully. She wasn't very sure how much to tell Joey. She knew quite well that something, at any rate, must be told. The family baby had joined in all their councils ever since she could understand what they were talking about, and she knew Joey well enough to be sure that she would be intensely hurt if she were left out now. Jo was very clannish in feeling. What injured her brother or sister injured her. She would be wondering what had been in Captain Carrick's letter, and the chances were that if she were not told she would guess. Madge decided that it was better to tell her the whole truth rather than leave things to her vivid imagination.

"Jo," she said abruptly, "I'm going to trust you. I don't want any of the others to know, but you've always shared with us, and I'm not going to leave you out now. That letter from Captain Carrick told me that he was leaving Juliet on our hands. He can't afford to keep her, so he says, so he's dropped her on to us. It's very hard luck on her, poor kiddy, because she has no one for the present but us. He did suggest that we might send her to an institution if we didn't want to keep her. But that's impossible, of course."

"Oh, of course!" agreed Joey, her impressionable little heart filling with pity for the girl who was looked on as a nuisance by her own parents. "Oh, Madge! Poor Juliet! I'll be as decent to her as I can!"

"Don't let her know you know," warned the elder girl. "She would hate that. Just be nice to her as you are to Grizel, or Gisela, or Bernhilda. Remember, Jo, I've trusted you. Dick's cable was warning me about the Carricks, but it's too late now. The only thing we can do is to be as kind as we can to Juliet, and make the best of it."

"Rather!" But Joey's bright little face looked puzzled.

"Well! What now?" demanded Madge. "What are you thinking, Jo?"

"I was thinking, it seems such a horrid thing to do, to desert your own child! Mother and father wouldn't have done it."

"I should think not!" Madge's thoughts went back to the long-dead father and mother who had loved their children so tenderly. "I've never heard of any other parents doing it either. Don't think about it more than you can help, Joey-Baba. Now tell me about yesterday."

"We'd a lovely time," responded Joey eagerly. "You'd have loved it at the Alte Post. And oh, the mountains! Madge, I love mountains!"

"Well, you've certainly got plenty of them here," said her sister. "Go on. Tell me what you did. Oh, and about that Berlin woman! What did Grizel say? I imagine she was frightfully rude, though Herr Marani didn't actually say so. But I know what she is by this time. Tell me all about it, Joey."

Thus encouraged, Jo gave a fairly accurate account of their various encounters with Frau Berlin, leaving Madge divided between laughter at the humour of it all, and horror at Grizel's behaviour.

"Grizel really is dreadful," she said at last. "I do hope you didn't join in, Joey."

"Madge! Is it likely? I've got a little common-sense!" cried Joey, distinctly outraged.

"I should hope so," returned her sister; "but one never knows. Now don't get excited. I didn't really suppose you did. Well, it's time to go back now, so we'd better turn. Have you got any ideas for Thursday besides the Mond-scheinspitze expedition? I've asked Frau Pfeifen to make some of the cakes for us, and I thought we'd get some tobacco. Herr Braun says the herdsmen always appreciate it, because, of course, they can't get it up there."

"Oh, that reminds me, Herr Marani is going to ask his mother to make some cakes for us," said Jo. "Gisela says she makes gorgeous cakes—all honey and nuts! The kind that melt in your mouth. Oh, and, Madge, I nearly forgot! He told me to tell you that Frau von Eschenau is coming to see you. He thinks she wants Wanda and Marie to be boarders. Won't it be topping if she does?"

"No, really?" said Madge, with quick interest. "Are you sure, Joey?"

"Well, that's what he said," replied Jo. "I say, aren't we growing?"

Madge laughed. "We are indeed! If we get any more boarders, I shall have to take another chalet for us to live in, or have school in, or something. Here we are! Now, Joey, remember! Not a word of what I have told you to anyone else."

Joey trotted off, and Madge turned into the dining-room, where baskets piled high with brown rolls and glass dishes full of amber honey gave colour to the clothless table. The big, hand-made cups and plates, with their cheerful decoration of unknown flowers painted in vivid colours, which stood at each place had come from Tiern

105

Kirche. The table looked un-English in the extreme, but very pleasant and inviting. Presently Marie came in bearing a huge earthenware jug in which steamed delicious coffee such as one rarely gets in England. She filled the cups by the simple method of dipping a mug into the boiling liquid and pouring its contents into each cup, while Madge arranged plates of the sugar oblongs, which were the joy of Joey, at convenient intervals down the long table. Her task completed, Marie carried the jug back to the kitchen, and then rang the bell which brought them all, fresh and summery in their white frocks, to the table.

Breakfast on Sunday was always a gay meal, for rules were then relaxed, and everyone chattered in her native language. Mademoiselle, Simone, and Joey were carrying on an animated conversation in French, while Grizel and Margia Stevens argued amiably in English about the probable ending of some book they were both reading, and Miss Maynard and Juliet were describing to the others the walk they had taken on the previous day. Juliet, it is true, had little to say, but Madge noted thankfully that she looked more natural than she had done last night. On the whole, the elder girl felt glad that she had taken her little sister into her confidence. It would make things easier, for she hated having any secrets from Jo. Besides, if anyone should be surprised when the next term found Juliet helping, Madge felt certain that her sister would put a stop to that by her own attitude in the matter.

After breakfast, the girls fled upstairs to make their beds, and the staff foregathered in the little sitting-room, where Madge told Miss Maynard that Juliet Carrick was to be a kind of student teacher next term, as her people had lost money, and had left her at the Chalet School for the present. Miss Maynard was interested, but showed no curiosity. When Miss Bettany suggested that perhaps she might like to go and write her letters, she went off cheerfully, putting Juliet and her affairs completely out of her mind.

Madge turned to Mademoiselle with a sigh of relief.

"Thank goodness! I wasn't sure whether she would want to ask questions, and it would have been awkward if she had. I've told Jo about it, Elise. If I hadn't, she might have imagined things as being worse than they are And it's quite safe with her; she won't talk."

"No, that is true," agreed Mademoiselle. "Have you seen Juliette yet?"

"No; I'm going to see her presently and tell her what I've decided. Now I must hunt up my book." She turned to the bookshelves as she spoke, hunting for *The Little Flowers of St. Francis*, which she was reading to the girls. Mademoiselle watched her with a sympathetic smile.

"You are very tender of Juliette's feelings, *chérie*. I can but trust that she will repay all your kindness to her! She has not proved an attractive member of the school so far."

Madge said, "I'm sure Juliet will do her best now, poor child."

There was a moment's silence, then Mademoiselle turned to the door with a little nod. "Perhaps you are right; we shall see! You are not wanting me this morning? Then I will ask Herr Braun to row me across to Buchau for High Mass."

"Yes, do," replied her friend absently. "Elise, why are those children so excited? Look at them!"

Mademoiselle looked out of the open window, to behold Margia, Amy, and Simone racing across the grass with eager faces. At the same moment music was wafted to them on the warm summer air.

"A band! A band!" cried Margia, who had shot ahead of the others. "Oh, Madame, a band—all violins and flutes and things!"

"Well, but why get excited about that?" asked Madge. "We've had bands here before—there was one last Sunday."

"Oh, but not like this! Big, very dark men, with flashing eyes!"

"They wear hankies round their heads," put in Amy, who had come up, panting, together with Simone. "Very bright hankies—all blue, and red, and yellow, and green! And huge silver rings in their ears! "

"The Tzigane! " exclaimed Madge, her eyes brightening. "Why, what fun! I wondered if there would be any of them round here this year. They're gipsies, children, and

107

their music is often very wonderful. We must go and listen to them this afternoon. I wonder where they will be playing?"

"Gipsies? The people who make gipsy tunes like in Liszt's Hungarian Rhapsodies?" queried Margia, who was intensely musical, and meant to be a pianiste some day.

"Yes, just exactly those tunes. You'll love them, Margia. They aren't a bit like other music, but something wild and untamed like the gipsies themselves. I do hope they've a good band! If so, we shall have a treat this afternoon."

At this point the others came to join them, ready for the reading, and as they made their way slowly through the flower-sprinkled grass to the shade of the pines, Madge told them of the old superstition that the gipsies were cursed with wandering because one of their race had once denied rest and shelter to our Lord. The girls were delighted, and seeing this, she repeated the old legend of the attempt to steal the nails which pierced Christ's hands. "It was a gipsy who did it—or tried to do it," she said. "Partly, he wanted the iron; but partly, also, he had pity on Christ. For that pity, so the gipsies say, thieving is not counted by God as a sin in them, and they think nothing of it. They are a strange people. They are to be found in most parts of the world, and the Romany tongue is practically the same the whole world over. A gipsy from India would talk with a gipsy from our New Forest, and each would be able to understand what the other said. A true gipsy can never be happy within four walls. It is misery to them to be imprisoned in any way. They are very revengeful, too, and never forget a wrong. But then, it is said, they never forget a kindness either."

By this time they had reached their favourite spot, so they settled down, and, putting the Tzigane out of her mind for the time being, Madge read aloud to them about the gentle "Brother to all things."

When the reading was over she got up, closed the book, and strolled away, leaving the girls to chatter eagerly about the visitors. Every now and then bursts of music, sometimes gay and swinging, sometimes sad and wistful, but always with a peculiar haunting wildness in it, came across the meadow to them as they sat talking together, or wandered about among the dark pine trees at the edge of the forest. Joey, who had read *The Romany Rye* and *Lavengro*, told them all she knew, and the fascinating subject had still not been exhausted when the "tinkle-tinkle" of Marie's bell summoned them back to dinner. When the meal was over, they were wildly anxious to go to the Kron Prinz Karl at once, but Madge insisted on an hour's rest first.

"And no talking," she added. "Run along, all of you, at once."

When they had gone, she turned to the other two mistresses with a smile.

"Don't they think me unkind!" she said gaily. "Well, I don't know what you two people are going to do, but I'm going to write letters. Be ready in about three-quarters of an hour, if you want to come."

Left to herself, Madge sat down and scribbled a long letter to Dick, telling him the full story of the Carricks and the decision she had made about Juliet. The hour was just ended as she signed it, so she got up and went out to the meadow to summon her girls.

Presently they were all ready, and set off along the lake-shore road. Marie followed them behind, for Miss Bettany had decided that they should have tea at the Kron Prinz Karl, so had given her a holiday.

Good Herr Braun, the proprietor of the hotel, met them with a beaming face, and escorted them to three of the tables with their huge scarlet umbrellas nearest the Tzigane. How they all enjoyed that afternoon—even Juliet, and Simone, who was suffering from pangs of jealousy because Joey and Grizel had foregathered at another table! Many of their friends were there—Herr Marani, who brought over Frau von Eschenau for a chat with Madge; the Mensches, who had a table nearby; Monsieur and Madame Mercier with Suzanne and Yvette; and many others.

As Grizel said afterwards, it was so unlike England. There were the gaily dressed Tzigane playing as though they were music-possessed; the merry cosmopolitan crowd seated at the umbrella-shaded tables; the vivid blue lake-waters before them; and, surrounding all, the great mountains, beautiful in the bright July sunshine.

They stayed a couple of hours, and then wandered back for their quiet talk, which was never omitted.

As they were going to bed that night, Grizel spoke what was in the minds of all of them.

"I think this has been a beautiful Sunday," she said. "If things were always like this it wouldn't be half so hard to keep rules."

"I s'pose it wouldn't really do if things were jolly always," said Jo. "It's because they're unjolly sometimes that we find other things topping, I think. It would be awfully dull if things were always the same."

"Yes, but some excitements are horrid, and we could do without them easily," replied Grizel.

In which she spoke more truly than she then realised.

CHAPTER SIXTEEN

The Mondscheinspitze

IT MIGHT HAVE BEEN expected that, after the delightful Sunday described in the foregoing chapter, things would take a contrary turn, and that there would be direful happenings. But for once Fate proved kind, and the week progressed quietly, such small events as Suzanne Mercier pouring ink over herself, and Grizel and Joey having what nearly amounted to a stand-up fight over Simone Lecoutier, not counting at all. The morning of the Head's birthday dawned in a kind of pandemonium, however. Margia Stevens had, the night before, hit on the original idea of serenading Miss Bettany under her window. The idea appealed greatly to them all, and, after a good deal of argument and squabbling, they had decided on "Who is Sylvia?"

"Of course, the name is wrong," said Margia, "but she'll know who it's meant for."

Six o'clock the next morning saw the long dormitory in the throes of getting up. From behind the yellow curtain which divided off the cubicles came subdued giggles and whispered remarks.

"Joey, is it fine? What's it like over the mountains?"

"Glorious," returned Joey, who had stripped her bed and was now sitting on it, waiting for her turn to go to the bathroom. "It's going to be a ripping day."

"Be quiet!" hissed Juliet. "You'll waken Miss Maynard if you shriek so."

"She's prob'ly awake already," returned Joey, not a whit disturbed. "Thank goodness! Here's Grizel at last! I thought you'd drowned yourself!"

"Rot! I've only been six minutes!" protested Grizel. "Buck up yourself! Margia and Simone have to come after you."

"What about my bath?" asked a little voice from the other corner of the room where Amy Stevens slept. "It's all cold still, isn't it?"

"Oh, bother! I quite forgot you hadn't to have cold baths!" Grizel paused in the act of putting on one of her stockings. "Juliet, what shall we do?"

"Marie will be up. Shall I go down and ask her for a kettleful of hot water? I'm just ready," suggested Juliet.

"Will you? That'd be topping of you. Yes, do go!" urged Grizel. "Hullo, Joey, old thing! You can't have had much of a bath! You haven't been a minute!"

"Have, though! Tootle on, Margia! You're next, aren't you?"

Margia and Juliet vanished together, and presently Juliet came back with a big jug of warm water supplied by good-natured Marie.

"Come along, Amy," she said cheerfully. "I'll tub you this morning. We can't wait till Mademoiselle comes."

"Oh, thank you, Juliet," replied Amy shyly; while Grizel stopped in the act of brushing out her curly mop to gape open-mouthed at her curtains. When had Juliet ever offered to help anyone like that before?

Amy herself was very startled. She had never liked

Juliet, but was too shy to refuse the older girl's help, so submitted in silence to being bathed with much vigour and goodwill, if with some clumsiness. Juliet's whole-hearted rubbing with the towel brought an involuntary "Ow!" from her, but when the Senior, conscience-striken, asked, "Did I hurt you?" she replied hastily, "No, oh, no, Juliet! And it's very kind of you to bath me. Thank you so much."

"Call me if you want anything tied or buttoned," said Juliet, as she returned to her own cubicle. "Margia will have to dress herself, and I'm practically ready, so I can help you easily."

Grizel restrained an exclamation of surprise in time. She stripped her bed in an awestruck silence which lasted until they were all ready to leave the room. Then Joey roused her.

"Aren't you feeling well?" she demanded bluntly.

"Yes, quite well! Why?" queried Grizel somewhat incautiously.

"You're so silent! You've scarcely spoken at all!" grinned Jo. "I thought something must be the matter!"

"So it is, Joey! Juliet did practically everything for Amy! Did you ever?"

"Well, that's nothing to be wondered at!" returned Joey smartly. "She's the oldest of us, and someone had to help Amy or else she'd never have been ready! You know what a perfect baby she is."

"Oh, yes, of course:" said Grizel uncertainly. "I expect you're right, Joey!"

"Course I am! Now come on."

They all slipped down the stairs and out into the glorious sunlight, collecting in a gay little group under Miss Bettany's wide-open windows.

"Let's start with 'Good King Wenceslas'," giggled Joey.

"Yes; I feel rather like Christmas carols too," agreed Grizel.

"Stop ragging, you two! We're waiting for you! This is the note." And Margia sang "Loo!" in a very true little treble. "Now! One, two!"

They all started off, and Madge, who had been sleeping the sleep of the justly weary, was roused by the notes of "Who is Sylvia?" sung *fortissimo* by the whole band.

She quickly guessed the meaning of the serenade, and sat up in bed with a chuckle. As they finished, she got into her kimono, and ran across to the window.

"Hullo, everybody!" she called. "What a jolly awakening!"

"It's to wish you many happy returns, Miss Bettany," called up Grizel. "It was Margia's idea, really. Did you like it?"

"Yes; it was delightful. Thank you all very much! Now I'm going to dress." She withdrew her head just as a tap at the door heralded Joey's advent.

"Hullo! Many happy returns of your birthday," she said. "I've brought you this." She presented her parcel, and Madge opened it with delight.

"A picture of the Tiernsee! Joey! You gem! It's just what I've wanted," she cried. "You couldn't have given me anything better!"

"Glad you like it," returned Jo, as she turned her cheek for her sister's kiss. "Herr Marani helped me to choose it last Saturday. I say, can I help you to dress? I'll strip your bed; shall I?"

She suited the action to the word, and presently Madge sauntered downstairs, ready for the day, in her pale green frock. Marie was scurrying round getting breakfast ready. She stopped to offer her good wishes together with a bouquet of Alpen roses, which she had gathered the evening before.

"Für Madame," she said shyly.

"Oh, Marie! How good of you! And I love Alpen roses so much!"

Breakfast was a hilarious meal, followed by a gay rush to put in bedmaking and practice. Nine o'clock brought all the boarders, flower-laden and beaming. Gisela and Bette carried the basket containing the precious china between them, and Maria had another, full of *Grossmutter's* delicious cakes.

"Hurry up! Hurry up!" exclaimed Joey, dancing with impatience. "I've got the tray from Marie, and Mademoiselle is keeping Madame talking in the dining-room till we're ready! Here you are! Now buck up!"

In the big schoolroom they arranged the dainty coffee-

113

service on the big black tray Joey had produced. Then they formed up in their usual lines, and Amy was sent to ring the bell. She came scampering back, proclaiming in a stage whisper, "She's coming!"

The sound of light, rapid footsteps followed, and then Miss Bettany came in and took her place on the dais. As she did so, a chorus of birthday greetings in German, French, and English came from the eighteen girls assembled below her. As they spoke, they all raised their bouquets—the day-girls had brought flowers for the boarders—and the beauty of the flowers, the goodwill and affection in the girlish faces before her, brought a little thrill to the young headmistress, and touched her charming face with rather more colour than usual. Then Gisela and Gertrud came forward, carrying between them the tray with its dainty burden of china.

The Head Girl looked rather flushed and nervous with her responsibilities, but she rose to the occasion bravely, and said in her clear, carrying voice, "Madame, be pleased to accept from us all this so small token of our feelings for you on this your feast-day."

"Thank you, girls," said Madge, a little shyly. "It is very good of you indeed, and I cannot tell you how much I appreciate your kindness to me. If anything could have made it a happier birthday for me—the first birthday I have spent in the Tyrol—your thought could."

Then came the business of presenting the bouquets, and soon the table on the dais was heaped with lilies, roses, marguerites, gentians, single dahlias, Alpen roses, and peonies, until that end of the room was glowing with their colour and beauty. When, finally, little Giovanna Rincini had trotted up with her armful of lilies and dahlias, Gisela called for three cheers for "Our dear Madame!" which were given heartily, and then the serious business of the day was over.

"In half an hour we shall start," said Madge, smiling at them over the great heap of flowers. "First, I must place these in water and put them in a cool place. Then we must collect up all our possessions, and then we can set off! Joey, please go and fetch me some big bowls; and Grizel and Juliet, I want some water. Take them into the dining-

114

room; that is the coolest place, I think. Miss Maynard, if you will look after the younger girls, Mademoiselle will see to the food, and the Prefects will help me to arrange the flowers."

They all flew off to do her bidding, and by ten o'clock a long string of girls was to be seen setting off up the path which led to the Lauterbach Valley, through which they would have to walk in order to reach the mountain-path that led up the Mondscheinspitze.

As long as they kept to the beaten track—that is, until they reached the white wooden railings that fenced off Briesau from the Lauterbach Valley—they walked in "croc", but as soon as the gate had swung behind them, they broke file, and wandered happily along in little groups, chattering gaily among themselves. Gisela, Gertrud, Bette, and Bernhilda attached themselves to Miss Bettany, and were soon eagerly comparing the differences of Cornish picnics and Tyrolean ones. Miss Maynard and Mademoiselle were discussing Paris, which the former knew very well, since she had been at school there. The little ones, needless to state, chased butterflies and gathered flowers; while Joey, Grizel, and Simone, for once in complete accord, strolled along amiably talking about their climb. Presently they came within sight of the Tiernjoch, even in this day of glorious sunshine dark and gloomy, with a hint of menace in its towering crags. Grizel stopped and tilted back her head, looking at it with a determined gleam in her eyes.

"I'll go up there some day," she said aloud.

Joey followed her eyes. "The Tiernjoch? Oh, Grizel, I wish you wouldn't!"

"Don't be silly! It's only a little climb! 'Tisn't even as if there were any glacier to cross!" retorted Grizel. "Why, there's no snow or anything!"

"It's such a cruel-looking mountain!" said Jo with a little shiver. "It looks as if it didn't care how many people were killed on it!"

"Joey! Tosh! That's only your silly imaginings!" began Grizel. Then the sudden whiteness of her friend's face made her sorry she had mentioned it, so she added,

115

"Anyway, I'm not going today—or this week either—so keep your hair on!"

"I think you are unkind, Grizel!" broke in Simone unexpectedly. "Always you tease, tease Joey! And she hates the Tiernjoch!"

" 'Tisn't your business!" Grizel was beginning heatedly, when Joey stopped her.

"Oh, shut up quarrelling, you two! An' if you mention that beastly Tiernjoch again, Grizel Cochrane, I'll go away, an' you can walk with someone else! So there!" And she marched ahead, leaving Grizel and Simone to follow meekly after her.

Luckily, at that moment, loud screams from Amy Stevens distracted everyone's attention to her, as she came flying down the slope, yelling at the full pitch of her lungs, "Ooh! Ooh! A snake! A snake!"

"What!" exclaimed Madge. She started forward, catching up the frightened child. "Amy! Are you hurt? Stop crying, dear, and tell me!"

"No, she isn't!" Margia supplied the information disgustedly. "She saw a little greeny snake curled up asleep by that stone, and so she howled! It never came near her!"

"Thank Heaven!" Madge set the child on her feet again with a sigh of relief. There were very few snakes found round the Tiernsee, and, so far as she knew, the only venomous ones were vipers, which were even more rarely seen than the harmless green variety; but Amy's shrieks had scared her for the moment. "There's nothing to cry about, Amy," she added. "If you scream when you only see a snake, you aren't a very plucky person, are you? Now dry your eyes and stop crying. And, girls, don't go into the long grass, please."

"It will be all right, Madame," said Gisela seriously. "Snakes prefer the sun, and that grass is in the shadow, and is cold."

"Nevertheless, I shall feel safer if you keep more to the path," returned her headmistress decidedly. "Frieda, I'm sure you've carried that basket long enough. Give it to Joey. And Grizel, take Juliet's for a while."

They went on again, Madge keeping a rather nervous eye on the Juniors. However, they soon had to leave the

116

track, and strike across the valley to get to the mountain-path.

"Do we cross here?" demanded Miss Bettany, eyeing what looked like the stony bed of a dried-up river somewhat doubtfully. "Isn't there a bridge?"

"Only a log further down," said Bernhilda. "You see, Madame, when the storms of autumn come, this is a torrent, and already three bridges have been swept away. The water comes suddenly, and there is nothing to break its strength. It is easy to reach, though. See; down here." And she pointed to some rough, natural steps which led down to the stony bed.

Already more than half the girls were struggling across, the unfortunate bearers of baskets uttering wild shrieks as the stones slipped under their feet, and they more than once nearly went headlong. At length they were all safely at the other side, and once more on the beaten path which led through grass and wild flowers to the foot of the mountain, where they all paused for a rest.

"Ouf! Isn't it hot!" panted Margia, as she mopped her crimson face.

"I'm just comfortable," said Joey with an exasperatingly superior air, "but I'm awfully hungry! What's the time, anyone?"

"It is half after eleven," said Gisela, glancing at her pretty little watch.

"You must be slow, Gisela," laughed Juliet, showing hers. "I make it ten past twelve."

"So do I," said Madge, "and mine was right this morning. Miss Maynard, what does yours say?"

"Nearly quarter past," replied Miss Maynard, "but I may be a little fast."

"Well, anyhow, it's time for lunch," said Joey. "Do let's have it here!"

"Oh, yes!" agreed several voices at once. "I am hungry!"

Madge laughed and gave way. "Very well. I'm rather hungry myself; and it would certainly lighten the baskets!"

Accordingly they all sat down, and in a very few minutes the baskets were considerably lighter than they had been.

"It's funny how much hungrier one is out of doors than

117

in," said Grizel presently, as she tackled her sixth sandwich.

"It is!" agreed Joey. "But I'm not so hungry as I was," she added pensively.

"After having only five sandwiches and six biscuits and two apples!" jeered Grizel. "There must be something up with you, Joey, old thing!"

"You can't talk! " said Joey contentedly. "You've had just as much. I say," she added in rather changed tones, "where's the lemonade?"

"Bette has it," said Gisela.

"I haven't," replied Bette. "I thought you had it!"

"No; I was carrying the apples. I was certain you had it!"

"Oh, no! I never had it!"

Madge began to gurgle with laughter. It was only too plain what had occurred to that lemonade.

"Sitting in the passage at home," she choked.

"*Oh!* And I'm dying of thirst!"

"And I! " "And I! " rose on all sides. "What are we to do?"

"Wait until we reach the Alpe. We can get plenty of milk from the herdsmen," said Miss Bettany somewhat unfeelingly. "I'm sorry, but it's your own faults."

"Then," said Jo, scrambling to her feet, "there's only one thing to be done—get up to the Alpe as soon as we can. Come on!"

There was common sense in her statement, so with loud groans the girls repacked the baskets and set off.

The climb up the Mondscheinspitze is remarkably easy. There is a well-defined path, which winds in and out among the dark pine trees, every now and then coming out into narrow—very narrow—grassy ledges. Presently, however, it left the woods, and they climbed up the bare limestone face of the mountain beneath the glare of the July sun. Tufts of grass, with wild scabious and white marguerites, punctuated the way, and gorgeous butterflies, brown and orange and scarlet and yellow, fluttered round them, so little afraid, that often they settled on hat or frock, and little Amy Stevens cried out in delight when one balanced itself on her outstretched fingers, resting there for a moment before it fluttered off.

Madge was thankful for the distraction the dainty creatures afforded the girls; otherwise, the Juniors at any rate would have found the path more difficult than they did. As it was, she was very thankful when a triumphant cry from Joey, Simone, and Frieda Mensch, who had raced on, announced that they had reached the Alpe.

"Isn't it a gorgeous view?" demanded Jo, when they were all standing on the short, sweet grass. "Just look!"

They looked. At their feet lay the valley they had crossed that morning, cool and green, with the empty river-bed stretching like a white ribbon down its length. In the distance they could see Briesau, lying like a toy village some giant child had set out; and beyond it, blue—blue—blue, the Tiernsee, a living sapphire, gleamed beneath the sun.

"Oh, wonderful!" breathed Madge softly.

They did not gaze long, however; they were all too thirsty. With one accord, presently, they turned, and made for the herdsmen's hut—and milk.

CHAPTER SEVENTEEN

On the Alpe

ALTHOUGH BOTH Joey and Grizel had been up the Bären-bad Alpe many times since their arrival at Briesau, they had never been inside a herdsman's hut, and great was their interest in it.

Only one man was there when they reached the place— a tall, lanky young fellow, in weather-stained green breeches and ragged shirt, open at the throat. His black hair was rough and long, and his face burnt brown with the weather. He wore the little green Tyrolese hat with its cock-feather, and was sitting contentedly smoking a long china-bowled pipe, such as most men smoke in the Tyrol. On seeing them coming, he rose to his feet with a smile of welcome and a hoarse-voiced "Grüss' Gott!"

"Grüss Gott!" replied Madge briskly. "Can you sell us some milk and cheese?"

"Yes, gracious lady. Will the gracious lady and the young ladies come in?"

Only the English girls availed themselves of this offer, so that they might look round at the little bare room, with its huge well in one corner, where a wood fire was burning although the day was so hot. A broad shelf ran round the room, well above their heads, and on this stood enormous earthenware pans for the milk and big cream-coloured cheeses. The one window was about two feet square, and set high up in the wall; a long wooden bench stood at one side, and next to it a huge cheese press; a door opened into another room beyond, where trusses of hay were to be seen. The atmosphere of the place was indescribable—a mixture of cheese, garlic, tobacco, and burning wood. The visitors soon left the hut for the sweeter atmosphere of the Alpe, where the others were gravely taking it in turn to drink out of an enormous bowl, full of rich, creamy milk, while their host stood nearby, still smoking, and gazing vacantly across to the mighty peaks on the other side of the lake.

When Miss Bettany presently brought back the empty bowl, together with the tobacco she had brought, and some *Kroner* notes to pay for the milk, he smiled again, and answered her questions in his curiously hoarse tones.

Yes, he and four others were there for the summer. They had come up early in May, and would stay there till the end of September if the weather was good. Then the cattle must be brought down to the valley before the autumn storms began.

"But aren't you ever lonely?" queried Joey, who had accompanied her sister to the hut. "Don't you ever want to go down to Briesau?"

He turned indifferent dark eyes on her. "No, gnädiges Fräulein. There are the cows and the mountains. We are five, and I have my pipe."

"What do the cows do in the winter?" asked Madge, a

fine instinct preventing her from asking what he did, though she felt curious about it.

"They live in the sheds in the winter," he replied, "and I go to my home in Scholastika. They do not need us in the winter, so we all go to our homes, and pray to *der liebe Gott* and the blessed Saints for an early spring. Last winter it did not come, and some of us went hungry for a time."

"How dreadful!" said Joey with wholehearted sympathy. "I hope it's a good autumn."

"It will be as *der liebe Gott* wills," he replied, with the curious fatalism of his race.

Madge made arrangements for milk and cheese for the tea, and then went back to her flock. She found them all lying about in exhausted attitudes, and promptly proposed that they should have a rest before exploring the Alpe any further.

"It will be easier going down than coming up," she said. "We climbed in the noon-day heat, but by then it will be cool, so we shall go twice as quickly. Half an hour, or even an hour's sleep won't do any of you any harm. I've got a book in my pocket, so I'll read and keep an eye on the time."

They promptly curled up in various attitudes, Mademoiselle and Miss Maynard among them, and Madge was soon the only one awake. She glanced at her watch with a smile.

"A quarter past three," she thought. "I'll let them sleep for another half-hour, and then we must have tea."

She turned back to her book. It was terribly hot—almost oppressively so, although the sun was not shining so brilliantly as it had done earlier in the day. The German print looked all funny and jumbled up; the page wasn't there any more. Madge was asleep.

Meanwhile, the sunlight faded away, hidden by the huge black clouds that began to marshal themselves in terrifying squadrons in the north-west. Even the faint breeze which had stirred the Alpine flowers in the short grass had died away. There was a waiting stillness, broken only by the occasional cry of a wild bird, frightened at what it felt was coming.

Joey was the first to feel it. She woke up with a sensation that something was wrong. The next minute she knew what it was. The electricity in the air was tingling through and through her. She sprang to her feet with a little cry, gazing wildly round her. The sunshine was gone; the whole place was wrapped in gloom. At the other side of the valley the mountains reared ghastly white heads against the blackness of the sky, and every now and then the lightning flashed across the awful inkiness, seeming to rip it open for a moment. There was no thunder yet, which made it all the more terrifying. Dashing to her sister's side, she shook her vigorously.

"Madge! Madge! Wake up! Wake up! Madge! I'm frightened!"

In a moment Madge sat up and regarded the awesome scene with horror in her eyes. The next instant she was on her feet.

"Thunder! What a fool I was not to think of it! We must get down at once! Girls! Wake up!"

They woke up at her urgent cries, and Simone and Amy promptly burst into tears. The Tyroleans were too accustomed to the terrible thunderstorms which come up with such terrifying suddenness to be scared, although the elder girls looked serious. They knew what thunder from the north-west meant.

Meanwhile, the three elders were taking rapid counsel, while Juliet and Gisela tried to console the two weepers. Joey was watching her sister's face anxiously, and Grizel was too excited to feel afraid.

Then, even as Miss Bettany turned to bid the girls hurry to the mountain-path, there was a vivid glare, that seemed to rend the very clouds asunder, followed by a terrific crash, which scared what few wits Simone had left completely from her. She clung to Mademoiselle, screaming hysterically, and Madge realised that if they were to get her down the path at all they would have to carry her.

A sudden shout coming out of the gloom which had descended so rapidly made her turn, and there was the herdsman running towards them, beckoning to them as he did so. In a flash she realised that he meant them to come to the hut. The next moment the darkness descended completely, and overhead the lightning flickered and the thunder crashed almost incessantly. There was no question of going down yet. Even if Simone had kept her head it would have been impossible. The path was easy enough in daylight, but there were great tree roots sprawling across it at intervals, as well as occasional boulders which had worked loose and rolled into it. Any attempt to descend it now was more than likely to end in sprained ankles, if nothing worse. She made a swift decision. Even as the panting herd reached them, she spoke.

"Come! We must go to the hut! It is the only thing to do, and we can stay there till it is over."

Gisela, Bette, and Bernhilda had already collected the baskets together, and now they all turned and followed the man, who had picked up Simone with as much ceremony as if she were a bundle of hay, and was now leading them across the little plateau to the hut.

It was really quite a short distance, but to Madge it seemed never-ending, that strange walk—half walk, half run—in almost pitchy blackness, lightened only by the fearful glare of the lightning, while all round them the thunder roared frighteningly. Little Amy Stevens was between her and Miss Maynard, while the elder girls looked after the other Juniors, and Mademoiselle hurried gaspingly after them, with an arm round Margia Stevens.

Once they were all safely inside, the herd shut the door and set Simone down on the bench. She had stopped screaming now, but little heart-rending moans came from her lips every now and then. Leaving Amy to Miss Maynard's care, Madge went over to her.

"Simone," she said sternly, "you must stop crying at once—at once! Do you hear?"

"I—I have such fear!" sobbed Simone in her own language.

"So have the others," replied her headmistress, "but you are the only one who is behaving like a baby. Come! You must stop at once or I shall slap you!"

She nearly burst out laughing when she finished, for, as she glanced up, she had happened to catch sight of Joey's face, with eyes and mouth round O's of wonder. However, her dramatic speech had its effect on Simone, who

123

gradually began to recover her self-control, and presently was able to sit up and drink the milk Gisela brought her.

Meanwhile, the herdsman had drawn the young headmistress aside.

"The gracious lady must stay here tonight." he said. "There is hay, and we can give bread and milk and cheese. To go down the path would be dangerous while the storm rages."

"But surely it cannot go on long?" said Madge in startled tones. "It is too heavy to last."

"It is from the north-west," he replied. "It will last many hours yet—four, or perhaps five; and then it will be night."

"Good heavens! How awful!"

She stood silent for a few moments, going over the state of affairs in her mind. Then she turned to the Seniors. "Gisela! Bette! Is this true? Are we storm-stayed here for the night?"

"I am afraid so," replied Gisela. "When a storm comes from the north-west it does not die quickly."

"But how appalling! What will your parents think?"

"They will know we took refuge here," said Bette. "Everyone at Tiernsee knows of the hut, and they will know that we should stay here. These storms come so quickly; often there is no time to do anything. Don't worry, Madame. They will be sure we shall be here, and quite safe."

"I wish I could think so!" murmured her headmistress. "Well, I suppose there is nothing else for it."

"Do you mean we're going to stay here all night?" gasped Grizel, who had been standing near. "How simply thrilling!"

"I'm glad you think so!" returned Madge dryly. "I'd be thankful to know we were all safe in our beds."

The herdsman, having given his opinion, was now busily engaged in carrying in great armfuls of fresh, sweet hay from a little shed which stood nearby. The rain had not yet come, and he had evidently made up his mind to prepare for the night before it did.

Grizel sprang forward. "Let me help!" she said in her pretty broken German. "Yes, do! I'd like it!"

"Oh, so would I!" exclaimed Margia. "I'll come too!"

The man made no attempt to stop them, so they followed him out; and very soon one end of the room was thickly littered with the hay, which the elder girls shook up and covered with their raincoats. When that was done, he shut the door once more, cast a couple of logs on the fire, and then sat down on the bench and lighted his pipe. He had done all he could, and now he was prepared to sit and smoke contentedly until he was sleepy, when he would go to bed in the next room.

A little silence fell on them all, which was suddenly broken by a "swish-swish!" and the rain had come. Such rain! Joey, opening the door to see, had to shut it again in a hurry or they would have been flooded out.

"Gracious Peter!" she remarked, as she came back to the others. "It's like the Flood! This is Mount Ararat, I shouldn't wonder!"

"Tosh!" retorted Grizel. "Mount Ararat has snow on it—I think!"

She finished rather doubtfully.

"Well, *this* has in winter," argued Jo amiably. "Anyhow, it's some rain!"

"Not unlike the rainy season in India," laughed Madge —the thunder had died away for the moment. "Do you remember how I told you about the time when we were flooded out the year before we came home?"

"Rather! Tell the others now!" said Joey. "It's like a story in a book!"

"It will take too long," replied her sister. "Ask me about it some time when there isn't a thunderstorm going on. Just listen to it!" as a fresh rumble forced her to shriek the last words.

"It often does that," said Gisela. "It travels round and round the lake till it dies away. It will come back again and again before it is over tonight."

"Where are we going to sleep?" asked Amy with interest. "And oh, Miss Bettany, what is that funny thing on the wall?"

She pointed as she spoke to a zither which was hung up by a loop of soiled ribbons. The herdsman, seeing her point to it, got up from his seat and, taking it down, produced a little twist of wire attached to a silver ring

125

which he fitted on his thumb, and then ran it across the string, producing a shower of silvery sounds.

"A zither!" cried Miss Maynard. "And I never noticed it!"

"Gnädiges Fräulein plays the zither?" queried the man, holding it to her.

"Yes; but you play first," she said, smiling at him.

He bowed somewhat clumsily, and then played them a simple little air, whose notes rippled through the hut like bird-notes. When he had finished, he handed it to Miss Maynard, and she played a song which, she told them, she had learnt from the New Forest gipsies. Every now and then the thunder roared above the tinkling music, and made the nervous people start. The first awful gloom was wearing off, but the lightning flashes were as vivid as ever, and the rain still poured down ceaselessly.

Presently the herdsman produced a huge pot, which he slung on a hook hung over the fire by an iron chain. Into this he poured a panful of milk, and, when it was heated, he invited them to dip big earthenware mugs, which he had brought from the inner room, into it, and drink. It proved very good if it did have a smoky flavour. Certainly, drunk in that room as an accompaniment to black bread and milk-cheese, it had a taste all its own.

When they had finished it, there was silence for a little. The close atmosphere and the warmth were doing their work. It was barely seven o'clock, but most of the Juniors were already nodding sleepily, and presently Amy turned to Miss Bettany with a request for bed.

"Please may I go to bed? I'm so sleepy!" she pleaded.

"I think most of you would be better in bed," said the young headmistress. "Come along, you people! You can slip off your frocks and lie down in the hay, and then we'll cover you up."

"In the hay?" Amy wasn't sure whether to laugh or cry.

Luckily, Maria Marani settled it for her. "It is topping!" she said cheerfully.

"Just like camping out!" added Grizel approvingly. "Oh, this is something like an adventure!"

The herdsman, seeing that bed seemed to be the order of the day, got up, lit two lanterns, hanging one on a nail

126

near the door, and, taking the other, slouched into the inner room with a muttered "Gute Nacht!"

"And that's that!" observed Joey, wriggling out of her frock. "I say, supposing the others come back, what a shock they will get if they walk in and see us lying round!"

"I hadn't thought of that!" Madge looked disturbed.

"I do not think they will come," said Gisela consolingly. "See, the door is barred. I think there is another hut at the other side, and they will spend the night there."

"Do you? Shunt along, Grizel! You've got three times your share of the hay—I mean bed! Righto, Simone! You can come next me—if you can keep your arms to yourself, that is!"

Thus Joey, as she slipped off her shoes and curled herself up. She suddenly sat up again to ask, "I say, does anyone snore?"

"Not unless it's yourself! retorted Grizel promptly.

"Girls! Girls! Be quiet!" put in Madge, laughing. "You really must settle down and get to sleep! We shall have to be up at six, to get down before Briesau is awake to see what scarecrows we are!"

Joey lay down, and presently they were all settled. Madge put out the lantern and lay down in her own place. It took her a little time to drop off, though everyone else quickly fell asleep—or so it seemed. But just as she was getting drowsy, a low voice said, "Madge!"

"Well?" she asked sleepily.

"We'll have a holiday tomorrow after this, shan't we?" Madge sat up, fully awake.

"Joey Bettany, lie down at once and go to sleep, and don't let me hear you again till the morning!" she said severely.

There was a rustle in the hay and a little chuckle. Then silence.

CHAPTER EIGHTEEN

The Chalet Magazine is Discussed

"OH, IT WAS PRICELESS!" Grizel gave a little chuckle. "There we were, all grubby and untidy, and our hair full of hay-seed, and all that walk to take! You'd have screamed if you had seen us!"

She laughed again at the memory, and Wanda von Eschenau joined her. Arrangements had been made for the next term, and Wanda and Marie were to join the Chalet School as boarders. In the meantime, they were to be with the girls as much as possible, partly with a view to learning English, so that they should be able to follow the lessons easily. Wanda already spoke fairly well, but Marie made funny mistakes at times. She and Joey and Simone were sitting in the grass some little distance away, revelling in the warmth of the sun, while Wanda and Grizel were perched on the railings which cut off the path to Geisalm. Farther along, Juliet was lying on the bank reading, while Margia, Amy, and the two little Merciers were making wreaths of the big white marguerites which grew everywhere.

It was a Saturday morning; practice was finished, and the boarders were free to amuse themselves. Grizel was telling Wanda about the birthday expedition with its unexpected ending. The young Viennese, who led the sheltered life of most girls of her class, was deeply thrilled, for Grizel told the tale well.

"It must have been full of terror up there on the Alpe," she said in her slow, careful English. "The storm was terrible, even here!"

"It was ghastly," agreed Grizel. "Simone shrieked like

mad and Amy cried, and I'm sure I don't wonder! It must be awful if you are afraid of thunder! I'm not! But then, I'm not afraid of anything much!"

"You must be very courageous," replied Wanda simply.

Grizel coloured to the roots of her hair. She had not meant to boast, but she had to admit that her last speech sounded uncommonly like boasting.

"Sorry! I'm afraid that was swank," she said.

"Swank? *Was ist denn* 'swank'?" queried Wanda.

"Oh, bucking—er—boasting," returned Grizel hastily. "Er—I wouldn't use it if I were you, Wanda. It isn't good English—not proper, you know."

"What you call 'slang'. I see," replied the other girl. "But go on, Grizel. Did you meet with anybody?"

"Only cowherds," said Grizel. "Oh, but it was lovely, so early in the morning! Everything looked so new and well-washed after the rain!—except us, of course! I don't know about the others, but all us boarders had a hot bath and washed our hair. We had to, to get the hay-seed out! Then we all went to bed and to sleep. I never knew bed could be so nice before," she added meditatively. "Sleeping on hay is fun all right, but you don't get much sleep! First of all, a beetle walked across Joey's face, and she yelled and hung on to my hair—suppose it was the handiest thing there was to hang on to! Then, when we had got over that excitement, Amy began to cry because the hay-seed had gone down her neck and was tickling her. Then, just before dawn, an owl of sorts started to screech, and so did some of the little ones!"

"But how could you enjoy such happenings?" asked Wanda, wide-eyed.

"Oh, I don't know! You do, you know! It's something fresh—I s'pose that's it."

"Perhaps," said Wanda doubtfully. "But I should not like it."

"Oh, you will when you've been with us a while," said Grizel confidently. "Only, of course, there won't be any mountain expeditions next term."

"No, not with the snow here," agreed the young Austrian. "How shall we amuse ourselves, then, my Grizel?"

129

"Oh, I don't know! Dancing and games, I suppose. P'r'aps we shall get up a play. Just the usual things one does do in the winter. I'm tired of these old railings now—they're so jolly hard! Let's walk along to the other end. Gisela may be coming. She often does on Saturdays, and so do Bernhilda and Frieda Mensch. It makes it jollier for Juliet and me. Most of the others are rather babies, you see. Coming, Juliet?"

Juliet raised her head. "Where to? Oh, the other gate? No, thanks, Grizel. I want to get on with my book; and anyway, it's too hot to move."

"Lazy old object!" laughed Grizel. "All right! Come on, Wanda! Let's leave her to it!"

They went off, laughing and talking gaily, while Juliet, uncurling herself from the little heap in which she had been lying, gazed after them thoughtfully.

She was not jealous, although Grizel had very little to say to her nowadays. In Grizel's eyes, Juliet had become suddenly and tiresomely "good"; Wanda was fresh, and the English girl was rather given to running after fresh things. One thing, thought Juliet, as she sat hugging her knees in a brown study, Grizel could come to no harm with Wanda, who had been trained on the most conventional lines, and was often horrified at her new friend's tomboyish ways. It was rather a relief to the elder girl to know this, for she could not forget Grizel's declaration of a fortnight or so ago that she would be off up the Tiernjoch the first chance she got, and she didn't care who said what! City-bred Wanda was most unlikely to attempt such an expedition. The Bärenbad Alpe was as much as she could manage, though Marie and Wolfram were ready for anything, and Kurt, the elder boy, went on climbing and hunting expeditions with his father every day.

Meanwhile, the younger children had grown tired of their wreaths, and were making their way slowly towards the boat-landing to watch the steamer come in. As they strolled along, they saw a couple of big boys come racing down the path towards them, followed by a little girl of about nine. Instinctively the children moved to one side, and the two lads tore past them without giving them a glance. The little girl turned and looked at them, however, with a look of friendly curiosity, before she galloped after the others.

"Wonder who they are?" commented Jo in German, which language she now spoke as fluently as she did English. "They looked rather jolly, didn't they?"

"I think they are English," said Simone gravely.

"Das Mädchen was not," corrected Marie. "She hadn't the English view."

"Appearance, you mean," observed Margia. "Amy, come back! You'll fall in."

"It wouldn't matter if I did—'cept for having to change," replied Amy.

"Well, that would be bother enough," said Margia, as she hauled her little sister back into safety.

"It wouldn't be yours anyhow!" snapped Amy.

Margia released her little sister in sheer amazement. It was the first time that Amy had ever attempted to have an opinion apart from her, and she gasped with wonder.

Joey laughed at her startled face. "Margia, if you open your mouth like that the mosquitoes will dash in to their doom. Be always kind to animals, wherever you may be. If a mosquito *is* an animal!"

"Oh, don't talk rubbish!" burst out Margia. "Amy, you must be ill!"

"No, I'm not!" returned Amy pettishly. "But I'm not going to be pulled about."

"Oh, say no more, Margia!" interposed Simone. "It is but that Amy grows up."

"Well—but——" If her gentle little sister had slapped her in the face, Margia could not have been more surprised.

"Never mind now," said Joey tactfully. "I want to talk about my idea—at least, it's Gisela's really," she added truthfully; "but don't you think it would be topping to have a school mag.?"

"Gorgeous!" said Simone, who had picked up this expression from Jo.

"It would be like the school tales," said Marie thoughtfully.

"There's the Mondscheinspitze picnic for one thing," said Joey. "That would be a topping thing for a mag!"

"And your day at Innsbruck and Frau Berlin," added

Margia; for all the school knew of that episode by this time.

"Yes; and the day we went boating and the storm came on. And we do play cricket and tennis with ourselves," said Jo thoughtfully.

"Then let us ask Gisela, shall we not?" suggested Marie.

"An'—an' I'll write a poem for you," proposed Amy cheerfully.

They all stopped still with one accord and stared at her. She blushed crimson, but stood her ground.

Joey was the first to speak. "I say!" she said, and whistled loudly.

"Amy!" cried Margia. "What do you mean? You know you can't write poetry."

"I can, then!" retorted Amy. "I writed some last night!"

"Let's see it, then!"

"Can't! It's in my cubey under my pillow!"

"What is it about?" demanded Marie.

"A river. The one beside the Kron Prinz Karl."

"That's not a river; it's not big enough," declared Margia.

"Well, I've called it a little river," returned Amy defiantly.

"Oh, Amy, do let us see it!" pleaded Simone. "I think you are awfullee clevaire! I could not do it. I! No, truly!"

"I tell you it's in my cubey," said Amy, nevertheless softening before Simone's compliments. "I'll get it when I go to wash my hands for *Mittagessen*."

"There's Gisela, with Wanda and Grizel," put in Joey. "Let's scoot and ask her."

But Amy had caught at her arm. "Joey, don't let Grizel know!"

"Why ever not?" demanded Joey in surprise.

"She'll laugh if you do! Don't tell her, Joey! Not yet, anyhow!"

"Grizel Cochrane shan't laugh at you!" said Margia determinedly. "Why should she?"

But all Amy could be got to say was, "She will! I know she will!"

"Oh, all right, then! But we can ask Gisela about the mag.," said Joey. "Come on, everybody! Gisela! Gi—se—la!"

Gisela, who had been chattering gaily with Wanda and Grizel, lifted her head.

"Yes! I come!" she called back, and set off at a run, heedless of Grizel's impatient "Oh, don't bother with the kids just now, Gisela!"

"What is it?" asked the big girl, as she reached the Juniors. "Is there anything wrong?"

"No, nothing. Only, do you remember what we were talking about the day we decided to get my sister's birthday present? Gisela, let's have a school mag.!"

"Yes; and you be editor," added Margia.

Gisela looked thoughtful, and at this moment Wanda and Grizel came up with them.

"Well! What's the worry?" demanded Grizel. "Anyone dead yet?"

Joey turned on her like a flash. "Grizel! I hate that horrid sneery way of talking you've got lately! You're always making fun of us! It's horrid of you!"

"Keep your hair on!" said Grizel easily. "No need to get hot about nothing!"

"I'm not!" retorted Joey. "And anyhow," as an unholy memory came to her, "anyhow, I didn't ask to have my hair rinsed in holy water!"

"Joey! What do you mean?" cried Wanda, astounded.

"Ask Grizel! She knows!" said Joey with somewhat malicious delight.

Grizel, crimson and furious, glared at her tormentor. "You little pig, Joey!"

"Well, you did—didn't you?" Then Joey's malice vanished in a chuckle. "I say! Do you remember the man's face when he heard you? Oh, wasn't it funny?"

"It was only a mistake," said Grizel with an unwilling laugh.

"But what was it?" asked Gisela, bewildered. "Please tell us, Grizel."

"Oh, it was only that I mixed up *heisses* and *heiliges*," explained Grizel. "Jo's a horror to drag it up like that! Oh, well, let it alone now, and let's get on to the magazine."

"It is an English institution," observed Wanda. "I have read of it in my story-books. Papa has given me several,

133

you know, as he wished Marie and I should know something about life in the English schools."

"But you can't always go by stories," said Joey. "Some of them are awful tosh—like that *Denise of the Fourth* one you showed me, Gisela."

"There is one about a girl who was a Guide," began Gisela doubtfully, "but I did not quite understand it. It is not the kind of guide we know here."

"Girl Guides, was it?" asked Joey with interest.

"It was a Girl Guide," said Wanda. "Her name was the same as yours, Gisela, but they called her 'Gilly.' I liked the book very good."

"You should say 'very much'," Grizel corrected her. "Well, we can't do anything about the Guides just now, though it's jolly well worth thinking about. Let's get on to the magazine. And this afternoon, I vote we play cricket. Wanda is keen to learn; aren't you, old thing?"

"I should love it," said Wanda.

"It is a tophole game," said Grizel. "You'll soon learn it. Now, about the magazine."

"I have never seen an English school magazine," began Gisela, "but I have read of them. We must have for editor one who can write the—the—editorial, and also arrange. Then we must have articles upon our games and the happenings of this term. There should be stories and poetry, and a letter from our Head. There are only eighteen of us, but I think we might do it. It is an English custom, as Wanda says, and we are an English school, and I should like to do it. Bette and Gertrud and Bernhilda wish it too. What do you think, Joey? Would Madame allow it?"

"Rather!" said Joey enthusiastically. "She'd be awfully keen, I know."

"Then what do you say? Shall we see what we can do about it?"

"Yes, let's!"

"It's a ripping scheme, Gisela!"

"But we—we, too, Gisela! We shall be members of the school soon. May we not write for it?"

"Well, I—I—I'll let you have some poetry!"

This last was Amy, of course. The Seniors looked at her

134

with much the same surprise as the others had done.

"Poetry, Amy? Why, you don't even know what poetry is, do you?" teased Grizel.

"Yes, I do! It's lines that rhyme! So there, Grizel Cochrane!" flashed Amy, her fair little face burning with a mixture of shyness and indignation.

"Oh my hat! There is a cat! On the mat!" mocked Grizel. "Your poetry anything like that, Amy?"

"It's a jolly sight better than anything you could do, anyway!" declared Margia, coming valiantly to Amy's assistance. She might sit on her little sister for her own good, but she wasn't going to have Grizel Cochrane doing it if she could help it.

Grizel tilted back her pretty head and laughed aggravatingly. But Joey now took up the cudgels.

"You're horrid just now, Grizel! I don't know what's the matter with you!" she said with more vehemence than politeness.

"Don't get excited, babies——"

"Grizel!"

"What is the matter with you, girls?" asked Miss Bettany, as they faced her.

Gisela rushed into the breach. "Madame, it was just a little argument. And please may we have a magazine for the school?"

"A school magazine?" She looked at them with twinkling eyes. "Yes, if you will promise not to quarrel over it, and not to leave all the work to one person, I think you may."

And so was the idea of *The Chaletian* born.

CHAPTER NINETEEN

Some Pranks

"ONLY THREE WEEKS till the end of term! Nothing much can happen in three weeks!" Thus Madge Bettany, as she sat in her bedroom, talking things over with Mademoiselle La Pâttre. "Our first term," she went on dreamily. "Well, it hasn't been a bit what I thought it would. For one thing, I never expected we should get such a large school together so quickly. Eight or ten was the most I had hoped for. But here we are with eighteen, and at least seven more for next term! It isn't bad, is it?"

Mademoiselle nodded her head slowly. "It has gone well, *ma chérie*," she said gravely.

"The girls are so keen on being really English," went on the young headmistress. "Even the Juniors are infected with the desire. The other day I heard Suzanne Mercier and Berta Hamel discussing some prank or other, and Suzanne asked very seriously, "Are you sure it's English?" Berta wasn't certain, so they went off to discuss it with Joey."

"Has it occurred yet?" asked Mademoiselle with a smile.

"I haven't heard anything, so I don't suppose it has."

"I wonder what it is?" ruminated the elder woman. "They think of things so extraordinary, these little ones. I am sure Simone would never have thought of cutting off her hair a year ago."

"It's far better for her," said Madge decidedly. "She really had too much. She's much better in every way, I think; and she's losing that tragic look she used to have, and she does things—well—off her own bat!"

"My dear!" Mademoiselle was genuinely horrified at the slang, but Madge only laughed.

"Awful, isn't it?" she said gaily. "Mercifully none of the girls heard me. Do remember, Elise, that I've not been a Head for three months yet! You must allow me a little slang just very occasionally."

Mademoiselle joined in her laughter, which was cut short by a piercing shriek.

"Mercy!" gasped Madge. "What on earth has happened?"

She fled to the door, tore it open, and ran down the stairs, to meet a scared and horrified Bette and Bernhilda, who both exclaimed, "Oh, Madame! Come quickly! Come at once!"

"What is it? An accident?" she gasped with whitening face.

"No—no! It is much worse! It is witchcraft!" wailed Bette.

"Witchcraft! Nonsense! There is no such thing as witchcraft!" she said sharply, nevertheless following them along the narrow passage to the little boarded-off compartment where the "splasheries" were. Arrived there, she gasped at what she saw. Then, realising what had happened, she burst into laughter. Each of the two basins was full to the brim of sparkling, sizzling bubbles! Even as they looked, the foaming began to subside, and in another minute or two the bowls held only ordinary water—or what looked like ordinary water.

"Oh, Madame, what is it?" sobbed Bette in German. "I did nothing! I only poured in the water, and Bernhilda also, and it foamed up at once! Oh, is it witchcraft?"

A sudden gurgle outside the window, followed by a "Hush!" drew the Head's attention for a second, but she took no further notice.

"Oh, Bette! You silly child!" she said rather impatiently. "Of course it isn't! Haven't I told you there is no such thing as witchcraft? All that has happened is that those young monkeys have powdered the bowls with sherbet or salts or some fizzy stuff! Of course it bubbled up when you poured the water in! But that's all it is!"

Had she been able to see through the bushes which grew against the side of the house, she would have seen four faces grow rather blank at her omniscience.

137

"I say!" murmured Joey. "I forgot they would probably fetch my sister, and it's a trick my brother told us of. He did at at his school."

"Will she be angry?" asked Berta, a trifle apprehensively.

Joey considered, her head on one side. "Shouldn't think so," she said finally. "There's nothing wrong in it— it's only a lark, and it doesn't hurt anyone. That idiot, Bette! Fancy believing in witchcraft at her age!"

"But lots of them do," argued Simone, with somewhat incautious loudness.

"Shut up, idiot!" hissed Joey. "D'you want them to come and catch us? Come along! We'd better clear out now!" And they promptly vacated their position and decamped to the ferry-landing.

Meanwhile, Madge was busy soothing the injured feelings of the Seniors. Bette was furiously angry at having been so taken in, and even Bernhilda the gentle was inclined to be indignant.

"It is an impertinence," she said in her soft, careful English. "Is it not, Madame?"

Madge nodded. "Oh, yes! But it is the kind of thing that often happens with Juniors, and I advise you to take no notice this time. If they do it again, of course, the Prefects should take it up. It's not bad mischief. You people must learn to distinguish between bad mischief and nonsense like this."

With this she left them, to go and relate the occurrence to their compeers, while she herself chuckled over it with Mademoiselle and Miss Maynard, who had just come in.

"It's healthy mischief anyhow," she said, "so I shan't interfere. There's *Mittagessen*."

At *Mittagessen* the four Juniors kept giggling together, and many were the meaning glances shot at Bette, who held her head very high, and was remarkably chilly in her behaviour to them. Bernhilda had cooled down, and was able to laugh at the affair, but Bette was half Italian, and her indignation still ran hot. Gisela and the others had enjoyed the joke, even while they admitted that it was "an impertinence", and, as the Head Girl said, it was better than the defiance of Grizel and Juliet of the previous week.

There were three bedtimes during the week at the Chalet. Amy and Margia Stevens, and the two little Merciers, who were boarders till the end of term, as their parents had been obliged to go to Paris owing to the sudden illness of Madame Mercier's mother, went at seven, Joey and Simone at eight, and Juliet and Grizel at nine. On Saturdays and Sundays they all went at the same time—half-past eight on Saturdays and eight on Sundays. When seven o'clock came that evening, the four Juniors trotted off quite happily. Miss Maynard went up to brush hair at half-past seven, and see that they were all safely in bed. She found them, as she afterwards said, "rather gigglesome", but as the story of the powdered basins—they had used sherbet, as Madge had surmised—had gone round the school by that time, she set it down to that. At eight o'clock punctually Joey and Simone said good-night and retired in their turn. It was Mademoiselle's duty to go up half an hour later to see that they were all right. Juliet and Grizel were considered old enough to be responsible for themselves.

When half-past eight came, Mademoiselle was in the middle of writing a letter, so Miss Maynard good-naturedly offered to run up for her. The Frenchwoman accepted the offer, and the mathematics mistress ascended the stairs lightly. She expected to find the two in bed, ready to bid her "good-night", so she was considerably startled to find Joey in her dressing-gown, grimly unpicking the top of her pyjama legs, while Simone was wrestling with a sleeve of her nightdress.

"Girls!" exclaimed the mistress. "What is the meaning of this?"

"All our night garments are sewn up," said Simone mournfully.

"Some joke!" remarked Joey. "Look, Miss Maynard! Stitched top and bottom of legs and sleeves, and the top of my trousers too!"

Miss Maynard's eyes twinkled, and she bit her lips. "H'm! So the biters were bitten," she said softly. "Well, I will give you five minutes longer. Be quick!"

She knew better than to look through the other curtains to see if the Juniors were asleep. Certain little rustles and

139

snorts made it quite evident that they were not. She took no notice of the suspicious sounds, but simply waited by the window until the other two were safely in bed, and then withdrew, remarking that she hoped they would all—with an emphasis on the "all"—get off to sleep quickly.

"Pigs!" remarked Joey, as soon as she was well out of the way. "Little horrors!"

Four separate giggles answered her, but no one spoke. She gave a snort and turned over, burying herself beneath the sheets. Simone had done the same.

"An' the worst of it is that it completely put the lid on our stunt!" she groaned next morning when she and Simone had finished telling the other four what they thought of them. "We'd intended ragging the Senior cubicles, but I thought we'd better get ready for bed first, and then we found what you'd done! An' Maynie came up before we were half ready."

"Well, why didn't you tell us?" demanded Margia. "Then we'd have helped, and left you till tonight!"

"Well! Of all the cool cheek!" gasped Joey. "Margia, you're the limit!"

"It's your own fault!" retorted Margia. "You said we hadn't any rags yet, and it would be a pity to finish the term without."

"Yes; but I never meant you to rag us! An' that reminds me. Is the piano done?"

"Uh-huh! Amy did it when she had finished her practice."

"Good enoughsky! No one saw you, did they, Amy?"

Little Amy shook her head till all her curls danced. "No one! It will be fun!"

"Well, it's Grizel's practice first! Won't she be mad?"

"Hopping mad," agreed Marcia. "There's the bell! Come on!"

The conspirators scurried in to lessons, and only saved themselves from complete disgrace by the most valiant efforts. Amy, her mind wandering to the latest joke, when asked to explain what a delta was, said dreamily, "It's another name for the keyboard of the piano—the white keys!"

Miss Bettany dropped the blackboard chalk in her surprise. "Amy!"

"I beg your pardon, Madame," she faltered. "I—I——" She stopped, unable to go on.

"I see," said Madge dryly. "Will you kindly pay attention to the lesson? What is a delta?"

Amy managed to stumble through a fairly accurate if somewhat lengthy explanation.

Joey and Simone, doing algebra, came off little better. Joey's simple equations were a hopeless muddle, while Simone's had neither beginning nor ending.

Frieda, Anita, and Sophie stared at them in amazement, while Miss Maynard scolded them sharply for carelessness and inattention.

Much they cared, however! They were only longing for two o'clock and the beginning of practice-time. They had not dared to meddle with the music-room piano, for this was one of the days on which Herr Anserl came up from Spärtz to give music lessons. He was a magnificent teacher, and a musician to his finger-tips, but he was terribly short-tempered, and any pranks would have sent him storming off to Miss Bettany. His pupils all regarded his lessons with a mixture of terror and amusement. He told Grizel that she had the fingers of a machine, and the soul of one too, which offended her dreadfully, but she dared not show it. Joey he raved at for her lack of a sense of time, while Juliet's stumbling performances brought German phrases and epithets rumbling from his very boots. On the other hand, he had once told Margia Stevens that if she worked hard and thoroughly for the next six years, she might make a performer who would not disgrace him. Margia was the only one of the younger girls to go to him, the others being taken by Mademoiselle.

Simone learnt the violin, and so did Gisela Marani and Gertrud Steinbrücke, so they three went down to Spärtz on one afternoon in the week for their lesson.

After *Mittagessen*, they were allowed to do as they liked until two o'clock, when preparation and practice were the order of the afternoon. The schoolroom piano stood in the Senior classroom, and while the Juniors did prep. under Miss Maynard, the Seniors had an English literature lesson

141

with Miss Bettany, and Grizel practised under Mademoiselle's eye, so that she should work as accurately as possible. The partition between the preparation-room and the Senior room was of light matchboarding only; the windows were wide open, and it was possible to hear everything that went on in the next room. The Juniors listened eagerly. They heard Grizel settle herself down and touch the notes tentatively before she began. Then Joey stood up.

"Please, Miss Maynard, may I take my French to Mademoiselle?" she said. "I don't quite understand her corrections."

"Yes, Joey, if you must," said Miss Maynard, glancing up from her work.

Joey escaped, and hastened into the other room. It was no part of their plan to let Mademoiselle find out what they had done. She would probably be angry, and report them to the Head, and they did not want that.

"*Eh bien*, Joey, what is it?" asked Mademoiselle, as she made her appearance.

"It's this exercise, Mademoiselle," replied Joey meekly. "I don't quite see where I've gone wrong. Should I have used the subjunctive mood?"

Unsuspectingly, Mademoiselle took the book from her and looked it over.

"Yes, my child, it is here," she said. "If you use '*est-ce que*', you must follow it with the *subjonctif*, which you have not done. Grizel! What, then, are you doing?"

She might well ask! Grizel was supposed to be practising modulatory exercises, but even they were no excuse for the hideous noise she was producing.

"I—it's the geys, Mademoiselle," said Grizel. "They are so slippery."

"Slippery? Bah! It is your own abominable carelessness! Begin again, and with more care, I pray you!"

Hunching her shoulders and compressing her lips, Grizel started again, with much the same results. For once, it was a cool day, and chilly fingers combined with slippery keys proved too much for her. Suddenly it dawned on her to look at her finger-tips. They were powdered with white! In a flash she realised what had happened: the Juniors had covered the keys with French chalk! Nearly choking with anger, Grizel took out her handkerchief and dusted the keyboard as unobtrusively as she could. Furious though she was, she could not give them away to Mademoiselle, who was busy instructing an extraordinary stupid Jo.

As for Jo herself, it was all she could do to keep a straight face. She was unable to see Grizel's expression, but a back can be very expressive at times, and Grizel's looked as if she had swallowed a poker whole. When, presently, she had apparently listened to all Mademoiselle's explanations, and was dismissed, the Middle girl literally fled out of the room, and, collapsing at the foot of the stairs, rocked backwards and forwards with laughter. The sound of footsteps overhead made her pull herself together with a mighty effort, and getting up, she went back to the prep.-room, where, for all the amount of work she did, she might just as well not have been.

Never had the afternoon seemed so long to the Juniors. When at length Miss Maynard said, "Five minutes to four! Pack up your books and get ready for tea!" they all sighed audibly with relief, much to her astonishment. She had barely taken her departure before a righteously indignant Grizel dashed in.

"Where's Joey Bettany?" she cried. "Jo, you little horror, how dared you mess up the keys like that?"

"I didn't!"

"She didn't!" "It wasn't Jo!" exclaimed several voices at once.

"But she knew all about it! I know that!"

"Jolly well I did! But I didn't do it," returned Jo stoutly.

"Then who did? I never heard of such nerve in my life! Who did it?"

"Me," said a small voice, and Grizel turned to stare incredulously at the baby of the school.

"Amy! You!"

Amy raised angelic blue eyes to the startled face above her. "Yes. It was a joke!"

"Well! I—I'm jiggered!" declared Grizel flatly.

She went slowly out of the room to her own quarters, where all the coaxing and teasing of the other Seniors could not get out of her what was wrong with her, and

143

it was only after Gisela and Bette had heard from the delighted Juniors what had occurred that they understood. Then they were almost as startled as Grizel herself. Amy was the last person they would have suspected of such a trick. Margia, Joey, Maria, even Suzanne might have done it. But Amy! The Seniors were completely flabbergasted.

As for Amy herself, she was in high glee over it, and cut capers to such an extent that she called down upon herself a sharp reprimand from Miss Maynard, who coached them for tennis, and who, of course, had no idea why Amy Stevens was behaving with such sudden wildness.

On their way home after tennis in the evening, Gisela summed up the state of affairs rather neatly to Bette.

"Amy is becoming a schoolgirl and ceasing to be a baby," she said. "But one doesn't expect it so suddenly."

"No," agreed Bette—they were talking in their own language—"but I think you are right."

"I know I am," said the Head Girl with finality.

CHAPTER TWENTY

And Still More!

THE JUNIORS, having begun to play pranks—all, it must be admitted, of fairly harmless character—found it too pleasant a pastime to give up. The night after the affair of the French-chalked piano keys, Juliet, on going to bed, barely suppressed a wild yell when she entered her cubicle, for there, sitting up in her bed, was a figure that looked curiously lifelike in the half light. A closer inspection informed her that the creature was made of her own pillow, decked in her own pyjama jacket, with a boudoir cap, hastily manufactured out of two handkerchiefs, stuck on top, while beneath this an amiably smiling face drawn in coloured chalks on a sheet of white paper made the thing natural enough to have scared her badly for the moment.

Grasping the ridiculous object, she marched into the cubicle where Joey Bettany, who had caught the extra-ordinary sound she had made, was choking her laughter with the sheet.

"Joey!" said Juliet indignantly, "did you do this?"

"I—I——" Joey was incapable of uttering more at the moment. The sight of the weird object completely upset her.

Dropping it, Juliet took her by the shoulders and shook her. "Joey! Stop giggling, and tell me if you were so stupid!"

"Well, stop shaking me then!" retorted Joey, as well as she could for lack of breath.

"You deserve more than shaking, you little horror!" declared Juliet, releasing her as she spoke.

"If anyone hears you, there'll be a row," said Joey calmly. "It's 'lights-out' for me, and you're not supposed to talk to me now."

Juliet was rendered speechless by her virtuous air, but she soon recovered herself.

"Well, upon my word!" she said. "For cool cheek, that beats everything! It would serve you right if I took this thing to Madame!"

"You won't, though," returned Joey with confidence. She was leaning back against her pillow, smiling up at the older girl as she spoke.

Juliet suddenly laughed back at her. "No; you're quite right—I won't! But be careful, my child! I'll have my r—r—revenge, so don't forget!"

"I won't," replied Jo cheerfully. "What! Must you go? So sorry! Good-night!"

She turned over on her side and snuggled down, and Juliet, with rather a grim smile, left her. All the time she was preparing for bed she was turning ideas over in her mind. Just as she was kneeling down to say her prayers, a smothered shriek from Grizel brought her to her feet with a bound.

"Grizel! What on earth's the matter? Are you hurt? Oh——"

"Those little beasts!" spluttered Grizel, as she drew her curtain back. "Look at that! Two brushes in my bed!" She held them out as she spoke.

"Little horrors!" laughed Juliet. "I had an effigy in mine!"

"They must have gone mad!" declared Grizel. "It's all Joey, of course! She thinks of the things, even if she doesn't do them."

"She does not!" said a third voice indignantly. " 'Twas me did that!"

"Girls! What are you thinking of? Juliet! Grizel! Why are you not in bed?"

They all jumped, as the outer curtains parted to show Miss Bettany.

"Why are you not in bed?" she repeated. "And why have you drawn back the curtains between your cubicle and Juliet's, Grizel? You know it is against the rules!"

Silence answered her. On hearing her voice, Grizel had dropped the brushes, so she did not see them. As no one seemed to have an answer ready, she bade the two Seniors hurry into bed.

"I will see you in the morning," she said coldly. "I am very disappointed in both of you. I thought you could be trusted to keep the rules!"

With this she left the room, while two unhappy people stared at each other. Then Grizel drew the curtain again and retired to her bed, after she had pushed the brushes underneath it. Juliet followed suit, and a deadly silence filled the room. It continued next morning, and, when Grizel met Simone on the stairs, she drew to one side. Simone lifted her dark eyes to the Senior's face with the glimmer of a smile, but Grizel tilted her head and stalked downstairs with an offended dignity, that was rather marred by her missing the last step and staggering somewhat ignominiously across the hall.

"Grizel is furious!" reported Simone to the others. "She would not regard me."

"If you mean 'look at', I'd say so," murmured Joey. "When are you going to my sister to say it's your fault?"

146

Simone's eyes fell, and she began to play nervously with the end of her girdle. "I—I don't know," she stammered.

"Why not? I should go after breakfast an' get it over."

"Ye—yes!"

Joey turned and looked at her incredulously. "You surely don't mean you're goin' to funk it?" she demanded.

"N—no! No! Of course I will go! Will—will Madame be very angry?"

"Couldn't say! Shouldn't think so," was the laconic response.

"Oh, Joey, do not be angry with me!" pleaded Simone, half crying. "I will go certainly, and say it was my fault."

"Righto!" said Joey. "Come on to breakfast—there's the bell!"

Simone would have made only a poor breakfast had Joey not kept a watchful eye on her. As it was, she was persuaded to eat her usual meal. And then Joey went with her as far as the study door.

"Buck up, old thing!" she said cheerfully. "She can't eat you, an' I'll wait for you here."

Thus adjured, Simone went in after tapping at the door. Miss Bettany looked up in surprise when she saw her; she had been expecting Grizel and Juliet.

"Well, Simone," she said, "what is it, dear?"

"Please, Madame, I am come to say that it was my fault," said Simone.

"Your fault? What is your fault? I don't understand."

Simone took hold of her rapidly departing courage with both hands and said, "The—the disturbance last night—I did it!"

"You did it? But it had nothing to do with you!"

"Yes, Madame. I had put two brushes in Grizel's bed."

For a moment Madge's lips twitched. Simone's expression was so serious. Then she pulled herself together. "That was very silly," she said gravely.

"Yes, Madame. I know it was," agreed Simone. "But you will forgive them, since the fault is to me?"

"'The fault is mine'," corrected her headmistress. "I will see Grizel and Juliet, Simone. And please don't do such a silly thing again. Run away, now."

Greatly relieved, Simone trotted off, and a minute or so later Grizel and Juliet presented themselves, inwardly quaking a little. They met with an agreeable surprise.

"Simone has been to me," said Miss Bettany soberly, "and she tells me that it was her fault that there was a disturbance in the dormitory last night, so we will say no more about it. But remember that for the future even brushes in your bed will not be accepted as an excuse for breaking rules. You may go now."

"Jolly good for Simone," said Grizel. "I didn't think she had it in her."

The next joke was a harmless one, that nobody minded except the perpetrators, but which had far-reaching consequences. Two days after Simone's confession, Joey and Grizel came up to Gisela and solemnly informed her that on the fifteenth of July, which was St. Swithun's Day, it was the custom in all good English schools to sip a cup of water, which was passed round, and wish as one did so.

"But first you must take it to any foreign mistress in the school," said Grizel impressively, meaning, of course, that the water should be offered to Mademoiselle.

As the two practical jokers had already played tricks of a similar nature on her, Gisela looked at them sharply. Neither had the ghost of a smile on her face, and Joey's expression was super-angelic—a bad sign, which her sister would have recognised at once. Gisela, however, was not so experienced, and she was completely taken in.

"The fifteenth—that is tomorrow," she said seriously. "I will remember!"

"What a lark! Didn't think she'd be had so easily!" chuckled Joey.

"Neither did I," replied Grizel. "Shan't we crow over them tomorrow!"

Unfortunately, Gisela had misinterpreted one part of Grizel's speech. In her eyes, of course, all three mistresses were foreigners, and both Joey and Grizel were thunderstruck when, just before prayers, the Head Girl advanced to the little dais where the staff was, and offering the cup of water, murmured in her pretty English, "The cup of water for a wish, as is the custom in all English schools on St. Swithun's Day."

148

There was a moment's silence. Miss Bettany looked puzzled, Miss Maynard choked audibly, and Mademoiselle wore an outraged expression. Then the headmistress, with one rapid glance round the room, took in the affair at once. Quietly she accepted the cup, and drank from it.

"Thank you, Gisela," she said, as she returned it. "And now we will have prayers."

The ensuing events were lost on Joey and Grizel, who were almost petrified with horror. They were more horrified when, after she had given out the notices for the day, Miss Bettany added, "I should like to see Josephine and Grizel in my study now, before lessons." Then she dismissed the school and went to her own room.

The culprits presently appeared. She waited till they had shut the door.

"Now," she said, "I want to know what Gisela meant."

"It—it was only a lark," mumbled Joey at last.

"Please speak correct English, Josephine. Repeat your sentence."

"It—it was only a joke," repeated her small sister rather faintly.

Miss Bettany's eyebrows went up at the statement.

"A joke? I'm afraid your sense of fun is too elemental to appeal to me. I see nothing humorous in a silly trick like that. Who suggested it?"

Joey went scarlet; Grizel hung her head and said nothing. Truth to tell, she was rather scared. She had never encountered her headmistress in this mood.

"Who suggested it?" repeated Miss Bettany, in a voice that intimated that she meant to know sooner or later.

"It was me," said Grizel at last, as sulkily as she dared.

"Indeed? Your grammar seems to stand in as much need of correction as your idea of humour. Well, I am going to send for Gisela, and you will both apologise to her before me for your silly impertinence towards her." She rang her little bell as she spoke, and presently Marie appeared and was dispatched for Gisela.

Presently Gisela appeared, wearing a rather startled expression. "You have sent for me, Madame?" she said.

"Yes, Gisela. Josephine and Grizel wish to express their

149

regret for being impertinent enough to play a silly trick on you about St. Swithun's Day observances."

Gisela's face cleared at that. "But it is all right," she said. "I knew when I had offered you the water that it was a—a take-in!"

"Nevertheless, it was very impertinent of them," replied Miss Bettany. "Girls!"

"I'm sorry," said Joey. "I suppose it was cheek, Gisela, but I didn't think of it; honest Injun!"

"It is all right," repeated Gisela.

"Now, Grizel," said the headmistress.

"I'm sorry," mumbled Grizel.

After dismissing the Head Girl, Miss Bettany said a few more words on practical joking, and then sent them to their form-rooms, where Jo, at any rate, was soon immersed in her history. Not so Grizel. She was intensely proud, and hated apologising to anyone. Besides this, her headmistress's strictures on her sense of humour had offended her dreadfully. She sulked till half-way through the morning, then the sudden memory of a joke she had once heard of as being played on a master at her cousin's school came to her.

"I'll do that!" she thought. "Perhaps that may not seem kiddish! At any rate it'll be something to rag me for! That idiot of a Gisela!"

The joke in question required careful preparation, and Grizel was rather doubtful as to whether she could get the materials she required. Fortune, however, favoured her. On the landing near the big dormitory stood an old armoire in which Mademoiselle kept such simple medicines as they were likely to need. As a rule it was kept locked, but Amy had fallen down and bumped her head, so Mademoiselle went to fetch some cold cream for the lump. She left the cupboard open, and Grizel, passing at the time, saw her chance—and took it.

The fun started next morning when Mademoiselle came to give B division their German lessons. Both Grizel and Jo came for this. Jo's German was fluent enough, but her written composition was weak, so Madge had ordained that she must attend the lessons of B division as well as those of A. Happy-go-lucky Jo accepted her lot quite calmly, and rejoiced in the fact that, at any rate, she was missing hated geometry, and might have been much worse off.

The first half of the lesson was devoted to the correction of a previous composition; then Mademoiselle turned to the blackboard.

"We will now do some oral composition," she said in German. "I will write the title on the board, and then we will all make sentences. We will, today, talk of the mountains. Margia, give me the German for 'the mountains'."

"*Gebirge*," said Margia promptly.

"The article?" said Mademoiselle, waiting, chalk in hand.

"Oh—'*die*', I think," said Margia, somewhat doubtfully this time.

Mademoiselle beamed approval on her, and turned to write it up. In vain she struggled with the chalk. Not one mark could she make.

"I do not understand," she said, lapsing into her own language in the stress of the moment.

"P'r'aps the chalk is wet," suggested Joey. "If it is, it doesn't write, I know."

"Perhaps that is the reason," agreed Mademoiselle, looking at the chalk dubiously. "Margia, my child, go to the stationery cupboard and fetch me a fresh piece, if you please. There is no more in the desk."

Margia darted away, and presently returned with a new stick. But for all the impression it made, she might just as well never have fetched it.

"But this is an extraordinary occurrence," Mademoiselle was beginning, when the door opened and the headmistress entered, white with anger. Mademoiselle was too full of the unusual behaviour of the chalk to notice anything wrong.

"Madame," she began eagerly, "the chalk will not write!"

"I know," said her Head in low tones. She advanced to the board and drew her hand down it in one sweep. Then she looked at her palm. "As I thought," she said. "Which of you has vaselined all the blackboards?"

There was a deathly silence. Everyone was staring with

151

fascinated eyes at the headmistress, whom they seemed to be seeing for the first time. Miss Bettany suddenly struck the desk with her hand. Everyone jumped.

"Who did it?" she demanded. "Is there a coward in the school?"

On the word, Grizel sprang to her feet, head up, eyes blazing defiance.

"I did it!" she said, as insolently as she dared. "I——"

"Hush!" There was that in the one word which checked the rush of speech to her lips. "You say you did it, Grizel Cochrane?"

"Yes."

"Go to your room," said Miss Bettany quietly, "and wait there till I come to you. I am ashamed to think a girl I had counted as a Senior should cause so much trouble by her childishness and impertinence. Go at once!"

Grizel went.

CHAPTER TWENTY-ONE

Plans

JUDGMENT HAD GONE forth. Grizel was to be left severely alone by the rest of the school. No one was to speak to her, and she was to speak to nobody. She was to sit by herself in classes, and her meals would be brought to her in the schoolroom. When the others were at games, she was to go for a walk with whichever member of the staff could take her. This was to last for two days, and it was the severest punishment that had ever been given at the Chalet School.

In vain did Joey plead that the fault was largely hers, since it was she who had suggested that it would be a pity to let the term go by without some practical jokes. In vain did Mademoiselle, who was fond of the troublesome child, appeal against the sentence. Not even could Gisela, speaking for the school, avail anything. Miss Bettany had made up her mind that punished Grizel was going to be, and nothing would save her.

In the interview she had had with the girl, Grizel had proved herself defiant in the extreme. She possessed a temper which, once aroused, took some time to cool off. She had hated having to apologise to Gisela the day before, and the two affairs together had roused all the worst in her. Finally, Miss Bettany had given up trying to make her see reason, had named her punishment, and left her to herself, hoping that a little solitude would bring her to her senses.

"Oh dear!" sighed Joey in the dinner-hour, when they were all wandering about doing nothing in particular. "I wish I'd never heard of the word 'joke'!"

"Is Madame very angry?" asked Gisela, slipping an arm through hers.

"She's rather mad," acknowledged Joey. "I think Grizel cheeked her."

She threw a wistful glance at the window of the little room where Grizel was, presumably, confined. Then, turning to the elder girl, she went on: "Grizel's got such a beast of a temper. When she gets her monkey up, she doesn't much care what she does."

" 'Gets her monkey up?' " repeated Gisela with a puzzled frown. "I do not understand."

"Sorry! That's slang, I'm 'fraid," apologised Joey. "Loses her temper, you know."

"Your English slang is sometimes so incomprehensible," complained the Head Girl.

"Yes, I s'pose it is. But it's jolly expressive. Hullo! Here's the postman! He is late today. Grüss' Gott, Herr Sneider!"

The postman returned her greeting amiably, handed her the letters, and departed.

"One from Dick—that's my brother—for Madame," commented Joey, "two for Maynie, and one for Margia and Amy. None for me. What a swizz!"

"There is the bell for *Mittagessen*," said Gisela. "Come! Let us go in!"

They went in, Joey leaving the Tyrolean in order to take the letters to her sister. Madge was standing by the window, her lips set and her eyes thoughtful.

"Hullo," she said, when she saw her small sister, "what is it? Oh, letters!"

"Letter from Dick," said Joey, "and it's *Mittagessen* now!"

Madge's face relaxed as she took the letters. "All right. You can come here after, and we'll read it together. Take the others to their owners, will you?"

Mittagessen seemed never-ending to Joey. She bolted her own food, and when Simone accepted a second helping of *Pflaumekuchen*, cast a look of deep reproach at her.

However, everything comes to an end sooner or later, and at last they all rose, and grace was said. To Madge, two minutes later, appeared a flushed and excited Joey, who could scarcely be induced to sit down.

"Buck up and get on! Do!" she urged. "I'm dying to hear what Dick says."

Madge laughed. "Here goes, then!" she said, as she smoothed out the thin foreign paper.

"DEAR KIDS," Dick had written,—"Thanks awfully for your last letters, though it took me all my time to read Joey's. What on earth she wrote with I suppose she knows! Some of the words looked as though a good-sized black beetle had fallen into the inkpot and then staggered about on the paper. They don't seem to teach the young to write nowadays."

"Cheek!" interjected Joey swiftly. "He needn't talk; his own fist's bad enough for anything!"

"I'm glad the school's going so well; but, my dear kid, have nothing to do with Carrick. He's an awfully bad hat. They do say that he was practically kicked out of here— had made the place too hot to hold him. But it's only gossip so far, and there may be no foundation for it. All the same, a chap from the Hills told me that they'd sent that unfortunate kid of theirs to some school up there, and then tried to clear out and leave her on the Head's hands. Luckily, the old lady contrived to track them, and they were obliged to stump up what they owed and take the girl with them. One's awfully sorry for her. She seems to have a rotten time from all I can gather. Mrs. C. has a vile temper, they say, and he isn't much better. It's an awful life for a girl to go dragging about like that! If Carrick wants you to have Juliet—isn't that her name?—as a boarder, don't you do it! I wish to goodness you had someone more reliable to look after you than Mlle. La Pâttre. I know she's a jolly good sort, but women are so helpless! They ought to have a man to look after them.

"I'm awfully glad to hear that the piccaninny is going strong and getting fat. Austria seems to suit her. That cinema stunt was rather cheek, I thought. I'm thankful it got no further. I certainly don't want my sisters stuck up in every cinema for any idiot to see!

"There's precious little news to tell you. We are busy with some experiments at present. The Gobbler (Dick's superior) has some wild notion of growing European fruit-trees here, so we're mucking about in a fair-sized clearing growing good old plum and apple. This, of course, is in addition to our ordinary work. I blessed him the other day, I can tell you. He had us pruning and planting the whole day, and the mercury doing the high jump for all it was worth.

"The rains are going well, and there's a chorus of frogs outside my bungalow at the moment. This is beastly weather. The one consolation is, that anyhow the snakes are lying pretty low. My bearer caught a whacker the other night—a king cobra—so he's introduced a mongoose to the household in case the mate is anywhere round. We've called the little lad 'Binjamin', after 'Stalky's' Binjamin. Remember? Well, there's nothing more to tell you, and I'm dead tired, and just going to turn in when I've finished this screed. Remember what I say, and leave Carrick alone. Salaams.—DICK."

There was a little silence when Madge had finished. Then Joey broke it.

"Dick's too late," she said. "We've been and gone and done it! Poor Juliet!"

"Poor Juliet indeed!" sighed Madge. "Oh, Joey Bettany, you've a lot to be thankful for, let me tell you!"

"I know," said Joey soberly. "You're a sport to me, Madge! And Dick's another!"

"We're all you've got," said Madge briefly.

"Some people haven't as much," replied Joey, leaning her head against her sister. "Look at Juliet! And then Grizel hasn't anyone much. You can't say her father's up to much, can you? Poor old Grizel!"

Madge slipped an arm round her little sister. "You're right there, old lady. But Grizel must come into line with the rest of you. You're up to monkey tricks as well, I know, but you haven't been impertinent too. I know you think I'm being a perfect beast to her, but she can't be left to go on like that, can she?"

Joey acknowledged the truth of this. "No; I see your point. But, Madge, old thing, I do think she's sorry by this time! Can't you go and see?"

Madge shook her head. "No, Joey! She won't be sorry yet. Now it's time for prep., and you must toddle off. Come along early tomorrow morning and we'll have a palaver. It's only a fortnight to the holidays now, and then we'll have a good time together." She gave her sister a little squeeze and then sent her off to her preparation.

Left to herself, she faced the Grizel problem once more. She knew that it would take a lot to make that young lady say she was sorry, and yet she had determined that apologise Grizel must and should. The point was, how was she to be brought to it? She recognised the truth of Joey's statement that Grizel hadn't "anyone much". In some ways she was more to be pitied than Juliet. From all accounts, the latter had been accustomed to little different treatment from what she had received; but Grizel for five years of her life had been the spoilt darling of her grandmother, the next few years had been a hard discipline for a wilful, petted child; and apparently too much freedom from such discipline had gone to Grizel's head. Nothing else could explain her present defiance.

Later in the day she went to see Grizel again, but found

her stonily silent and absolutely unrepentant. The interview did no good, and she left the girl with a hopeless feeling that something was all wrong here. Grizel herself was still too miserably angry to care what happened.

"I hate her—I hate them all!" she thought to herself. "I'd run away if I'd anywhere to run to! Oh, I wish I was dead, I do!"

She leant her forehead against the edge of the window-frame, staring miserably out at the dark pinewoods and the slopes of the Bärenbad Alpe. Presently she shifted her position, so that she could look up the long valley towards the Mondscheinspitze, with the Bärenkopf in the distance, and, towering over all, the Tiernjoch, with its sinister shadows. Even on a summer's day, when the other peaks gleamed white in the glory of the afternoon sun, it looked dark and lowering. Her mind went back to the stories Herr Mensch had told them about it. How, one winter, sixty years ago, there had been a fearful avalanche down its slopes, which had partly buried a little hamlet that stood at the foot of it, and how, when spring had brought the thaw and the snow had melted, the houses were so buried in rocks and earth that it had been well-nigh impossible to dig them out. There were other gruesome stories, too, of travellers who had been caught in the treacherous mist on its slopes and had never been seen again—or else had been found, a little heap of broken bones, at the bottom of the ravine which made one of its chief dangers. As she stood looking dreamily into the distance, she heard footsteps under the window, and then Wanda's precise English.

"Where is Grizel, Margia? I should like with her to speak."

"Grizel's in a row," replied Margia's voice. "She vaselined the blackboards, and was awfully rude to Madame about it. So she's not to be with any of us till she says she's sorry."

"Oh, I am so sorry!" said Wanda. "Poor Grizel! How unhappy she must feel at having been rude! But how did she dare?"

"Goodness knows! She dares anything! She's going to

157

climb that old Tiernjoch some day, she says," floated up Margia's clear notes.

"Oh, but I do not think she can mean that!" replied the young Viennese. "That is only talking, as Joey says."

They moved on then, but the mischief had been done. So that was what they thought, was it? That it was all talk on her part? Well, she would jolly well show them! She would show them that very day! No, the next day! She would get up early, and when they came to find her she would be gone! She'd show them all what she dared to do and what she daren't! She'd make them sorry they'd treated her like this!

Miss Maynard entered at that moment to tell her to get ready for a walk, and she had to change her shoes and find her hat. Throughout the hour and a half, during which they went round the lower end of the lake to Buchau, where they caught the steamer back to Briesau, she remained obstinately dumb. Miss Maynard made one or two remarks, then, finding her efforts vain, lapsed into thoughtfulness on her own part, leaving Grizel to herself.

When they returned, the young lady was taken back to her room, and Miss Maynard brought her a couple of books and her embroidery before she withdrew, closing the door quietly behind her. There was no question of locking her in; the door was merely shut. Naughty as she had been, it never dawned on Miss Bettany to think that the girl would abuse the trust reposed in her; and in her normal frame of mind, Grizel would as soon have thought of trying to fly as of betraying that trust. But she was not normal at present. The one idea of "showing them" filled her mind to the exclusion of everything else.

It would be an easy matter to get away. She must wake early—by four o'clock at latest. That would give her a start of four hours, since nobody was likely to come near her much before eight. By that time she hoped to be well on her way to the little Alpe or Alm half-way up the mountain, where herdsmen attended to the cattle which were grazed there in the summer. The question of food was rather a difficulty, for the one little shop the place boasted would not be open at that hour, and Grizel knew that bread and cheese was all she was likely to get from the herdsmen; and the bread would most likely be reeking of garlic, which she detested. Finally, she decided that she must save all she could from her supper. She hoped they would bring her plenty.

She strayed over to the window, and stood with her head thrown back gazing at the great gloomy mountain. Joey Bettany, passing beneath with Simone on her way to tennis, glanced up and saw her, though she did not see Joey.

Half-past seven brought Marie and her supper. Grizel's spirits went up with a bound as she took in the bowl of soup, the rolls and the butter, the large slice of *Kuchen*, and the glass of new milk. The soup and the milk would do for the supper, and the rest she must put away for the morning. Perhaps there would be some apples in the kitchen. Things were going well for her.

Later, she heard the others coming back from cricket and tennis. Joey was talking. "Look! Alpengluck!" she said, her words carrying easily on the still air.

"Bother!" Juliet chimed in. "No games tomorrow, then, and it's Saturday!"

She heard no more, for just then the Head came in to say "good-night", and see that everything she needed was there.

Miss Bettany had meant to say something to her, but the hard, defiant look 'Grizel turned on her forbade anything of the kind. She realised that, in the girl's present mood, discussion would be worse than useless.

"Good-night, Grizel," she said quietly.

"Good-night," mumbled Grizel.

Then the door closed and she was alone.

159

CHAPTER TWENTY-TWO

Grizel Runs Away

"SATURDAY MORNING! Thank goodness, no lessons!" And Margia heaved a sigh of relief.

"Lazy bones!" jeered Juliet from her cubicle, where she had been reading for the last half-hour.

"The hols. will be here soon anyhow," said Joey Bettany. "Let's hope it's decenter weather than this! A horrid grey day! I do hate them so!"

"There's mist on the mountains!" Margia had climbed out of bed, and was contemplating the Bärenbad, the Bärenkopf, and their fellows with pensive eyes. "Can't see the top of old Mondy, and the Tiernjoch is lost!"

"It'll rain later," observed Juliet, shutting her book with a sigh for her disturbed peace. "We shan't even get a decent walk."

"Frau Mensch asked Simone and Grizel and me to tea today," observed Joey in rather muffled tones, since she was buried beneath her *plumeau*. "I suppose we'll go, but it's rotten for Grizel. I wish she hadn't cheeked my sister!"

"It is quiet without Grizel," observed Simone, who was sitting up in bed hugging her knees. "And it will be not nice—I mean horreed!" as a groan from Joey reached her —"to have to say Grizel is being punished."

"Don't you worry! They'll know all about it!" Joey assured her. "I saw Frieda's eyes nearly jumping out of her head yesterday when she answered Mad—my sister! Where's my dressing-gown?"

She scrambled out of bed, wriggled into her dressing-gown and bedroom slippers, and vanished in the direction of her sister's room.

"It's rotten for Joey," said Margia, who had gone back to bed again. "Madame is her sister and Grizel is her chum. Whichever she sides with, it looks mean for the other! I do think Grizel is an ass!"

"Whose turn is it to go first to the bathroom today?" inquired Juliet.

"It is me!" said Suzanne Mercier in her shy soft voice.

Both Suzanne and Yvette had very little to say at any time, and their voices were so seldom heard, that, as Grizel had once remarked, they might just as well never be there more than half the time. Now, Juliet nearly jumped.

"I always forget you two are there," she said. "If you're going, Suzanne, you'd better toddle along. I can hear Marie coming with Amy's water."

She got up as she spoke, and fished out her bedroom slippers and rolled up her sleeves, preparatory to giving Amy her bath. That she should do it had become quite a recognised thing now, and to Juliet it was a great thing that she could help even in so little, as some return for her Head's goodness to her. She could never help contrasting Miss Bettany's quiet acceptance of the state of things with the behaviour of her Anglo-Indian headmistress under similar circumstances. That lady had been mainly concerned about the loss of her fees. Of Juliet's feelings she had thought not one jot. Juliet had not suddenly become an angel as a result of her present Head's treatment of her. She was a very human girl; but she was deeply grateful, and since she was thorough in whatever she did, she was making valiant efforts to become the same sporting type of girl as that to which her headmistress belonged. This bathing of Amy, which had been a self-imposed task, sometimes bored her very much, but Miss Bettany's thanks had filled her with a determination to go on, and, as a result, she was learning that a duty undertaken for love of a person isn't half so tiresome as one which is thrust on one.

As for Amy, she had quite overcome her fear of Juliet, and chatted gaily as the elder girl sponged her down and then rubbed her dry.

"There you are!" said Juliet finally, as she finished drying between the little pink toes. "Now buck up and get into your clothes! Who's in the bathroom now?" she went on, raising her voice slightly.

"Simone," replied Joey, who had come back from her sister. "I'm next, an' then you. Oh, an' Madame says go past Grizel's door quietly, as she wants her to get a good sleep 'cos she seemed so tired last night."

"All right," said Juliet briefly. "Stripped your bed, Joey? I say, I don't think we'd better put the *plumeaux* over the balcony today. It looks as though there was going to be a splash!"

" 'Twon't come yet," said Joey the weather-wise. "Prob'ly not till this afternoon. It's going to be a beastly day," she added, shaking her pillow vindictively. "I jolly well wish it was over!"

Nobody seemed in a particularly happy mood this morning. The girls were subdued under the consciousness of Grizel's disgrace. The staff was worried for the same reason. In the kitchen, Marie was accusing her small brother Eigen, who came to help with odd jobs, of having helped himself to the apples she had left in a big dish overnight.

"Sixteen apples I leave," she scolded, "and now there are but ten! Where are the others, rascal? Thou hast eaten them! Thou hast stolen!"

Eigen, a stolid person of eleven, looked at his sister solemnly. "*Nein*, Marie," was all he said in answer to her accusations.

"But I say thou hast! Who would take them if thou didst not, *junge Taugenichts*?"

"*Nein*, Marie," said Eigen serenely. All he knew was that he hadn't touched the apples, whatever his sister might say, and he cared for nothing else.

Madge, hearing the disturbance in the kitchen, went to discover what it was all about.

"Why dost thou scold, Marie?" she inquired in fluent German.

"This rascal, Madame, he has stolen six apples—six."

"Good gracious!" observed Jo, who had followed her sister. "He'll be ill!"

"*Nein*, Marie," observed Eigen, still as placidly as ever.

Marie turned to her mistress with outflung hands of

162

helplessness. "You hear him, Madame! That is all that he says! He who has stolen!"

"*Nein*, Marie!" was the parrot-like response of the accused youth.

"Wait, Marie," said Miss Bettany, checking the flood of exclamations which she could see to be on Marie's tongue. "He is a good boy. If he says he did not touch the apples, then I do not think he did. Eigen, hast thou seen the apples of which Marie speaks?"

Eigen looked at her hopefully. He had quite given up expecting any sense from his sister. He said, "Nein, gnädiges Fräulein."

"Very well!" Miss Bettany turned to Marie. "I am sure he speaks the truth, Marie, and one of the young ladies may have felt hungry during the night and taken them. I will inquire, and, meantime, say no more about it."

Her young mistress left the kitchen, followed by Jo, who was wondering rather miserably how things would go that day.

"It's going to be simply horrid!" she decided, as she attacked her roll and honey with considerably less appetite than usual. "Oh, I wish it was over!"

Inquiries about the apples did not solve the mystery. No one had touched them, and Juliet, who was a light sleeper, and who had, in any case, awakened early, was positive that no one had left the dormitory till the rising-bell had rung. "Except Joey," she added.

"Joey came to see me," said Miss Bettany, "so that's all right. Well, I'm sure that if Eigen says he hasn't touched the fruit, he hasn't. I imagine Marie didn't count very carefully when she put them out. That's more likely than that Eigen should have taken them when he says he didn't. Now, go and make your beds and then get ready for a good walk. It's going to rain later on, so you won't get games this afternoon, I'm afraid. Jo, you and Simone are going to Seespitz to the Mensches, so you'd better not go with the others. Get your practising and mending done this morning instead of going for the walk, and change before *Mittagessen*. Herr Mensch rang me up last night to say he was going to take you all for a motor ride up the Tiern Valley, and would be at the fence gate for you at two o'clock, so you must be ready. What he will do if it rains I can't tell you!"—thus forestalling the question on Joey's lips. "Now run along, all of you, and get on. Please go quietly."

She had said grace previously, so they all got up and went upstairs in subdued manner. As she passed the door of Grizel's prison with Simone close beside her, Joey heaved a little sigh.

"What is it then, Joey?" demanded Simone.

"I don't know. I feel as though something horrid was going to happen," returned her friend. "Sort of fore-telling, you know! Spooky and awful!" she added incoherently.

"I do not understand," said Simone, who might well be forgiven for not understanding.

"Oh, well, I can't explain!" replied Jo impatiently. "Come and make your bed!"

They were half-way through, when the chink of china on a tray and the sound of careful footsteps told them that breakfast was going to Grizel.

"It's awfully jolly to have your breakfast in bed," grumbled Margia. "I wish I had! Worth being naughty for! I say! What's that?" as a startled cry reached her ears.

Before anyone could answer her, there came the sound of hurrying feet, and Miss Bettany flung open the door of the dormitory.

"Girls! Which of you has seen Grizel Cochrane this morning?"

A startled silence followed her question. Finally Juliet answered.

"I don't think any of us have, Madame. Isn't she in her room?"

"No. The windows are wide open and her clothes are gone! Are you sure you haven't seen her?"

You could have heard a pin drop as they digested this information.

"D'you mean you think she's—run away?" ventured Margia at last.

"Of course she hasn't!" exploded Joey. "She's broken bounds, that's all! An' I think she's a beast!"

"Hush, Joey!" said Miss Bettany. "Of course she hasn't run away, Margia! For one thing, she has no money, and for another, she hasn't anywhere to run to. But it's very trying! I did think I could trust you girls!"

She turned and left the room as she spoke, leaving a startled group behind her. They did not quite know what to think. Up till this moment they had felt a good deal of sympathy for Grizel; and her brilliant idea of vaselining the blackboards had rather captivated them. But this was quite another thing. It was untrustworthy, and, as Margia said later, "not cricket." With all her wilfulness, Grizel had never yet failed to play the game, and the shock of discovering that she could fail rather stunned them. Presently Juliet went back to her task of bed-making, and they all followed her example in a deathly silence that said far more about their feelings than any amount of speech could have done. When they had finished, Joey and Simone went to their practice, while the others got ready for their walk with Miss Maynard. Presently they set off, passing Madge and Mademoiselle on the way, the one going over to Buchau to make inquiries as to whether Grizel had been seen about there, while the other was going down to Spärtz by the mountain-path on the same quest.

For some forty minutes Joey worked away steadily at her scales, her mind anywhere but on what she was doing. Suddenly she jumped up.

"The Tiernjoch!" she gasped. "That's where she's gone! Up the Tiernjoch! Oh, she was looking at it last night! That's what she was thinking of! I must go and fetch her back!"

With Jo the impulsive, to think was to act. She dashed along to the cloakroom, tore madly into her mac., dashed into Simone, and gasped, "Simone, Grizel's gone up the Tiernjoch! I'm off to fetch her back! You must stay and tell Madge when she comes! Good-bye!"

Before the astounded Simone had taken in half the sense of what she said, she had gone. Thus it happened that a distracted and worn-out Madge was met some hour and a half later by a tearful Simone, who sobbed out that Joey had gone up the wicked Tiernjoch to find Grizel.

CHAPTER TWENTY-THREE

On the Tiernjoch

TO GO BACK a few hours to the time when Grizel awoke in the early greyness of the morning is now necessary. When she had got into bed, she had banged her head on her pillow four times, saying solemnly "Four o'clock!" as she did so. She woke up just as the old grandfather clock below chimed four times. For a minute she listened for the breathing of the others, then she remembered. She was by herself as a punishment, and she was going to climb the Tiernjoch that day. "At last!" she thought, as she climbed cautiously out of bed. Shivering a little with cold and excitement, Grizel began to dress in the half light. She was soon ready, and then, picking up her electric torch, she stole downstairs in her stockinged feet to the kitchen to see if Marie had, by chance, left any food about. She found the apples on the kitchen table and abstracted six, dropping five of them into her knapsack and beginning on the other. There was nothing else, however, and she dared not risk opening the cupboards in case any of the doors should creak. Still, six apples, two rolls of bread, and a slice of Marie's *kuchen* were not so bad.

The next thing was to get out. It would be madness to attempt to open the doors. What she decided on was almost as mad. The window of the room opened on to the balcony that ran all round the house. Grizel clambered over the railings, hung for a moment from the ledge of it, and then dropped. Mercifully, it was only ten feet above the ground, and she had learned how to fall easily, so beyond a bumped elbow she came to no harm.

When she reached the fence, the cows that were pastured

in the valley were coming along, led by the big cream-coloured bull who was lord of the herd. The boy who was herding them looked curiously at her, but made no comment. Probably he thought that she was waiting for the rest of a party. When they had passed, Grizel set off again, this time at a reasonable jog-trot pace, which she knew she could keep up for some time. When she had reached the tiny hamlet of Lauterbach, the last remnants of the darkness had gone and it was broad daylight.

A man was chopping wood for the fires outside one chalet, and he was whistling a gay tune as he worked. Two or three goats, tethered nearby, bleated at the sound of her footsteps, and a baby kid came skipping alongside of her, its head cocked inquiringly on one side, its yellow eyes full of innocent inquiry which won her heart instantly.

"Oh, you darling!" she cried, trying to catch him in her arms. But Master Billy was as shy as he was curious. With a terrified "Ma-a-a!" he made a side-dash away from her, and raced for home and mother.

Grizel threw back her head, laughing gaily at the sight. The peasant looked at her, and grunted "Grüss' Gott!" She answered him, and then went on. All remembrance of the fact that she was in disgrace and had no business to be there had faded from her mind in her enjoyment of the morning. Even the actual ascent of the great mountain that hung so threateningly over the upper end of the valley was forgotten.

Like a good many unimaginative people, Grizel possessed the gift of living in the immediate present. Where Joey and Madge would have been dreaming of the mountain summits and the joy of the hard climb, she was simply wild with delight in her present surroundings. As she swung along, she began to sing one of the folk-songs she had learnt in her English school. She finished the song with a wild flourish of her stick, and discovered herself at the foot of a narrow path that wound up and up between bushes and rocks. A tiny stream trickled down far above her, looking like a silver thread in the cold light.

Grizel stopped and debated with herself. Should she eat her breakfast where she was, or should she go on till she reached the Alm where she would buy her milk?

"I'll eat an apple," she decided, "then I'll go on. Coo! What a scramble!"

She sat down on a convenient rock and bit firmly into an apple. "Jolly it is, early in the morning!" she thought, as she flung the core into nearby bushes. "Well, I must pull up my socks and get on with it!"

Accordingly, she shouldered her knapsack once more, picked up her stick, and set off gaily up the narrow path, whistling cheerily as she went. Presently, however, the track left the bushes, and twisted about round boulders and over heaps of broken stones which she found tricky to negotiate. She had been right. It was a scramble! Up and up she clambered, unheeding of her legs and shoulders, which were beginning to ache with the unaccustomed exercise.

"The Sonnenscheinspitze was a circumstance to this," she thought, as she toiled onwards, "and as for the Mondscheinspitze, it was a baby's crawl! I hope it gets better farther on!"

Far from getting better, however, it got worse, and Grizel was forced to stop more than once to rest. "Oof! This is some climb!" she sighed, as she sat down for the third time to mop her streaming face. "However they get the cows up here is beyond me!"

As a matter of fact, the cows reached the Alm by a path, which came over the shoulder of the mountain, and was much easier; but Grizel could not know that. Presently she set off again, and this time she succeeded in reaching the Alm. She nearly came to grief over the last few steps. The Alm itself overhung the path, and, in order to get on to it, she had to catch at a tree root and haul herself up. She was almost there when her hand slipped and she nearly fell. If she had gone, it would have meant a fall of twenty feet or more, for just here the rock had broken away. Luckily, she managed to scramble to safety somehow, and reached the short, sweet turf, where she lay with beating heart for the next few minutes.

Presently she got to her feet. With all her faults, Grizel was no coward. A weaker character might have given in at this point, but she simply set her teeth and went on. The Alm is a long one here, and the herdsmen's hut is built in a crevice in the rock, so it was a good ten minutes before she reached it. The men had long since gone to their day's work, and there was only a lad of sixteen or seventeen in the hut. He stared at her, but made no comment. When she asked for milk in her best German, he brought it to her in a big earthenware mug, and stood watching her while she drank it. Never had anything tasted so delicious to her as that draught of sweet milk, rich with yellow cream. When she had finished, the boy took the mug, saying in curiously hoarse, thick tones something of which she caught only the last words *ein Nebelstreif*. Grizel did not understand, but she was not going to let him know that if she could help it; so she looked as intelligent as she knew how, nodded her head, and said, "Oh, ja-ja!"

Again the boy spoke, this time saying something about *keine Aussicht*. This, Grizel knew, meant "no view", so she shook her head this time, saying, "Nein, nein! keine Aussicht!" which seemed to satisfy him, for, with the usual "Grüss' Gott!" he turned and went back into the hut.

Grizel looked after him doubtfully before she turned and went on her way. Walking over the short, springy grass was a treat after the hard, toilsome scramble over the rocks and shale. She had got her second wind, and went on joyously, munching an apple as she went. It struck her that it was getting rather misty, but she had no means of knowing the time, as she was not wearing her watch, and she supposed it to be the morning mists, which would soon disappear. It was then about eleven o'clock, as a matter of fact; and at the foot of the mountain Joey Bettany was eyeing the path up which her friend had come with dubious eyes. Ten minutes took Grizel to the far edge of the Alm, and once more the path began to wind upwards. It was easy going at first, but soon became more difficult. The mist-clouds closed in round her, and presently she found herself struggling upwards, surrounded by white walls of mountain fog, which hid the path from her and deadened all sounds save those of her own footsteps. She was plucky enough, but the deadly silence and the eeriness began to frighten her. Some of the terrible stories Herr Mensch and Herr Marani told them came back to torment her now. She was worn out, and the climb

169

was becoming more and more difficult. Over and over again she was obliged to sit down and rest, and after each halt she felt herself becoming stiffer and stiffer. Then suddenly her foot struck a loosened stone and set it rolling. She heard it go a little way, then there was an awful silence, and at the same moment the clouds lifted just sufficiently to show her that she was standing on the edge of a precipice!

As the realisation of the fact came to her, Grizel felt the last remnant of her courage oozing away, and clutched at it desperately. If she had followed the inclination of the moment, she would have flung herself down on the ground and screamed. Luckily, she did nothing of the kind. More, she even tried to take a step or two forward. Then, as the mists came swirling back once more, she gave it up. She knew where she was, for Herr Mensch had described the ascent to her more than once. She had reached the worst bit of all. Here, for one hundred and fifty yards, the path, barely three feet wide in most places, and even less in some, crawled along the edge of a precipice which went sheer down to the valley below. On the other side a wall of stark rock rose, also sheerly, giving no hold of any kind. This was the part where anyone in the least degree nervous was roped, and it was where the worst accidents always occurred. What made things worse was the fact that she had no idea how far along she had come. With a pitiful attempt at self-control, she sat down, slowly and carefully, curling herself up against the rock-wall. Little shivers, partly of cold, partly of terror, ran up and down her. Lying there, with only a narrow shelf of rock between her and instant death, Grizel prayed as she had never prayed before. At first the words would not come. Then gradually the old familiar "Our Father" rose to her lips. That comforted her. "Our Father, which art in heaven," she prayed aloud, the sound of her own voice helping to steady her. "Our Father, oh, send someone! Please send someone quickly. Our Father——"

"Grizel! Grizel!" The cry came faintly through the mist.

She sat up. Joey! It was Joey's voice! "Our Father," she sobbed. Then, "Joey! Joey!"

"Hold on a tick! I'm coming! Where are you?"

Grizel pulled herself together. "Joey! I'm on the precipice! I'm lying down! Look out!"

Almost at once a figure loomed up out of the mist, and then Joey, feeling her way carefully, was beside her. She was sitting down, pulling her into her arms, holding her tightly, saying, "Grizel! Grizel!"

"Our Father," began Grizel dully. "Oh, Joey, He sent you at last!"

Then darkness swept over her, and, to Joey's utter dismay, she fainted. It was only for a few moments, however. She struggled back to consciousness, and with consciousness came terror, complete and overwhelming. She clung to the younger girl, shaking from head to foot, while Joey, with wide, straining eyes trying to see through the mists, held her tightly, murmuring words of comfort to her.

"Grizel! Darling! Don't cry! It's all right! Honest Injun, it is! There! Don't cry, Grizel! Joey's here! Joey's got you safely! It's all right!" Over and over again she repeated it, till finally the meaning of her words reached Grizel's brain, and she began to pull herself together.

"Joey!" she said presently. "Oh, Joey! How did you know?"

"Where to come to, d'you mean? I guessed! Grizel, are you better? Don't you think if we went on hands and knees you could get back to the rocks? We aren't awfully far along, I know. Two minutes would do it. Can't you try, Grizel?"

But Grizel dared not. "Joey, I daren't! Oh, Joey, I know I should slip and fall! I daren't move! Don't you move, either, Joey! If you do, we shall go over! Don't move, Joey! Please don't!"

"But, Grizel, old thing, it's awfully cold, and you're wet through! Do let's have a shot at it!"

But Grizel's nerve was gone. She could only clutch her friend, crying piteously, and, mercifully for both of them, she made no attempt to move. Had she done so in her present state of mind, there is little doubt but that both of them must have gone over the edge. Finally, Joey gave up her coaxing, and settled herself as comfortably as she could to await the rescue she felt sure would come soon. Grizel, lying closely against her, had ceased to cry. Now she seemed drowsy and dull. With a sudden throb of fear, Joey Bettany faced a new danger. She had read of the death sleep which continued cold brings on, and she realised that already Grizel was only semi-conscious. At all costs she must rouse her.

"Grizel!" she said imperatively. "Grizel! Wake up! You can't go to sleep!"

Grizel muttered something drowsily, but made no movement. Joey slapped her face smartly, and nearly brought disaster on them both as the elder girl stirred.

"Grizel! Grizel!"

"Yes, Joey! I'm here!"

"But you must stay here!" sobbed poor Joey. "Oh, Grizel, don't go to sleep!"

"I'm not; but I am so tired," murmured Grizel.

"I know, but oh, you mustn't! Oh, I can't bear it!"

Her tears fell on Grizel's face, and did more to wake her than anything else would have done. Joey crying was a wonder not to be understood.

"Don't cry, Joey! It's all my fault, and I'm sorry now! Oh, if we both die it will be my fault, and Miss Bettany will never forgive me or look at me again!"

Joey began to gurgle hysterically at that. "Don't be s—silly! If we both die we shall be d—— What's that?"

She sat with head upreared, listening for the sound her quick ears had caught. It came again—the long, melodious call of the mountaineer.

"Grizel!" she cried. "We're found!" Then, with all her strength, she cooeed.

The yodel came again, nearer this time, and, as she answered it, Joey noticed that, at long last, the mists were thinning. Then came the sound of careful footsteps, and, finally, the dear familiar figure of Herr Mensch, looking more like a benevolent giant than ever. Behind him came the slighter form of Herr Marani, and behind him again two of the herdsmen, who had been pressed into service. To a skilled mountaineer like Herr Mensch the narrow path presented no difficulties. With one big stride he had stepped across the two girls, then, turning round, he bent down and picked up Grizel, while Herr Marani helped Joey to her feet. The next few minutes were dangerous enough, for Joey's cramped muscles would not work, and she nearly fell. Luckily, Herr Marani had her firmly, and twenty minutes later they were on the Alm, where Madge awaited them with white face and eyes dark with the agony she had undergone. If Herr Marani would have allowed her, she would have carried Joey herself to the herdsmen's hut, where a potent drink of hot milk, mixed with brandy from Herr Mensch's flask, was given to them before they made the final descent to the valley.

Two hours later the sun appeared in full glory, gilding all the peaks and driving away the last rags of mist from the sinister mountain which had so nearly added two more to the toll of its victims.

CHAPTER TWENTY-FOUR

Consequences

IT WAS THE DAY after Grizel's grand escapade, which had so nearly ended in terrible disaster, and it was a day which none of the girls ever forgot. The sun shone gloriously the whole time, as if to make up for his behaviour of yesterday. The Tzigane band had come up the lake again, and was making music outside the Kron Prinz Karl. But all this meant nothing to the school, for Grizel was ill with bronchitis, and Joey Bettany had never come out of the sleep into which she had fallen after they had laid her in Herr Mensch's car, which had been awaiting them at the foot of the mountain.

Herr Marani had gone hotfoot to Innsbruck to fetch the doctor, and he had said that the awful nerve strain through which the imaginative, highly strung child had gone might result in brain fever. That could only be decided when she came out of the heavy stupor in which she lay, and which might last for two or three days yet. Grizel's case was far simpler. It was a straightforward attack of bronchitis, the natural result of having been for hours in the clinging mists. It was, of course, made worse by the fact that she had gone all to pieces when she found herself in her own bed; but with careful nursing—and they could be sure of that—she would soon be all right again. Joey's case was far more doubtful. Then he left them, promising to return the next day. Frau Mensch had appeared in the morning and carried off Amy and Margia, and Frau Rincini had sent Bette over to fetch the little Merciers. She had offered to have Simone as well, but Simone had begged to stay, and Juliet had offered to look after her, so they had given the child her way.

Midday had brought Frau Marani with an offer to nurse Grizel, and Madge herself had never left Joey for a minute until the doctor had arrived, and with one glance at her white face had sternly ordered her out.

"It will make things worse if you are ill," he told her. "Go and have some food, and then a little walk. Tonight you must sleep, while the young lady—ah, Fräulein Maynard!—watches. Nothing will occur for some hours yet." Then the anguish in her eyes touched his compassion, and he added, "She looks better—seems more natural. Now go and rest."

Madge did as he told her as far as going out was concerned. She had gone to the pine-wood, and was wandering up and down, when Simone had caught sight of her, and, breaking away from Juliet, had rushed across the meadow and caught her arm with hot little hands. Now, as she saw the child's face, all puffed and swollen with crying, Miss Bettany felt suddenly that she had been neglecting her duty. She slipped an arm round Simone, who promptly began to sniff again.

"The doctor says nothing will happen for some hours yet, but he thinks she looks more natural. Don't cry, Simone."

Simone made a valiant attempt to check her tears, and

succeeded. "I do love Joey so much!" she said quaveringly. "Oh, Madame, if there is one little thing I can do you will tell me?"

"Yes," said Madge. "I can tell you of one little thing now. You can stop crying and try to be brave. Tomorrow there will be school as usual. Joey is far above the schoolrooms, and I know you will all be quiet. We shall break up on Tuesday or Wednesday, instead of a week later as I had intended. I want you to be very brave, and work as steadily as you can for the two days. If the others see you and Juliet"—she smiled at the other girl, who had now come up with them—"trying to go on as usual, they will try too, and that will make things easier for us all."

"I will try," said Simone very soberly. "I will try ver' hard."

"I'll do my level best," Juliet promised, "and I will look after Simone, Madame."

"Thank you, both of you," said Madge. "Now I must go back, as I may be needed."

She turned and went back to the Chalet, feeling fresher for her little rest, and more able to cope with things. She found Joey lying as she had left her, with the doctor sitting by her side. He looked up as the girl entered, but made no other movement. Madge bent over the bed, looking at the dear, funny little face with a world of love in her eyes. Was it her imagination, or did Joey really look more like herself. She glanced up at the doctor inquiringly, and he nodded his head.

"Yes, it is really so. I begin to have hopes of her. We cannot yet say definitely, but the pulse is stronger, and the temperature has risen no further. Now go and change your clothes, and have a bath and wash your hair!"

Madge quite literally gaped at him, wondering if she had heard aright.

"Yes, I mean that," he said, nodding his head again.

"Go to the hotel with this note and have your hair shampooed. There is more than time for it, and it is a better tonic than any I can mix for you in my dispensary."

Sheer astonishment rendered her dumb and obedient. She had thought as she mounted the stairs that she could only leave the bedroom again when she knew that Joey was safe. Now, clutching his note, she made her way to the Kron Prinz Karl, where the Tzigane were playing a plaintive, haunting waltz, to which people were dancing on the grass at the side.

The Von Eschenaus were sitting at one of the little tables, and when Frau von Eschenau saw her, she came quickly over, taking her arm.

"Mein Fräulein, we are so grieved—Marie has cried herself sick for grief! Tell us, how is das Mädchen, and if there is anything we can do?"

"Thank you," said Madge. "There is really nothing. Joey is much the same, and I've come to get my hair shampooed—the doctor sent me."

Frau von Eschenau stared. "To get your hair shampooed?" she repeated doubtfully.

"Yes. I have a note for Herr Braun."

"Then come this way, and we will find him. Doubtless he will be in the *Speisesaal*."

The good-natured Viennese led her into the big dining-room, where Herr Braun was engaged in directing the laying of the tables for dinner. When he saw them, he hurried forward, exclaiming. Madge gave him the doctor's note, and he read it through with wonderment in his eyes. Then he nodded his head wisely.

"It is well, gnädiges Fräulein. If das Fräulein will come through here, it shall be done."

He led her into the hairdressing-room, and forty minutes later Madge was going back to the Chalet feeling refreshed and ready for anything. She peeped into Grizel's room, where good Frau Mensch sat knitting, one watchful eye on the bronchitis kettle. Grizel was sleeping, propped up with pillows to relieve the breathing. She looked flushed, but there was nothing alarming. The illness would take its natural course, and the doctor was not alarmed about her. So much Frau Mensch told the young headmistress, her busy fingers never ceasing their work.

"He will stay here for tonight," she continued in her low, murmurous voice that made the guttural German sound soft and musical. "I think he expects that little Jo will come to herself before the morning. Mademoiselle has come in, but she knows nothing about sick-nursing and would be useless. Frau Marani will come tonight and watch by das Mädchen, for Fräulein Maynard must sleep, and you will be with the little sister. *Na, mein Liebling,*" as Madge tried to thank her, "it is nothing—we are glad to do what we can. You and she are very dear to us all, and we of the Tyrol do not show ingratitude. See! das Mädchen is waking —she opens her eyes."

"What is it, dear?" said Madge. "Do you want to know about Joey? She is still asleep. The doctor is staying here for a while."

"Will—she—be—very—ill?" The words came slowly.

"She is very tired," said Madge evasively, "but she hasn't got bronchitis like you. Now you must rest, you naughty child. We want you to get well again as quickly as possible. The holidays are very near, you know." She bent to kiss the girl, and Grizel relaxed.

"I'm glad," she said. "It wouldn't have been—fair if Joey—had to be ill—for me."

Madge left her after that, and went back to the other sick-room. The doctor looked at her keenly, but, beyond a grunt, he said nothing. Throughout the long night he sat there, watching the little white face on the pillow, Madge watching with him. Once only he left her, to go and see Grizel, and came back with the news that she was decidedly stronger. At ten o'clock Frau Marani appeared, and Frau Mensch went back to the hotel at Seespitz. Five o'clock in the morning brought Miss Maynard to insist that Madge should lie down on the couch and rest for a couple of hours, while she watched in her turn. At seven the doctor went to ring up his partner in Innsbruck and warn him that he should stay where he was for that day. Later, Marie came with hot coffee, rolls, and butter, of which the doctor insisted Madge should partake, and at five to nine she went downstairs to see to work for the day.

The girls came with grave faces, and kind messages and offers of help from their parents. The whole lake-side knew of poor Grizel's escapade, and a good many people had since learned of the dreadful possible result for Joey, so there were many inquiries.

Amy Stevens' first care was to grab Juliet and demand

177

in an awestruck whisper, "How is Joey? Has she come awake yet?"

"Not yet," said Juliet, who looked white and heavy-eyed. "Don't ask Madame any questions, Amy, will you? She's so fearfully worried."

"Course I shan't!" returned Amy indignantly. "I say, isn't the bell late?"

"There won't be any bell at all today," explained Juliet. "Just go straight in to prayers."

"Juliet, will you come here one minute?" said Gisela. "We want to know about Joey and Grizel too. How are they both?"

"Grizel is getting on fairly well," replied Juliet. "Joey hasn't roused up yet. They can't say till she does what will happen. The doctor expects it will be today, and he is staying. He was here all last night too."

Prayers were very solemn that morning, and when they were over, there was a little stir among the girls. Madge looked at them.

"Joey is much the same," she said. "There is no change —yet."

She left the actual schoolwork to Mademoiselle and Miss Maynard, flitting in and out at intervals.

The weary day wore on, and still there was no news from the room at the top of the house. The girls behaved like angels, as Miss Maynard said afterwards. There could be no music lessons, of course, and Mademoiselle had rung up Herr Anserl to tell him.

The one bright spot during the day was the fact that Grizel, reassured by their repeated statements that Joey was asleep, and also by Madge's obvious forgiveness, was improving rapidly, temperature going down, breathing easier.

At about three o'clock, as Madge was wearily trying to help Amy Stevens disentangle a glorious muddle of rivers and lakes in her map of Asia, word came down that the doctor would like to see her for a moment. She fled up the stairs to her bedroom. The doctor was standing by the bedside, one hand on Joey's wrist. He looked up as her sister entered.

"Ah, mein Fräulein, I have sent for you, for I think she

is beginning to arouse. Please stand just there, where she can see you."

Madge took up the position he pointed out, and stood, her eyes fixed on Joey's face. There was no doubt that she was coming out of the stupor. Her lashes flickered more than once, her lips were parted. The only question was, Would she wake up the old Joey, or would it be to the babbling delirium of fever?

There was a silence in the room that could be felt. The only sound to be heard was the breathing of the four people—Frau Mensch was by the window—and the ticking of the doctor's watch. Then, slowly, slowly, the long black lashes lifted, and Joey looked full at her sister.

"Hullo!" she murmured. "I'm awfully tired! Hai-yah!" She finished with a little yawn, turned slightly, snuggling down into the pillow, and fell asleep.

"Gott sie Dank!" said the doctor quietly. "She will do now; there is no further danger. Hush, *mein Kind*," for Madge had begun to cry. "It is well now!"

"I know," sobbed Madge. "But oh, Herr Doktor, the relief!"

He signed to Frau Mensch, who led her down to the study, and let her cry away the last of the awful weight that had been hanging over her. When, finally, the tears were all dried, she found a dainty meal of soup, roll, and grapes awaiting her, and when she had finished, Frau Mensch suggested bed.

"I must tell the girls first," said Madge. "I will make myself tidy, and go and tell them."

Ten minutes later Miss Bettany, who looked like herself once more, entered the room where they were all anxiously awaiting her news. She looked at them, but no words would come to her lips. It was Bernhilda the quiet who helped her out.

"Ah, Madame," she said, "there is no need to say anything. Joey will get well."

Madge found her voice. "Yes," she said. "She is sleeping now, and all is safe once more."

And there were rejoicings in the Chalet School that afternoon.

CHAPTER TWENTY-FIVE

Frau Berlin Again

"Oh, I say! Isn't this perfectly golloptious!"

"Joey! What an appalling expression! Where on earth did you get it?"

"What? 'Golloptious'? I heard those schoolboys we ran into at Tiernsee use it."

"Well, I wish you wouldn't. It's all very well for schoolboys, but it isn't pretty for schoolgirls, so cut it out!"

Joey cocked her black head on one side consideringly. "Getting a bit old-maidish, aren't you, old thing?" she said. "Don't do it, Madgie Machree!"

"Joey, you little brute! I won't be called such awful names! And you might show a little more respect for your headmistress. You get worse and worse every day!"

"Poor old darling! Never mind! Wait till we get back to school again, and then you can be as crushing as you like. This is holiday-time, and there's no one to hear us for once. I think it was topping of the Maranis to take Grizel and Juliet away for the week and let us be on our own for a bit. And this really is a gorgeous place! I never imagined anything like it!"

Madge nodded as she glanced up at the great peaks of the Rosengarten Gebirge which towered above them. Their own limestone crags in the North Tyrol were magnificent, but they were not to be compared with these. As far as they could see, lofty pinnacles of rose-hued rock lifted magnificent heads to the summer skies. Every here and there, cataracts flung themselves downwards in silver ribbons which leaped from rock to rock, all hurrying to join the river which dashed past, making thunderous music as it went, for the two previous days had been very wet, and all the springs and mountain streams were flooded.

Neither Madge nor Jo had been in the South Tyrol before, though both knew the North Tyrol very well, and when Frau Marani had come with the suggestion that Grizel and Juliet should go to Vienna with them for a week while the two sisters had a little holiday to themselves, it had been Joey's idea that they should come here.

"We can't go too far," she argued. "For one thing, we can't afford it. We've never seen Meran, or Botzen, or Primeiro, or any of those other places, and the Mensches say the Dolomites are just gorgeous. It's warm there, so it'll suit us both, and it's been rather chilly here lately. So let's go there, shall us?"

Madge had laughed and agreed. There was nothing to keep them at Tiernsee. Miss Maynard was spending the holiday with her family in the high Alps, and Mademoiselle had gone home to her beloved Paris, taking Simone and the two little Stevens with her. The Maranis' kind invitation had settled Juliet and Grizel, and so, seven days previously, the two Bettanys had left Innsbruck, *en route* for Botzen, by way of the magnificent Kuntersweg Gorge. Botzen they had loved, and Meran was a dream of delight. They had left the little Roman town only that morning to establish themselves in the tiny village of Paneirimo, in the Rosengarten Valley; and here, on the morrow, the other two girls would join them. Joey now turned and slipped an arm through her sister's. "It's been jolly on our own!"

Madge nodded, but said, "I told them at the Chalet to forward letters here. You might run and see if there are any, Jo. I forgot to ask."

"Righto!" And Joey dashed off, to return in a very few minutes waving a whole budget. "Here you are! Dozens of them! At least there are ten—eight for you and two for me. This is from Simone, and this looks like Marie von Eschenau. Madge! You aren't paying any attention! What on earth's the matter? Who's your letter from? Is there anything wrong? What is it?"

Madge pulled herself together with an effort and turned

to her little sister. "It's rather dreadful news in one way, Joey. There has been a terrible motor accident in Rome, and Captain and Mrs. Carrick were in it."

Joey looked serious. "Are they awfully hurt?"

"Mrs. Carrick was killed at once," said Madge, "and Captain Carrick died two days ago. He has left me Juliet to bring up, as they have no relations."

Madge gathered up her letters and went to her bedroom.

Joey sat looking after her. She was silent for a minute, then she turned to her own letters. "Let's see what Simone's got to say!"

Meanwhile, Madge Bettany sat in their bedroom re-reading the letter written by a doctor of the hospital where Captain Carrick had died. After describing generally his injuries, the writer had continued: "Captain Carrick told me that his daughter was with you, and that you would be her guardian. He made a will before he died, leaving all he possessed, including some very valuable jewellery belonging to his wife and a sum of one hundred thousand lire, in trust to you for the girl. He asked me to say he hoped you had forgiven the trick he played on you, and would undertake the trust. The money, I gathered, he had won at the tables at Monte Carlo. He died three hours after he had made the will."

The letter concluded with a request to know how the jewels and money were to be sent, and a suggestion that Madge should come to Rome to fetch them, when "my wife will be delighted to welcome you to our home as our guest."

When she had finished re-reading this startling communication, Madge sat thinking hard. In one way, this event settled the Juliet difficulty, but it by no means completely solved it. Pondering over the problem seemed to bring her no nearer its solution, so she shelved the matter for the moment and turned her attention to her other letters. One was from Mrs. Dene, who had written to make final arrangements for Rosalie, who was coming to the Chalet School next term. Another came from Mrs. Stevens, thanking her for her care of Margia and Amy, and enclosing a very welcome cheque for the next term's fees. The third she took up was on very expensive paper, in a most illiterate hand, and bore the postmark of Bradford, which puzzled her extremely.

"Bradford!" she said aloud. "Who on earth do I know in Bradford?"

"Open the letter, old thing, then you'll find out!" observed Joey's voice from the doorway.

Madge literally jumped. Joey happened to be wearing plimsolls, and her steps had been quite noiseless.

"Sorry!" she observed, as she dropped down beside her sister. "I didn't mean to startle you. I'd finished my letters, so I thought I'd come to see what you were doing. I say! If Captain Carrick has left Juliet to you, how does he imagine you're going to manage for money?"

"There's money for her," returned Madge. "You needn't worry, Joey. But I'm rather afraid we shall have to go back to Tiernsee tomorrow. They want me to go to Rome to see about Juliet's affairs."

"And who is your Bradford pal?" said Joey.

Madge opened the letter and glanced at the beginning. "Honoured and respected Madam." "Good heavens! Who on earth can it be from?" She turned to the end, but found no enlightenment there. The signature, finished off with a flourish, was "James H. Kettlewell."

"James H. Kettlewell! Never heard of him!" began Joey.

"No; and yet it's vaguely familiar." Madge thought hard for a minute. "Joey! I've got it! Do you remember the man in the Paris train who gave us gooseberries? His name was Kettlewell, and he told us he lived at Bradford!"

"So he did! Whatever can he be writing about? Buck up and see!"

"Ahem! 'Honoured and respected Madam,'" began Madge, "'I take my pen in hand to inscribe this present epistle to you.'"

"Coo! What elegant English!" commented Joey.

"Be quiet! If you interrupt, I won't read it to you at all!"

"Sorry! I'll be good! Do get on! I'm dying to know what it's about!"

"Where was I? Oh, yes! 'It is with the greatest diffidence that I venture to approach you on such a subject, knowing, as I do, the delicacy with which it should be treated, especially to a high-up lady like you——' What on earth—— Is the man mad?"

"Oh, get on!" implored Joey impatiently. "Don't be so aggravating!"

"All right! It's my letter, remember! Let's see—'lady like you. Believe me, honoured Madam, I should not have the—the—oh—the temerity to approach you thus were it not that I feel——'." Her voice died away as her eyes wandered down the page. Then she suddenly sat bolt upright with horror. "Joey! It's a very private letter! I——"

"I s'pose you mean it's a proposal!" Joey interrupted her. "Oh, I knew what was coming after the very first sentence! Oh, I say!" And she went off into fits of laughter.

Madge shook her slightly. "Joey, behave yourself! It's not a thing to laugh at! If I'd known, I'd never have read it to you. I thought it was just an ordinary letter. You must give me your word of honour never to mention it to a soul!"

"What do you take me for?" Joey was righteously indignant. "Of course I shan't."

"Oh dear! This is dreadful!" Madge had turned over the page and was reading on.

"But of all the weird things to happen!" Joey got up and strolled over to the window. "I scarcely ever thought of him again. He was awfully sweet and kind, of course; but I must say it seems a mad thing to do when he'd only seen you once. Why, he couldn't know if you were good-tempered, or a decent housekeeper, or—or truthful, or anything!"

"Oh, Joey, be quiet!" exclaimed the exasperated Madge. "You'd talk the hind-leg off a donkey! Oh dear! Why does everything come at once?"

"It's rotten luck, old thing!" Joey's teasing mood had suddenly vanished. "You have had a time of it since we came to Austria! Let's hope next term is quieter than this has been! One thing, Grizel can't go off climbing mountains!"

Madge got up, folding her letter and putting it back into its envelope.

"Joey, I don't want you to think I'm always saying

'don't', but I'd rather not talk about that affair just yet. It's too soon after!"

She cast a thought to those dreadful hours when it had been doubtful what was going to happen to the speaker, and suddenly hugged her. "It was all very horrible. We won't talk about it at all, Joey. Let's see what the other letters are."

There was nothing exciting in them. Two of them were from the aunts in England, one from an old school-friend of Madge's, and the last asked for a prospectus of the school.

Later they strolled along by the banks of a rushing stream.

"It's been a weird affair all round!" said Jo, as she stood throwing in pebbles, trying to make them skim the surface of the water.

"What has?" demanded her sister.

"Why, all this—coming to Austria, and having the school, and Juliet, and—and James H. Kettlewell's letter, and everything!"

"Yes; but I don't see why you call it a weird affair!" Madge was deeply interested. Jo's imagination often helped to throw new light on matters, and she wondered what new light was going to be thrown on the Chalet School.

"Why, it's this way. We come out to Tiernsee because we're frantically poor. You decide to start a school, and it goes like—like fun. We do heaps of things in one term, and we grow from three to eighteen. Then, when the school is just going like everything, you get a chance to chuck it if you want to, and get married. We're jolly lucky, I think!"

Madge nodded. "Yes, that's quite true. But oh, if we're going to have the same sort of excitements each term that we've had this, I shall want to give it up!"

"Still, they haven't been bad excitements, 'cept the last—not really bad! Madge! Did you ever! There's Frau Berlin!"

"Frau Berlin? Where? Joey, don't point! It's frightfully rude!"

"There! By that house! Well, I be gumswizzled!"

"Joey! "

185

"Well, but did you ever! Glory! She's coming along! Wonder if she'll know me?"

But she passed them without a look, while Joey gazed at her with wide-open eyes.

"She'll recognise Grizel," she said, when the tartan-clad lady had finally waddled out of hearing. "Oh, Madge, if she does!"

"I'm not going to risk any more fusses." said Madge with determination. "If there's the slightest chance of that, back we go tomorrow."

"P'r'aps it would be best. I say, I'm awfully hungry! Let's go back an' see if we can get anything to eat. It must be nearly dinner-time."

As Madge was hungry too, she agreed, and presently they were enjoying a substantial meal. Just as they had reached the dessert stage the door opened, and in rolled Frau Berlin!

"That settles it!" murmured Miss Bettany. "You may pack up tonight, for as soon as Grizel and Juliet arrive we go back to Tiernsee. I think I must go to Rome after all, so that will be all right. It will just fit in nicely."

As soon as they could, they left the *Speisesaal* and retired to their room.

"That's the finish!" said Jo, as she finally rolled into bed at about half-past nine. "There can't be anything more after this."

However, the morrow was to bring them just one surprise more.

CHAPTER TWENTY-SIX

A Grand Wind-up

"WHAT DO YOU THINK? An old pal of yours is here, Grizel —a very dear friend!"

Grizel, thus greeted by a wildly excited Joey on her arrival at Paneirimo, looked at her suspiciously.

"Who on earth is it?"

"Guess!"

"Can't! Can't you think of a soul likely to be in Austria! Who is it, Joey?"

"Think, Griselda! Think of someone you met a short while ago!"

"But I haven't met anyone except people you have too. Why is it a pal of mine?"

"Someone you had a fearful row with," Joey prompted her, jumping tantalisingly up and down.

"I can't think— Joey! You don't mean Frau Berlin? Oh, it is—it is!"

"Well done you! Yes, it is. Well, what do you think of it?"

"My dear! It's awful! Has she seen you yet? Does she know, d'you think?"

Joey shook her head. "Don't think so! Anyway, we're not staying. Madge won't risk it."

"What d'you mean by not staying? Where are we going?"

"Home! Oh, you don't know yet, of course!" Joey cast a wary eye at Madge and Juliet, who were walking ahead. "Come on down to the river. We aren't going till the afternoon train, and we're to spend the night at Innsbruck.

It's rather awful in some ways, but, on the whole, I think it might be worse. My sister had a letter from Rome yesterday, and Juliet's father and mother are dead."

Grizel gasped. "Joey! Oh, how dreadful! Poor Juliet! What will she do?"

"Her father's asked Madge to look after her, and he's left her some money to do it with," said Joey. "That's one reason why we're going home. Madge has to go to Rome to get it. We're going back to Briesau, and Miss Maynard is coming to look after us. She was coming anyhow, so that's all right. What sort of a time did you have in Vienna?"

"Tophole!" And Grizel plunged straightway into an account of her adventures. When, finally, they turned their steps towards the hotel, they saw Madge coming to meet them. She was by herself and was walking rather slowly.

"Have you told Juliet?" said Joey in hushed tones as she reached them.

"Yes; I want you two to be very kind to Juliet. She's been through a good deal lately, and, naturally, she is very much upset. I needn't tell you not to hang round her or do anything silly like that, but just be as nice as you can to her. We are going back to Innsbruck this afternoon, and then tomorrow we shall go up to Tiernsee, and I shall have to leave you there, as I must go to Rome to settle up affairs for her. Miss Maynard will be with you, and I want you to give her as little trouble as possible. I'm sorry I can't send for her to come here, but, under the circumstances, I'm afraid it's rather impossible."

Grizel coloured furiously, although her headmistress had not attempted to make the last remark specially pointed. She knew well enough, however, that her behaviour at the Alte Post was mainly the cause of their leaving Paneirimo that afternoon. She said nothing, but followed Joey into the hotel with unaccustomed meekness. Madge, herself, had said nothing about what had occurred on that Saturday when Grizel had followed her own wilful way and tried to climb the Tiernjoch; but Frau Marani had had no scruples, and she had told the girl very plainly of what they had feared for Joey during the two long days which had followed. Grizel had had a dreadful shock, and she was never again so thoughtless.

"Where is Juliet?" asked Joey, as they reached the foot of the stairs.

"Upstairs in our room," replied Madge. "Yes, go to her, you two. Take them both out and show them the place, Joey. There are one or two odds and ends of packing I want to finish up, and I'd rather not risk a fuss with that Frau Berlin, as you call her. So keep out of the way till luncheon. Our train goes at three, so you won't have much time here. Make the most of it."

Upstairs in the big airy room with its twin beds they found Juliet standing at the window staring listlessly out at the mountains. She was not crying, as Joey had half feared, but she had a white, worn look, as though she had been ill, and her eyes were heavy and weary.

"Come an' see the mountains, old Ju!" said Joey, slipping her hand into the elder girl's. "They're topping, though not a bit like ours at home, of course!"

"Yes, do come!" urged Grizel. "And oh, Juliet, that awful woman's here!"

"Which one?" asked Juliet, though with a complete lack of interest in her voice.

"Frau Berlin—the one who was such a pig the day we went to Innsbruck to get Madame's birthday gift. Don't you remember?"

"Oh, yes, I remember. All right, Joey, I'll come."

But though she let them pull her downstairs and out into the sunshine, it seemed as though she didn't really care much what she did. The shock of hearing what Madge had told her, even though the news had been broken to her with great tenderness, had dazed her for the time being. Through all the chatter of the other two she was conscious of just one thought—"If only I could have felt they loved me!"

However, the fresh air and sunshine did her good, and when, finally, Miss Bettany came to summon them to lunch, she looked better than she had done.

No contretemps occurred with Frau Berlin, for she did not appear. Nevertheless, Madge felt very thankful when she found herself safely in the Innsbruck train without having had a scene. Juliet settled herself in a corner with a book, but she did not appear to read much. Most of the time she was gazing unseeingly out of the window. The other two had retired to the far end of the compartment, which they had to themselves, and at Joey's bright suggestion embarked on a game of Roadside Cribbage. Madge, sitting with one eye on the silent girl opposite her and the other on the *Wiener Zeitung*, occasionally heard exclamations of "Three goats—thirty!" "Waterfall—five!" "Mule —oh, bust it! Back to the beginning!" but paid no attention. She was not desperately interested in her paper either. For the most part, her thoughts were with the coming term. She would have twenty-six girls this time, and of these, twelve would be boarders. If the school went on growing, she knew that she must either build on to the present Chalet, or else take another somewhere near. She was not quite certain what to do. Herr Marani and Herr Mensch were very good friends to her, but she wished heartily that Dick were at hand to advise her.

As she was thinking of this, she suddenly became aware that the train was slackening speed, and even as she looked up to see where they were, it began to rock violently backwards and forwards with a sickening motion. She had barely time to leap to her feet before, with a mighty crash, the carriage gave a final lurch and collapsed on its side. Above the noise she heard the screams of the three girls, mingling with shrieks from the other passengers. Mercifully, Joey had flung herself on the floor, dragging Grizel with her; and, by a positive miracle, neither Madge nor Juliet had been badly hurt, though the former was, like everyone else, slightly stunned, and Juliet, as they found out after, was badly bruised. Also, being thoroughly English, they had had the window wide open, and so had a means of exit. The door, when Miss Bettany tried it, was jammed.

"It's a good thing none of us are fat," she said with a shaky laugh. "Come along, you three; I'm going to push you through the window. Grizel first."

Grizel had the sense to make no protests; besides, she was still rather dazed, so she allowed her headmistress to push and tug till she was through, and then, as the fresh air began to clear her stupefied brain, she reached down and helped to pull Juliet up. Joey was an easy matter, and she was soon standing on a heap of stones, looking very white and scared, while the two big girls dragged her sister out. They had just pulled her clear when, from the front of the train, came the dreaded cry of "Fire!"

"Das Feuer! Das Feuer!" shrieked a fat woman, who was badly jammed in the window-frame of the next compartment.

Madge flung a hasty "Stay where you are! Don't dare to move!" at the terrified girls and dashed to the rescue. The scene was becoming ghastly. The big engine and three of the long carriages lay on their sides in a narrow gorge-like way. The foremost carriage was already wrapped in flames, and their roaring rose above the screams and cries of the people still imprisoned in the other carriages. The three remaining on their wheels had disgorged all their passengers, and already men were tearing along, working madly to save those in such deadly peril. Madge Bettany contrived to take in all these things as she made that frantic scramble on to the side of the carriage, where a terrified fat woman, with grey hair streaming wildly round her, was struggling madly to get free of the window-frame, which held her gripped as in a vice.

Through all the horror of it the English girl contrived to keep her head.

"Steady!" she said, as she took the gripping hands, and though the language was a foreign one and a hated one, her voice brought self-control to the maddened woman.

"I cannot get free," she panted in German. "Fräulein ____"

"Keep still a moment! Now! Ready! Then, as hard as you can!"

There was a struggle, a sound of rending and tearing, a sudden gasp, and then the other woman suddenly shot out over the wheels and on to the heap of stones, her clothes in shreds, but otherwise safe. Madge sprang down beside her, and then she felt the world turning black, and she fainted. When she came to herself she was lying on a coat in a field. Joey was kneeling beside her, crying vehemently, and a big fair man whom she did not know was

191

holding something to her lips. With an effort she pulled herself together and pushed it away.

"No, no," she said.

"Oh, Madge!" sobbed Joey. "O—ooh! I thought you—you w—were dead!"

"Hush!" said the man. "She'll be all right in a minute, kiddy. It's only whisky-and-water I'm giving you, Madam. Better take a little to buck you up!"

"No; I'm all right!" With an effort she sat up, pushing the hair off her face. Joey promptly flung her arms round her, hugging her tightly. Juliet and Grizel seemed to have vanished.

"Oh, Madge darling! Oh, I had such a fright! Oh, Madge!"

"There! That'll do," said their benefactor. "You're not helping her, kid. Let her alone for a minute or two to come round. It's quite all right—the other kids are safe enough, and—oh, you plucky girl! It was one of the bravest things I've ever seen!"

"It was nothing," returned Madge, who was rapidly coming to herself. "Joey! Don't strangle me, child! Let me get up!"

She contrived to get on to her feet, but was glad enough of the arm the stranger flung round her as she swayed for a moment.

"There!" he said rather roughly. "Come over here and sit down a minute! You can't do everything at once! I'll send the other kids along, and you'll be all right in a minute. No, there's nothing you can do. Everyone got clear but the driver. He fell on his head, poor chap! Even your fat rescue is recovered enough to fuss about having no skirt on——"

"Yes; and oh, Madge, who do you think it is?" interrupted Joey, with considerable lack of both manners and grammar. "It's Frau Berlin!"

"Oh, goodness!" And Madge began to laugh weakly.

"Isn't it rum? And we left Paneirimo because of her and Grizel, and then you save her life! Yes, you did. The carriage got on fire just as you slithered down. If it hadn't been for you, she'd have been burnt to death! She was only bumped a bit, and she wanted to kiss you, only that man came and hiked you off into this field, and she suddenly found her clothes were all torn, so she wouldn't follow us! Grizel and Juliet are over there. They aren't hurt, and nor am I. Do buck up, Madge!"

Thus Joey, in a breathless, hurrying tumult of words.

"That man" stood to one side, smiling, as the elder girl managed to take it all in. Then Grizel and Juliet appeared, and all the excitement began over again. At length he interfered.

"Now then, you kids, let's go and see what we can do about getting on. I know this place, and we're about ten miles from anywhere. Besides, Miss——?"

"Bettany," supplied Madge. "These are my sister Joey, and two of my pupils—Grizel Cochrane and Juliet Carrick."

"Ah, thank you," he replied. "My name's Russell— James Russell, at your service. Well, as I was going to say, Miss Bettany, you had better get somewhere where you can lie down for a bit. There's a main road goes past here somewhere, and, with luck, we ought to get a lift in something. If you will take my arm, I think we can get there all right, and we can't do anything here."

There was common sense in what he said, so they set off, Madge beginning to realise how very shaky she still felt. The girls were upset too, and it took them some time to make the high-road. Luckily, just as they reached it, a peasant came past with an empty hay-cart. Mr. Russell quickly came to an arrangement with him, and a couple of hours later they were safely in the *Gasthaus* of a tiny village. They stayed there all night, their new friend going on to Innsbruck after leaving his card with Joey and getting the Chalet address, so that he could wire to Miss Maynard not to expect them for another day. The morning found them all very tired and worn out, but Madge wanted to get back to Tiernsee and home, so they set off, and finally arrived at the Chalet, where they were rapturously welcomed by an anxious Miss Maynard, who had been feeling very worried. Mr. James Russell had been better than his word, for he had gone up to Tiernsee and given her a full description of what had occurred.

"I'm thankful you've all arrived safely," said the young mathematics mistress. "I couldn't feel sure you wouldn't have another awful adventure."

"I think I'd rather keep out of adventures for some time to come," laughed Madge rather shakily. "Teaching and school generally will be enough for me for the next three or four years, I can assure you."

"Oh, I expect we'll have some more adventures presently," said Joey.

And so they did. But that, as Mr. Kipling says, is another story.

THE END

Jo of the Chalet School

First published in a single volume in hardback in 1926 by
W & R Chambers Ltd
First published in paperback in 1967 in Armada

Copyright reserved W & R Chambers Ltd

The author asserts the moral right to be identified as
the author of the work

CHAPTER ONE

The Three

"Charlie's neat, and Charlie's sweet, and Charlie
  is a dandy;
Charlie, he's a nice young man, and feeds the
  girls on candy."

"Oh Jo! Do stop that awful thing! I'm sick of it! "

Joey Bettany kicked her heels against the fence on which
she was sitting, and gave a chuckle. "I think it's jolly nice."

"Well, *I* don't; and I just wish you'd stop it! " retorted
Grizel Cochrane, frowning.

"Poor old thing! You *are* in a bad way! " laughed Joey
teasingly.

"I just wish term would begin, and the others come
back! " declared Grizel.

She looked round at the lake beside which she was
standing, Ringed in by big mountains, with a long, narrow
valley stretching away to the west, and water-meadows at
its southern extremity the Tiernsee in the North Tyrol is
surely one of the loveliest places in the world, and an ideal
spot for such a school as the Chalet School. Here Joey
Bettany's sister, Madge, had established herself at the end
of the previous April, beginning with nine pupils—Joey,
Grizel, and Simone Lecoutier (niece of the French lady who
had joined in the enterprise), and six Tyrolean girls who
came from the summer chalets which have grown up
round the lake—and ending the first term with just twice
that number.

The new term would begin in ten days' time. Meanwhile,

Joey, Grizel, and one other pupil, Juliet Carrick, an orphan and the ward of Miss Bettany, were finding time hang rather heavily on their hands. They missed their other friends, especially Grizel, who was a gregarious little soul, and, unlike the other two, had no resources of her own.

Grizel was an active tomboyish person, who was happiest when she was rushing about, climbing the steep mountain-paths, or rowing over the blue lake in one of the clumsy but serviceable boats which were kept there, largely for the use of the many tourists who came there during the summer months.

To make matters worse, Miss Maynard, the mathematics mistress, had brought back for Joey a copy of *The Appalachian Nursery Song-Book*, and Joey had sung them in season and out of season, till even the donor of the gift was beginning to regret that she had ever brought it. Grizel was not musical—Herr Anserl, the music-master who came every week to the Chalet from Spärtz, declared that she had as much soul as a machine, and played like one—and before many days were over she hated those nursery songs, a fact of which naughty Jo was not slow to take advantage.

Now, the songstress swung herself down from her precarious position on the top of the fence that divided Briesau, the little village where the Chalet School was, from the rough pathway that leads round the lake to Geisalm, the next hamlet, and demanded briskly, "What are you so humpy about?"

"It's all so slow," returned Grizel. "You and Juliet are always reading—unless you're reading, and she's working. I wish we could have an expedition somewhere! "

"P'r'aps we can." Joey considered for a moment. "Where'd you like to go?"

"D'you think Miss Bettany would take us into Innsbruck the next time she goes? If we wrote to the Maranis they might meet us. Gisela said in her last letter that she and Maria would be staying there till term began."

"That's rather an idea. I'd love to see Gisela again; I think she's a splendid girl."

"Some of the others might be there too! " Grizel was

growing enthusiastic over her own plan. "Wouldn't it be lovely if we could all meet and do something together?"

"Splendiferous!" Joey gave a little leap into the air. "Let's go and hunt up my sister, and ask her at once!"

"We can't this minute. She's gone down to Spärtz to see Herr Anserl about the new people, and to buy some more china."

"How do you know?" demanded Joey, her face falling.

"I went as far as the top of the mountain-path with her and Miss Maynard. Never mind! Let's go as far as Seespitz and see the train come in. We can get some apples from old Grete, too."

"All right," agreed Joey. "But it's no fun meeting the trains now; everyone's going away—not coming."

"It does seem lonely, now all the visitors are going," sighed Grizel.

Joey glanced at her. "It'll be all right when the others come back," she said. "What crowds of us there'll be! All the old girls, and Wanda and Marie, and their cousin Paula, and Rosalie Dene, and that American girl Evadne Lannis, and Vanna di Ricci."

"It's gorgeous to think we're growing like this. Why, Madge thinks we may get up to thirty by Christmas—and it's only our second term!"

"I know. And I thought your sister said you weren't to use her Christian name in school," put in Grizel a trifle maliciously.

"I know she did; and I don't! 'Tisn't term yet!" retorted Jo.—"I say, there's the smoke of the train! We'll have to hurry!"

They set off running at their best pace, but the train with its procession of funny little open cars got there before them, and, when they had reached it, its small load of passengers were already making their way to the boat-landing where the little white steamer awaited them. There were only ten visitors. The remainder were dwellers in the valleys round about. Some might even have come from Tiernkirche, a large village some four or five miles away from Scholastika, the hamlet at the head of the lake.

Many of those who lived on the lakeside recognised the

girls in their short brown gym tunics and brown blazers, and called out a friendly *"Grüss Gott!"* as they passed.

The strangers looked curiously at the two children, so obviously not Tyrolean, and commented on them. Grizel, with floating brown curls, tanned rosy cheeks, and dancing eyes, was typically English; and Jo Bettany of the pointed face with straight black hair, neatly bobbed, and eyes like pools of ink, was apt to attract notice wherever she went. Years of delicacy had left her with hollowed cheeks which had not yet filled out; and even a summer spent in the life-giving atmosphere of the mountains and at an altitude of some three thousand feet had not altogether taken away the fragility of her appearance, though she was stronger and healthier than she had been since she was a very small child.

Of these inquisitive visitors, none showed greater interest than two Italian girls of fifteen and twelve. They turned and stared at the pair with such concentration that the younger one tripped over some wood that happened to be lying in the path. Joey and Grizel promptly made a rush, and hauled her to her feet, Joey chattering the whole time.

"Are you hurt?—*Etes-vous blessée?*" she demanded, dropping rapidly from English into French as the other child looked at her blankly. "Oh, bother! She doesn't understand! *Haben Sie sich weh getan?*"

The little Italian shook her head and smiled. She had no idea what Joey was saying, as she spoke only Italian. Her sister, however, understood French, and caught at the word *blessée*.

"She asks if you are hurt," she said to the younger child in their own tongue.

At the sound of the musical syllables Jo's face lightened. She knew very little Italian, although her French and German were both fluent. She hastily recast her sentence.

"*Nuocete?*" she demanded.

The two girls laughed; and at that moment a gentleman, obviously their father, called them imperatively, "Bianca! Luigia! *Venite—adesso!*"

They went immediately, the elder pausing to say, "*Addio; e grazie!*"

200

"Goodbye; and thank you," translated Joey for the benefit of the less learned Grizel.

"They're rather jolly, aren't they?"

"Yes. But their father is a bossy old thing," commented Grizel.

"Here's Grete," cried Joey. "*Grüss Gott*, Grete!"

Grete, an old shrivelled apple woman, greeted them with an outburst of Tyrolean German, to which Jo responded with much fluency, and Grizel with a few somewhat halting sentences. She was very slow at picking up languages, and often had to think before she got the word she wanted. Jo, on the other hand, never had the smallest difficulty, and chattered away as rapidly and as gaily as the old woman.

"There is snow on the mountains," she remarked presently, as old Grete picked out her best apples for them.

"Yes, *mein Fräulein*. The winter will come quickly now. Soon the snow will descend from the skies; the lake will freeze; and then we shall sit all day by the stove, and shiver—shiver, and long for the spring to come again."

"I shan't," observed Grizel in her own language after she had got the sense of this. "I shall go for walks, and skate."

"Rather! Heaps of skating here, I should think!" agreed Joey. She turned to the old woman. "One skates, *nicht wahr*?"

"Oh yes; one skates. But it is not always safe. There are springs in the lake, and the ice is thin, there. Then, one day, someone more daring or more foolish rushes over, and—there is a crack—a cry! And it is finished! One recovers the bodies in the spring!"

"B-r-r-r-r!" shivered Grizel. "How horrid!"

"We shan't smash in," said Joey confidently. "Herr Mensch and Herr Marani will show us where to go, and they will take care of us!"

"They won't be here all the time." Grizel reminded her.

"Oh well! Herr Braun will, and he will show us where the springs are.—How much, *meine Frau*?"

Grete told her; and when they had paid they strolled slowly homewards, eating the apples. At the little gate they

201

were met by Juliet, who had got tired of her sewing, and come to find them.

"You mean creatures! How dare you go off like that and leave me!" she demanded, laughing. "What have you got? Apples?"

Joey nodded and held out the big paper bag and said "Have one?" Juliet accepted the invitation, and they went on to the Chalet, munching happily.

The Chalet was a very large wooden building which had been designed for a hotel. Miss Bettany had rented it from Herr Braun, the proprietor of the big white-washed hotel which stood near the boat-landing, and had converted it into her school. Up to the present it had proved quite large enough; but now, with the prospect of additional pupils and another mistress, she had been obliged to take the smaller chalet that stood a little way from it, and was making it into a junior house, with a couple of class-rooms, so that she could keep the little ones entirely by themselves. There had been six of them in the previous term, but now their numbers were to be enlarged by four, and the young head-mistress had decided to let the "babies" have their own department this term.

"Won't they be *thrilled*?" said Joey, nodding her head towards this building.

"They certainly will," laughed Grizel. "Heigh-ho! I *shall* be glad when we start school again! I'm longing to see the others!"

"So am I!" said Joey. "I say! I'm hungry. Let's go and see if *Mittagessen* is ready."

They all went in to find Marie Pfeifen, the head of the domestic staff, awaiting them in the *Speisesaal* with bowls of delicious soup, such as she only knew the secret of making.

"I'm glad of a hot dinner!" said Joey. "It's cold today!"

"No wonder! There's snow on the mountains," returned Juliet.

"Two new girls came on the train," Joey remarked presently as she laid down her spoon. "Italians! And they can't speak a word of English!"

"Or German," supplemented Grizel. "And the little one didn't seem to understand French either."

"How do you know?" asked Juliet.

"Oh; the little one fell down and we helped her up, and Jo asked if she was hurt. She looked rather silly, and Jo tried her in German, and then the older one spoke to her in Italian; so, of course, we knew they were Italians."

"Surely it's awfully late for visitors? There are only the Kron Prinz Karl and the Post open. I wonder why they've come?"

"They didn't say, and we didn't ask them. Their father called them away. They've got jolly names—Luigia and Bianca."

"Perhaps they're new pupils," suggested Joey as she turned her attention to the *Kalbsbraten* Marie had just placed in front of her.

"Perhaps they aren't! I think they're just tourists come up for a few days," was Grizel's answer to this—"I wonder why it is the things always taste so nice here? I used to loathe veal at home!"

"Something to do with the cooking," said Juliet wisely. "Marie's a jolly good cook! —*Sehr gut*, Marie." This last to Marie, who stood watching them with a smile on her pleasant face.

Marie nodded, well pleased. She liked all the girls at the Chalet, and adored Miss Bettany, who was such a kind mistress, and took such an interest in her younger brothers and sisters. It was worth while working one's hardest for anyone so good, thought Marie. What made it seem better was the fact that Madame also made Fräulein speak politely to her always, and they followed the head-mistress's example, and were interested, as well as polite. Marie's conversation sometimes made her less fortunate friends quite green with envy.

When *Mittagessen* was over, the three girls made for the railway once more. They knew that Madame—as they called Miss Bettany—and Miss Maynard, the mathematics mistress, would be coming back that way, and, as they would be laden with parcels, Juliet suggested that a little help in carrying them would be appreciated.

203

When the train arrived the two mistresses looked out of the window and the first thing they saw was the three girls waiting for them.

CHAPTER TWO

The Robin Arrives

"GOOD GIRLS! " said Miss Bettany as she descended. "Yes; you can take those two baskets, Grizel, but carry them carefully—they are full of china. Will you take this suitcase, Juliet? And, Joey, here's a parcel for you—can you manage it? It's rather on the large side! "

"Rather! " said Joey cheerfully. "I say! What heaps of things you must have bought! Is there much more?"

Miss Bettany smiled rather queerly. "Only two suitcases, and I'll manage those. Miss Maynard is going back to Spärtz, and then she's going on to Innsbruck; so we must do without her."

The three gasped. Miss Maynard going to Innsbruck? *Now?*

Their head-mistress knew what was in their minds, but she said nothing, though her dark eyes twinkled with fun. She sent Joey across to the little ticket-office to buy the new ticket for Miss Maynard, and stood with them until the train had vanished round a curve. Then she bade them pick up their burdens and come home.

"But—but what's the joke?" demanded Joey as they set out. "Why have you got all these things? What is Miss Maynard going back to Innsbruck for? What's it all about? Why——"

"Stop—stop, Joey! " cried her sister in laughing protest. "Let me answer those questions before you ask any more!

Now, let me see. There's no joke at all—not the faintest shadow of one. We've got all these things because they had to be brought up, and we guessed that you would meet us. As to why Miss Maynard has gone to Innsbruck and what it's all about, that is a story which can wait until we get home. It's rather a long one, and I'm too chilly to tell stories just now. It's much warmer in the valley than it is up here."

Joey said, "Won't you really tell us anything?"

"Not until we're at home," said Miss Bettany decidedly. "Tell me what you've been doing instead."

"Oh, just the usual things! We went down to meet the last train, and there were two Italian girls on it," began Grizel. "I thought they looked awfully jolly."

Miss Bettany nodded. "Yes; I saw them in Spärtz. Did Marie give you a good dinner?"

"Topping—I mean very nice," said Jo, correcting herself hastily. Her sister had inaugurated a crusade against slang, declaring that she would not allow the foreigners to pick up the appalling expressions that the English girls very frequently used. All three felt this edict. Perhaps Grizel came off the worst. But, young as she was, Madge Bettany always made herself obeyed, and they were doing their best to speak good English only.

"Miss Bettany," said Grizel at this point, "whatever will Evadne Lannis do about not talking slang when she comes?"

"My dear girl, why should you imagine that it will be worse for her than it is for you? I shall be sorry for the rest of us if it *is*! "

"But Americans do use a great deal of slang, don't they! " queried Juliet.

"Not at all," replied Miss Bettany. "I have known Americans who used as pure English as anyone could wish. Quite possibly Evadne will; and, if she doesn't, then you people must try to remember not to pick up any of her expressions."

"Hurrah! Here comes Marie and Eigen! " cried Jo suddenly, as Marie and her little brother who helped with the rough work came running towards them.

Eigen was a sturdy little fellow of eleven, and quite accustomed to carrying loads, so he took two of the cases with a cheerful grin, and Marie commandeered the other as well as Joey's big parcel, and they were soon inside the *Speisesaal*, with its green-washed walls, and long dark wood tables with their cloths of blue and white checked material.

"Coffee, Marie, as hot as ever you can! *Auch Brötchen*," ordered Miss Bettany as she threw aside her coat and hat and warmed her hands at the great white porcelain stove that stood in one corner of the room. "Get chairs, girls, and come and sit down. I know you're all aching to hear my story."

"Aching? I shall expire from sheer curiosity if I don't hear soon!" Jo declared as she hauled up a couple of wooden stools for herself and her sister, and collapsed on one of them.

Madge laughed. "Poor old thing! I hope you won't do that! Here's the coffee, thank goodness! It's positively wintry up here today! Just look at the lake!" Three pairs of eyes glanced casually at the Tiernsee, which had a cold grey look, and then everyone turned imploringly to the Head. "Take your coffee," she said. "Thank you, Marie. We shan't need anything now till sixteen o'clock. Fräulein Juliet will bring the bowls along to the kitchen when we have finished."

Marie curtsied and trotted off to her own domains, and Jo, Grizel, and Juliet turned eagerly to Miss Bettany, who was drinking her coffee slowly and with a meditative air. "Joey," she said, "do you remember a Captain Humphries who stayed with us in Cornwall some years ago?"

Joey shook her head. "No; I'm sorry, but I don't."

"I suppose you wouldn't really." Miss Bettany set down her bowl. "It was years and years ago. He was a great friend of our father's." Madge Bettany paused a moment. "He came to see us in the summer holidays, and he took us all over—Dick and me. He was very good to us, and Dick adored him. When he went back to France—he was home on leave—he used to write at first. Then, when peace was signed, he was sent up the Rhine: he was in the army of occupation, you see. Then, somehow, we drifted apart. I had you," she smiled at her small sister, "to look after, and Dick was training for his forestry work. I've often thought of him, because he was so good to us, but I've never seen or heard of him till I met him in Spärtz today."

"In Spärtz? Did you meet him there? What's he like? Is he coming here? Why did he stop writing?" Needless to say, it was Joey who poured forth these questions. The other two sat deeply thrilled, but silent.

"For asking questions, I'd back you against anyone, Joey Bettany!" declared her sister. "Yes; it was in Spärtz. I was bargaining with an old lady for some crocks, and he saw me. He is on his way to Vienna, really, and from there he is going to Russia. He recognised me at once, and came over and spoke to me. He's had a very bad time, poor fellow! He married a Polish girl whom he met in Cologne, and they were very happy, I believe. They had a little girl whom they both worshipped, and, after the Rhine was evacuated and he was demobilised, they stayed on in Germany, living in Munich, where he had got some post or other—I didn't quite gather *what*. Mrs Humphries taught the baby, and kept house, and made all her own and the child's clothes, and seems to have done pretty well everything. They were poor, you see; but there was always enough, and she—Marya, he called her—was a good manager. Then, eleven months ago, Captain Humphries noticed that his wife was looking thin and poorly, and that she was easily tired. But she only laughed at him when he worried. Well, things went on like this for another fortnight, and then he insisted on having the doctor, and she gave in."

Here Madge made a pause so long that Joey gave her a little shove, asking plaintively, "That isn't all, is it? Go on; what was wrong with her?"

"It was what people used to call 'rapid decline'," replied her sister gravely. "She had suffered terribly during the war, of course, and the doctor said it was a wonder the trouble hadn't shown itself sooner. He thought that probably her great happiness and the quiet life they had led had helped to keep the disease back. There was nothing they could do for her, of course. That sort of thing can't be cured when it is like that. They could only keep her as happy as possible, and see that things were made easy for her. Captain Humphries did everything he could; but she died in six weeks. Up to the very end she was hopeful, always talking about what they would do when she was strong again, and making heaps of plans for the baby. He told me that it was only the evening before she died that she realised what was going to happen."

"Oh, Madge!" Joey choked.

Madge flung an arm round her little sister. "Joey! Don't cry! Even then she was happy, for they had had seven perfect years together. She died; and for months he has been just looking after the baby, and doing his work, and trying to get used to doing without Marya. Then someone who knew him got him this post in Russia, and, as he can't take the baby with him and has no one with whom he can leave her at Munich, he remembered that his old friend, Herr Anserl, had talked about this English school at Briesau. Funnily enough, dear old Herr Anserl had never mentioned our name. He just talked about 'Madame' and 'Fräulein Joey', as far as I can gather. Captain Humphries decided to bring the baby here if we would take her, and brought her as far as Innsbruck. He was just going to hunt up Herr Anserl and get our proper address from him, when he saw me."

"Then is she coming here tonight?" queried Grizel, who had listened to the story with wide-eyed sympathy.

"Yes; he got a wire this morning, saying that he must be in Petrograd by next Friday, and as he has some business to attend to in Vienna, he must get it done before he goes on to Russia. He will have to set out at once, so I've undertaken the care of the Robin, and Miss Maynard has gone into Innsbruck to fetch her."

"*What* did you say she was called?" demanded Joey.

"Her real name is Cecilia Marya, but they have always called her the Robin."

"How old is she, Madame?" asked Juliet.

"Just six. He says she is a happy little soul and accustomed to living with older people, so we shan't find her too much of a baby. I have told you three her story because

I want you to be very kind to her. Captain Humphries will be away for at least a year, so she will have to spend all her holidays with us, and this will have to be her home."

"Where will she sleep?" Grizel wanted to know.

"In your dormitory for the present. In term-time she will be with the other little ones, over at Le Petit Chalet, of course."

"What time is she coming?" asked Joey.

"They will be here by the eighteen o'clock boat, I expect," replied Madge. "And that reminds me, I must go and see about having her bed made properly. Joey, it's your turn to help. Coming?"

"Rather!" Joey jumped up and followed her sister out of the room, leaving the other two alone together.

There was a little silence; then Grizel spoke. "Isn't it weird how everyone seems to come to Madame for help?"

Juliet shook her head. "I don't think so. She's the sort of person people *do* come to. She's a dear, and I adore her!"

"Oh, so do I," agreed Grizel.

Juliet opened her book, and then there was a silence, which remained unbroken until Marie brought in *Kaffee und Kuchen*, and the two Bettanys joined them. After that, they got into their coats, and rushed wildly to the boat-landing, for the steamer was already stopping at Buchau on the other side of the lake. From the windows of the Kron Prinz Karl the two little Italians of the afternoon watched them go racing past and envied them. Neither Joey nor Grizel remembered them. Miss Bettany's story had driven everything else out of their minds. They were literally dancing with excitement as the boat neared the landing-place, and they saw Miss Maynard with a bundle in her arms, standing at the side.

Madge met her as she came off the boat. "Asleep?" she queried in low tones.

"Yes—poor little dear! She's tired out with the travelling and the good-byes," replied Miss Maynard in the same key. "Here's Fritzi with the little trunk.—*Danke sehr, Fritzi.*"

"The girls can take that between them," said Miss Bettany. "Give the baby to me. Your arms must be aching by this time if you've carried her the whole way."

"She was so upset at parting from her father," explained Miss Maynard as she gave up her burden. "Hullo, you people! Can you manage that trunk?"

"Oh, rather! But we want to see the Robin!"

"Please let us see the Robin, Madame!"

"Just turn back a tiny bit of the rug, and let us see her! Please do."

The three exclamations came simultaneously.

Miss Bettany shook her head. "You must wait till we get indoors. I don't want her to be out in this awful wind any longer than can be helped. Remember, she's not accustomed to it as you are, and she's not very strong."

They hurried back to the Chalet. In the warm *Speisesaal* Miss Bettany sat down and carefully drew back the rug in which the Robin had been wrapped. The girls pressed forward eagerly.

Such a lovely baby-face! With curly black hair clustering over the small head, and long black lashes resting on the rosy cheeks, which were tear-stained. She was very fast asleep—so fast, that the two mistresses were able to undress her and put her to bed all without waking her, and the upcurling lashes never even fluttered. They lighted the night-light to which she was accustomed and they crept out of the room and ran downstairs to join the others.

The Robin had arrived!

CHAPTER THREE

The Chalet School Grows

THE WHOLE of the next day was devoted by the girls to the Robin, with whom they all fell in love at once. She was a dear little girl, very happy and sunshiny, as her father had said, and not at all shy. The very first morning of her coming, when she awoke, she sat up in bed, looking curiously round at the little curtained-off cubicle with its dainty yellow curtains and pretty touches, rubbed her eyes, and said, "But where am I now?" in the prettiest French.

Joey, who had been lying reading, tumbled out of bed and trotted in to her. "Hullo, Robin!" she said. "Can you speak English?"

"A ver' leetle," replied the Robin. Then she went back to her French. "Who are you? Where am I? And where is papa?" she asked.

"I am Joey Bettany," replied the owner of the name. "You are in Briesau, at the Chalet School; but I don't know where your father is."

"Joey?" The baby made a valiant effort at pronouncing the word, but it failed, and came out something like "Zhoey".

Grizel, in her dressing-gown, appeared. "Hullo," she said. "I'm Grizel—Grizel Cochrane."

"Grizelle," repeated the Robin.—They found that it was a trick of hers to repeat the names of people she met for the first time.—"Zat is easy to say. And ze ozzer demoiselle —what does she call herself?"

"Her name's Juliet," replied Joey in French. "You'll have to buck up and learn to speak English, you know."

"I understand him verree well," replied the Robin with dignity. "It is but zat I do not speak him well. At home, wiz mamma, we speak ze French. Mamma has gone a long way," she went on, dropping into the more familiar language, "and papa is going a long way too, and I cannot go with him, so I must stay with you. Who will give me my bath and dress me and brush my hair?"

"I will," responded Juliet, who had just come out of her cubicle and into the one where the Robin was holding her little court. "Will you get up now, Robin, please? It is time we *began* to get up.—Joey and Grizel, you must hurry up, or you will be late as usual."

The Robin turned her great dark eyes on the tall girl with the long fair hair, who was standing smiling down at her. "Are you Juliet?" she asked.

"Yes, I'm Juliet. Will you get up now?"

The Robin clambered out of bed, and dropped on to the floor with a bump. "I can't bath myself," she informed the older girl.

"Never mind." Juliet's French was by no means as fluent as Joey's, and she often had to pause before she got the right words. "I'll do the bathing for you. See, here comes Marie with your tub."

Marie, with a broad smile, appeared between the curtains, carrying a wooden tub and a large jug of hot water. *"Grüss Gott, mein Fräulein,"* she said to Juliet Then, as she looked at the baby, *"Ah, das Engelkind! Grüss Gott, mein Liebling!"*

"Guten Morgen," replied the Robin politely.

She was not at all overcome by being called an angel-child, and Juliet gathered from her chatter as she was tubbed and dressed that pet-names and tender words had been a matter of course in her little life. Just as the little frock of pink woollen material was slipped over her head there came a tap at the door, followed by the entry of Miss Bettany, come to see how her new pupil was faring. "Good morning, girls," she said as she came into the room. "Well, Robin, so you are dressed?—That was kind of you, Juliet. Run along and finish your own dressing now, dear, or you will be late. Robin can come downstairs with me."

The Robin slid her hand into the slender one held out to her. "Good morning, Mademoiselle. Juliet had been so good to me, and Zoë and Grizelle are kind too."

Miss Bettany nodded her head. "Of course! Come along now, dear."

She led the child away, and presently Joey, helping to hang out the *plumeaux* over the balcony railings so that they might be aired, saw them going down to the lake together, the Robin chattering at breathless speed.

"She'll be baby now," she said. "Won't Amy be thankful?"

"Shriek for joy, I should think," laughed Grizel. "It's just as well. She might have been jealous. I say, Joey! Look! There's those girls we saw yesterday. They're staring at the Chalet like anything! See them, Juliet? Don't they look topping—I mean jolly?"

212

"Awfully jolly," agreed Juliet. "I wonder if they're thinking of coming here to school? They're staring hard enough."

The three hung out the *plumeaux*, watching the two Italian girls with such interest that they never heard the bell ring, and Miss Maynard had to come to fetch them. "Now then, you people," she observed cheerfully from the door, "don't you want any breakfast this morning? Whatever are you doing?"

They turned round, all very red at being caught like this. "Miss Maynard, I'm so sorry!" cried Juliet. "We never heard the bell."

"So it seems," returned Miss Maynard dryly. "Well, are you coming?"

They followed her meekly downstairs, and into the *Speisesaal*, where the Robin was making short work of a bowl of hot milk before she attacked her roll and honey.

"Why are you three so late?" demanded Miss Bettany as they came in.

"We were watching those girls," explained Joey as she slid into her seat.

"Which girls? Do you mean those two you talked about yesterday?"

"Yes. They were standing on the lake-path, by the bushes, and staring at the Chalet."

Madge Bettany was interested. "Really?"

"Yes. Oh, *do* you think they might be coming here?" implored Grizel.

Her head-mistress laughed. "My dear girl, I have no idea! They would hear about us, of course, at the Kron Prinz Karl, and that would probably account for their interest."

"It would be gorgeous if they did!" Juliet contributed her share to the conversation. "How many would it make us, Madame?"

"Over thirty."

"Oo-oh, how decent! I do hope they come."

"Wouldn't it be magnificent?"

Miss Bettany laughed again. "You're startling the

213

Robin. She won't understand such wild enthusiasm.—
Do you like honey, Robin? Will you have some more?"

The Robin accepted some more honey and another roll.
She was very quiet, watching everything with big eyes, and
listening to everything that was said.

"What are you people going to do?" asked the young
head-mistress as they finished their *Frühstück*. "I'm going
down to Innsbruck tomorrow, and I'll take you all with me
to help to carry the parcels, and so on. What do you want
to do today?"

They considered. "May we take the boat to Buchau and
walk to Seehof?" asked Joey finally. "We can carry the
Robin if she gets tired. We might go directly after
Mittagessen, and get tea there, and then come back by the
boat. They give you such gorgeous cakes at the Seehof
hotel!"

"Very well; you may do that. This morning, I think you
had better show the Robin Briesau. Don't tire her, though!"
Miss Bettany smiled at the small eager face under the
black curls which was raised to hers. "Do you like walking,
Robin?"

"Veree much, t'ank you," replied the Robin promptly.

"Very well, then. That's arranged. Now trot along and
make your beds. Do you want to go with them, *Bübchen*?"

The Robin nodded, and slipped down from her chair,
and trotted happily out of the room with them.

Miss Maynard stood looking after them. "Poor little
soul!" she murmured.

Miss Bettany nodded. "Yes, indeed! I don't like the
idea of Captain Humphries going to Russia! One hears
such dreadful stories about happenings there."

"She's such a baby," said her colleague. "Well, talking
won't alter things. What shall we do today?"

"I want the new dormitory over here put right," replied
Miss Bettany. "We can put the curtains up, now that the
beds are in place. Then, there's Mademoiselle's at Le Petit
Chalet, and yours here to put in order. Shall we go up and
do the long dormitory first?"

Miss Maynard agreed, and they were soon busy with the
pretty pale-green curtains of the big dormitory that ran

right across the house from back to front. It was under the roof, so that in the middle it was quite lofty, and at the sides it was very low. A long window ran across the wall at each end, and the door was in the middle at one side. There was room here for four cubicles, and Madge had planned to put Gisela Marani, the head girl here, also Bernhilda Mensch, Grizel Cochrane, and Bette Rincini, the other senior boarders. Juliet Carrick was to remain head of the big dormitory immediately beneath, which had eight beds in it.

The room which Miss Maynard had occupied during the previous term was to be made into a bedroom for two, and Mademoiselle's old room would hold three. Over at Le Petit Chalet there would be nine small girls, with Mademoiselle in charge.

"And," said Miss Bettany as she finished draping the last pretty curtain, "if we get any more older girls as boarders, I must send Simone Lecoutier and Margia Stevens over as well. That will mean arranging another dormitory."

"Who will be in the lower one?" queried Miss Maynard.

"Oh, Juliet, Joey, Gertrud, and the four new girls, Paula von Rothenfels, Rosalie Dene, Vanna di Ricci, and Evadne Lannis. The Hamels have taken that little chalet near the Post; and Anita and Giovanna Rincini may come, or they may not! "

"Are the Merciers going to Le Petit Chalet?"

Miss Bettany stopped short. "My dear! I had absolutely forgotten about the Merciers! "

"And you haven't given Simone and Margia a place yet. Are you putting them in Mademoiselle's old room?"

"Yes. They're about the same age; and for Joey's sake I think it better to separate her and Simone. Well, Suzanne can go with them, and Yvette will, of course, go over to Le Petit Chalet! " She sat down on the nearest bed. "Well, I never for one moment imagined we should grow like this. Of course, people like the Maranis and the Steinbrückes and the Mensches are only boarders for the winter. Still, it's extraordinary; isn't it?"

Miss Maynard nodded. "In a way, I suppose it is, but

they all like you enormously; and, after all, you are doing a lot for their girls, you know."

"It's easy," replied Miss Bettany, as she pencilled her dormitory list. "They're all such dears, and the girls are so keen on the school! Then, they've recommended us to their friends as well. The Maranis spoke to the von Eschenaus, and, of course, Paula is coming because her cousins are. The Eriksens are coming through the Stevens; and so it goes."

"And there goes the bell for *Mittagessen!*" laughed Miss Maynard.

They went downstairs, and presently the six were sitting round the table eating *Nudelsuppe*, followed by chicken, cooked in some delicious way which was Marie's own secret, and *Apfeltorte*, a kind of cake with baked apples on the top. When it was over, the two mistresses accompanied their charges to the boat-landing, and saw them on to the boat. It was a lovely day. Once more the September sun was shining, and the Tiernsee was blue with the blueness which adds so much to its beauty. The Robin was delightfully happy over everything, and she shrieked with joy at "*Le lac si bleu!*" as she danced along the path. The bright day had tempted out the few visitors that still remained, and among them they saw once more the two Italian girls and their father.

Joey nudged her sister. "Look! Those are the girls we saw yesterday," she said.

Madge looked at them with interest. She approved of the pair. They had a fresh, well-groomed appearance, and they seemed nice girls. They, on their part, gazed at the group, which had reached the landing and stood waiting for the little steamer, with more than ordinary gazing.

Miss Maynard noticed it too. "I believe the girls are right," she said. "I shouldn't be a bit surprised if you received a visit from their father, or whoever he is, before very long."

"Here's the boat!" said Grizel ecstatically. "Oh, isn't it a topping day?"

Miss Bettany raised her eyebrows at the forbidden slang, but she felt that she couldn't be continually nagging at them, though she wished that Grizel would try to remember. Juliet saw, though the culprit didn't, and determined to say something if she got the chance later on. Meanwhile, she turned her attention to the passengers coming off the boat.

The next minute Joey uttered a shriek: "Gisela! Gisela Marani!"

A tall dark girl, who was walking sedately down the gangway, turned her head. "Joey!" she cried.—"Papa! Here is Joey!"

"Oh, Gisela!" exclaimed Grizel. "How lovely! I thought you weren't coming till next week. We are going over to Seehof for tea. Can't you come too?"

Gisela glanced at her father for permission. "Certainly," he said, smiling, as he raised his hat.

"Thank you, papa," said Gisela. "That will be so nice.— All right, Joey; I'm coming."

She ran round to join the others, while Herr Marani moved over to where Miss Bettany stood waving to them.

"Grüss Gott, Fräulein Bettany!" he said, greeting her with the pretty Tyrolean greeting. "How goes it with you?"

"It goes well, Herr Marani," she replied, giving him her hand. "How good of you to let Gisela go! Now I shall feel quite happy, as our head girl is with them. You see we have a very small new pupil?"

"Yes; she is indeed a baby one," returned Herr Marani with a smile.

"And how goes it with you? Is Frau Marani well? And where is Maria?"

"My wife is very well," he said. "She and Maria are still in Wien, where they will stay until Wednesday of next week. Then they will come home to Innsbruck. I am sorry," he went on, "that we cannot use our summer home up here for the winter months as I had arranged; but my mother has been very ill, and wishes us to be with her this winter. I am glad you can make room for my girls as boarders. They are very happy with you."

"I am glad," said Miss Bettany simply. "I am very pleased to have them—especially Gisela. She makes a splendid head girl."

There was a little more conversation, and then Herr Marani took his departure.

The two English girls went back to the Chalet School, and there set to work on the other dormitories. They were still very busy when Marie appeared with a card in her hand.

"Signor di Ferrara," repeated Miss Bettany. "Who on earth can he be?"

"Better go down and see," suggested Miss Maynard. "I can finish this quite well by myself. Perhaps it is the father of those two girls come to arrange with you for them to be boarders."

"Very well, Marie; I will come at once."

The Head vanished, and Miss Maynard went on with the task of hanging up the pretty mauve curtains that divided the cubicles of the three-bed dormitory. Half-an-hour later, just as she was sitting down to her *Tee mit Citron* and cream and honey-cakes from Innsbruck, Miss Bettany came into the *Speisesaal*.

"Well?" said Miss Maynard.

Madge Bettany nodded. "Yes; Luigia and Bianca di Ferrara are coming here; and, my dear, we shall start this term with thirty-three pupils! "

CHAPTER FOUR

Term Begins

"GRIZEL! I'm going to meet the boat! Are you coming?" shouted Joey, outside the Chalet School.

Grizel poked her curly head out of the east window in her new dormitory, and looked across the lake to Buchau, where the little lake steamer was lying. "All right! Wait a tick, and I'll come! "

She hunted madly for her blazer, struggled into it, and fled downstairs and out to the path where Joey was waiting for her.

"At last! Thought you were never coming! Come on; we must buck up!"

They tore along the path to the landing, where the nine o'clock steamer was just tying up.

"There's Mademoiselle!" shrieked Joey. "Simone's beside her. I s'pose the other kid's her sister Renée!"

"I can see Bernhilda!" proclaimed Grizel. "The von Eschenaus are over there! See them? Cooo-eeee!"

The excitement of the pair sent a smile round the people standing near, but they cared nothing for that. From the boat the other girls were waving and calling, and when at last they all met on the path the noise they made was simply terrific. Mademoiselle was quite as bad as anybody; and there were so many questions to be asked and answered, that the boat was well on its way to Seehof before any of them moved on.

"How many are we this term?" inquired Bernhilda Mensch of Joey as they set off for the Chalet.

"Heaps more than last term, anyway," replied Joey. "Thirty-three."

"Thirty-three? But how delightful! Who are there?"

"Well—Wanda and Marie von Eschenau and their cousin," began Joey.

"Yes—yes! I know that!" replied Bernhilda with an impatient movement of her hands. "Also that Gertrud brings her little sister. But who else?"

Joey thought. "There's the Robin. You won't know about her, of course. Her father was a friend of my father's years ago. She's six, and a darling, and her mother is dead. Her father is in Vienna just now, but he is going to Russia. You'll love her, Bernhilda."

"I am sorry for her." Bernhilda's blue eyes were very soft. She was a tall, pretty girl of the fair German type, with long fair plaits and an apple-blossom skin. Her younger sister, Frieda, was very like her, but there was much less character in her face, and she was a quiet little mouse, while Bernhilda was quite a leader in the school.

Simone Lecoutier, the little French girl who clung closely to Joey's other side, was as typically of France as Bernhilda was of the North Tyrol, with big dark eyes set in a little sallow face, black hair, and very neat hands and feet. She was intensely sentimental, and cherished a tremendous admiration for unsentimental Jo, who was thoroughly bored by it, but was too kind to say so. The von Eschenau girls, Wanda and Marie, who followed with Grizel, and their own cousin, Paula von Rothenfels, were a lovely pair, with thick golden hair, violet eyes, and skins of roses and cream. Grizel was pretty, and so were the two Mensches, but Wanda and Marie von Eschenau made them quite commonplace. As for Paula, she was dark and very ordinary; and Renée Lecoutier, Simone's little sister, who was a second edition of Simone.

Meanwhile, Grizel was pouring forth much the same information as Joey had given, with the added news that Gisela and Maria Marani had already arrived, and that the new mistress, Miss Durrant, was also at school. "She's sleeping over at Le Petit Chalet," chattered Grizel. "*We* shan't have much to do with her—only drawing. She seems quite jolly, and she's keen on hockey. Miss Maynard told me she had played for her county."

"Where is Juliet?" asked Bernhilda, as they reached the Kron Prinz Karl.

"My sister wouldn't let us all come," explained Joey. "She said we'd deafen the whole lake if we did. So we drew lots to see who should come first, and it came to Grizel and me. Juliet and Gisela are going to meet the eleven o'clock boat; crowds of people are coming by that— the Stevens, and the Merciers, and the Rincinis, and some others."

"Have the English and American girls of whom we heard last term arrived yet?" asked Bernhilda.

"Gracious! What a sentence! Oh, it's correct English all right, but it's so—so *correct*!" complained Jo, who often found the English of her foreign friends very boring. "You mean Rosalie Dene and Evadne Lannis, don't you? No; they aren't here yet. I don't think they're coming till the sixteen o'clock boat, as a matter of fact."

"Then, are Gisela and Maria the only early ones?"

"M'm," was Jo's reply. "Unless the new Italian girls have turned up, of course."

"*What* Italian girls, Joey?" asked Simone, speaking for almost the first time.

"Oh, two quite new ones. They came up last week, and their father landed the next day to make arrangements. He's Italian consul somewhere, and he heard of this school through someone—I forget who—and came up to see it. He's quite mad on English things 'cos he went to an English public school himself, and he liked the Chalet awfully, so they're coming. One's fifteen, and the other's twelve, and their names are Bianca and Luigia."

At that moment Miss Bettany appeared with Miss Maynard, and everyone promptly surrounded the two mistresses.

"Madame, it is so nice to see you again! You are well, I hope?"

"Yes, thank you, Bernhilda; I am very well. No need to ask how *you* are! You look splendid, all of you. Have you had pleasant holidays? Where is Mademoiselle, by the way? I thought she was coming by this boat."

"She went round to Le Petit Chalet, Madame," explained Grizel. "She said she would see you afterwards."

"Oh, I see! Wanda, I am so glad to see you and Marie. Is this your cousin? Welcome to the Chalet, all of you! Now come along and see our new arrangements. Grizel will take you up to your dormitory, Bernhilda; and, Frieda and Paula, go with Joey. Wanda, I've put you and Marie together for the present, as you asked for it until Marie gets accustomed to school. And, Simone, we've moved you into a new dormitory with Margia and Suzanne. Renée is over at Le Petit Chalet with the other small folk, and you shall take her over when you've seen your new quarters. Ah, here come Juliet and Gisela! Come along, you two! I want you to take these people to their dormitories, and then you can all go over to Le Petit Chalet and inspect it thoroughly. Now hurry up, for there's still heaps to be done."

They scattered, laughing. Bernhilda and Grizel ran up

to the top dormitory, where Bernhilda was introduced to one of the lake-window cubicles.

"Gisela has the other," explained Grizel. "Bette and I have the valley windows between us. Aren't they decent? Gisela is head here, and we are to have some privileges, as we are the oldest. Juliet is head of the yellow room—this is the green room—and she is to share our privileges."

In the room below Jo was explaining to Frieda and Paula where they were to keep their possessions, and all about dormitory rules. Shy Frieda listened in silence, and Paula was rather too much overawed to say anything. In any case, Jo's English was distinctly difficult for her to follow since that young lady forgot all about rules against slang in her excitement, and "topping—ripping—vile—absolutely *It*! " and other forbidden expressions freely sprinkled her speech. Miss Bettany, coming in to see that all was well, stood in the doorway, smiling grimly as the unconscious Jo informed the new members of the dormitory that "It's simply ripping having such crowds this term! Even if the kids don't play hockey, we'll have enough for two teams, which is top-hole luck! "

"Josephine! " said her sister's voice at that moment.

Joey swung round, and turned beetroot colour. "I forgot," she said lamely.

"It sounds like it," said Miss Bettany, a twinkle in her eyes. "Please don't forget again." Then she turned and left them to go to the blue room, where Gisela, Wanda, and Marie were all standing by the window, chattering.

"Here is Madame," said Gisela as she entered.

Wanda turned with a smile. "Oh, Madame! It is such a charming room! And the colour is de-light-ful! "

She spoke slowly and carefully, for English was still a difficulty to her.

"You like it?" said Madge. "That's splendid! Has Gisela shown you the form rooms yet? Show them all over, Gisela. You old girls will have to look after the new ones."

She withdrew, and went to the last dormitory with a little quaking sensation. She was not at all sure how Simone would take this separation from her beloved Jo. She and Mademoiselle, who was a distant cousin of Simone's, had talked it over at the end of the previous term, and had decided that it would be better for both children if they were parted. Simone must learn to make other friends besides Joey; and Joey ought to have a little freedom sometimes. She was one of the most unsentimental of schoolgirls, and the French child's adoration had often been trying to her during the past term.

"All the same," thought Miss Bettany, "I *do* hope Simone won't spend all her spare time in tears, or I shall regret our decision."

She went into the room, but it was empty. Evidently Simone had taken her small sister over to Le Petit Chalet. Miss Bettany heaved a sigh of relief, and went off to her own quarters. It was now half-past ten, and in half-an-hour there would be a fresh inflow of pupils. She had barely settled herself down to copying the time-table before Miss Maynard appeared, waving a dormitory list at her.

"What *is* the matter?" demanded the Head.

"We've forgotten those new Italian children!" gasped Miss Maynard.

"Goodness! How awful! Let me have the list." Miss Bettany took the neatly-written list and skimmed it through. "Yes; I have it! Simone can go over to Le Petit Chalet as I said, and Frieda Mensch too. Then Bianca can have Simone's cubicle, and Luigia, Frieda's. What a good thing we got that extra dorm. ready in case of need! Go and tell Frieda, will you? and send Joey to take Simone's things over. I'll run across and settle it with Mademoiselle. We must fly."

Fly they did; and, as Bernhilda and Gisela came to the rescue, the two cubicles were soon rearranged, and Simone and Frieda were settled.

"In a way," said Miss Maynard, "it ought to be a good thing. They're a colourless pair, and they would certainly never have had a chance in those other rooms. Now, one of them will be bound to take the lead, which will be just as well."

The two people concerned didn't think so. Simone promptly dissolved into tears at the thought, and Frieda wondered unhappily how she would get on so far away from Bernhilda. However, when they all assembled for *Mittagessen* at thirteen o'clock they were as cheery as anyone.

Miss Bettany glanced down the two long tablefuls of girls with pride. They all looked so fresh and trim in their brown tunics with tussore tops. The people with long hair had it fastened with ribbons to match, and, as she afterwards said to Mademoiselle, the Chalet *Speisesaal* really looked like a school dining-room. Twenty of the boarders had now arrived. The others would be arriving during the afternoon, and on the morrow work would begin. The girls were all together today, but, except at the week-ends, the juniors would in future have all their meals in the little *Speisesaal* at Le Petit Chalet. As far as possible they would be kept there, having their own class-rooms over there, and their own music-room and play-room. Yvette Mercier, the oldest of them, was nine, and the others were mainly eight-year-olds, so it had been decided that it would be best for them to have their own quarters away from the elder girls.

Yvette, who had just been informed that she would be head of the Junior School, was very proud of herself. She was a quick, clever child, with any amount of personality, and her mistresses felt fairly sure that under her the juniors would soon grow in unity of spirit, and later on, would be able to make themselves felt in school affairs.

After *Mittagessen* they scattered to unpack, and the rest of the day was spent in getting their books ready for the morrow, settling about seats in the form-rooms, and racing about in the bright September sunshine, and *talking*—any amount of talking. On the morrow they would have to speak in English most of the time; but today they might use their own languages, and the effect was reminiscent of the Tower of Babel. German and French predominated, naturally, but there was a good deal of Italian; and two new juniors, Thyra and Ingeborg Eriksen, could speak very little but their native Norwegian.

Joey chattered a polyglot mixture, for she was as much at home in French and German as in English, and Juliet and Grizel stuck to their own language as much as possible;

while Rosalie Dene, the new English girl, felt literally tongue-tied with most of the others.

When twenty-one o'clock brought the bedtime of the senior dormitory, and Juliet and Luigia, Miss Bettany drew a sigh of relief.

"I feel," she said to her three colleagues—Marie Pfeifen was in charge at Le Petit Chalet for the moment—"just as though no one had stopped talking *once* today! Thank goodness for a little peace!"

"Hear, hear!" laughed Miss Maynard. "And I'm off to bed if you will all excuse me!"

"I think we'll all go," said her Head.

Mademoiselle assented. "I too. Come, Mademoiselle," to Miss Durrant, "let us seek our own chalet."

They all went to the door.

"Good-night," said Miss Bettany; "I think it's going to be a good term."

"Tophole!" said Miss Maynard wickedly.

And with that they retired for the night.

CHAPTER FIVE

New Interests

"GISELA—GISELA! Do stop a minute! I want to speak to you!"

Gisela Marani halted and turned round to see Joey Bettany racing after her. "I am sorry, Joey," she said as the younger girl reached her. "I did not know you were following me."

"'Course you didn't! I say, are you in a hurry? 'Cos if not, I want to speak to you."

"Yes? What is it? Some important event you wish to celebrate?"

"No fear! It's nothing like *that*! Only, do you remember that book you showed me last term—'Somebody or other of the Fourth'?"

"Yes," said Gisela. "It was from that that we took our idea of celebrating Madame's birthday."

"So it was! I'd forgotten that. By the way, what *was* the name of the girl?"

"Her name was Denise. But do you wish to read it? I will ask mamma to post it if you would like it."

"Thanks awfully, but I'd rather not. It looked awful tosh, really! No; all I meant was about the school magazine. What about it?"

Gisela had frowned at the word "tosh", which sounded to her uncommonly like forbidden slang, but now her frown vanished as she exclaimed, "Of course, I had not forgotten; but we are always so busy!"

"I know we are. The bell will ring for *Mittagessen* in a minute! Oh, Gisela, *do* get started! There's a gem!"

"I should like a magazine," said Gisela thoughtfully. "How shall we begin?"

"I should call a meeting and ask the others," said Joey promptly. "My idea is, ask the day-girls to come tomorrow morning at nine, just like ordinary school-days, and hold a meeting in the dining-room. I'm sure my sister would agree."

"She said we might have a magazine last term," said Gisela. "I will ask her if we may call the meeting, and, if she gives permission, we will do as you suggest, and perhaps we may begin this term."

"Good! That's splendid of you, Gisela! You *are* a gem! And there goes the bell. Come on! I'll race you back!"

Gisela, however, as head girl, had a certain amount of dignity to uphold, and she refused the challenge, so Joey set off by herself, and arrived at the Chalet, panting for breath. Her sister was standing at the lakeside, looking at the grey waters, and raised startled eyes as she dashed up.

"Jo! Why are you racing about like that? It's enough to start you coughing again!"

"But it hasn't," retorted Jo with perfect truth. "I say! Do you think there's going to be a storm?"

"I don't know. The lake looks rather like it. I've a good mind to send the Hamels and the Rincinis home now. They all have to get to Torteswald, since the Hamels have had to turn out of the chalet by the Post; and, if the wind comes, it will blow from the north-east, and that means waves breaking on the path if it's a strong wind."

"Well, before you *do* send them home, Gisela wants to know if we may have a meeting tomorrow to discuss the magazine," said Jo eagerly.—"Don't you, Gisela?"

Gisela, who had come up in time to hear the last sentence, smiled. "If we may, Madame, it might be well. See, it is now October, and we should begin at once, *nicht wahr?*"

Miss Bettany nodded. "Yes. If you want a magazine this year you certainly ought to begin now. Have the meeting tomorrow by all means. I am going to send the Hamels and the Rincinis home now, as I think we are going to have a storm, so come along and tell them."

The second bell sounded at that moment; so Gisela, flinging her dignity to the winds, raced into the house to find the four day-girls who lived at Torteswald, a little village beyond Seespitz, and bid them come next morning for the meeting. Her head-mistress followed to send them home.

The news of the meeting thrilled the girls enormously, and they could talk of nothing else. Even the rising of the storm scarcely distracted their attention. After *Mittagessen*, Gisela ran across to Le Petit Chalet to let the juniors know about it. Coming back, she could scarcely keep her feet. In these narrow valleys the wind roars down as through a funnel, and its violence is doubled. The lake was already covered with white-capped waves that dashed themselves against the shore, bespattering the path with spray and foam.

"Isn't it a good thing," said Joey as she struggled with her sewing, "that the Hamels have left Scholastika? It would have been an awful walk."

"They couldn't have come every day," replied Juliet. "Either they'd have had to be boarders, or they'd have had to have a governess, now the steamers have stopped."

"The railway will have closed in a fortnight's time," put in Gisela. "After that we shall have to take the mountain-path when we want to go to Spärtz."

"Coo! Won't it be cheery when the snow comes?" commented Joey.

"You know what the winter is like here, Gisela. You'd better write an article on it for the magazine," suggested Juliet. "Lots of us have no idea."

"You will know when this term has reached its end," laughed Gisela as she laid aside her own beautifully-done work to see what Jo was doing. "*Joey!*"

"Why, what's wrong?" demanded the owner of the work. "It's quite neat, and the stitches are *nearly* all the same size."

"But it is the wrong stitch!" wailed Gisela. "Give me your scissors."

"Oh, I say!" protested Jo. "You're not going to take it out, are you?"

"But it cannot remain like that! It is all wrong! It will spoil the garment!"

"Well, I don't mind that. I'd rather it was spoilt alto-gether as have to do the horrid thing all over again! I simply *loathe* sewing!" returned Jo, who, till last term, had scarcely ever touched a needle.

To the foreign girls this was a shocking state of affairs. They could all do exquisite plain sewing themselves, and the older ones, at least, embroidered beautifully. Juliet Carrick, Margia Stevens, and Rosalie Dene were the only ones among the English girls whose work would pass muster with Mademoiselle. Jo Bettany and Grizel Cochrane were considered worse than the juniors, and the American child, Evadne Lannis, had scarcely known one end of a needle from the other when she first came. Some of the elder girls had promptly constituted themselves teachers to Grizel and Joey in the previous term, and Bernhilda Mensch did her best for Evadne, who hated sewing even worse than Joey did, and did everything she could to get out of it.

On Mondays and Wednesdays a book was read; but on Fridays discipline was somewhat relaxed, and the girls were allowed to talk, so long as they spoke English and did not make too much noise over it.

"I must send a copy of the *Chaletian* to England to my old school." said Joey, as she resignedly watched Gisela snipping out her stitches. "They'll be awfully interested. I wonder who'll be editor?"

"It ought to be one of you English," replied Gisela, re-threading Jo's needle and beginning the work again. "See, Joey. I have begun for you. Make your stitches thus, and keep them very even."

"Well, I'll try," sighed Joey, "but I shall never sew like that."

"You will if you try," returned her friend. "See, I have made them a little larger than usual, so that you may keep yours the same size."

Joey took her work, and stitched slowly; while Gisela, who was doing elaborate smocking on a frock intended for her little sister, went on with her own.

"We must have a page for correspondence," observed Juliet presently.

"Oh, rather! And I think someone ought to write a description of that picnic to the Mondscheinspitze last term," added Joey. "Herr Mensch told us some jolly legends about the mountains, too. I should think someone might write out at least one of them. Bernhilda could do that."

"Please fold up your work," Mademoiselle said at this juncture.

"What are we going to do, Mademoiselle?" asked Joey eagerly. "We can't go out today."

"Miss Durrant is coming to teach you a new dance," replied Mademoiselle. "Please carry all the chairs into the little class-room, and leave this one empty."

In less than ten minutes the big double form-room was cleared of all chairs save the one at the piano, and the girls stood ready, wondering what this new dance might be. They knew very little of Miss Durrant, really. She came over to the Chalet two afternoons in the week, and taught them drawing; but otherwise they rarely saw her. They looked at her with interest as she came into the room, followed by Miss Bettany, who was carrying some music.

"All ready? That's right," said Miss Durrant briskly. "Will you please get partners, and then form in two lines down the room. One over, is there? Well, never mind, Rosalie. I'll come in a minute. Now, girls, I'm going to teach you some of the old English folk-dances. We'll learn two very simple ones today, and I'll teach you the movements, and then another time we'll learn more. One thing let me impress on you now. You must never dance on your toes or point them, because that's not folk-dancing. I'll tell you more about it when we've done some, and then you'll see why. All face me."

They turned and faced her in two long files. They were all interested, and one or two people were thrilling with excitement.

"Take hands," said Miss Durrant. "Now run three steps forward, and then three back. Begin with your right foot always, *and don't bend your knees*; give at the ankles."

With shrieks of laughter they began, and soon they were running backwards and forwards as lightly as they could, while Miss Durrant walked up and down, criticising them.

"Don't point your toes, Wanda! —Grizel! Stop jumping —*run*! —Joey, you aren't an elephant; so don't try to be one! —Straighter knees, Gisela! That's better! —Come along, Rosalie; try with me."

Two minutes later she stopped them. "That's called 'leading up a double'," she explained. "If you do it without holding hands, it's called 'running up a double'. Heaps of the dances begin in that way. Now join hands with your partners, and I'll teach you slipping step."

This was easier, and before long they were all slipping, first up, then down, while Miss Bettany played for them. Finally, they learned "setting to partners" and "turning single", and this last movement proved full of pitfalls for them.

"Joey! You aren't a spider! " cried Miss Durrant. "And you'll certainly kick your next-door neighbour if you do it like that. Make your steps as neat as possible —You ought to be able to turn single in—in a soup-plate! "

"Turn to your right, child! " This was to Evadne. "*Never* turn single to your left unless you're definitely told to do so —*Four* steps, Grizel; not two.—Now let's begin again, and go straight through them."

When, finally, they were all sure of those five movements, Miss Durrant turned her attention to skipping, and had them all skipping round the room till they were breathless. Then she let them rest for a few minutes while she told them of Cecil Sharp, and his great work for English folk-dancing, and England.

"You all know *some* of the folk-songs," she concluded with a twinkle. "I have even heard some of you objecting to the constant repetition of a few of them. Joey's Appalachian nursery songs are very 'folk'. Now form your lines again, and I'll teach you 'Gallopede' and 'We Won't Go Home Till Morning'."

When four o'clock came, they were all rosy and breathless with exercise, and, when Miss Durrant give the order to dismiss, they all crowded round her, begging for more.

She laughed at them. "Oh, you'll have a good deal of folk-dancing," she assured them. "I hear that the weather is often very violent here in the winter; so, whenever you can't have walks or games, you will dance, and by next spring I hope you'll all know at least twenty dances! "

"Coo! " said Jo. "That'll take some learning! But I like this. It's heaps more sensible than foxtrots and onesteps! I say, Gisela! Something more for the mag."

Gisela nodded. "Yes. We must also teach the others what we have learned today."

They all trooped off to tidy themselves for *Kaffee*.

CHAPTER SIX

The "Chaletian"

THE WHOLE SCHOOL was waiting in the big double form-room by nine o'clock the next morning. The wind was still blowing hard, but it had veered to the north; so the lake-path, though wet from its bath of the previous day, was not continually washed by the waves now, though the water meadows which lay between Seespitz and Torteswald were, to quote Jo, "thoroughly squelchy". The four day-girls who lived in the latter place had, therefore, managed to come, and Lisa Bernaldi, the other one, was living at the Post Hotel, and had been at school on the Friday afternoon. The wind had stopped blowing continuously, too, and only came in great gusts now. Between these, the juniors were rushed across to the Chalet, even the Robin arriving without mishap.

"I'm thankful to know the mountains protect us from east winds," said Miss Bettany as she stood at the window watching the angry waves tossing madly to and fro. "If it were not for them, I should be afraid that some day we should be washed away. We are very near the shore here, and the water is never more than a few inches below the path."

"Mercifully, *ma chère*, it is an impossibility," said Mademoiselle, to whom she had been speaking. "What are the children to do today?"

"I hope the storm will have gone down by this afternoon," replied her Head. "If it does, they shall have a long walk to the head of the valley. This morning they will have their meeting, and mending, and home-letters. Tonight, they shall dance and play games."

232

"They are very much interested in this magazine," said Mademoiselle pensively.

"Yes—thank goodness! It will give them something to think about!"

The school had no idea of the interest the staff were taking in their latest venture. They assembled in the greatest excitement, and, as usual, when they were in their places, Grizel's was the first voice to be heard, though what she said had nothing to do with the magazine."

"Joey Bettany!" she cried. "For goodness sake stop that *wretched* humming!"

"What for? I can hum if I like!" protested Joey in injured tones.

"No, you can't! You've got to think of other people a little. I'm sick to death of those ghastly Appalachian things! I wish Miss Maynard had never brought them for you!"

" 'Twasn't one of the Appalachian songs!" retorted Jo triumphantly.

"Well, whatever it was, dry up! It's enough to make anyone ill!"

Luckily, Gisela saw fit to interfere, or the squabble might have become serious. "Grizel, will you please sit down," she said. "And, Joey, we are going to discuss our magazine now."

The pair subsided at once. Gisela was an excellent head girl, and knew how to make her authority felt. She gave the meeting no time to ponder on the wrangle, but plunged straight into the cause for its being held.

"We wish, some of us, to have a school magazine," she began. "We shall arrange it for ourselves, and we shall have in it accounts of our concerts, and picnics, and schoolwork. We also hope that there may be stories and poems, and letters to the editor. Before we go any further, we should like to know that you all wish such a thing; so will any who do not, please hold up their hands?"

Needless to say, not a hand was raised.

"It goes well," said Gisela. "Then we must now elect our editor."

Joey rose to her feet. "I beg to propose Gisela Marani as editor," she said.

"I'll second that!" said Juliet, following up the proposal.

Gisela shook her head. "It is very good of you—I am grateful. But, indeed, I should prefer that someone else had the position. I do not know enough about it, and I already have much to do."

The members of the assembly looked at each other blankly. They had quite taken it for granted that Gisela would fill the post, and they had not troubled to think of anyone else. There was a silence.

"What about Bernhilda?" asked Juliet at length, somewhat doubtfully.

The shy colour flooded Bernhilda's face. "Oh, no! Please no! I could not!"

"What about yourself?" demanded Grizel of Juliet.

"If I was any use at English, I might," replied that young lady. "As it is, you might as well have the Robin for editor. She'd be as much use!"

There were giggles over this at the idea of the Robin wielding the editorial pen, but they soon died as the girls once more faced the problem of the editorship. A suggestion put forward by Wanda that Grizel might manage it was promptly squashed by Joey.

"Grizel? She hasn't any more imagination than a—a cheese!"

"I've got common-sense, anyway!" retorted Grizel hotly. "That's better than——"

"Stop it, you two!" interrupted Juliet. "If you want to scrap, you can do it outside!"

Once more the pair desisted, but there seemed a good deal of truth in Bette Rincini's remark to Bernhilda that Joey and Grizel were simply spoiling for a fight, and it would come off before the day was over.

Then, no less a person than Simone Lecoutier addressed the meeting. "Will not Joey do?" she said shyly. "She speaks the English; she has the imagination; she is not a prefect, as are Gisela, and Bernhilda, and Juliet, and Bette, and Gertrud; so she is not busy."

There was a dubious pause. The idea certainly had its

points; but to set against them was the fact that Jo was not thirteen for a month yet, and she had no experience.

Then Wanda spoke once more. "I think it is a good idea," she said. "Would not Miss Maynard help with it, so that Joey shall not have too big trouble to worry her?"

"A bit muddled," remarked Joey genially, "but I see what you mean. I don't mind taking it on if Miss Maynard will give a hand with it. But I've never run a magazine before, any more than anyone else here, and I can't do it off my own bat, that's certain."

Then Juliet had an inspiration. "Look here, why not divide it into pages and give various people a page each to be responsible for? Then Joey would only have to collect the pages in, and write her editorial, and arrange the thing!" They jumped at the suggestion, for there was common-sense in this. It solved all their difficulties at one blow; for people who might feel too busy to tackle the whole magazine would scarcely grumble at having one page to look after.

"Then, shall we appoint Joey as the editor?" inquired Gisela. "Will you hold up your hands if you agree?"

A forest of hands was promptly waved in the air, and the motion was carried.

The next thing was to decide on the pages. At the invitation of the prefects, Joey joined them on the little dais, and was called on to make suggestions.

She screwed up her eyes, ran her fingers through her hair till it got into the wildest confusion, and then said, "Well, who will do the School Notes? That's the first thing."

"Gisela will, of course," said Juliet. "Grizel must do the Sports Page, and I propose that Bernhilda does a page on the folklore of the district. She must know heaps about it, because her father knows so many legends."

"Oh, jolly good!" declared the editor joyfully. "That's three pages settled, then. Who's going to do the stories?"

"Oh, has only one person to do the stories?" said little Amy Stevens disappointedly.

"Oh no! Anyone can; but there must be someone to choose them," explained Joey.

"Miss Maynard might do that," suggested Gisela; "and ought we not to ask the mistresses to contribute to it?"

"Yes, of course. And, if any of you have interesting things to write about, you can write me a letter, and I'll put it in if it's decent enough," promised the editor kindly.

"What about poetry?" someone wanted to know.

"If we get any that's good enough, we'll put it in."

"And everything must, of course, be in English," added Gisela. "I think we ought to have all our—our——"

"Contributions? Is that what you are driving at?" asked Joey.

"Thank you, Joey. Yes; that is what I want. I think they ought to be in by the end of the month."

"That's a fortnight," pondered the editor. "All right. October the thirty-first is the last day for sending things in.—And they must be decently written!"

A tap at the door interrupted proceedings. The Robin ran to open it. Miss Bettany was there.

"Do you people know that it's nearly eleven o'clock?" she said. "Haven't you finished?"

"Yes, thank you, Madame," replied Gisela. "All is prepared, and Joey is to be editor."

"Joey?" The Head had not expected this. "My dear girls, I don't want to interfere, but surely it would be better to have someone a little older?"

"I'm almost thirteen," said Joey, a little resentfully.

"Also, Madame, Joey has read so much; and we thought if Fräulein Maynard would help her. We are to have Pages, you see."

"I don't quite understand. Explain, please."

Gisela explained, and Joey and Grizel supplemented her remarks. "Don't you think we can manage?" asked the latter anxiously when they had finished.

The Head nodded slowly. "Yes; I think you can. It is a good idea to have the Pages. I should think it would answer very well. Now come for your milk to the *Speisesaal*, and then, if you seniors like to walk back with the Torteswald people as far as Seespitz, you may—all except Grizel; she has a cold, and will be better indoors today."

Grizel made no attempt to question this decision. She

knew a certain tone in Miss Bettany's voice, and there was no argument possible when it was heard.

"Us too?" questioned Margia.

"No; it's getting very wild now. If you people want a walk, you may go up the valley a little way; but you'll have to keep very tightly hold of each other. I think the wind must be veering round to the north-east, to judge by the lake and the trees. The juniors can't go at all, I'm afraid; and, if the rest of you are going, you must hurry up about it, and get ready."

They ran off at full speed, and presently they were all standing ready in long brown coats, brown tam-o'-shanters, and stout boots. Miss Maynard and Miss Durrant were waiting for them, and, as the former joined the lakeside walk, Gisela turned an imploring face to her Head, who had come to see them start off.

"Oh, Madame! May Joey come with us? We can then talk about the magazine."

Miss Bettany nodded. "Very well. Don't get any wetter than you can help, though." Then they set off.

The wind was blowing steadily again, and, as Miss Bettany said, was coming from the north-east. Out on the lake the waves were big, considering that the Tiernsee is only three miles in length, and never more than a mile wide. They formed a choppy sea, battling with the strong current that flows about due north to become the Tiern River below Scholastika at the northern end. The path, barely ten inches above the water's surface, was drenched with spray, and every now and then a wave, larger than the rest, would roll up, and actually break on it, so that it was well under water.

As long as they were in the Briesau triangle this did not really matter, as they were able to get away from it on to the grass. But once they had passed the fence, which divides the lake-path from the peninsula, the mountain-side rose steeply up from the path, and the most they could do under the circumstances was to dash wildly to one side and wait there until the water had retreated, when they tore along again at full speed. As Miss Maynard afterwards said, whatever else you called it, it wasn't a walk.

237

"Ow! Here's a *huge* one coming!" shrieked Jo, as a rather larger wave than usual swept towards them. "Ow—ow!"

Crash! Down it came. The water swirled over the road, then receded, and they all fled along in the direction of Seespitz.

"Quick, girls!" called Miss Maynard. "Here's another! Climb up on to those stones!"

They scrambled up, clinging to the rock wall, as another wave sent its volume over the way. Then, down again, and another wild scamper, this time finishing by the boat-landing, where the mountain curved round, and they were able to rush out of reach. Jo declared afterwards that it was the maddest walk she had ever taken, save one.

"Which was that?" asked Grizel with interest.

"Never you mind!" Joey told her.

But Grizel was in a teasing mood, and worried until her friend told her.

"One I took last term."

Grizel went crimson. Last term, she had run away and tried to climb the great Tiernjoch, with results that were very nearly disastrous; for a mist had come down, and she had found herself on the verge of a precipice. Joey had come after her, and had succeeded in keeping her quiet until help came, but Grizel herself had gone down with bronchitis, and for three days they had feared brain-fever for Joey. It was not an exploit of which Grizel was proud, and she would have liked to forget it.

Jo had had no thought of unkindness when she had referred to it, and, at the sight of Grizel's face, she promptly declared herself to be a beast.

"It is all over," said Gisela, who had overheard their conversation. "But, Joey, we have still not talked with Miss Maynard about the magazine."

"Well, how could we?" demanded the editor. "Going was bad enough; but coming back was the limit! We had the wind against us the whole time, and the lake got wilder and wilder!"

"Shall we go to her now?" asked the head girl.

"Righto!" agreed Jo easily.

They went to the little music-room where they knew Miss Maynard was to be found, and tapped at the door.

"Come in," she called. Then, as they entered, "Well! What can I do for you?"

"It's the magazine," explained Jo. "Will you help us?"

"Yes, of course! What do you want? Sit down and let us discuss it."

They sat down, and Joey poured out their plans, Gisela explaining here and there—rather a necessary thing, for Joey, enthusiastic, was very apt to be incoherent.

When they had finished, Miss Maynard nodded. "I see," she said thoughtfully. "You really want me to act as a final court of appeal."

"Ye—yes, I suppose so." But Joey looked rather crest-fallen.

"Well, what else *did* you want me to do?" demanded the young mistress. "It's your magazine, and you've got to manage it. I'll be there when I'm needed, but you must do the work yourselves."

Joey got to her feet. "Thank you, Miss Maynard," she said.—"Come on, Gisela. I'm going to begin *now!* "

CHAPTER SEVEN

Rufus is Adopted

"GIRLS," said Miss Bettany in worried tones as she came into the big school-room early on the following Saturday, "have you any idea where Joey is?"

The fourteen people variously employed in the room at the moment looked up in surprise at her question. They had supposed—those of them who had thought about it at all—that Joey was either practising, or else in the little form-room, struggling with her editorial. For the past week

—in fact, ever since the preceding Saturday—she had thought of little else. She had managed to control herself during lessons, her sister's threat of putting a stop to the whole thing having settled *that*; but, out of them, she thought, talked, and, the others declared, *dreamed* magazine.

"Is she not in the little room, Madame?" asked Gisela.

"No; I have looked there. She isn't practising, and she's not in her cubicle. She seems to be nowhere in the house. Have any of you any idea as to her whereabouts?"

"Perhaps she's over at Le Petit Chalet," suggested Grizel. "She *did* say something at *Frühstück* about finding a quiet place to write her editorial."

But Miss Bettany shook her head. "No. She isn't there either. I knew she wanted a quiet spot, because she told me so herself. That is why I came here last. Don't any of you know where she would be likely to be?"

Nobody did.

"Who is practising?" asked the Head.

Gisela glanced at the list nearby. "Simone Lecoutier, Vanna di Ricci, and Marie von Eschenau, Madame," she replied. "Simone might know, perhaps."

"Grizel, please go and fetch Simone here," said Miss Bettany. "It really is extraordinary where Joey can be. You're all *sure* you haven't seen her?"

No one had, however, and just then Grizel returned, bringing Simone with her. Simone looked badly scared, for Grizel had simply said, "You're to come to the schoolroom; Madame wants you! " and left it at that.

Miss Bettany nearly laughed at her big startled eyes, for she looked *all* eyes. As it was, she merely said, "Simone, have you any idea where Joey is?"

"*Mais non, Madame!*" replied Simone. "*Est ce qu'on ne peut pas la trouver?*"

"No," replied the Head, too worried to notice that the little French girl was not speaking the regulation English. "When did you last see her?"

Simone thought hard for a minute. "*Je ne l'ai pas vu dépuis neuf heures,*" she said finally.

"Has anyone seen her since nine this morning?"

No; no one had. They had had school prayers as usual at nine o'clock, and since then Miss Joey seemed to have vanished.

"Perhaps the Tzigane have been here and have stolen her," suggested Simone.

"Nonsense, Simone!" Miss Bettany spoke sharply. "It's the last thing the Tzigane would be likely to do! They have children enough of their own! Please try to control your imagination, and don't make silly suggestions!"

"Has she perhaps gone to Torteswald?" This was Gisela.

"Did she say anything about going?" demanded Miss Bettany.

"No, Madame. Indeed, I thought her here with us until you came in."

"Have you others heard her speak of it?"

"No, Madame," they chorused.

"Shall we look everywhere for her once again?" proposed Bernhilda.

Miss Bettany assented. "Yes; you might do that. Two of you go to Le Petit Chalet, and the rest of you hunt through the house. Please report to me in the study when you have finished. If you find her before that send her there to me at once."

With this she withdrew, and the girls started their search. Gisela and Bernhilda went over to Le Petit Chalet; Juliet and Grizel tackled the dormitories, and the others hunted all over the lower part of the house. They dived into the stationery cupboard; they looked behind the book-lockers; they moved all the desks—though how they thought even Robin, much less Joey, could have hidden in them was beyond anyone with any common-sense! They peered under the tables in the *Speisesaal*, and took down every coat hanging up in the cloak-rooms; they invaded the *Küche*, to Marie's disgust, and insisted on opening every single cupboard and poking about it. Margia Stevens even peeped inquiringly into the great jar where the flour was kept. Needless to state, no Jo was there. Simone climbed on to the music-stool and looked down into the piano, undeterred by Bette Rincini's suggestion that, thin as Joey Bettany was, she was not thin enough to be there. When, finally, they had driven neary everyone distracted, and Simone and one or two of the babies were quite convinced that something awful must have happened to their missing friend, and had accordingly dissolved into tears, they went to inform Miss Bettany that, wherever else her small sister was, she was not in the lower part of the house.

At the study door they met Grizel and Juliet, bound on the same errand, and ten minutes later Gisela and Bernhilda came back from Le Petit Chalet, knowing as much of Jo's whereabouts as they did. No one seemed to have seen anything of her since prayers that morning, and she had certainly not been over to the juniors' quarters.

A kind of eloquent silence fell on the school after Gisela had finished speaking, even Simone choking down her sobs. The general attitude was one of surprise. Had it been Grizel, who could be thoroughly wrong-headed when she chose, or Simone, who was quite famous for doing silly things, it would not have come with quite such a shock. But Joey was a level-headed young person as a rule. Mademoiselle, who came fussing over from Le Petit Chalet, said as much to Miss Bettany, who was standing looking thoroughly puzzled and worried.

"Joey has common-sense!" cried the Frenchwoman in her own tongue. "She will not have run to climb mountains, or to cut off her hair!"

Grizel and Simone both went crimson at this allusion to their exploits of the previous term. They felt that Mademoiselle was not playing fair in raking up past events, and their faces said as much.

"Can she have gone to Torteswald?" pondered Miss Bettany aloud.

Mademoiselle glanced out of the window. "But regard you the rain, *ma chère*! It pours like a torrent!"

"I can't imagine her doing such a thing without telling me first!" went on her sister. "Still, she might have done so! Or she may have gone to see the Brauns. She is very fond of them.—Gisela, go and ring up the Villa Maurach and—where is it your cousins are staying, Bette? Wald Villa?—Well, ring them up, Gisela; and also Die Rosen, the Brauns' chalet at Buchau, and ask if any of them know anything about her."

Gisela went off to the telephone, but presently returned, saying that nobody had seen Jo that day.

Miss Bettany frowned as she turned away, after thanking the head girl. It was so totally unlike Jo to go off by herself in this fashion. She was a gregarious little soul, and was generally to be found with crowds. Where she could be now was a mystery, and the girls, streaming back to their own quarters, were thoroughly curious. Some of them inclined to Simone's suggestion that the Tzigane had carried her off; the others declared that she must have gone for a stroll somewhere.

"But it isn't the weather *for* strolls!" Grizel pointed out, with an eloquent wave of her hand towards the window. "The rain's simply *emptying* down! Just look at it!"

"Well, anyway, there's no truth in that idiotic Tzigane idea!" declared Juliet. "I think you ought to be ashamed of yourself for saying anything about it, Simone! Madame's worried enough without your suggesting such ghastly things!"

"I d—didn't!" sobbed Simone in her own language. "I love Madame!"

"It looks like it, I must say!" retorted Juliet grimly. "Well, Robin? What do *you* want?"

The Robin, who had been tugging at her sleeve, said, "I don't think you ought to speak so unkindly to Simone, Julie!" (Her name for Juliet.) "I think also that Zoë is with Eigen."

"Eigen?" The big girls crowded round her at once.

"But why do you think that, Robin?" asked Gisela.

"Eigen isn't here," returned the mite. "He was talking this morning with Zoë, and perhaps they went somewhere."

"Come and tell Madame," said Gisela. "She will like to know."

Accordingly, as Madge Bettany was pacing up and down her study, trying to puzzle out where Joey could have gone, she heard a tap at her door, and then the head girl and the school baby entered.

"Robin thinks Joey may be with Marie's little brother

Eigen, Madame," explained Gisela as she made her little regulation curtsy.

The Head stared at that. "Joey with Eigen! But why?"

"She was talking with Eigen this morning, Madame," said the Robin in her pretty French.

Miss Bettany sat down and held out her hand. "Come here, Robin. Now, tell me just when you saw Joey and Eigen together, and where."

The Robin leaned up against her knee, and looked up at her with confident brown eyes. "It was when we came from Le Petit Chalet, Madame. They were standing by the stationery cupboard, and Zoë"—she still could not manage the English J—"was looking very angry—but *very* angry, and she stamped her foot and said, 'Oh—ze—brutal—*beasts*!'"

The Robin repeated the English words with great care and a distinctness which would have been laughable under any other circumstances. But nobody felt very much like laughing just then.

"You're sure that is what she said?" asked the young head-mistress.

The curly head was nodded emphatically. "But yes, Madame. I heard her."

"Gisela, would you ring for Marie?" asked Miss Bettany.

Gisela rang, and presently Marie appeared. At first when she was questioned, she declared that she had no idea as to what the two missing children could have been talking about. She was very angry with Eigen, for he should have been in the kitchen, helping her, and she had seen nothing of him all the morning. Then, after a little more urging from her mistress, she suddenly remembered that the dog of a neighbour of theirs had had a litter of pups, and she had heard that the little things were to be drowned that day.

"If that is what Eigen was telling Joey," said Miss Bettany with great decision, "then that is where they are! But she had no right to go off without telling me!" Then a sudden thought struck her. "Is it that beautiful St. Bernard dog?"

"Yes, *mein Fräulein*," replied Marie. "They are too poor

to keep the pups, for they eat much; and, indeed, they spoke of shooting Zita."

"Oh, what a shame!" The Bettanys all adored animals, and the same spirit which must have sent Jo off in an attempt to save the puppies boiled up in her sister now. "Poor Zita! If they can't afford to keep her, why don't they sell her to someone who can?"

Marie stood respectfully silent. It was not for her to speak, but she thought that if Madame had seven children to clothe and feed, and a husband who could earn money only during the summer, since he was a cowherd, she would not have been so indignant over the proposed shooting of a mere big dog who ate far more than she ought to do. Of course, if the pups had arrived during the tourist season, they would most likely have sold, in which case there would have been plenty to buy food for all. But Zita had not done what was expected of her, and so they must go. That was a matter of course.

Madge, looking up, guessed what was passing through the girl's mind. "Are they very poor, Marie?" she asked gently.

"They can live, *mein Fräulein*," replied Marie dryly.

A wild shriek of "Joey! Joey!" broke across the conversation, and Madge, running to the window, beheld her small sister and Eigen racing madly along. Eigen looked much as usual, but Joey was a sight to behold. She was soaking, and her hair was on end. Her face was splashed with mud; her gym tunic was torn so that a great triangular piece hung down in front. She was crying, too—an unusual thing for her; and in her arms was a soft little roly-poly ball, which she cuddled to her.

Leaving the people in the study to do as they chose, Madge fled to the door, and caught the child in her arms. "Joey! How could you?" she cried reproachfully.

"Oh, Madge! Oh, Madge!" sobbed Joey exhaustedly; "I could only save him! The rest were all drowned! Oh, Madge! Such little *young* things! But I pulled him out and saved him! And, oh! the poor old mother! If you'd seen her eyes! Oh, I *can* keep him, can't I?" She thrust the little wet bundle against her sister. "He's such a baby!"

"Hush, Joey! Don't cry so, darling! Yes; of course you shall keep him! —Eigen! Go and change at once, and tell Marie to give you some hot coffee! —Come, Joey! Come and have a bath!"

An hour later, Joey, cleansed and in her right mind, with her new possession cuddled up to her, told her story to an attentive audience.

Eigen had told her about the two-week-old pups; and their destiny, and she had torn off with him as soon as prayers were over. They had arrived too late to do anything but save this last pup, even though they had scrambled over rocks and through thorns to do it. Joey, clutching the poor baby-thing to her, had harangued the man fiercely in a mixture of French, German, and English, which luckily he had not understood. She had cried all the way home over the memory of poor Zita's frantic grief; and Eigen had cried too—mainly out of sympathy, Madge suspected.

"I can keep him, can't I?" wound up Joey passionately.

"Yes; you may keep him," said her sister. "He must go back to his mother for a few weeks, and I will pay for him, so that they can keep her. I'm going now, to see about it. If things are very bad, Zita had better come here for the present. We can feed her better than they can, I imagine, and that will be my birthday present to you, Joey. Until I come back, you can give him some warm milk and water with a very little sugar in it."

She set off, and on reaching the little hut found that things were as Marie had said. The people had enough to do to feed themselves, and there was no margin for keeping such a huge animal as Zita. The herdsman at once fell in with her suggestion that the poor brute should go to the Chalet for the winter. He also agreed to accept some money for the pup, and his wife wept for joy when the kroner notes were laid on the table. The money would make all the difference to them. Then Zita was unchained and handed over to her temporary owner, and Madge arrived back at the Chalet with her.

The joy of the poor mother over her restored baby made Joey cry again. Zita washed her puppy thoroughly, and then lay down with him snuggled up to her, thumping the floor ecstatically with her big tail, and looking her gratitude out of her pathetic eyes. She had reached a dog-paradise. For the first time in months she had had a good meal. She was in a warm place, with plenty of fresh, sweet hay for her bed, and she had got back one of the babies they had taken away from her. What more could a sensible dog ask?

"I shall call him Rufus," said Joey, as she reluctantly shut the door of the shed where they were, and went in to *Kaffee*. "I love him, and it's the nicest birthday present I ever had!"

CHAPTER EIGHT

The New Singing-Master

HAVING DISTINGUISHED herself by scaring everybody and rescuing Rufus from a watery grave, and Zita from an untimely end, Joey "lay low" for a while. As a matter of fact, nobody did anything specially striking for the next week or two; little things, such as Amy Stevens tilting her chair over backwards during *Mittagessen*, or Grizel Cochrane handing in her diary instead of her composition-book, not being sufficiently important to count. True, Grizel was fearfully teased over her exploit, but that was to be expected. Things jogged along very comfortably and quietly, till one break, when Margia Stevens, who had been having a music-lesson with Herr Anserl, the master who came up twice a week from Spärtz, rushed into the little form-room where the middles were, obviously bursting with news.

"Guess what!"

"What is it to do with?" asked Rosalie Dene un-grammatically.

"Oh, school, of course! Go on! Give you three guesses!"

"We're going to the theatre at Innsbruck!" suggested Joey.

"No!"

"Madame has arranged for a dance on Saturday," volunteered Frieda Mensch.

"No—no! Nothing like that! You've only one more guess!"

"Someone has given us more new books for ze librairie!" This was Simone's idea.

"No! Not that at all!"

"Then what is it, please?" asked Paula von Rothenfels.

Margia drew a deep breath. "We're to have a singing-master! He's an Englishman, and—— Oh bother! There's the bell for silence!"

The others echoed her exclamation, but, as they had had a long lecture—much needed—on the necessity of keeping the few rules of the school only that morning, they dared not speak after the silence-bell had gone. In the meantime, Mademoiselle and Miss Maynard couldn't imagine what had happened to make them so stupid this morning.

When finally the bell rang and Mademoiselle had left the room, they all thronged round Margia demanding to know all details of the new singing-master.

"I don't know *much*," she said, "but he's come to live at the Villa Adalbert for the winter. His sister is with him, and he's very good, and awfully keen. He wants to teach singing here because he likes to have something to do; so he came and asked Madame if he might."

"I wonder why he has come?" said Simone thoughtfully. "He is ill, perhaps?"

"I wonder what kind of songs he teaches," said Joey.

"Let's hope it's not those awful folk-songs you're for ever shrieking!" observed Margia with point.

"I hope it isn't beastly tuneless things like the rubbish you play!" retaliated Joey.

"Jo Bettany!" said Gisela's horrified voice. "You must pay a slang fine."

Jo grumbled under her breath; but after all, as the others assured her when Gisela had gone, she had simply *asked* for it. "Topping" and "ripping" and kindred expressions

248

were banned to them, but most people were a little lenient about their use; but nobody showed any lenience over such words as "beastly", and she knew it. The crusade against unpleasant slang was being carried on thoroughly, and already the girls were improving in that direction. Luckily for everyone, the bell rang for *Mittagessen* at this point, and they all had to stop talking until they were seated at the table. When the meal was over, and before she said grace, Miss Bettany informed the school of the new arrangements she had made for their singing-classes.

"Mr. Denny," she said, "is spending the winter here for his health. He is a singing-master in England, and loves his work, so he came to see if I would allow him to take you. I have agreed, and he is coming this afternoon to have the first classes. You will be divided into three divisions as you are for lessons, and I hope you will show Mr. Denny that you can sing, and also behave well."

At half-past two punctually Mr. Denny came, and the whole school was assembled at his request in the big school-room. When they were all in their places, with Mademoiselle at the piano, Miss Bettany appeared, and following her was one of the weirdest creatures the girls had ever seen. He was tall and gaunt, with long brown hair falling wildly into his eyes and on to the wide collar of his shirt. His suit was of brown velveteen, and he wore an enormous brown bow at his open shirt-throat. There was something untamed about him, and his vivid pink-and-white skin added to his unusual looks.

"These are my girls," said Miss Bettany with a very grave face. "Girls, this is Mr. Denny. Please sing your best for him."

Then she turned and left the room abruptly, and Mr. Denny and the school faced each other. "Will you sit down?" he said in a deep musical voice.

They sat down and waited to hear what he had to say. He put an arm on the music-stand that had been set on the dais for him, and surveyed them solemnly. "Years ago," he began, "in the time of the Greeks, music was considered to be one of the necessary foundations of a good education. Read Plato's *Republic*, and you will see that it is so.

249

Nowadays, music is *not* so regarded. In many schools it is taken as an 'extra'. Music! The gift of the gods to this earth! "

"Quite mad! " murmured Joey to her next-door neighbour, Simone. Then she stopped, for Mademoiselle was regarding her with a baleful glare.

"Fortunately for you girls, your mistress knows better. A lover herself of good music—I do not speak of the appalling amount of syncopated trash that is now flooding the world! —she has resolved to see that your knowledge of the heavenly art shall be a full one. She is right—very right! "

"More than he is! " decided Grizel. "He looks absolutely touched! "

The lecturer was concluding his remarks. "I am here to act, not as a teacher—I, who am only a learner myself, would not presume to that rank! No! but, as a *guide*, I will do my best for you. Will you all please stand and sing to me?"

The school rose to its feet, vaguely wondering what it was to sing. Mademoiselle promptly settled that question by playing the opening bars of "Where'er You Walk", which had been one of their last term's songs. Those who knew it sang with all their might, and Mr. Denny listened with a beaming face. "Excellent! " he said, when it was over. "But now we will sing a song we can *all* learn. Will you, little maiden, distribute these to your compeers?"

He held out a sheaf of songs to the Robin, who took them and gazed wonderingly at him. She didn't understand him in the least. Luckily, Joey held out her hand for a few and passed them along, so the school baby guessed what he wanted and gave out the rest in her usual composed little way.

The girls looked at their copies eagerly. They were a setting of Henry Maughan's "Song of St. Francis":

There was a Knight of Bethlehem
    Whose wealth was tears and sorrows;
His men-at-arms were little lambs,
    His trumpeters were sparrows.

His castle was a wooden Cross
   On which He hung so high;
His Helmet was a crown of thorns
   Whose crest did touch the sky.

It was new to all of them—even Joey had never seen it before. Mr. Denny gave them a minute or two to look at it; then he tapped on the stand with his baton.

"If Mademoiselle will be so kind as to give us the keynote, we will begin."

Mademoiselle meekly sounded the note, and the school made an effort at humming the air. It was easy to read, and they did it well. Once they had got the notes, they were switched on to the words. Finally, Mr. Denny made them sit down, and sang it to them himself in a sweet baritone, and with the utmost simplicity, as the music demanded.

When it was over, the master looked across at Gisela. "What do you think of the song?" he demanded embarrassingly.

"It is a beautiful song," said the head girl thoughtfully.

"Why is it beautiful?" He turned to Joey, who could think of nothing to say, and just gaped at him.

Margia answered for her. "It is beautiful because the words are simple, and so is the music."

"Right!" he said promptly. "We will now sing it again, and then we will turn our attention to another kind of song. Attend, little maidens!"

They sang it straight through once more, and he nodded his satisfaction.

"That went well. Now if the tiny maiden"—he indicated the Robin again—"will bring me the first song, we will ask this next little elf to distribute these!"

He waved a second bunch of papers at Amy Stevens, and presently the girls found themselves looking at another song they did not know at all—one entitled "Brittany".

Once again they were given the keynote, and then had to read the melody. This was more difficult than the last, though, again, it was perfectly simple. The girls liked it. These two songs, both by the same composer—an Englishman who, they learned later, had fallen in the war—were

251

totally unlike anything they had ever done. They wound up with another song of very much the same type, "A Page's Road Song", and then the first lesson was over.

"We will have three divisions next lesson," explained Mr. Denny, tossing back his long hair out of his eyes. "The elder maidens will sing first; then, we will have the little lasses; and, finally, our small elves. I wish you adieu until then."

He bowed deeply to Mademoiselle, smiled at the girls, and strode out, leaving a gasping class behind him. Miss Maynard appeared almost at once.

"Be quick and tidy up the room, girls," she said. "Then go and get ready for a walk. No talking until you are outside!"

That last command was a rather necessary one. The girls were bursting to discuss their new master, and, as he was only in the study across the passage, he would probably have heard every word that they said. So they cleared the room, and scrambled into their coats and hats without a word; but, once they were safely round the lake, the comments came thick and furious.

"What a weird soul!" exclaimed Grizel.

"He is—unusual," said Gisela hesitatingly. "I liked the songs."

"Yes, so did I. Thank goodness he kept off folk-songs!"

Joey was too far behind to hear this comment, which was, perhaps, just as well. She and Simone were chattering in French about Mr. Denny. Simone considered that he looked "romantic".

"He looked an ass!" returned Joey briskly. "I loathe men who have their hair bobbed! And why couldn't he wear a decent collar and tie like other folks?" which put a complete stopper on the one thing Madge had feared when she had finally agreed to letting him have the singing.

It was Margia who sealed it. "Who was that Greek man he talked about who said music was education?" she inquired when they had broken ranks.

"Plato," replied the omniscient Jo. "Why?"

"It would be a jolly good name for *him*! Don't you think so?"

"Fine! We'll call him that!"

And "Plato" he remained from then onwards.

As the Head said when she came to hear of it, "It would be rather difficult to be sentimental over Plato!"

CHAPTER NINE

Shakespeariana

"I'M FED UP!" observed Evadne one day, shortly after Mr. Denny had made his début at the Chalet School. "I think Gisela is right-down mean!"

"Why!" demanded Margia, who was sitting on the top of her desk, swinging her legs. "What's she done to you?"

"Fined me!"

"Oh! Why? Was it slang?"

"You know real well it was! I think she's a—a rubber-necked four-flusher!"

"Those prefects are getting very trying about slang," said Joey Bettany thoughtfully. "I think it's about time we choked them off a bit! Bette actually fined me for saying something was awfully decent!"

"Juliet's just as bad as the rest," put in Rosalie Dene. "I'm sure Madame never meant we were to stop saying 'jolly' and 'decent'. Why, *Shakespeare* used them—'jolly', at any rate!"

A gleam lit up Joey's eyes. "What is it, Joey?" asked Simone, who noticed it.

"An idea," replied her friend laconically.

"What *sort* of an idea? Something to down the prefects?"

"Goodness, Margia! What English! If Gisela heard you now, she *would* have a fit."

"Oh, let her! Tell us your idea, Joey! Go on!"

"Can't! 'Tisn't ready, yet! I'll tell you when it is!"

And Jo slipped off to visit Zita and Rufus, who by this time had his eyes open, and was beginning to stagger about on four unsteady legs, while his proud mother looked on.

After *Kaffee* that afternoon she condescended to reveal her idea to the others, and they listened with breathless interest.

"Won't it mean an awful lot of work?" said Margia doubtfully.

"Well, we'll have to read it up a bit, of course," conceded Joey; "but it's quite easy, really! Don't do it if you'd rather not, though!"

"Jo! Don't be an ass! Of course I will! We *all* will!"

While this was going on, Miss Bettany had opened the fines box and was frowning over the amount in it.

"It's really disgraceful!" she said. "The number of fines the middles have is simply appalling! We must do something to stop this silly slang. Put it away with the rest, Gisela, please; and then we must think of some other punishment, I think."

"Perhaps if you were to speak to them, Madame," suggested Gisela. "It is Evadne who is worst. She speaks so much that seems ugly."

"All slang is ugly," said the Head absently. "Some is worse than the rest, of course. I've no wish for you all to talk like the heroines of goody-goody books, but at the same time there is a line to be drawn somewhere, and I draw it at expressions like 'gumswizzled', and 'jim-dandy'!"

"Yes," said Gisela. Then she added unexpectedly, "Madame, what is a rubber-neck?"

Miss Bettany gasped. "My dear Gisela?"

"I heard one of the juniors talking—ah, no, *saying* it to another!"

The Head got to her feet. "I am going to put a stop to this, once for all! I will not have the babies using such expressions! Please go and assemble the seniors and the middles in the big school-room at once!"

Gisela fled; and ten minutes later the school was assembled, and waiting to know what it was Miss Bettany had to say to them. They hadn't long to wait.

Three minutes after the last of the middles had been hauled away from her private affairs, and hunted into the big school-room, the Head appeared and read them all a lecture on the iniquities of slang that left them gasping and breathless.

"I will not allow it!" she wound up. "You can surely speak English without descending to these ugly, meaningless, slang phrases. At any rate, they are strictly forbidden! Please understand that I shall punish most severely any girl who is reported to me for using slang!"

Then she left them, and went over to Le Petit Chalet to impress on the juniors the evils of such expressions as "rubber-neck".

The middles clustered together in a corner to discuss the affair, while the prefects went off to their own room, and the other seniors retreated to the little form-room. It had taken the younger members of what was unofficially known as "the big school" nearly all the term to become a united body. The difference of their nationalities had had something to do with it; also their want of a common tongue. Many of the new girls found English terribly difficult, and Rosalie Dene and Evadne Lannis were still unable to carry on a conversation of any length in either French or German. Jo Bettany's facility and fluency in all three tongues were the envy of the others. She could even chatter in Italian now, for she had persuaded Vanna di Ricci and Bianca di Ferrara to talk to her whenever it was permissible. It was natural, therefore, that she should be the leader of the middles. Now they gathered round her to hear what she proposed doing.

"We've got to speak good English," she said slowly. "Well, I don't see any reason why we shouldn't! *Shakespeare* spoke very good English. Of course, lots of it is rather out of date now, still we can't go wrong if we copy him!"

The English girls saw the point of her remarks at once, and as soon as it had been carefully explained to the others they saw too.

"But, Joey, how shall we do it?" asked Simone. "I only know so little of Shakespeare."

"We'll read all we can," said Joey. "Whenever we get a chance, we'll talk to each other; but mind, no one's to say a word till I tell you. We don't want to let the others know before we're ready. I want it to burst on them like—like—a hurricane, sort of!"

For the rest of that week the middles were surprisingly quiet and studious for them. Gisela, under the impression that this was the result of the Head's lecture, was quite jubilant about it. There were very few fines, and all seemed to be going well. Saturday was a wild stormy day, with a tearing gale from the north-west, and a heavy grey sky. Bernhilda, the weather-wise, declared that if the wind shifted to the north the snow would come. It was later this year than it had been last, and when it came it would probably be a regular blizzard. The wind was blowing too heavily for anyone to go out; and mistresses and prefects prepared for a strenuous day. They need not have worried. Every one of the eleven people who were responsible for most of the mischief going on in the school read nearly the whole day, and Sunday was the same. The great surprise was to begin on Monday, and everyone wanted to know as much Shakespearian English as possible before then.

In the yellow room Joey Bettany still had one of the window cubicles; Juliet, as head of the dormitory, had the other. Paula von Rothenfels and Luigia di Ferrara had their little domains at the other end of the room. In between came Evadne and Gertrud, Rosalie and Vanna. It was the usual thing for one of the "door" people to ask Joey what the weather was like, when they first woke, and Juliet had got so accustomed to the query that she never paid any heed to it. So this morning, when she heard a rustling from Paula's cubicle, she merely snuggled sleepily down under the *plumeau* after a glance at her watch. The next minute she was widely awake, for, instead of the usual "Joey—Joey! *Quel temps fait-il?*" Paula had remarked, slowly and distinctly, "Joey! Prithee tell me, wench, doth it yet snow?" And Joey had replied, "Nay! But I'll warrant me 'twill come down yet ere the nightfall!"

A smothered giggle came from Luigia's direction, followed by, "Mayhap 'tis time we were arising!"

Then, Joey, "Prithee, fair Juliet, shall we not arise?"

Just then the bell rang, and five separate mumps told her that her dormitory was up—a fact which gave her further cause for wonder, since, as a rule, there were groans when getting-up time came.

"Marry, how dark 'tis!" observed Rosalie. "In sooth, the night hath not given place to day! Lights, ho!"

In response, Paula switched on the electric lights, and then a scurry of feet told the senior that the first two girls were making for the bathroom. She was longing to get down to the other prefects to discuss things with them, but she had to wait until the last junior had flung up her curtains over the rod and stripped her bed. Then, leaving them, to wedge open the door, she sped down to the big school-room, where Gisela, Bernhilda, and Wanda von Eschenau were standing round the huge porcelain stove, warming themselves. She poured out her tale to them amid their exclamations, and then demanded their opinion.

"I think we will wait and see what they will do," said Gisela in her careful English. "At least, it is not slang!"

"No; it isn't slang," agreed Juliet, "but it sounds so odd!"

The door banged open at that moment, and Frieda and Simone, who slept over at Le Petit Chalet, came racing in.

"Good-morning!" said Gisela pleasantly.

"Good—good-morrow, sweeting!" replied Simone rather nervously.

Gisela could scarcely believe her ears, and she received a further shock; for just then the members of the yellow room, with Mari von Eschenau, entered, and Joey, who was a little in advance of the rest, cried, "Well met, Gisela! How is't with thee, sweet chuck?"

Juliet gurgled. She really couldn't help it.

"Joey!" exclaimed Gisela. "You must not use slang!"

"Nor did I, pretty mistress!" replied Jo, her black eyes dancing wickedly.

"Surely 'sweet ch—chuck' is slang!" exclaimed Gisela, stumbling slightly over the unusual term.

"Nay; 'tis the English of Will Shakespeare," responded naughty Jo.

Gisela had nothing to reply to that, and, as the bell for *Frühstück* rang just then, they all filed into the *Speisesaal* in silence.

When they had sat down, Simone passed Frieda the rolls, saying, "Come! Fall to!" and Frieda accepted, saying with a giggle, "I thank ye; and be blessed for your good comfort!"

Miss Maynard, who was at the head of the table, raised her eyebrows, but said nothing. Meanwhile, Evadne, at the other table, turned to Bernhilda, and said, "How thinkest thou, gentle Bernhilda; will it snow?"

Bernhilda, dumbfounded at this unusual mode of address, said nothing. There really was little that could be said. Miss Bettany had told them to read the classics and see how little slang was used there, and to try to model their own speech rather more on them than on that of cheap magazines filled with Americanese and language which might be suitable for boys, but was not allowable for girls.

The middles had taken her at her word, and *were* modelling their language on the classics. They had only gone rather further back than she had intended.

Miss Maynard was thoughtful throughout the meal. The head-mistress was not there. She had wakened up with a violent headache, and had had to stay in bed for the present. Jo, glancing round, had just realised that her sister was absent, and was wondering uneasily what was wrong. She was recalled to herself by Margia, who leant across the table, remarking sweetly, "How now! Thou dreamst! Where lies your grief?"

"Margia, sit up!" said Miss Maynard authoritatively. "You must not lean forward like that!"

"I crave pardon, Madam," replied Margia.

A gasp went round the table, but the mistress took no further notice of it than to say, "Go on with your meal!"

Conversation rather languished after that. The others wanted Jo to give them a lead; but Jo was worrying over her sister's absence, and never opened her mouth. As soon as *Frühstück* was over, she dashed off upstairs to the little room on the second landing where Madge slept, and tapped gently at the door.

"Is that you, Joey?" said Miss Bettany. "You can come in for a minute."

Joey stole in, and came over to the bed. "What's wrong, Madge?"

"Just a headache," replied her sister wearily. "Oh, it's better than it was, so you needn't look so scared."

"Would you like some tea?" Joey asked softly.

"No; nothing, thanks! I've had some, and some aspirin, and I shall go to sleep, I think. Run downstairs now, Joey," she murmured. "Tell Miss Maynard not to worry; I shall be quite all right. You can come up and see if I am awake at eleven if you like. Don't tap; just come straight in. Bye-bye for the present! " She stretched out a slender hand and squeezed Joey's, then she settled back, and her small sister went quietly out of the room to find Miss Maynard and give her message.

The other middles found her decidedly quiet and dull. It was such an unusual thing for Madge to be poorly, that Jo felt scared. She adored her sister, though wild horses wouldn't have dragged it out of her, and she felt rather miserable. Bernhilda and Gisela, understanding, took her off with them when they went over to Le Petit Chalet to explain things to Mademoiselle, so that the others might not bother her with questions.

Luckily, when eleven o'clock came, Jo found her sister sleeping quietly, and went downstairs, much relieved; and *Kaffee* at sixteen o'clock brought a message to her from the study, where Madge, her headache completely gone, sat waiting for her. Jo went into the room rather apprehensively.

"You goose! " laughed Miss Bettany. "You look scared out of your existence! "

"I was! " returned Joey truthfully. "It isn't often *you're* ill, you know! "

"No; I know that! But I can't help having a headache now and then! Now, you know how I feel when there's anything wrong with *you*; so perhaps you'll try to avoid doing mad things that give you cold! "

"I haven't had *one* cold all this year! " cried Joey in injured tones.

259

"I know! I'm only warning you! Now sit down and pour out the tea, will you?"

"Well, rather! "

Joey had a joyful hour with her sister, and then went back to the others in high spirits.

Gisela came over to her at once. "How is Madame?" she asked.

"Nearly all right, thanks awfully! " replied Jo. "She's not coming into school at all today, but she'll be there tomorrow."

"I am so glad," returned Gisela. "We do not like it when Madame is ill! "

Then she sent the middle back to her own quarters, where she was promptly seized on by the others, who demanded to know how Madame was.

"I am glad she is better," said Simone. "It has been so *triste* all day!"

"In sooth it hath been a weary length," returned Joey, suddenly remembering their plans. "I pray you, tell me, doth it yet snow?"

"Nay, damsel, but the wind is howling much! " replied Evadne promptly.

The spirits of all the middles had gone up with a bound. How they managed to get through prep without any trouble was a mystery.

After prep Bernhilda appeared to say that there would be no dancing that night, but that they were all to get their sewing, and Miss Durrant had offered to read aloud to them.

"Woe is me! " sighed Jo. "I cannot stomach sewing! "

Bernhilda gasped. "Will you all please hurry," she said, when she had recovered her breath. Then she left them.

"I'll warrant me I startled her full sore! " laughed Joey, as she got out her much-abused petticoat. "Oh dear! How I hate sewing! "

Work in hand, they trotted off to the big school-room, where they found the others ready, waiting for Miss Durrant, who happened to be late.

"Here's snip, and nip, and cut, and slish, and slash! " quoted Margia as she shook out her sewing.

"Away, thou rag!" retorted Jo as she sat down. Then she turned to Bernhilda: "What sweeting; all amort?"

"Joey, be quiet," said Gisela. "And please do not use such language! I am sure Madame would not like it!"

"Nay; this to me!" retorted Jo. "Thou very paltry knave——"

"Josephine," said a quiet voice behind her.

Jo turned round in dismay. There stood her sister.

"When I told you to model your language on that of the classics," said Madge, "I never meant you to use Shakespearian expressions, and you knew it!"

Eleven people looked down, their cheeks scarlet. Miss Bettany surveyed them, a little smile twitching at the corners of her mouth.

"Please don't do it again," she said, and then left them.

"I suppose it was your plan, Joey?" she said later to her small sister, who had come to say "Good-night" to her.

"Oh, don't be cross!" pleaded Joey. "We spent *ages* reading Shakespeare, and now it's been nearly all wasted!"

"And serve you right!" was the answer.

Joey looked at her doubtfully. "We know a lot more about him, anyway," she said irrelevantly. "And it's awfully hard not to be able to say 'jolly', and 'decent', and 'awful'! Really, it is, Madge! And Shakespeare used such *gorgeous* words!"

Madge gave it up and laughed. "Go to bed," she said.

"I won't use Shakespeare's expressions any more," promised Joey. "And we *may* say 'jolly', and things like that, mayn't we?"

"Good-night, you baby!" was the only reply she got.

However, as the prefects relaxed their vigilance a little, the middles thought it was fairly safe to take it for granted that Miss Bettany did not mind a *little* slang; so their Shakespearian studies had not been in vain.

CHAPTER TEN

"It was all my own Fault!"

NEXT DAY the snow came, and with it the winter. All that day and the next it snowed, a huge whirling blizzard, and the clouds were so heavy with it that they seemed to be lying on the mountain-tops, and still the snow fell. On the Thursday there was a lull which lasted for two hours, and the girls, well wrapped up, played about the Chalet during the whole time. As Miss Bettany said, they would have to take advantage of fine weather when they could. So from ten o'clock until twelve they rushed about in the dry, powdery white, which was so unlike English snow, and had a glorious time. Just before twelve the great flakes began drifting down again, and they had to go in, and then once more everything was veiled in whirling white, and the blizzard raged until the Sunday. When the girls got up in the morning the wind had gone down, the snow had ceased to fall, and it was freezing hard.

Joey, sitting up in bed gazing out of the window, gave a cry of ecstasy as she saw the beauty before her. Mountains, path, and level grass were thickly covered with a white mantle against which the lake lay, still and black beneath its veiling of thin ice.

"Oh, wonderful!" gasped Joey. "Juliet! Wake up! Isn't it glorious?"

There was a groan from the other occupants of the dormitory.

"Joey, *do* be quiet! It's Sunday—the only day we get a really decent time in bed!" complained Juliet. "I can see it's stopped snowing without sitting up. It's going to come down again, though! Just look at that sky!"

"How it is cold!" shuddered Gertrud in her own language. "Joey! Does it freeze?"

"I should think it did! The lake's absolutely black, and the snow looks so white!"

The members of the yellow room hopped out of bed, and dressed as quickly as possible.

Downstairs, Simone was waiting in the passage; and Marie von Eschenau, who was noted for being a quick dresser, came racing down too. The three little girls ran to the door and opened it, letting in a rush of icy-cold air that made them shiver.

"B-r-r-r! Isn't it *cold*?" gasped Joey. "We'll be able to have a walk today!"

"Yes—if it does not snow again," said Simone pessimistically. "Here is Frieda!"

Frieda, with her long blue cloak pulled tightly round her, and her pretty flaxen hair waving loosely over her shoulders, came flying across from Le Petit Chalet. "*Grüss Gott!*" she smiled as she reached them. "How it freezes!"

"*Grüss Gott*, Frieda!" said Joey. Then, eagerly, "I say! *You* know the weather about here. Do you think it will snow again today? Or do you think it'll hold off till tonight?"

Frieda looked seriously at the sullen sky above them. "I cannot tell," she replied. "The sky is very full of snow, but it freezes, and so no more may fall until the night. There is no wind, of course. If a south or a west wind should rise, then I think we should have much more snow —wet snow. A north wind might bring hail. As long as it does not blow, there will be frost. If the lake freezes, will Madame give permission for skating, Joey?"

"Sure to," replied Jo. "How long will it be before the lake bears, Frieda?"

Frieda shook her head. "I do not know. It depends on how long the frost holds, and how keen it is. Shall I go and put my cloak away? The bell will be ringing for *Frühstück*."

"And we shall be rowed for standing here without any coats on!" supplemented Jo.

They went in, shutting the door behind them, and ran into the cloak-room just as Miss Bettany came downstairs.

"Just in time!" murmured Joey under her breath. "Coo! It was cold standing there! Let's go and get warm at the stove!"

They went into the big school-room where some of the others were, and presently the bell summoned them to the *Speisesaal*. After breakfast Miss Bettany told them that she intended arranging for walks that morning. In the meantime, no one was to go outside without a coat, as there was an icy wind getting up. Everyone was overjoyed at the idea of getting out after two days' imprisonment.

There was a service in the little white-washed chapel today, so all the Roman Catholics—which meant the greater part of the school—would attend. The remainder, eight girls, Miss Bettany herself, and Miss Maynard, would have a little service of their own. Then they would have a kind of scratch meal and a long walk, having *Kaffee* at the usual time, and a semi-dinner at seven in the evening.

"Splendid scheme!" declared Margia. "Isn't it, Joey?"

"Awfully jolly!" agreed Jo, suppressing with difficulty a shiver.

She cast a little rueful glance at her sister, who was laughing at something Gisela had been saying. No one knew better than Jo what was going to happen. Oh, how bitterly she regretted those few minutes at the open door! She had been standing there such a little time, but she had felt the icy cold grip her, and she hadn't been warm since. There was nothing for it but to tell Madge, and all the laughter would vanish from her face, and the old anxious expression would come back into her brown eyes, and Jo hadn't seen it since April.

She shivered violently; and Grizel, standing near, noticed it. "Joey! You're shivering!" she cried. "Whatever's the matter? You can't be cold!"

The words reached Miss Bettany, and she swung round at once. "Jo! Aren't you well?"

"I—I'm sorry," said Jo limply. "I—I was standing at the door before *Frühstück*——"

"Joey! How could you! You must go to bed at once!—

Grizel—no, Gisela, run to Marie and ask her for two hot-water bottles! Grizel, you can turn on the bath.—Come, Joey! Come *at once*!—Miss Maynard, please look after the girls!"

Joey was hurried away and into a hot bath. Then she was put into pyjamas heated at the stove, and rolled in a blanket and carried up to Madge's room, where she was tucked into bed with two hot-water bottles and sundry pillows to lift her up to help the breathing that was already becoming difficult. Nearly all her life her colds had been serious matters, to be dealt with immediately and given no chance to get any hold. The old bronchitis kettle was routed out and set going, and then Madge went over to the window and stood looking out with compressed lips. A croak from the bed brought her to it.

"What is it, Joey? Don't try to talk! You will only tire yourself. Would you like a drink?"

"Yes, please," croaked Joey. But when it came she gripped her sister's hand. "Madge—I'm sorry! "

Madge held the glass to her lips before answering. "All right," she said curtly as she set it down. Then she sat down on the side of the bed, and lifted the child up against her shoulder. "That easier, old lady? Mademoiselle is hunting up some medicine."

"Shall I ring up Doctor Erckhardt?" Mademoiselle asked her young head-mistress. "It might be well to have him. He would come, for he loves *la petite*."

Madge nodded. "Yes; better send. We can't afford to take risks where Jo is concerned."

Later came the sound of voices as the girls returned from High Mass, and then the bell ringing them to *Mittagessen*. Miss Bettany ran down for this, leaving Mademoiselle in charge of the invalid. Joey's breathing was quick and hard, and her cheeks were flushed with the rising fever. An unpleasant little cough had developed too. Mademoiselle readjusted the bronchitis kettle, and saw that the hot-water bottles were all they ought to be, then she went off in charge of the senior walk.

Miss Bettany had brought back with her some calves-foot jelly, and she fed her small sister with it, forbidding her to put her arms out of bed. "Try to sleep a little, Joey," she said, when the jelly had vanished. "Are you comfortable? Like another pillow?"

"No, thanks! " croaked Joey.

She closed her eyes obediently, but sleep wouldn't come. Her chest felt as though there were tight iron bands round it, and a little sharp pain kept stabbing her in the side. She had a queer idea that the walls of the room were closing in on her, and she cried out in sudden fear. Madge, sitting at the window watching for the doctor, was with her in an instant.

"All right, Joey—it's quite all right! " said the low, sweet voice that Joey loved. "Drink this, honey! "

Joey drank it—cool water with orange-juice in it, and then the kettle was attended to again, and breathing became a little easier for a while. Presently she raised her eyes. "It's the pain in my side," she said weakly.

An hour later, the doctor arrived.

After that, Jo had no very clear idea what happened during the next day or two. She came to herself late on Tuesday night, to find that the horrid tightness in her chest and the pain in her side had vanished, and she was lying down comfortably with only one pillow under her head. A night-light was burning on the little table by the window, and on a camp-bedstead lay her sister. Jo lay for a minute or two, pondering matters; then she made a slight movement, and at once Madge sat up, shaking the dark-brown curls out of her eyes.

"Hallo! " said Joey. "What's up? Have I been ill?"

"No; just a warning not to do silly things," replied Madge as she got up and slipped into her dressing-gown. "Drink this, Joey, and then go to sleep again."

Joey obediently drank what was given her, and then snuggled down; the long lashes fell on her cheeks almost at once. Madge stood for a minute, looking down at her. It had been a narrow shave. Not until that afternoon had the doctor told her that all fear of pleuro-pneumonia was at an end, and that, given ordinary care, Joey would be herself in another week. It was a tremendous relief, and not the least part of it was that the doctor had assured her that her small sister was much stronger than she had been in the summer, and that he quite thought she would out-grow her childish delicacy.

"That's something pleasant to write to Dick!" she murmured, her thoughts going to her twin-brother who was in the Forestry Department in India. "He will be pleased!"

She leaned over the child again, listening to the soft, even breathing. Then she pulled up the *plumeau*, tucking it in more closely round her, and retired to her own bed, where she speedily fell asleep, only awaking when the rising-bell sounded.

Joey slept through it, and through her sister's dressing. Indeed she only woke up when her breakfast tray appeared at nine o'clock. Her eyes went to the window. It was a gloriously sunny day, and she could see the mountains opposite arrayed in sparkling robes of snowy white. "Isn't it gorgeous!" she said. "When can I get up, please?"

"Not for a day or two yet," replied her sister, as she wrapped her in a thick woolly shawl, and banked her up with pillows. "That's what you get for doing mad things!"

Joey chuckled; then she turned wistful eyes to the delicate face above her. "It was all my own fault," she said humbly.

Madge nodded gravely as she laid the tray on her knees. "Yes—I know! Joey, do you remember Monday of last week when I had a headache?"

Jo paused in the act of peeling the top of her egg. "Yes, of course! why?"

"You told me that you were worried."

"I *was*! Horribly worried."

"How do you think I've felt since Sunday?"

Joey's eyes fell. "I didn't think," she murmured.

"Exactly! I'm not going to preach; but if you could realise all I've suffered since then, I think you'd do all you could to remember!"

Madge's lips twitched as she spoke. She had had a bad fright, and still had not recovered from it. Tender-hearted Joey saw it, and, at imminent danger of upsetting her tray, she flung her ams round her sister. "Madge, I'm a pig! I'll try—honest injun, I will! "

Madge returned the hug heartily. "Yes, *do*, Joey! I shall feel happier about you now you've made that promise! I must go now; but I'll look in about eleven."

"Can I see any of the others later on?" demanded Jo, still clinging to her sister.

"Oh yes; so long as you don't get excited."

"You—you've forgiven me?"

"Yes! Haven't I said so?" Madge paused a moment, then she bent down and kissed the little white face.

Joey sat back contentedly. "*That's* all right! " she said happily. "Oh, Madge, I do love you so! And please couldn't the Robin come and see me a bit?"

Madge laughed. "Yes; I don't think *she* will excite you. Eat your breakfast, and she shall come up about ten."

At ten sharp the Robin arrived, carrying carefully some jigsaw puzzles, and when Miss Bettany came shortly after eleven, bringing with her the doctor, she found them disputing about the pieces, and wrangling joyfully.

The doctor smiled when he saw them. "I shan't keep my patient much longer," he said in his big rumbling voice. "We shall have you back into school next week, Fräulein Joey! "

"Good! " said Jo contentedly. "And please, when may I get up?"

He looked at Miss Bettany with a twinkle in his eye. "She is impatient, *gnädiges Fräulein, nicht wahr*? However, it is well, and *das Mädchen* may arise on Thursday for a few hours. I shall see her on Saturday, and perhaps she may be skating to Buchau on the following Saturday."

"Oh, tophole! " said Jo. "I'm sorry, Madge, but honour bright it *is*."

And what could Madge do but laugh?

CHAPTER ELEVEN

The First Issue of the "Chaletian"

JO WAS RECEIVED with enthusiasm when she appeared in school on the Monday. She had been kept right away from the others until then, so that she might have a thorough rest, for she was growing very quickly, and Dr. Erckhardt had said it was a good thing that the holidays were coming so soon. Not that they were long holidays. Miss Bettany had decided to break up five days before Christmas, and start again on the seventh of January.

"Easter comes at the end of March," she said; "so we'll have only the fortnight or so at Christmas, and then I shall give the whole of April at Easter, when the weather will be better."

"What about Simone and Renée and the Merciers?" asked Joey. "Will they go home?"

"Mademoiselle is going to take them to Vienna, and Miss Maynard will take the three Italian girls up to Munich. You and I, Joey, are going to Innsbruck."

"To a hotel?" demanded Jo eagerly.

Madge shook her head. "Not for worlds! No; we're going to stay a week with the Mensches, and the rest of the time with the Maranis. The von Eschenaus have invited Juliet to go to them, and the Robin will come with us."

"What about Grizel?" asked Joey.

"Grizel is going home to England," replied Madge. "Her grandmother is very ill, and has asked for her; so she is going, and will not return till the end of January. Mr. and Mrs. Stevens are coming to Salzburg; so Amy and Margia will go to them. There'll only be the Robin with us, and you won't mind her?"

"Oh no! I love the Robin!" said Jo gaily. "What will

the Robin call you in the holidays?" said Joey.

"She told me quite seriously this morning that when it wasn't school time, she would like to call me *Tante Marguerite*, as she hadn't any aunts, and would like one! "

"Shall you let her?" asked Jo curiously.

"Yes. The poor baby hasn't any people of her own near her. If she wants to think of me as *ma tante*, I don't mind in the least! "

"It'll seem *weird*," commented Joey. "It must be *horrid* for her! "

There the conversation had ceased, and today Joey was back in school once more, and was received with acclamation, which she certainly didn't deserve.

"But it is so delightful to have you back, my Jo! " said Simone wistfully.

"Splendid to see you again, old thing! " was Grizel's cheery greeting.

"We have missed you, *mein Liebling*," observed Gisela.

It snowed all next day, making yet deeper the deep mantle which lay on the land; but towards evening it ceased, and Bernhilda the weatherwise proclaimed that it was going to freeze, and that soon the lake would be fit for skating, provided no wind got up to ruffle the ice.

She was right. When they tumbled out of bed the next morning, every single liquid that was not near a stove was frozen like a stone. The lake lay black against the snow, and the snow itself was hard as a rock. There was no wind, and the sky above was a clear pale blue; and almost cloudless. The girls were overjoyed, especially the English girls, for they had never known a winter like this. In the houses the great porcelain stoves were kept at full pitch, and the windows were covered with marvellous fairy designs, through which it was impossible to see. Jo, with a vivid remembrance of Hans Andersen's fairy-tales, warmed a penny and made little round holes on the panes, just as Kay and Gerda did, and the middles gazed out entranced on what she insisted on calling "Storybook-land".

At twelve o'clock everyone wrapped up warmly, and they went out and raced about, shouting and laughing. Even Jo, with "two of everything on, and one over, for luck, of some things!" to quote herself, trotted forth to enjoy the fresh, icy air. The glare of the snow under the December sun was terrific, so they all wore coloured spectacles, and shrieked with laughter at each other.

"We shall skate tomorrow," said Gisela, looking at the lake. "See! There are people on it already!" And she pointed to the Seespitz end of the Tiernsee, where two or three figures were to be seen circling about on the ice.

"Gorgeous!" cried Joey ecstatically. "T've never really skated in my life!"

"Have you not?" asked Wanda von Eschenau with wonder in her eyes. "But how strange!"

"Not at all," replied Jo. "We lived in the south of England, and there was never a long enough frost for the ice to reach the bearing stage—not that *I* can remember, anyway! Is it *frightfully* difficult to get your balance?"

The girls who were accustomed to skating every winter, and had been so from their earliest days, were rather non-plussed by this question, which they did not know how to answer.

"I do not think it is so very hard," said Bernhilda at length. "I do not remember."

"Here is Madame," said Gisela. "She comes to call you into the house, Joey!"

"Blow!" said Joey. "It's quite warm in the sun!"

However, when Madge called her, she went obediently.

"Sorry, Joey," said Miss Bettany, "but it's too soon after your last cold to take any risks!"

"It's hard luck, all the same!" sighed Jo. "Yes; I know it's my own fault, but it doesn't make it any nicer! Can I skate tomorrow if the ice holds?"

"We'll see what you're like after today," replied Madge cautiously.

Jo ran into the Chalet, and was met by Marie, bearing a large parcel. "For you, Fräulein Joey," she smiled.

"For me?" Joey stared. "Whatever is it?" She examined the label. "'*Gebrüder Hertzing, Drucker*'! Oh! *It's the magazines!*" She snatched the precious bundle from Marie. "How gorgeous! I didn't think they'd be here so soon! Marie, *bringen Sie Fräulein Bettany! Beeilen Sie sich!*"

271

Marie dashed out into the snow, to return presently with an anxious-looking Madge. "Joey! What is it? Don't you feel well?" she demanded.

"Goodness, yes! But look! The *Chaletian* has come! That's why I wanted you!"

Miss Bettany drew a long breath of relief. "Oh, what a fright I got! Marie simply said you wanted me at once! I quite thought you must be feeling ill again!"

"Well, I'm not! Come on! Let's go into the study and look at them! I'm dying to see it—the first magazine I've ever edited in my life!"

They went into the study, Jo hugging the big parcel affectionately to her, and presently the brown paper covering was off, and there, before them, lay the first number of the *Chaletian*. She picked up a copy and held it out to her sister. "There you are, Madame, the head-mistress! With the editor's compliments!"

"Jo, you *are* an idiot!" declared Madge. "Don't let the others see you like this!"

"Let's call them in to see it," suggested Jo.

"The people responsible for Pages, if you like! I don't want the whole school!"

Jo flew to the window and banged on it, till Gisela saw her frantic gestures and came to see if Madame had had a fit, or Marie had upset the dinner all over the floor. *"Was ist es?"* she demanded.

For answer Jo held up the *Chaletian*. The head girl's eyes widened. Then she vanished, and they could hear her calling, "Bernhilda! Grizel! Bette! *Kommen sie! Das Chaletian ist hier!*"

There was a wild rush as everyone surrounded her. The two people in the study couldn't hear what was going on, but the rapid gestures and shrill voices were sufficient signs of their excitement. It was fairly obvious that they all wanted to come, and that Gisela was having hard work to prevent them. Miss Bettany decided to take a hand herself. "Run and find Miss Maynard and tell her, Joey," she said. "Ask her to come to the study, and I'll fetch the others."

Joey dashed off in the direction of the little music-room, and the Head strolled out to the excited girls.

"Madame! When may we see the *Chaletian*, please?" asked Amy Stevens.

"You shall all see it this afternoon," said Miss Bettany. "In the meantime, I want the magazine committee to come to see it now in my study. Oh, and while I remember, will you all please try to remember the rule about speaking English? I heard a good deal that was *not* English as I came up."

She turned back to the Chalet, followed by the committee. Gisela left them, and ran on to join her headmistress. "Madame, I have spoken in German all the while! I am so sorry; please pardon me! "

"I heard you," said Miss Bettany dryly. "Of course, if the head girl doesn't remember, Gisela, I can scarcely expect the others to do so, can I?"

Gisela coloured. "I know! Indeed, Madame, I am very sorry! Shall I enter my name in the Order Book?"

Miss Bettany shook her head. "No; don't do that. It would be very bad for the juniors and the middles to see the head girl's name there. But do remember that your position makes carelessness a serious matter. Now go and get your things off and come along to my study."

Gisela went off to do as she was told, while the young head-mistress marched into the study, to find Miss Maynard already there.

"It looks very well, doesn't it?" said the mathematics mistress as she turned over a copy. "I think the girls are to be congratulated."

"So do I," smiled Miss Bettany.—"Come in! " as a tap sounded at the door.

In response, the members of the magazine committee solemnly filed into the room and sat down at her invitation. Then Joey doled out one copy each of the *Chaletian*, and there was silence while they all looked through it.

It was a very well-arranged little magazine, and, for a first number, quite good. Jo's Editorial, setting forth the aims and ideas of the *Chaletian*, was well written for a girl of thirteen, and very original. The School Notes, attended to by Gisela, were accurate, and their English would have shamed that of many English girls' efforts—

did shame Grizel's Sports Notes. That young lady, in her attempt to avoid slanginess, had gone to the other extreme, and become almost unbearably stilted. The two mistresses were hard put to it to keep straight faces over such statements as, "Tennis has been most enjoyable during the past season," "All have endeavoured to do well in cricket," and the like, from slangy Grizel. Bernhilda's narratives of how the Tiernsee became a lake, and the origin of the Wolfenkopf, a grim, dark mountain peak at the northern extremity of the lake, were interesting, but no one save Jo gave them more than a passing glance. Miss Durrant had contributed a delightful account of a summer school held by the English Folk Dance Society at Cambridge, and Mademoiselle had written a description of her own first term as a pupil in a big convent school in the south of France. But it was the Fiction Page which most interested the committee. At least ten girls had sent in contributions to this page, and four had been chosen by Joey for Miss Maynard to select from. As this had been done at the last minute, no one but she knew whose had been taken, so they were all agog to know. A groan of dismay went up as they discovered that the contributions had been printed unsigned, and only Jo and the authors themselves could know whose they were.

" 'The Wooden Bowl of Hans Sneeman'," read Gisela. "But who, then, wrote that? It is a story of Kobolds." She glanced up in time to catch the expression on Jo's face. That young lady was staring at Miss Maynard with startled eyes and wide-open mouth. "Jo!" exclaimed the head girl. "*You* have written it!"

"But it is charming!" cried Bernhilda, who had been eagerly reading it. "Joey, I make you my compliments!"

"But—but——" gasped Joey. "I never *gave* it to you, Miss Maynard. I didn't give *anything*!"

"I know you didn't," replied Miss Maynard calmly. "I found it lying on the floor under your desk one day, and liked it so much, I decided to use it."

"Splendid!" Grizel put her word in. "It's simply gorgeous, Jo! I can't think how you did it!"

Jo remained dumbfounded. It was so unexpected that,

for once, she hadn't a word to say for herself, while the rest exclaimed delightedly over it.

It was a very simple little tale, following well-known lines. A poor forester met an old woman, who begged food and shelter from him. He had only a little log hut, and a wooden bowl he himself had made. In the bowl was a very little vegetable stew, which formed his one daily meal. Nevertheless, he gave it up to the stranger, who ate it, and then suddenly vanished. The next morning, as Hans Sneeman the forester was working, hungry and somewhat disheartened, a radiant angel appeared to him, who informed him that it was she whom he had helped the night before, and for his generosity and unselfishness the help he had given should always be his, and he should never be in want again so long as he lived. Then the angel vanished; but, from that time forth, everything went well with Hans Sneeman, who remained always humble-minded, generous, and unselfish; and to remind him of his days of poverty, and to keep himself from becoming proud, always ate his meals out of his old wooden bowl, which was buried with him when he died.

It was slender enough, but it was gracefully written, with a certain sense of humour to flavour it. All things considered, it was a remarkable thing for a schoolgirl to have produced. Madge Bettany read it with wonder. She had always known that her little sister was gifted in this way, but she had had no idea that the gift was so unusual. In the years to come Jo Bettany was to astonish those who knew her, again and again, with her writings; but her sister never forgot that icy winter's day at the Tiernsee when she first discovered that the family baby was going to write.

The other story, an account of the adventures of an old trunk, had been written by Bette Rincini, and was quite well done, though there was nothing to distinguish it from similar work by most clever schoolgirls. Bette had a marvellous command over the English language, and the little tale ran easily, and was told with a humour and freshness which made it very readable.

The Poetry Corner came next, and the *Chaletian* discovered the interesting fact that the Chalet School contained quite a number of would-be poets. Like the stories, all the verses were unsigned, but it was a comparatively easy matter to name the writers.

Rosalie Dene, an otherwise undistinguished member of the school, had sent in some pretty lines on "Roses"; Gisela had contributed a couple of stanzas on Spring; and Gertrud had given a very charming word picture of the lake. The surprise of this page lay in four lines entitled "A Rime".

> Lilies in the garden; roses on the wall;
> Apples in the orchard—there's plenty for us all.
> Some prefer the apples, and some prefer the rose;
> But I always think the lily is the fairest flower
> that grows.

"Who wrote that, Joey?" queried her sister. "It's rather pretty."

"Which is?" demanded Joey, rousing up from her rapture at first seeing herself in print with some difficulty.

"The little verse called 'A Rime'," replied Miss Bettany.

"That? Oh, Amy Stevens sent it in."

"*Amy!* Jo! Are you *sure*?"

"Of course I am! " Jo sounded distinctly injured.

Miss Bettany made haste to apologise for her seeming doubt. "I'm sorry, Joey; but—well—it's very good for such a little girl. She's only eight! "

"Yes; it *is* decent, isn't it?" observed the editor complacently as she turned to the Correspondence Page, and then, finally, the Head's letter. "I say. I don't want to buck, but don't you think it's a good mag. for our first, everyone?"

A chorus of assent answered her. They were all agreed; it *was* a good magazine for the first.

"And," said Miss Maynard later on when she and Miss Bettany were alone, "it looks to me as though *two* of the contributors to the first number of the *Chaletian* will be writers some day."

The head-mistress nodded. "Yes; at least I hope so. At any rate, we must see that they have every help and every encouragement."

Miss Maynard collected her possessions and turned to leave the room. "When we are old women," she observed as she opened the door, "I expect we shall be proud to say that we helped with the education of Amy Stevens the poetess, and Josephine Bettany, the well-known novelist! There are a good many consolations in our profession!"

Then she went out, and left the sister of the future "well-known novelist" to groan over a map of that young person's and wonder why Joey never seemed able to put in contour lines correctly.

CHAPTER TWELVE

The Hobbies Club

"Ow! You've upset my cards! You *are* mean, Grizel Cochrane!"

"Well, you shouldn't have them all over the place, then!" retorted Grizel as she hastily stooped and began sweeping the postcards together.

She was stopped by a wild shriek from Margia. "Leave them alone! You're muddling them up. *Oh!* and I'd just got them all sorted out!"

"Well, I'm sorry," said Grizel impatiently, "but I couldn't help it!"

"Why don't you pick them up in their sets?" suggested Joey Bettany, looking up for a minute from her collection of crests. "It would save trouble later. I'll help, shall I?"

She dropped on to all fours, and began gathering up views of Italy with great goodwill, while Margia, adopting her suggestion, collected Germany, and Grizel sorted out "pretty" ones.

It was Saturday afternoon. All day, a fierce wind had blown from the icy north, and it had been impossible for any of them to go out. In England it is difficult to realise just how furious the great winds *can* be that in the winter sweep across the central plains of Europe from the Arctic regions. Even in the Tyrol, with its mountain-ranges to protect it from the worst, the gales swirl down with devastating fury, and, of course, up in the mountains at the Tiernsee, three thousand feet and more above sea-level, there was no such protection.

Marie Pfeifen, who ruled in the kitchen at the Chalet, shook her head as she listened to the howling of the wind round the house, and prophesied a hard winter. Even—it was possible—the wolves might come! Certainly they would appear on the plains.

With the weather like this, the girls had to content themselves indoors as best they might. They had done country-dancing in the morning under Miss Durrant's instruction, going through all they had learned, and then joyfully making the acquaintance of two new ones—"Pop Goes the Weasel," a longways dance for as many as will, and going on to "If All the World were Paper," with its sung chorus and pretty figures in between the "arms to the centre," "siding," and "arming."

In the afternoon Miss Bettany, with an eye to the needs of her staff, had suggested that the girls should bring their hobbies into the big double school-room, and amuse themselves quietly, while the mistresses retired to their own rooms for a well-earned rest. Nearly everyone "collected" —in fact, there was quite a craze for it this term. Most of the younger girls went in for postcards or stamps. Jo's crests were unique, and so was her other craze— "Napoleoniana", to coin an expression to fit it. She begged postcards, cuttings and photographs of the famous man, also of his possessions, his battles, and his family.

Grizel collected photographs of notable sportsmen, and also owned forty-seven postcards of the Prince of Wales and other members of Britain's Royal Family. The elder girls went in for autographs, pressed leaves, and flowers; and Gisela collected feathers of various kinds of birds. Pretty Bette was quite a keen geologist, and was very proud of her "rocks". Wanda von Eschenau possessed a very good collection of copies of famous pictures; and Bernhilda Mensch had a large exercise-book into which she copied all her favourite quotations and extracts, a hobby in which her younger sister, Frieda, shared. Marie von Eschenau collected tiny models of animals, and at the present moment her corner of the huge trestle-table, at which most of them were sitting, looked rather like a zoo and a farmyard combined. The Robin, who adored these playthings, was curled up beside her, helping to arrange them.

It was left to Simone, in many ways the most colourless and unoriginal of them all, to have the funniest collection. *Her* craze was for paper dolls. She had over one hundred of these: some, the variety bought in boxes with their various garments all ready to slip on; others, figures cut out of magazines and books, and pasted on to cardboard. Many of these were celebrities, and Simone's favourite game was to pretend that one was holding a reception, to which the others came.

These, with Marie's animals, were decidedly the most popular of all the collections with the juniors, who would listen for hours to Simone's plays if she would only let them.

Grizel suddenly made a suggestion which thrilled them all. "I say," she remarked, "why don't we have a Hobbies Club?"

A Hobbies Club!

There was an instant hubbub, for everyone wanted to give her views on this magnificent idea, and nobody was at all disposed to listen to anyone else.

"What a tophole scheme!" cried Joey, her good resolutions with regard to slang completely forgotten.

"Grizel! But how charming!" remarked Bernhilda.

"*Splendid!*" "*Wunderschön!*" "*Epatant!*" "*Magnifico!*" The various exclamations rose in a perfect babel of languages.

Grizel stood trying to look modest, and failing utterly. It really was a good idea, and she knew it.

They made so much noise that Miss Bettany came across to them from the study to inquire what it was all about. She was almost overwhelmed by their explanations, but at length she managed to gather something of what they were saying.

"Start a Hobbies Club?" she repeated, as she accepted the chair Gisela was offering her. "Well, I don't know. Whose idea is it?"

"Grizel's!" replied Joey.

"How do you propose to run it, then?" queried Miss Bettany. "What are your aims?"

Grizel looked rather floored over this. Finally, "I— I don't know," she said.

Joey's black eyes flashed. "*I* do, though. You want us to have jolly times together with our c'llections, don't you? An' do proper swopping an' see who can get the best, an' have shows——"

"Yes! And do all kinds of work too!" Grizel knew what she wanted *now*. "Gisela and Bernhilda are awfully keen on embroidery, and some of the others make lace, and some of us wood-carve. *I've* always wanted to do leather-work," she added reflectively.

The Head nodded. "I see! Well, it's a very good idea, and I see no reason why you should not carry it out. You may have definite meetings from four till five one afternoon in the week, and, in bad weather, on Saturday afternoons if you like. I propose that you all choose some handcraft, and work during the winter months——"

"Oh! And have a show at the end of next term!" cried Joey eagerly.

"Oh yes, Madame! We shall all like that!" said Gisela enthusiastically.

Miss Bettany glanced at them. There was no mistaking their feelings. One and all, they were longing to begin. "Very well," she said briskly. "You may do it. We can't do much this term, of course! Exams begin next week, and then we shall break up. But next term you shall begin in real earnest, every one of you, and I hope we shall have a good show!"

"But what can *we* do?" demanded little Amy Stevens.

"You can make scrap-books," replied Miss Bettany without an instant's hesitation. "We'll get raffia as well, and you can learn to make mats and baskets and napkin-rings—oh, there are plenty of things you can do!"

The juniors, who had been hanging on her words, heaved

sighs of satisfaction, and forthwith departed to the other end of the room to discuss their views on the subject. The head-mistress strolled out, and the seniors and the middles gathered together to decide what crafts they should take up.

"Leather-work for me!" declared Grizel. "I'll make bags, and book-marks, and moccasins!"

"I'm going in for fretwork," decided Joey. "I'll cut jigsaw puzzles. It looks easy, and they make jolly presents. What's anyone else going to do?"

There was a variety of ideas. Two or three of the elder girls meant to stick to embroidery; Gertrud Steinbrucke and Vanna di Ricci could both make pillow-lace, and had their pillows with them; some were interested in wood-carving, and others in sketching. Wanda von Eschenau proved to be the most original here, for she decided to take up painting on china.

"I wish there was something one could do with *music*," said Margia Stevens discontentedly, "but there isn't. I shall have to stick to knitting."

"Couldn't you write a song?" suggested Joey, "or, if you like, I've got a *real* musical idea for you."

"Well, what is it?" Margia's curiosity was aroused.

"Why," said Jo, "you just collect pictures of great musicians, and then stick the picture on one page and put down all you can about the man on the other. Like: 'Beethoven. A great German composer. Born at Bonn seventeen and something or other. Went deaf quite young,' and a list of his chief works, and where he died, and so on."

Margia was gazing before her with the eyes of one who sees visions. "Joey! What a *splendacious* idea! It's simply gorgeous! You *are* a brain!"

"I thought you'd like it," replied the originator of the idea as off-handedly as she could.

"Oh, I *do*! I'll make a topping book of it!" Margia's voice died away as she sat visualising her book. She would have brown pastel paper for the picture sides, and the nicest writing-paper she could get for the notes. Miss Bettany would get them for her the next time she was in Innsbruck, she knew. She would make holes through the sheets with a large knitting-needle, and tie them together with brown ribbon. They should have a cover of brown——

"Hi! Margia Stevens! Wake up and take your coffee!" said Grizel's voice in her ear at that moment, and Margia came back to earth with a start, to find that *Kaffee und Kuchen* had been brought in, and Grizel was standing before her and offering her a large cup of coffee, while Bernhilda was just behind with the cakes. They always had it picnic fashion on Saturdays, and no one ever interfered with them. Miss Bettany liked her girls to feel that there was at least one meal in the week which was absolutely theirs. Mademoiselle La Pâttre rather distrusted the idea, but the young head-mistress held to it firmly, and so far there had been nothing to prove it an impossible idea. The girls always behaved nicely, and the prefects kept an eye on the juniors.

Naturally, everyone was full of the new club this afternoon. Gisela had some idea of combining a concert with the "show" at the end of next term, and inviting parents to come. "We could perform some of our new dances," she said. "I have heard Miss Durrant talk of several very pretty ones we might learn when we come back next term, and our parents would enjoy watching, for the English country-dances are so different from those of our own people."

"Our new English songs too," added Bernhilda. "I do like the last one Herr Denny taught us! I like the song so much," said Bernhilda. "It is a folk-song, is it not?"

"Rather! Just as my 'Appalachian Nursery Rhymes' are," replied Jo.

"Why not give a 'folk' entertainment?" suggested Juliet. "Vanna and Luigia and Bianca could dance the Tarantella for us; and some of you Tyrolese could give us one of your Schuhplättler; and the French girls could sing 'Monsieur de Cramoisie', and 'L'Arbre d'Amour'; and the babies could do nursery rhymes of all kinds; and we could *all* show the country-dances."

"We seem to be literally *spurting* with ideas this afternoon!" laughed Jo. "That's a jolly one, Juliet.—Hullo, Robin! What's the trouble?"

The Robin danced forward, curls dancing, cheeks

crimson with excitement. "Me, I will sing 'Ze Red Sarafan' in ze Russian!" she cried, and promptly lifted up a sweet baby voice in the well-known Russian folk-song.

They all clapped her, laughing at the pretty picture she made. She nodded her head at them joyously. Then suddenly the little voice quivered and broke, and she buried her face in her dimpled hands in a perfect storm of tears. "*Maman! Maman!*" she sobbed. "*Oh, je veux toujours Maman!*"

They were round her in an instant, petting her and trying to soothe her; but all their efforts were vain, and she sobbed on. Nearly in tears herself—for there was something so desolate in the baby's little wail—Joey dashed out of the room and into the study, where Miss Bettany was entertaining her staff. At Joey's unceremonious entry they all looked up amazed.

"Jo!" exclaimed her sister severely. "What does this mean?"

"I'm sorry!" gasped Joey incoherently. "It's the Robin —crying! She was singing—'The Red Scavenger', or something like that; and then she wanted her mother! *Do* come!"

Miss Bettany was on her feet in a moment, and across the passage to where the poor mite was still sobbing out her pathetic little appeal, "*Maman! Maman! Viens, je te prie! Maman!*"

Tender arms were round about her; soft dark curls, so like the lost mother's, were against her cheek; then Miss Bettany bore her off to be cuddled back to serenity, while the girls finished their *Kaffee* rather more soberly.

"She is so happy always," said Gisela, "that one forgets how short a time it is since the little mother left her."

"I suppose *she* used to sing that song," added Juliet. "Poor baby!"

Presently they turned back to the subject of the Hobbies Club again, and when a cheered-up and once more placid Robin joined them later on, they were very busy discussing hobbies and collections, and no more was said that night about the concert.

CHAPTER THIRTEEN

The Nativity Play

THE REMAINDER of the term simply flew. Exam week followed the inauguration of the Hobbies Club, and various people wished on different days that they had worked a little harder during the term.

Jo Bettany groaned over every one of the maths papers. "That was a—a—*disgusting* fraction!" she proclaimed to all and sundry after the arithmetic paper.

Margia, who was standing near, opened her eyes widely. "Why Joey, it was easy! It came out to 2/13ths!"

"*What!*" gasped Jo. "I say! I got 67685/107676!"

"Joey! You *couldn't*! What on earth have you done?"

"Goodness knows!" Jo resigned herself to her fate. "I never *could* do maths, and I never shall!"

But if the paper was, as Miss Maynard characterised it, "disgraceful!" her English, French, and German were all excellent, and so were her history and literature, in all of which Margia was only average. Frieda Mensch came out strongly in geography; and of the seniors, Bernhilda headed the mathematics lists, with Grizel a good second, while Gisela and Juliet divided the languages honours between them, and Wanda von Eschenau proved to be an easy first in drawing.

The last afternoon was given up to a concert, which was attended by the people in the valleys round about, Herr Anserl and one or two of his friends from Spärtz, and a few parents, who managed to get up the snowy paths to the Tiern valley. Needless to state, everyone was wild with excitement at the prospect. *Mittagessen* took place at twelve, and by half-past one all the girls were attired in white frocks. They had spent the morning in decorating the big school-room with branches of evergreen. A couple of screens cut off the upper end of the room, and the other part was filled with chairs and forms for the visitors, who began to arrive shortly after two. By half-past the room was full, and then Miss Bettany came forward and announced the first item, a madrigal, "How Fair the Sun". The screens were drawn aside, showing the rows of white-frocked girls, with Mr. Denny in front of them to conduct.

"Plato" might be a freak, as Joey declared, but he certainly knew how to teach singing, and the harmony of fresh voices that filled the room was something to be proud of. Like all Austrians, the Tiernsee people are musical, and they listened in a breathless silence, which told how they enjoyed it.

It was followed by the girls' own favourite, "My Bonny Lass, She Smileth"; and then they sang one of Martini's canons.

Herr Anserl sat looking unusually pleased. *"Herrgott!"* he observed to Miss Bettany, "but he has made something of them, this young man!"

The Head nodded. "They sing well, *nicht wahr?*"

"Excellently well! I must greet him, Herr Denny!"

The singing was followed by a piano solo by Margia, who was some day to surprise the world with her music; and Gisela gave a charming rendering of Martini's *Preghiera* for the violin. Grizel and Frieda played a pianoforte duet, Mendelssohn's "Fingal's Cave", with strict attention to time, and very little to anything else, and then they all sang again—one of the folk-songs this time, "Come, all you valiant Christian men".

After this there was an interval, during which Amy Stevens, Simone Lecoutier, and Maria Marani distributed papers among the audience, on which were written the words of the German carol, *Stille Nacht, Heilige Nacht,* and also the Latin hymn, *Adeste Fideles.* Then Miss Bettany came forward once more and explained: "We are going to give you a little Nativity play," she said. "It is in English, and is called *The Youngest Shepherd.* As you all know, it was to the 'shepherds abiding in the field, keeping watch over their flocks by night' that the angel of the Nativity told the good news of Christ's birth. Our little play is based on that story, and we should like you, when we come to them, to join us in the Christmas songs written on the sheets given you."

Then she vanished, and the screens were drawn, to show an ordinary room with modern children in it. It was Christmas Eve, and the children were talking—quarrelling —till a carol outside made them stop: such a lovely càrol —"Good Christian men, rejoice", sung as only Mr. Denny's pupils could sing.

The four children hushed their wrangling then, and spoke instead of the next day, and what it brought to the world. Then the curtains parted, and the Youngest Shepherd stood before them. He told them of the Angel Song, and explained that, as he was the youngest of all the shepherds, he had had to stay behind to look after the sheep, but God had sent an angel down to guard them, so that he, too, might go and worship at the Manger; and he invited the children to go with him. They all sprang to their feet, ready to go. Then they remembered that all who had gone to worship the Baby King had taken Him gifts; so they caught up their own favourite possessions to give. The young shepherd drew aside the curtains, saying, "See! Listen! "

A throng of angels were there, and they were singing the English carol, "In the Fields with their Flocks Abiding".

The children stood listening, till the lights dimmed, and the song died away into the pealing of Christmas-bells, and the screens were swiftly drawn across the stage. The next scene was out of doors. The children came in wearily with the Youngest Shepherd. It was a long way, and they were so tired! A poor Man came by them, and asked where they were going. They told him, and asked him to come with them, but he said kings never gave audience to the poor and needy such as he. For reply, they told him that this was the King of the poor and needy. He laughed at them, and then the Youngest Shepherd, as a final answer, sang the old "Cherry Tree" carol. They had all known that Joey could sing, but no one had quite realised the beauty of her voice before. It was not a very strong voice, but each note was round and pure, with the bell-like quality to be found in some boy-choristers' voices. She was utterly unself-conscious, and had, in fact, forgotten everything but the fact that she must get this Man to realise that the King wanted him too.

There was a low murmur as the last clear note died away, but the audience were too deeply interested in the story to applaud.

Then the Man agreed to come; but, just as they were about to move on, a great Lady, clad in whispering silks with many jewels about her, met them, and asked their destination. They told her they were going to see the King, and she sneered at their manner of going. Kings, she told them, could only be visited in great pomp. They begged her to come and see, and at first she refused. Then the smallest child held out her hand and said "Do come Oh, do come!" and she gave way and came, and so they passed on.

There was a little silence at that; then suddenly the lovely chorus rang out, "There came three Kings", and the Magi appeared, bearing their gifts of gold, frankincense, and myrrh. Caspar, Melchior, and Balthazar paused in their following of the Star to rest and discuss the meaning of their gifts. Then they too went forward, and the screens were drawn once more.

During the three minutes' interval there came another carol, "When the Crimson Sun had Set", with its wonderful chorus of *Gloria in excelsis Deo*. When it was finished, the stage was revealed once more—the door of the Stable. An archangel stood there, the white lily of peace in his hand. Music stole out into the room, and as one the audience rose, and the old German carol, *Stille Nacht, Heilige Nacht*, was sung with full throats. When it was over, and they were all sitting once more, the Angel-chorus sang again, the "Bird" carol this time. Then silence fell, and the shepherds appeared.

How weary they were—and how eager! At the door they paused. Would the King be pleased to see them? Yes; surely He would. He had sent the angel to tell them. So they passed in, and the chorus sang "The First Nowell".

Next came the Wise Men, and they paused in wonderment before the humble place. *This* was no King's abode But the Star had stopped, so it must be right, and they, too, passed in.

Finally came the Youngest Shepherd and his little group. To the singing of the children's carol, "Come to the Manger in Bethlehem", the children pressed forward into the Stable. The Man and the Lady followed more slowly. Last came the Youngest Shepherd. He had no gift but himself to offer. He was scarcely even a shepherd; just a servant to help the others. But at last he, too, went slowly in, and the screens were drawn back once more across the stage.

The well-known tune of the *Adeste Fideles* sounded, and everyone sang it, so that it rang out as even *Stille Nacht, Heilige Nacht* had not done. Then the screens were taken away for the last time, and the interior of the Stable was shown. They had done the whole thing very simply. As Miss Bettany had said, it would have been in bad taste to have elaborate scenery. An old wooden trough filled with hay stood at the back. Before it was seated the Madonna, Wanda von Eschenau, holding in her arm a bundle to represent the Holy Child. Behind her stood Luigia di Ferrara as Joseph, and at either side stood an archangel with bowed head. Child angels clustered round them, and kneeling at the Madonna's feet, her baby face full of awe and reverence, was a tiny cherub, the Robin. To the right and at the back stood the welcoming Archangel with his lilies.

There was a little silence. Then, once more, music swelled out, and once more Joey's silvery notes stole forth, though Joey herself was behind the scenes. The carol chosen for this was the Breton carol, "Sleep, Holy Babe". The poignant sweetness of the young voice struck home, even to those who could not understand what she was singing, and somehow the scene brought lumps into the throats of the audience.

Then, one by one, the worshippers stole in. The shepherds came first, offering their crooks; then the Wise Men with their symbolical gifts; then the children eagerly laying their treasured possessions before the Holy Child and His Mother. The poor Man had only his old blunt knife, but it was offered and accepted; the Lady tore off all her jewels and piled them at the Madonna's feet. Then the Youngest Shepherd came. He had nothing but himself to give. Humbly he knelt and a sudden strain of music swelled out as the Madonna rose, queenly, to her feet, and held out to him a silver crook. His was the richest gift of all, for he had brought other worshippers.

Then came the final carol, "Brightest and Best of the Sons of the Morning". As it ended, the screens were brought forward, and the lights in the room were turned up. Miss Bettany stood forward. "Thank you," she said in her sweet voice, "for your appreciation of our little play. We wish you all a very happy Christmas! "

A storm of good wishes promptly broke on all sides. Tyroleans are quick to answer emotion, and all were specially sensitive at the moment. The girls' performance, simple as it was, appealed to a people accustomed to giving and witnessing Mystery plays; and for many a day *The Youngest Shepherd* gave the lake people a topic for conversation.

As for the girls, it took them some time to come down to the earth. When they did, there was much chatter about Christmas plans. They were all going home early the next morning. Miss Bettany, Joey, and the Robin would be the only ones left, and they would be leaving the Chalet in the afternoon. The school was to be closed, and Marie and Eigen with Zita and Rufus were going home for Christmas. Jo had begged hard to take Rufus to Innsbruck with her, Bernhilda having assured her that he would be welcomed; but Madge was firm, and would not hear of it. Jo, therefore, had to content herself by giving the faithful Eigen reams of advice about him. "All the same, I know he'll miss me, the darling! " she mourned to Grizel.

"Rubbish! " retorted Grizel. "He'll be all right. Oh, Joey," she went on, "I do wish you were coming with me tomorrow! I hate the idea of being with only Mr. Stevens all the time! "

Mr. Stevens, father of Margia and Amy, was going to London to see the editor of the great daily paper to which he was foreign correspondent, and had offered to take Grizel so far. Her own father would meet her there, and take her to Cornwall.

"Mr. Stevens is awfully nice," said Jo, in answer to her friend's last remark. "And, anyway, you're going to have *weeks* more than the rest of us, so I don't see why you're grumbling! "

"I'm not *grumbling*! But—well—I'd like you and Miss Bettany too," replied Grizel. "I *did* want to be with you for Christmas! "

Jo looked at her curiously. "You'll have Easter with us! "

"I know! But Christmas is such a homey time! 'Tisn't much of a home at *home*! "

Joey was silenced. She knew that Grizel's stepmother had made home anything but happy for her, just as she knew that Grizel loved her life at school. Finally, "We'll miss you! " she jerked out. "Buck up, old thing! "

And with that Grizel had to be satisfied.

CHAPTER FOURTEEN

The Christmas Holidays Begin

"ISN'T IT QUIET?" said Joey suddenly.

It was one o'clock on the following afternoon, and she and her sister and the Robin were finishing a very picnicky meal before finally closing the Chalet and making the journey on foot to Spärtz, where the midday train from Salzburg would carry them off to Innsbruck and the Mensches' flat in the Mariahilfer Strasse at the other side of the Inn. Everyone had been up early, and the last of the girls had gone shortly after ten o'clock. Since then Miss Bettany and the two children had been busy packing their clothes in the light wicker baskets which Eigen and Marie would help to carry down the snow-covered footpath to the station at Spärtz. It would be easy walking, for the snow was frozen till it was like a rock, and the big nail-studded climbing-boots they all wore would give them a grip on the slippery surface.

"*Don't* you think it's deathly quiet now everyone else has gone?" said Joey.

"Yes; very quiet," agreed her sister. "If you two have finished, we may as well clear these things away so that Marie can clear up. We've a very fair walk before us, and it is dark by four, so I want to get off as quickly as possible. Hurry, children!"

They hurried. One usually did when Miss Bettany spoke in that tone. Marie was busily washing up the few crocks she and Eigen had used, and Joey sped to the *Speisesaal* to fold up and put away the blue-and-white checked table-cloth, and help the Robin to push the chairs into their places. Eigen came in while they were busy, and carefully raked out the remnants of fire left in the big porcelain stove. Like most of the houses along the Tiernsee, the Chalet was built of wood, so the precaution was a necessary one.

Just as he finished, Madge called them to get ready for their walk and the short railway journey, and saw to their wrapping-up herself.

"It's freezing hard outside, and we have a long walk," Madge said. "Run downstairs now, you two, and I'll come in a few minutes."

They clattered off, and ten minutes later Miss Bettany was locking the door, while Marie and Eigen were already trudging ahead, each carrying two of the baskets, while a much smaller one remained for Joey.

"At last!" exclaimed that young lady as her sister dropped the keys into her pocket. "Now we're really off. Oh, Madge, won't it be jolly to see the shops all decorated for Christmas? We've got nearly all our presents to get, you know. Won't it be fun?"

"Splendid," replied Madge. "But you don't want to live in the town always, do you, Joey?"

"Oh *no*! I love the Tiernsee and the mountains. But it's jolly to have a change!"

"What do you think, Robin?"

The Robin lifted a rosy face to the delicate one bent down to hers. "It will be *zolly!*" she said emphatically.

Madge laughed. "So it will! I expect we shall have a splendid Christmas."

"Will the Christ Child put bonbons in our shoes?" asked the Robin eagerly.

"Yes, if He thinks you have been good."

"And then there'll be the Christmas-tree," added Joey. "Frieda says they're going to have an extra nice one 'cos we're going to be there. Her brother's coming too, from Bonn."

"We shall go to the church," the Robin chimed in, "and see the Manger and the little Lord Jesus and His Mother."

"There's tobogganing too, and skating," went on Joey, waving gaily to the hostess of the *Gasthaus* at Seespitz, which they were passing. "Come on, Robin; *this* way now!" And she led off to the right through tall black pines to the narrow winding pathway that ran along the banks of what was usually a very turbulent little stream. Now, Winter held it in his iron grasp, and there was silence where before there had been the music of tossing water. Icicles hung on the boulders in its bed, and fringed the alder boughs that overhung it, and a black pathway of ice was all that showed its usual course.

"Isn't it still?" said Joey in half-awed tones. "Even the sawmill has stopped."

"Of course," said Madge. "It can't go on when the stream is frozen."

"I forgot that!" Joey gave a giggle. "What an ass I am!"

Down, down, they went. The voices of Marie and Eigen floated up to them clearly on the frosty air, and occasionally there was a sharp "crack," as a rotten bough snapped in the woods under its weight of snow. But, except for these sounds, there was silence—a silence that could be felt. Even excitable Joey stopped talking before long, and they went on without speaking.

When they had gone a third of the way, Miss Bettany stopped and picked up the Robin, who was beginning to lag behind.

"Why not take her on your back?" suggested Joey. "I

can give her a boost up, and then you'll be able to see your way better."

"That's a good idea," agreed Madge. "Climb up on that log, Robinette, and Joey will help you up. That's it! Put your arms round my neck, but don't strangle me if you can help it! Comfy?—Come along, then, Joey!"

They set off once more, and this time got on faster. The Robin was a light weight, and Madge, though slightly built, was strong. Joey stepped out manfully, and they made good time down the mountain-side.

Miss Bettany was beginning to feel anxious about Marie and Eigen. They meant to return that night, she knew, and it was growing dusk already under the pines. "Joey," she said presently, "if I send Marie and Eigen back as soon as we reach Spärtz, do you think you and I can manage the Japanese baskets between us? The Robin could carry your little one, I should think."

"Oh, rather!" said Joey enthusiastically. "It isn't far to the station."

"I don't like the idea of those two having to go back up there in the dark. It's clouding in, too, and I'm afraid we shall have more snow. I'll carry the Robin to the bottom, and then she'll be quite fresh. We can take the baskets, and I'll send those two straight back up the path."

"Good scheme!" agreed Joey. "But, I say, Madge, if you get tired, Robin can carry the basket now, and we can give her a queen's-chair."

"Perhaps that would be better," said Madge thoughtfully. "She's very light, but the baskets won't be. We'll stop now, and do as you suggest, Joey baba!"

"But I can walk," declared the Robin as she wriggled down to the ground.

"No, dearie, you will be so tired," replied Madge tenderly. "See, I'm going to tie the little basket to your belt. Then you can sit on our hands, and it will rest on your knees, so that you can hold on to us safely."

The Robin was always obedient. She sat down on their linked hands, settled the basket on her knees, and then put an arm round each neck. "Now I am ready," she said cheerfully.

They hurried on, and another twenty minutes saw them within sight of Spärtz, where already the lights twinkled out merrily.

Marie and Eigen were waiting for them. "Marie," said Miss Bettany, as she and Jo set their burden down, "I am afraid it is going to snow before long, so I want you and Eigen to give us the baskets and go straight back to Briesau at once. We can easily manage as far as the station."

Marie would have argued the matter, but her young mistress gave her no chance. She took the two largest baskets herself, and said firmly, "Jo, take the other baskets. —*Auf wiedersehn, Marie, und fröhliche Weihnachtsfest!*"

Marie curtsied, while Eigen saluted, and both wished the trio "*Fröhliche Weihnachtsfest!*" before they turned and set off on their long walk home.

"Oh, Madge, there's Herr Anserl!"

Herr Anserl, a shaggy-looking monster in his old fur coat, came hurrying across the road.

"*Guten Tag, Fräulein,*" he said to Madge, relieving her of her load. "But where, then, do you go?"

"We are going to Innsbruck for the Christmas holidays," explained Madge in his own language.

"'*Zist gut!*" he said. "I will myself bring you to the *Bahnhof*. Give me one of those basket cases, Fräulein Joey. Yes; I can take it. I will 'see you off,' as you say in England."

Madge was really very thankful for his escort. She was beginning to feel tired, and the baskets *were* heavy after their long trudge through the snow. She took the other one from Joey, who was beginning to look all eyes, an invariable sign of weariness with her, and they all meekly followed in the wake of Herr Anserl, who strode along, shouting greetings, so it seemed, to most of the people they met.

At length they reached the station, and, while Madge went to get the tickets, the somewhat eccentric music-master took the two little girls into the *Restauration* and ordered hot milky coffee for them, with new rolls—"And be sure they are *new!*" he added to the indignant attend-ant, who tossed her head, but nevertheless produced the coffee and delicious crusty rolls to break into it. When Madge appeared, he insisted that she should have the same.

"There is sufficient time before the train comes," he said. "Yes; eat, *gnädiges, Fräulein!* Here is sugar."

By the time they had finished their meal, the signals were down, and two minutes later the train swept into the station, and Herr Anserl was bundling them into a compartment and wishing them a merry Christmas, beaming widely all the time.

"Isn't he *decent*!" said Joey amazedly, as they steamed out of the station, for Herr Anserl was considerably more feared than loved at the Chalet School. "I'm going to send him a Christmas card."

Madge settled Robin comfortably in her arms, and before they had reached the old town of Schwaz she was far away in dreamland.

Joey turned her attention to the flying landscape. The train had one more stop before they reached Innsbruck—at Hall. Then, presently, came lights, and five minutes later they were on the platform of Innsbruck station, with Frau Mensch taking a very sleepy Robin from Madge's arms, and Frieda and Bernhilda kissing an ungrateful Jo on both cheeks, and welcoming them all very warmly.

"This, then, is all the luggage?" queried Frau Mensch. "We have a *Droschke* ready, and Gottfried will carry the packages. Fräulein, permit me to present my son to you."

She waved forward a tall fair young man, who bowed with his heels well together but said nothing. As he took the baskets, Joey reflected that he seemed to be as shy as his two pretty sisters, who evidently thought him one of the most wonderful beings in the world. Frieda walked beside him, looking up at him almost reverentially. Joey wondered what Dick would have said if she had ever looked at *him* like that. Bernhilda came round to her side, slipping an arm through hers. "It is so nice to have you with us, Joey!" she said. "We have looked forward to it for a long time. Gisela and Maria wished to come with us to meet you, but they live very far away, and there was no one to come with them, so Frau Marani refused permission."

By this time they had reached the *Droschke*. Joey sat silent as they were whirled down the brightly-lighted Landhaus Strasse, into the wide Maria Theresien Strasse, with its big modern shops, all lit up, and its wide pavements, full of merry, jostling crowds, through the much narrower Friedrich Herzog Strasse, where the shops are built under the Arcades, across the fine bridge, and so to the quieter suburb on the left bank of the Inn. They turned to the left from the bridge, and presently drew up before one of the tall narrow houses overlooking the river.

Gottfried jumped down, and helped out his mother and the girls, before he hurried to open the door, to disclose a narrow winding staircase of wood.

"We are on the third floor," said Frau Mensch. "It seems a long way when one is tired, but the air up there is always fresh, and it is a comfortable flat with plenty of room. Come, Fräulein Bettany. I am sure you are weary, and will be glad to rest; and this *Vöglein* should be in bed.—Are you waking up, *mein Liebling*?" for the Robin had opened wide brown eyes to gaze into the kind face above her.

They went upstairs, leaving Gottfried to wrestle with the cabman and the baskets. Frau Mensch stopped before a door on the third floor and unlocked it. "Enter," she said, "and be very welcome!"

She had set the Robin down to find her key, and now she stretched out her hand and drew Madge inside, kissing her heartily before she did the same to Joey.

"These little birds are very weary," she said in her soft voice, which made the guttural German sound musical. "We will have supper, and then they shall go to bed. You will like to see your room, *nicht wahr*?"

It was a typical Tyrolean room in which they stood, with walls and floor of polished pine-wood. There were a couple of mats on the floor, and in one corner was a huge wooden bed, with its big puffy *plumeau*, and pillows in pillow-cases edged with exquisite hand-made lace. Two tiny wooden washstands stood side by side, with the usual baby bowls and pitchers on them; but over the towel-horse hung towels of the finest hand-woven linen. A tall wardrobe, a chest of drawers with a mirror over them, and three chairs made up most of the furniture. At the foot of the bed stood the little cot, and over its head hung a beautiful copy of Guido's "Blue Madonna". The room was warm, but not stuffy, and the white sheets and pillow-cases made Joey long for bed at once.

A tap at the door ushered in a rosy, smiling girl, wearing a full white blouse, short blue skirt, and wonderfully embroidered apron. She was carrying a huge jug of hot water, which she set down by the washstands, beaming all the time.

"Gertlieb is a good girl," said Frau Mensch when Gertlieb had gone. "Now we will leave you to perform the toilet as soon as Gertlieb has carried in your baskets, and Frieda will come to bring you to our *Speisesaal* in ten minutes' time."

At this moment the smiling Gertlieb reappeared with two of their hampers, and a few minutes later she brought the others. Then she withdrew, followed by her mistress, and Madge set herself to "perform the toilets" of her two charges, who ungratefully clamoured for bed.

"I don't want any supper," said Joey, with a wistful look at the big downy pillows. "Oh, Madge, *can't* I just go straight to bed?"

But this, Madge would not allow. She insisted on Joey's changing; made her wash herself thoroughly, and then brushed the short black hair vigorously before she turned her attention to her own toilet, leaving Jo to see to the Robin.

Frieda came presently, looking very fresh and pretty in her dark-blue frock and white pinafore. Her hair hung loosely to her waist, and excitement had deepened the roses in her cheeks. She led them into the *Spiesesaal*, a low, wide room, with flowering plants in one window and a canary's cage, at present covered with a dark cloth, in the other. The long table had the usual blue-and-white checked cloth, and the china was white with a cheerful blue-and-yellow pattern on it. A big book-case, full of books, stood behind the door, and there were chairs set round the table.

As the girls came in, Gertlieb was just placing a big dish of delicious soup before her mistress, who sat at the head of the table. A flat dish piled with crisp little brown sausages stood before Gottfried, and Bernhilda was dispensing rolls.

"Come," said Frau Mensch cheerfully. "Sit down, everyone.—Frieda, *mein Kindchen*, ask *der liebe Gott* for a blessing on our food."

Frieda murmured the pretty Tyrolean grace, and the plates of soup were passed to Gottfried, who ladled a sausage into each before he sent it on to its destination. It was very good; and so were the great *Vanerkuchen* with jam, which formed the next course; but Joey and Robin were almost too tired to eat.

Frau Mensch smiled as she saw the baby's head nodding lower and lower.

"She is too sleepy for supper," she said. "Fräulein, if you will permit, Bernhilda shall take her away and put her to bed."

Bernhilda rose at once, and led the sleepy Robin off to bed, whither both Jo and Frieda were dismissed twenty minutes later.

"It is early yet," said Frau Mensch apologetically to Madge, "but I am old-fashioned, and I like early hours for young people. Also, little Jo is very weary, and should soon be asleep."

"She does not look too strong, Fräulein," said Gottfried gravely.

"She is not strong," replied Madge quietly. "She is much better, however, and Doctor Erckhardt thinks she will outgrow her delicacy."

"Oh, undoubtedly," replied her hostess, as she led the way into the *salon*, another long room, and rather narrow, but bright and cheerful with its pretty mats and blue-covered furniture.

There was the inevitable sofa with its little table before it, but there were no books arranged at mathematical angles, as Madge had expected. Instead, there was a bowl of Roman hyacinths. More flowering plants were in a long wicker stand near one of the windows; a grand piano was at the other end of the room; and in an alcove stood a harp. A beautifully-carved *Brautkasten*, or bridal-chest, was placed near, and on it was Bernhilda's violin. The Tyrolese are an artistic people, and the few pictures on the walls were reproductions of famous paintings, while the ornaments were mainly carved wooden ones, with a few dainty Dresden figures.

"My mother-in-law, who lives with us, thinks our *salon* very modern," said Frau Mensch as she waved Madge to a comfortable chair. "She is very old, you see, and she does not like modern ways. She lives in her own room most of the time, but on festival days she joins us, and then she amuses herself by criticising everything that is not exactly as it was when she was a bride. Well, she is nearly ninety-five now; my husband is her youngest son—and she has not much pleasure in life; so, if she enjoys it, why should we mind? She cannot be with us much longer. Now, *mein Liebling*, it is easy to see that you are tired, so, Bernhilda shall play for us a little, and then you shall go to bed.— Gottfried, will you and Bernhilda make music for us?"

Gottfried and Bernhilda promptly played several things together, he accompanying her violin. Then, at his mother's request, he sang two or three of Schubert's beautiful *Lieder* in a sweet, sympathetic baritone; and at nine o'clock Frau Mensch sent her guest off to bed.

"It is of no use to wait for my husband," she said. "He is always late at Christmas-time. There is much to see to tomorrow, so I will go to see that *Grossmütter* has all she needs, and then Bernhilda and I too will go to our beds."

She walked with Madge to the bedroom door, and then paused. "My child," she said gently, "while you stay with us, may we not treat you as one of ourselves, we older people, and use your pretty Christian name?"

"Oh, please do," replied Madge. "I should like it."

"Thank you! That will be more comfortable I think. Now, *mein Liebling*, good-night, and the angels guard you!"

"How kind!" thought Madge as she undressed as quietly as possible for fear of waking the two children who were sleeping soundly.

When she was ready for bed, she pushed Joey over to her own side, and then slipped in beside her with a sigh of pure pleasure for the relief of stretching her tired body.

"We shall have a splendid Christmas," she thought drowsily.

Three minutes later, Frau Mensch, peeping in, found all her visitors slumbering so profoundly that they never even stirred as she closed the door behind her.

CHAPTER FIFTEEN

A Jolly Day

JOEY WAS THE FIRST to wake up next morning. They all three slept through Gertlieb's brisk sweeping and polishing of the passage-floor, the sounds of Herr Mensch's rising, the tap-tap of the girls' feet as they hurried about helping their mother. But about eight o'clock Jo suddenly opened her eyes wide, and then sat up, fully awake in a moment. She glanced at the cot standing across the foot of the bed, but the Robin never stirred. Then she looked down at her sister, who lay flushed with sleep.

Joey slipped quietly out of bed, and tiptoed to the window. It was impossible to see anything, however, for the window-panes were covered with wonderful frost designs.

A tap at the door sent her flying across the room to open it on Frau Mensch, who exclaimed in horror at seeing her barefoot and without a dressing-gown.

"I've only *just* got out of bed," pleaded Joey in excuse. "Madge and the Robin are both sound asleep still."

"And you would like to get up now?" queried her hostess understandingly. "Will you bring your garments into my room, and you can dress there without fear of disturbing the others. Your sister is very tired, and we will let her and *das Vöglein* sleep as long as they will. Bring your clothes, my child, and you shall dress and breakfast with us."

Joey collected her possessions noiselessly, and then followed Frau Mensch into a room very like the one they had. Early as it was, it was specklessly tidy, and the bed had been made. Frau Mensch explained that they had all been up since six, as there was a great deal to do today. Gertlieb had been at work since half-past five, and already much of the ordinary housework was finished. Then she left Joey, bidding her come to the *Speisesaal* when she was ready. Jo never loitered over her dressing, and twenty minutes later she entered the big, bright dining-room, where Herr Mensch was already seated at the table, consuming coffee and rolls, with Frieda on one side of him and Bernhilda on the other, while his wife dispensed coffee from the other end. She looked up with a smile as Joey entered.

"Come, my child! Here is coffee for you—but, where is your pinafore?"

"I haven't any," explained Joey as she meekly allowed Herr Mensch to pat her head in fatherly fashion, while he asked if she had slept well.

"No pinafore!" Frau Mensch looked horrified. "Run, Frieda, my bird! Fetch Joey one of your pinafores from the drawer in my room.—You will wear it, will you not, *Mädchen*?"

"Yes, of course, if you want me to," replied Joey cheerfully.

Herr Mensch nodded approval. "That is a good, obedient *Mädchen*," he said, as Joey put on the useful black pinafore Frieda had brought her. "It will keep the little dress neat and dainty. Here, with us, all little maidens wear pinafores to save their pretty gowns. Does the baby have them?"

"Oh yes, Robin wears them," said Jo. "Madge packed them in for her."

"What will you do today?" asked Herr Mensch presently, while Joey attacked her coffee and rolls with good appetite.

"We've got Christmas gifts to buy," replied his small guest.

"Ah, then mamma must take you to the shops and the market this morning. And this afternoon, if it does not snow again, Gottfried shall take you to the toboggan run, and you shall see how like flying that feels."

"Perhaps Joey knows that already?" suggested Frau Mensch.

Joey shook her head. "I've never tobogganed in my life! I've read about it, though, and it sounds gorgeous! It would be nice if Herr Gottfried would take us."

Bernhilda laughed. "He will be very glad," she said. "And tonight we will go to church and hear the Christmas singing before we come home to supper and bed."

"I shall not go," said Frau Mensch decidedly. "I shall be busy with the tree. But papa will take you; and Gottfried also. Aunt Luise is coming to help me, so we shall have it finished in time. Remember, children, no one is to go into the *salon* today. Gottfried has gone to get the tree, and I shall lock the door when he has brought it. Frieda, my child, if you have finished, go and feed Minette in the kitchen."

"May I go too, please?" asked Joey. "I love cats."

"Yes; go if you wish," replied the lady, smiling. "Bernhilda, we will leave you to wash up the china and arrange the table again for Fräulein Bettany and the little Robin."

Then she bustled off to see about *Mittagessen*, while Joey and Frieda trotted into the kitchen to feed Minette, who was a magnificent tabby-cat, with a white dicky and white boots. Gertlieb smiled at them—she never seemed to do anything else but smile—but she went on steadily with her work. There was a great deal to do today, for all the mince-pies which would be eaten tomorrow had to be made; and Frau Mensch had suddenly been seized with a fear that there would not be enough sausages, so there were more to be prepared, and Gertlieb must work if she wanted her two hours in the afternoon, when she could go to the market and buy gifts for the little brothers and sisters at home.

When Minette's wants had been satisfied, Joey returned to the bedroom, where she found Madge was still sound asleep, though the Robin had roused and was sitting up in bed with her curls all on end. At sight of Joey she put her finger to her lips.

"Hssh! We must not talk, for Tante Marguérite sleeps yet."

Joey suggested that the Robin should get up.

"*Oui, vraiment!*" agreed the Robin, beaming at the suggestion. She was hungry.

Quietly Joey managed to get the small girl into her clothes, and brushed the short curls. She managed to remember one of the prettily-embroidered pinafores, which the Robin always wore to keep her frocks tidy. Robin never uttered a word till they were safely out of the room. Then she turned wide eyes on her new nurse. "I have not seen you to wear ze pinafore till yet, Zoë," she said curiously. "Why do you wear him now?"

"Frau Mensch told me to," replied Joey, glancing down at herself. "Come on and have *Frühstück*."

Frieda had brought in a little tray with the big cup of milky coffee and rolls and honey all ready for the Robin, who sat down and demolished three rolls with gusto. "I feel more full," she said with a sigh as she finished the last.

Joey smothered a laugh. "You mustn't say things like that, Robin," she said.

"Why?" demanded the Robin, as she rubbed sticky fingers on her bib.

" 'Cos it isn't polite! "

Frau Mensch, who had just taken her third guest's breakfast to her, returned in time to hear this admonition, and smiled broadly, for she understood a little English, though she could not speak it.

"Come," she said in her own language, "we will have no scoldings today. In one little hour Fräulein Bettany will be ready, and we shall go to the shops, and see what they have to offer us for Christmas."

"Oh, is Madge awake?" asked Joey. "May I go to her?"

"Yes, little heart! Go to thy dear sister, by all means! "

Jo darted out of the room, and across to the bedroom, where Madge, wrapped in her pretty yellow jersey, was sitting up in bed, eating her breakfast.

"*You* disgrace! " observed her small sister from the doorway. "You must have slept the clock round! "

"Just about," replied Miss Bettany cheerfully. "I didn't

know I was so tired till I got to bed—— Joey Bettany! That's never you in a pinafore! Wonders will never cease!"

"Frau Mensch nearly had a fit 'cos I hadn't any," explained Joey. "I didn't like to say I loathed pinnies when she sent Frieda for it."

"Who dressed the Robin?" asked Madge.

"Me, of course. Do buck up, Madge! I'm simply aching to go out! The sun's shining like anything, and it's a gorgeous day! We're to go shopping this morning; and this afternoon Gottfried is going to take us coasting. I say, what shall I get for Frieda? Bernie wants some hankies, so I'm going to get her some. I've got that fretwork bracket for Frau Mensch, and a pipe-rack for Herr Mensch——"

"Which he won't know what to do with," cut in her sister.

"Well, anyway, I've *got* it," said happy-go-lucky Jo. "We're getting a doll for the Robin, aren't we?"

"Yes. I've made most of the clothes. I don't know what you can get for Frieda. Would you like to join with me and give her a fountain-pen?"

"Madge, you ripper!" Joey gazed at her sister in wide-eyed admiration. "It's just the very thing!"

"More than your language is!" retorted Madge. "Take the tray, Joey; I'm going to get up now, so you can vanish!"

"Not before time—your getting up, I mean!" chuckled Jo as she grabbed the tray and made good her escape.

An hour later they were walking up the Maria Theresien Strasse, all well muffled up, for it was bitterly cold in spite of the bright sunshine which made every place sparkle gaily. All round the town lay the great mountains, ringing it round like kindly giants guarding a great treasure. Under foot the snow crunched as the busy shoppers hurried along. There was no sound of wheels to be heard; but the street rang with the jingle of bells as the horses trotted up and down, drawing *droschkes* and sleighs. The shop windows were brightly decorated and there was a general atmosphere of goodwill and merriment.

Frau Mensch undertook the charge of the Robin for half-an-hour, and a meeting-place was appointed at a café in the Landhaus Strasse, where they would drink chocolate at half-past eleven. Madge and Joey spent a pleasantly exciting time making their money go as far as possible. Joey contrived to slip off by herself for a few minutes, and rejoined her sister with a certain little parcel in the inside pocket of her coat; a beautiful doll was chosen for the Robin, and Frieda's fountain-pen and Bernhilda's handkerchiefs were bought. Madge added an embroidered tobacco-pouch for Herr Mensch, and a dainty little collar for his wife. They had to run to be in time for the others, and arrived flushed and panting with laughter and haste at the café, where the Robin's enormous importance proved that she had been shopping too.

"We must hasten," said Frau Mensch, "for there is much to do; and this afternoon some of us go to ski."

"Ski!" gasped Joey delightedly. "Oh, Frau Mensch, not really?"

Frau Mensch laughed. "But yes, my Joey. Why not?"

"Oh! I never thought we could *ski*!" Joey's voice and face were both filled with rapture at the bare idea. "I thought you had to go to Switzerland or Norway for that!"

"But why not here?" demanded Bernhilda. "We have deep snow, mountain-slopes, and a strong frost; so we ski."

"Well, I think it's gorgeous!" sighed her junior. "Better even than coasting!"

The Austrians laughed good-naturedly at her joy. Madge was hardly less excited at the prospect. The Robin didn't understand what it was all about, but she, too, was thrilled.

"I think," said Joey solemnly, as they gathered up their parcels to go, "that this is going to be the jolliest Christmas we've ever had!"

There was still some more shopping to do; then they hurried home to *Mittagessen*, which the smiling Gertlieb had waiting for them. Joey could hardly bear to sit through the meal, she was so excited, and Frau Mensch half regretted that she had said anything about the ski-ing till later on, as she saw the food left on her plate. Herr Mensch, however, came to the rescue.

"A *Mädchen* who wishes to ski this afternoon," he remarked, "will eat all her meat. Also she will enjoy the little *Kartoffeln* which a gruff old giant gives her." And he ladled on to her plate another heaped spoonful of the little buttery potato-balls.

Joey blushed; but she ate what he gave her, much to Madge's relief.

When the meal was over, there was a rush to get ready, and then Gottfried and Herr Mensch escorted the five girls to the place where ski-ing was going on. It was at their side of the river, only twenty minutes' walk away, and then they were at the foot of the slope which was used for the sport. They stood for a few minutes, admiring the graceful, swallow-like flight of the experts; and then Gottfried suggested that they should all go to a quieter spot where the three novices could make their first attempts.

"It looks fairly easy," observed Jo, as, the quieter spot reached, she allowed the young Tyrolean to strap on her skis, while Herr Mensch performed the same kind office for her sister. "*Is* it, Herr Gottfried?"

"Try for yourself," he suggested, as he rose to his full height. "Keep them straight—that is all."

"Right-ho!" Joey made a tentative step; then another; then a third. "Oh, this is jolly!" she called back over her shoulder. "Quite easy, too—ouf!" In some mysterious manner the points of her skis had rushed to embrace each other, and over she went! Bernhilda fled to the rescue.

"They—they didn't keep apart!" Joey said feebly.

"Never mind," replied Bernhilda consolingly. "That is what one always does in the beginning. Try again."

"Of course! I'm not going to be done by two bits of wood or whatever it is they're made of," returned Joey calmly. "Look at Madge!—I say! Look out, Madge, they're crossing!"

Too late! They crossed with that peculiar malignancy that seems to afflict them when beginners are wearing them, and over Madge went. The Robin fared no better; but, like the other two, she persevered, and by four o'clock, when the city below them was brilliant with lights, and the short winter afternoon was closing in, they could all manage to get along for a fair distance, and Herr Mensch prophesied that in another week's time they would be quite good.

"You like it? Yes?" asked Frau Mensch as she welcomed them to cakes and coffee.

"It's *glorious!*" stated Joey definitely. "I'm aching for another go!"

"I'm aching too—from a different cause!" laughed Madge.

Frau Mensch nodded. "You must have a hot bath tonight, all of you, and I will give you some liniment to rub on, that you may not be too stiff on the morrow. Well, Aunt Luise and I have finished the tree, so we shall be able to come with you to the Christmas Eve singing after all."

"How nice!" said Joey sincerely.

The two ladies looked pleased, and Aunt Luise, a younger and slimmer edition of her sister, said, "But that is kind, *mein Kindchen*."

"When do we go?" asked Madge.

"At eighteen o'clock," replied her hostess. "We go to the Hof-Kirche which lies across the river, so we must not be late. It is in the Burg-Graben, and you have surely seen the wonderful tomb of the Kaiser Maximilian the First? Your own King Arthur stands there."

"Yes; we have seen it," replied Madge.

"It's a *gorgeous* place," put in Joey. "How splendid to hear the Christmas music sung there!"

"But it is all splendid to you, Joey!" laughed Bernhilda as she offered Jo some tempting cakes, all almonds and honey and cream.

"Of course it is!" retorted Joey as she took one. "I'm having a—a *splendacious* time!"

"I am so glad!" replied the elder girl.

Then the conversation turned on to the music, and presently it was time to get ready and set out for the Westminster Abbey of the Tyrol.

CHAPTER SIXTEEN

Christmas in Innsbruck

"MADGE! Wake up, old thing! It's Christmas morning! Merry Christmas to you!"

Madge rolled over and blinked sleepily up at the excited face Joey bent down to hers. She had been dreaming of the wonder-music they had heard in the great Hof-Kirche the night before, when the boys' voices, soaring up and up in almost angelic melody, had brought tears to her eyes with their poignant sweetness. Then had come the walk home through the gay, lamp-lit streets, across the old bridge, beneath which the frozen river lay silent and up the much quieter streets of the suburb. Sometimes, as they passed the lit-up windows of the houses, gusts of melody came out to them. Through one, where the shutters had not been closed, they could catch a glimpse of a Christmas tree, and there floated out to them the sounds of merry voices and gay laughter. By this house stood a little girl, listening to the gay noise with a wistful face. With a vague remembrance of dear Hans Andersen's *Little Match Girl*, Joey the impetuous ran to her, and pressed what was left of her money into the purple hands. "Run!" she cried eagerly. "There are *heaps* of shops open still! Do go and get something to eat *now*!"

Joey spoke in English, but her tones and actions were unmistakable. The child gasped; then caught the kind little fingers pressing the paper into her own, and kissed them. "God bless thee!" she cried, before galloping off at full speed.

The Tyroleans are a simple race. Joey's little action seemed quite natural to the Mensches. Herr Mensch patted the little fur cap with a benevolent smile, and his wife said approvingly, "It was well done, my child! The little Christ Child will not forget!"

All this had got mixed up in Madge's dreams, so that when Jo shook her awake she had to think for a moment before she could realise where she was. Then she sat up, shaking back her hair vigorously as she rubbed her eyes. "Merry Christmas, Joey!" she said, when at length she had got her bearings. "Well, Robinette! Are you awake? Merry Christmas!"

The Robin stood up in her cot. "I give you ze greetings of Noël," she said solemnly. "Zoë, do lift me out, please."

Joey tumbled out of bed and assisted the small person on to the floor. The Robin promptly scrambled up beside Madge, and planted a fervent kiss on to her head-mistress's pretty chin before she trotted over to the stove where the three had put their shoes the night before, so that the Christ Child might fill them. Jo was after her in a minute, and echoed the baby's rapturous cry as she found the little shoe filled with chocolate bonbons and a tiny doll. Joey had chocolates too, and a dear little *Book of Saints and Heroes*, which she had long wanted. "Madge, you *gem*!" she cried, as she opened it, and gazed at the illustrations delightedly. "Oh! Here's *your* shoe!"

"Oh, there'll be nothing in mine!" laughed Madge, as she took it. Then she cried out in surprise. It was she who had filled the children's shoes, and she had tucked a handful of chocolates into her own, but she had expected nothing else. Now, on top of the chocolates was a round flat parcel. She opened it, and there lay a little miniature of Joey, set in a narrow silver frame. "Joey!" she cried. "Where did you get this?"

"Miss Durrant did it," explained Jo through a mouthful of chocolate. "She said I was to give it to you when we were by ourselves; so I thought I'd shove it into your shoe. Do you like it?"

"*Like* it!" Madge's eyes glowed as she looked from Joey of the picture to the pyjamaed figure curled up beside her in bed. "It is just what I most wanted, and exactly like you!"

Jo considered it with her head on one side. "No one on earth could call me beautiful, could they?" she said with unexpected wistfulness in her voice.

"No," said Madge truthfully; "they couldn't. You wouldn't be Joey if you were, either; we'd have to call you 'Josephine'!"

"I hate it when you call me 'Josephine'! I always know you're going to rag me about something."

"Exactly!" Madge's tone was dry. "Well now, you're going to get up and get dressed. Hurry up about it, too!"

Joey chuckled and tumbled out of bed. "What frock shall I put on?" she demanded presently, as she stood in her short white petticoat brushing her hair. "My brown velvet?"

"No," replied her sister, who was dressing the Robin. "You'll find your frock over there, on the chair."

"Madge!" Joey made two wild leaps across the floor, and stood enraptured before the little silky frock of soft dull green which lay over the back of the chair. "Oh! What a gorgeous colour! Where did it come from?"

"Dick sent the stuff, ages ago," replied Madge. "Mademoiselle made it for you. Like it?"

"It's beautiful!"

"Put it on," said her sister. "I want to see how it looks."

Joey slipped it on and turned round. The little frock suited her. The soft green brought out the faint flush of colour in her cheeks. It was very simply made, with a short skirt and a round neck, and the silky material fell in graceful folds, which helped to hide her angles.

Madge nodded. "Yes; you'll do," she said. "Now for *your* frock, Robin. Here we are!"

The Robin's frock, of the same silk, was a warm crimson, and had holly leaves embroidered round the hems of skirt, sleeves, and neck in very dark green. Madge had tied up her hair with a big dark-green bow, and with her rosy face and velvety eyes she looked like a Christmas fairy.

"What have you got, Madge?" asked Joey. "*You've* got something pretty too, haven't you?"

Madge nodded and waved her hand to a frock of vivid jade colour. "There you are—I hope it meets with your approval!"

"It's *topping*!" said Joey. "Do buck up and get into it! I think they're gorgeous presents, and Dick's a dear!"

"Oh, these are just extras," laughed Madge. "Dick's *real* presents are—but you'll see later!"

"Are what?" Joey pounced on her. "Do tell me, Madge!"

"Not one word! Get out of my way, Joey, or we shall be late for breakfast!"

They filed into the *Speisesaal* just as the bell rang for *Frühstück*, to find Frau Mensch and the girls already there in full Tyrolean dress. Frau Mensch wore the black full skirt gown of the elder women, with soft white lace kerchief knotted under the square-cut neck, and heavily embroidered apron of fine white linen. Bernhilda and Frieda had shorter skirts, and their dresses were dark green. Both wore their long flaxen hair in the double braids typical of the Tyroleans, and both looked as if they had just stepped out of a fairy tale. Jo cried out with delight when she saw them. "Oh, how jolly!" she exclaimed. "What topping dresses!"

"*Fröhliche Weihnachtsfest!*" said Frieda, dancing up to her friend and giving her a hearty kiss. "Do you like our dresses, then? It is to please *Grossmütter* that we wear it. She joins us today, you know. Papa and Gottfried are carrying her into the *salon* now, and we shall go there when we have finished *Frühstück*."

Meanwhile, Frau Mensch had been greeting her other guests, and leading them to their seats at the table. "My sister is with my mother-in-law," she explained; "and here come my husband and Gottfried."

Herr Mensch and his son were also in national costume, with the well-known green knee-breeches, belt with huge filigree silver buckle, full-sleeved white shirt, and green jacket. Their stockings were light fawn, and their shoes had big silver buckles. It was a dress that suited them both, and Joey voiced the feelings of her sister when she said, "It's like Hans Andersen, or Snow White and Rose Red come to life!"

Herr Mensch's deep laughter rumbled through the room at that, but Gottfried looked uncomfortable and shy. He was not accustomed to being likened to fairy-tale heroes. Luckily, Gertlieb brought in the coffee just then, so they sat down to breakfast.

When the meal was over, the girls helped to clear away, and then to tidy the room, after which they went into the *salon*.

"No one must go to the part we have hung curtains before," said Frau Mensch. "That will not be looked at till tonight. But we will sing carols, and *Grossmütter* will tell us stories of her youth. This afternoon we will hire a sleigh and go for a long drive into the country, if the snow has ceased; but now it falls heavily."

She was right. It was coming down almost like a blizzard. If it had been a fine morning, Madge had intended taking Joey to the English service held in one of the rooms at the Tiroler Hof Hotel; but it was out of the question now.

"You shall sing to us your English carols," said Herr Mensch, who had guessed at the disappointment the English girls felt. "*Sonntag*, perhaps it will be fine, and then you can worship at your own service."

He led the way into the *salon*, where Tante Luise sat with a little old woman. Very, very old she looked, with a face full of wrinkles, and snow-white hair under her fine muslin mutch; but her eyes were bright, and still blue; and when she smiled, she showed a set of teeth any girl might have envied. She was, indeed, one of the old school. Her granddaughters curtsied to her as they wished her "*Fröhliche Weihnachtsfest*," then Bernhilda took Joey by the hand and led her forward. "This is our English friend, Josephine Bettany, *Grossmütter*," she said.

Something in the old lady's bearing seemed to impel Joey to curtsy.

"She is well-mannered," observed old Frau Mensch—"Exactly as though I couldn't understand!" said Joey indignantly afterwards—"and she has a modest bearing."

Madge nearly choked over this, but Frau Mensch was introducing her, and under the circumstances she felt that she couldn't do better than follow her small sister's example, which pleased the old dame enormously. She patted a chair by her side and said, "You may sit here, *mein Fräulein*, and we will talk."

The autocratic Miss Bettany, head of the Chalet School, meekly took the seat assigned to her, and then it was the

Robin's turn. Old Frau Mensch looked at her with soft-ened eyes. *"Das Engelkind,"* she murmured. Then she turned abruptly to Madge. "I had a little daughter like that once," she said. *"Der Liebe Gott* gave her to me sixty-seven years ago on this very day. Sixty years ago on this very day He took her away to spend Christmas in Paradise. I pray that you, Fräulein, may never know such loss. My sons are good sons; but I can still hear my little Natalie's baby feet, and feel the clasp of her arms as I laid her down when she had wished me *Fröhliche Weihnachtsfest* for the last time."

The Robin came up to the old lady's knee. "Mamma is in Paradise also," she said. "Papa is very far away in Russia; but Tante Marguérite looks after me. Perhaps my mamma is playing with your little girl."

"It may be so," said old Frau Mensch. "Sit on that little stool, *mein Liebling*, and I will tell thee tales of when I, too, was a little maiden—nearly ninety years ago."

They sat down, and she began. And what tales she told them!

Tales of a little girl who lived in Innsbruck. *Grossmütter* told them, too, of one terrible winter spent in Vienna when the cold was so severe that the wolves came howling round the city walls, and the poor died like flies. "We get no winters like that now," she said. "It was cold—so cold! I was not allowed to go outside for fear I should be frost-bitten, and the great stoves had roaring fires in them day and night. I can remember old Klaus creeping into my room during the night to put more billets of wood into the stove, and coming to pull my *plumeau* closer over me."

"How thrilling!" said Joey. "Are there wolves in Austria still, please?"

"But yes, my child. But it needs very bitter weather to bring them to the towns from the forests. You need not fear."

"And it would be bears at the Tiernsee, not wolves," added Herr Mensch, who was seated on the other side of the stove, smoking his long china-bowled pipe, and listen-ing contentedly to his mother's stories. "Do not weary yourself, *Mamachen*, telling these naughty ones your interesting stories.—Shall we not sing a carol, my children?"

Bernhilda rose at once and went to the piano, and they sang *Stille Nacht, Heilige Nacht*, and *Adeste Fideles*, and several other carols. Then Frau Mensch said, smiling, "And now Joey will sing for us, *nicht wahr*?"

"Rather! if you want me to, that is," replied Joey. "What shall I sing?"

"Sing 'The Little Lord Jesus'," pleaded Frieda. "I love it so much!"

Madge went to the piano, and Joey stood facing them all, and sang with round golden notes, as sweet as any chorister's, Martin Luther's cradle hymn:

"Away in a manger, no crib for a bed,
The little Lord Jesus laid down His sweet head:
The stars in the bright sky looked down where He lay—
The little Lord Jesus asleep on the hay.

The cattle are lowing, the baby awakes,
But little Lord Jesus, no crying He makes;
I love Thee, Lord Jesus! Look down from the sky,
And stay by my cradle till morning is nigh."

When she finished, Frau Mensch wiped her eyes. "It is very beautiful," she said seriously. "Now I must go and see to my goose that it may be cooked properly!" And, with this funny mingling of the artistic and the matter-of-fact, she went off to overlook Gertlieb's attentions to the goose.

"Sing to us again, my child," said Herr Mensch. "There is time for one more song before we are called to *Mittagessen*."

So Joey sang again, "The Seven Joys of Mary," and then, since there was still time, the old Coventry carol, "Lullay, thou little tiny Child," with its quaint little refrain of "By, by, lully, lullay."

A frantic fantasia on the bell by Gertlieb summoned them to the *Speisesaal* after this, and they had a magnificent dinner, even though the English Christmas pudding was wanting. The home-made sausages were far nicer than anything the Bettanys had ever tasted in England, and the goose was a miracle of good cooking. The meal was finished off with raisins, nuts, and grapes; and a big box of crackers, which Madge had shyly offered Frau Mensch the day before.

"Now to get ready for our drive," said Herr Mensch. "The snow has ceased, and it freezes hard; so wrap up warmly, every *Mädchen*."

"Isn't this gorgeous fun?" giggled Joey as she snuggled down between Frieda and Bernhilda, with the Robin wedged in, in front of them, while Herr Mensch and Gottfried tucked in the bearskins round them. "O-o-o-oh! Listen to the bells! Isn't it *topping!* "

"Glorious! " agreed her sister as a loaded sleigh drawn by two horses dashed past, the bells on the harness making silvery music in the snowy world. "Joey, are you *sure* you are warm enough?"

"I'm cooked! " declared Joey. "I couldn't get on another thing if you paid me for it."

"Josephine," said Aunt Luise's voice, "here is my fur-lined cloak for you. We cannot have you ill at Christmas-time."

Joey groaned aloud. "I can't get out," she said.

But Aunt Luise was in the sleigh, fastening the great cloak round her, and tucking its folds well over her. "No," she said, "we cannot run any risk of bad colds. Now you will be safe, I think."

She climbed down, and went back to the house, while Gottfried got into the driver's seat with his father beside him. Frau Mensch and Madge sat facing the girls, and an extra rug or two was tucked into the bottom of the sleigh under the hot bricks which were to keep their feet warm. Aunt Luise was not going, for someone had to stay with old Frau Mensch, and Gertlieb was to have two hours off to go and see her mother, and take her Christmas gifts to her brothers and sisters.

They were going at a fine rate now. The horses were young and in excellent condition, and Gottfried was a good driver. They had left the main streets of the city, and were driving through the suburbs in the direction of the Brenner Road. Other sleighs were going in the same direction, and the usually quiet streets were gay with the jingle of sleigh-bells, the shouting of merry voices, and, here and there, bursts of song, as sleigh-loads of young men went flying along. All round lay the mountains, beautiful and remote in their snow-clad splendour, and over all the grey sky, heavy with snow yet to fall.

Herr Mensch, pointing to it, turned round. "We dare not go far," he shouted. "I had hoped to make the expedition to Berg Isel, but it will not be safe with that sky. We must return when we have reached Wilten. See, Fräulein, that is our University Klinik—where we take the sick. Now we shall turn out of the streets, and it is the country. Over there lies our cemetery, which we shall soon pass; and we return from Wilten by the road that winds out into the country, past the Exercier Platz and along the banks of the river."

Madge nodded. She was enjoying the drive as she had never enjoyed anything. Innsbruck under snow has a loveliness all its own, and out here in the country she felt as though she were living in a story.

"Christmas-card land!" laughed Joey. "This is topping —the jolliest ride I ever had! Just look at those trees!"

All too soon they reached Wilten, and there Gottfried turned the horses' heads to the west, driving towards the river. Just as they reached the Exercier Platz, which lay bare and white under its covering of snow, the first great flakes began to drift slowly down from the skies, and by the time they reached the bridge they were enveloped in a whirling white mist, which made driving difficult. Luckily they had not very far to go, and ten minutes later they drew up before the tall house in the Mariahilfe suburb, where Aunt Luise was standing at the door, looking anxiously out for them.

Herr Mensch and Gottfried carried the younger girls across the snow into the house, and they reached upstairs, thrilling wildly; for now there was coffee, and then—*then* there was the Christmas-tree and their presents. Frieda, Joey, and the Robin were so excited they could hardly eat anything, and Frau Mensch, laughingly remarking that they must make up for it at *Abendessen*, led the way into the *salon*, where the curtains had all been taken down and the Christmas-tree in all its blazing glory of tinsel, glass toys, candles, and frosting stood before them.

"Oh!" gasped Joey. "How *beautiful*!"

Bernhilda laughed. "It is a lovely tree, mamma—the best we have ever had. It is like the tree in the book of Märchen!"

"Come!" cried Frieda. "Come and see which is your table, Joey!"

Then Joey noticed that all the little tables in the house were set in a row, and that each was covered with parcels. A card gave the name of each owner, and Frieda was pulling her towards one marked "Joey," while Herr Mensch had carried the Robin to another, where the doll she and Madge had got the day before sat smiling.

It was thrilling work opening the parcels. Frieda was in raptures over her fountain-pen, and Frau Mensch exclaimed with delight at Madge's collar and Joey's bracket, while her husband regarded the fretwork pipe-rack with rather a puzzled air.

Jo herself found books, perfume, sweets, a kodak, a paint-box, and a fountain-pen like Frieda's. Madge was rejoicing over a copy of *Martin Pippin in the Apple Orchard*, and a string of fine amber beads; and the Robin sat on the floor cuddling her dolly, and alternately admiring a set of doll's furniture and a toy town.

It was nine o'clock before everyone had thoroughly examined everything, and finished exclaiming over it and thanking the giver. By that time supper was ready. When it was over, the Robin was carried off to bed by Madge, nodding like a sleepy fairy, while Jo and Frieda followed, clutching all their new possessions. When midnight came the elders went too. Joey woke up as her sister switched on the light. "Hullo!" she said sleepily. "Hasn't it been a glorious day?"

"Hssh!" said Madge warningly, coming over and sitting down on the bed beside her. "Don't wake the Robin."

But Jo was asleep once more, and Madge hurried up to join her as she lay dreaming of her first Christmas in the Tyrol.

CHAPTER SEVENTEEN

The New Term

"WELL, WE HAD a most glorious time, and the splendidest Christmas I've ever known!" Joey heaved a little sigh, partly for remembrance, partly for pleasure.

"*We* had a splendid time too," declared Margia, who was by no means prepared to allow Joey Bettany to carry off all the honours. "We had the *magnificentest* in Salzburg!"

"Joey, when does Grizel return?" demanded Simone Lecoutier at this moment, interrupting what looked like being a stormy argument.

"Hello, old thing!" Joey spun round to greet her French friend. "When did you come back?"

"I returned with Cousine Elise, of course," replied Simone with dignity. "I have been unpacking for Renée and myself, and then I came across to see *you!*—and y-you have not yet embraced me."

"Oh—bother! Get on with it, then!" And Joey presented her cheek for Simone's kiss, since that young lady sounded tearful.

"But when *does* Grizel return?" persisted the French child. "Will she come soon? Or has she left for always?"

Joey looked at Simone with a funny little smile. "Would that break your heart? No; she hasn't left—only gone to be with her grannie, who's very ill. My sister had a letter the other day, and they're afraid old Mrs. Cochrane won't live much longer. She adores Grizel, and it makes her happier to have her, so she'll just stay as long as she's wanted."

"I am sory for Grizel," said Simone, her black eyes growing very big and soft with sympathy. "She loves her grandmother, and it must be hard to lose those one loves."

"Are there any new girls, Joey?" asked Margia by way of changing the subject.

"Two," said Jo briefly; "one junior and one senior, so they won't trouble *us* very much. The senior will only be a day boarder, too. She lives up the valley in that huge chalet, just beyond the fencing. She was at school in Vienna, but her mother has been ill, so they brought Stéphanie home; but she's only sixteen, so she's coming here for a year."

"Hello, Joey!" cried a fresh voice, and Jo swung round to greet Evadne Lannis, leaving Margia to saunter off towards Frieda Mensch, who was talking at a great rate to Marie von Eschenau, Paula von Rothenfels, and Bianca di Ferrara.

It was the first day of term, and already most of the boarders were back.

Two days after Christmas Day, the whole of the North Tyrol had been swept by a tremendous blizzard, which had raged for nearly three days without ceasing. The snow was followed by such severe cold as no one could remember having known for the past sixty years at least. Reports came from the plains that the wolves were already becoming more daring than had ever been known before, and the mountain regions could say the same thing about the chamois.

New Year's Eve had found the Bettany girls and the Robin staying with the Maranis, where they had a very good time indeed. When the day arrived for them to return to the Chalet, Herr Marani came with them, and saw them comfortably settled in. The short rest had done them all good, and Jo proclaimed herself to be growing *fat*!

Joey said, "I say—Simone! You've had your hair cut again. How's that? I thought you were going to let it grow?"

"Maman says that she prefers I shall have it short while I am at school," replied Simone sedately. "I am very glad, because it is so easy to keep tidy."

"D'you think so?" Joey turned and regarded her reflection in the mirror for a minute or two. "It may be for you; but look at *me*!"

Two or three people, who were standing near, heard, and turned to look. They all shouted with laughter as they did so, for a bigger contrast than Simone's neat little black head like a well-polished boot-button, and Joey's tousled, gollywog locks could not be imagined.

"It certainly isn't tidy for you, Joey," chuckled Juliet. "As for Simone, I couldn't imagine *her* hair ever looking like yours. There's absolutely no comparison!"

"Oh, it is tidy—on occasion," returned Jo casually.

"I should think it *was* 'on occasion'! Pity it isn't that oftener!"

"Oh well; we can't all have the same virtues!"

"No," said Gisela, who had overheard the last part of this conversation, "but neatness is a virtue that one may acquire. Therefore, my Jo, go upstairs and brush your hair, for the bell for *Kaffee* will ring very soon, and it is not polite to Madame that you should appear looking like that."

"Oh, bother!" grumbled Jo. "You Austrians *do* insist on your twopence-halfpenny worth of manners! My sister wouldn't mind first day!"

"No; but I do. Come, Joey! Make haste, or you will be late."

Gisela spoke firmly, and Jo knew better than to disobey her; so she vanished upstairs, grumbling loudly all the time at the bother of having to do her hair. Margia accompanied her.

Joey laid down her brush and regarded her head with approval. "It's heaps better now, but goodness knows how long it'll stay that way. There's the bell! Come on!"

They fled downstairs, Jo with her hands clasped over her head so that she might arrive in the *Speisesaal* reasonably tidy. Unfortunately, she forgot the narrowness of the staircase, and banged her funnybone, which drew a low howl from her.

"What on earth's the matter?" demanded Margia, stopping short.

"Banged my elbow!" was the brief reply.

Margia turned back. "You poor old thing! It's a simply

sickening thing to do, isn't it? Almost as bad as biting your tongue!"

Jo got up from the stair on which she had been sitting. "Come on—we shall be late, and Gisela is sure to say it's rude to Madame!"

Margia wisely held her tongue, and they reached the big dining-room in silence.

By this time everyone had come except Grizel, whose absence seemed to make a huge gap. She was by no means one of the oldest there, but she certainly was one of the leaders. Miss Bettany had not yet made her a prefect, nor given her much responsibility; but there could be little doubt that she was one of the people who counted in their little world.

Gisela Marani voiced the fact for them. "It seems strange without Grizel," she said, as she poured out the last cup of coffee. "I hope she will return soon, Madame."

"I don't know when she will come," replied Miss Bettany. "We must go on with the games without her, Gisela."

"Ah, yes," said Gisela. "We shall have to appoint a new games captain for the time, until she returns."

"There'll be skating too," put in Joey. "The lake is bearing, and they say there will be no more snow for a few days. Marie says that if it's still all right they're going to have an ice carnival on Saturday night. They light up the Seespitz end with torches, and have huge bonfires burning on the banks. One of the Tzigane bands comes up and plays, and there is dancing and feasting and heaps of fun. People come from all round to see it—from the plains, and up the valleys. Doesn't it sound *thrilling*?"

"Yes," replied her sister, "it certainly does.—Mademoiselle, you have no coffee.—Joey, fetch Mademoiselle some more; and Miss Maynard hasn't any cake.—Margia, bring the cakes, dear."

The two did as they were told, but Joey's face wore a mutinous expression which deepened as Madge quietly turned the conversation on to some other subject. Later on in the evening she had to go to the study with some books. Madge was alone, writing letters at her desk.

"Madge," she said.

Miss Bettany looked up. "Well, Joey baba, what is it?"

Jo dropped down beside her. "Madge! Be a gem and say we can go to the carnival," she coaxed. "I want to see it ever so much!"

Madge laid down her pen and leant back in her chair. "Joey, I can't say anything definite till I know more about it. I don't intend for one instant to allow any of you actually to join in. There will be far too many strangers there, and I am sure it will be noisy and rough. But I will go over and see Herr Braun tomorrow, and ask him if it will be all right for you to go to Seespitz and look on. If he says that it will, then you shall go for an hour—all the seniors and middles shall, at least. But if he says *not*, then I'm afraid you'll have to content yourselves with looking on here."

"Oh, Madge!" Joey's voice was full of disappointment. "Nothing could happen to us! Why should it? And I do so want to see it."

"I'm sorry, Jo. I'll let you go if it's possible; but I can't promise."

"If such crowds of people come, p'r'aps they'll want the whole lake," suggested Joey hopefully.

"Then you'll be able to see from the dormitory windows," replied her sister. "Now I'm busy, and you must run away. Will you find the other mistresses and ask them to come and see me in half-an-hour's time? Gisela and Juliet can go over to Le Petit Chalet and take charge there."

Joey left the room and devoted the next ten minutes to delivering her messages. Then she turned back into the little class-room where her own clan were roasting chestnuts.

"Nothing doing," she reported gloomily as she flopped down on the floor between Simone and Margia. "At least, if Herr Braun thinks it'll be all right, we may be allowed to go and watch; but if not, then we mayn't!"

A chorus of groans arose. "Oh, what rotten luck!"— "Would Madame agree if we all went and asked her?" —"*Schrecklich!*"—"*Pfui!*"—"*Tristo!*"—"Oh, Joey!"

"It's no use fussing," declared Joey as she accepted the chestnut Frieda dropped into her lap. "Once my sister says a thing, she jolly well sticks to it! "

Finding her chestnut difficult to peel, she put it into her mouth to bite a hole in it. The next moment there was a loud "Pop! " accompanied by yells. The thing had burst in her mouth.

"Ow! Water! Water! " shrieked Joey, whose tongue was badly burnt.

"What on earth is the matter?" demanded Juliet from the doorway. She had been passing at the time of the mishap, and, hearing the noise, hurried to the rescue, quite convinced that someone was badly hurt.

They enlightened her, all talking at once, and she laughed when she understood. "Poor old Joey! No; don't drink cold water! I'll go and get some baking soda from Marie, and that will take the stinging out of it."

She hurried off, and presently returned with the soda, which she put on Jo's tongue.

"It's got a *beastly* taste! " said the patient disgustedly.

"Never mind. It'll help the burning.—The rest of you clear up that mess of shells," said Juliet. "It's nearly eight o'clock, and you can't go to bed and leave the room like that.—Better now, Jo?"

"Yes, thanks," said Joey, who was beginning to recover from her fright.

"Then I must go now. Gisela is waiting for me. Your tongue will be a bit sore tomorrow, I expect, Joey; but it'll soon be all right again. There's the bell. Finish tidying, and then run along to bed.—Frieda and Simone, you'd better come with us."

"And I only had that one chestnut! " mourned Joey as Juliet went off, accompanied by the two middles who slept at Le Petit Chalet.

"Never mind," said Margia consolingly. "There are heaps left, and you can have your share tomorrow."

Then they all trooped off to bed, but that chestnut had helped on something that was beginning to simmer in Joey's brain; and that something was to have direful results.

CHAPTER EIGHTEEN

The Ice Carnival

THE DECISION was made. There was to be no ice carnival for the pupils of the Chalet School. Herr Braun's horror when he heard Madge's queries on the subject had quite settled that.

"But the ice carnival for *die Mädchen!*" he had exclaimed. "Oh no, *gnädiges Fräulein*—it can never be! It is not becoming for young ladies. People come from far and near, and with them they bring beer and *Schnäpse*. That is bad, for they take too much, and there is much roughness and horseplay on the ice. Sometimes there are quarrels, and then we have fighting. Oh no, *mein Fräulein!* But you and *die Mädchen* must lock the doors, and shutter the windows, and go not out at all!"

Madge looked troubled. "Do you think it possible that our part of the lake may be in use?" she asked.

Herr Braun waved his hands in a gesture of helplessness. "I cannot say. It is probable, I think. But I will speak to those who build the bonfires, and ask that one is not placed near the Chalet. That will keep the skaters away. Also, I will have the fencing of the land finished, and we will put very strong padlocks on the gate; but it is all that I can do. At least, *mein Fräulein*, this occurs but once in the year, and it is quite possible that the better people only will come to your side of the lake. The wilder ones will stay at the Seespitz end, where there will be many bonfires and much light."

"You are very good, Herr Braun," said Madge gratefully. "I shall certainly not allow the girls to go outside after nightfall on Saturday, and the fence will be a great protection."

Then she had skated back across the lake to issue her

commands, while Herr Braun sent his men to get on with the fence, with which he was enclosing the Chalet School and its ground. The posts had been driven in before the snow came, and a part of the withe-weaving, which was to build up the fence, had been done. Now the men were set to continue the weaving; and by Friday it was finished; and the Chalet, Le Petit Chalet, the shed, and the cricket-ground and tennis-courts were safely enclosed within a six-foot barrier, which not only shut the school out from curious eyes, but also cut off interesting sights from in-attentive pupils—a rather necessary thing.

Miss Bettany issued her commands; but she omitted to give any reason for them, which was a mistake where one or two of her pupils were concerned. People like her own small sister are usually quite contented to obey orders if a reason is given to them; and Jo had been in many ways treated from a grown-up point of view. Because Madge had chosen to give no explanation of her edict, Joey became restless, irritable, and, finally, downright rebellious.

"It's a mean shame!" she declared to her own special coterie of friends, which consisted of Margia, Simone, Frieda, Marie von Eschenau, and Paula von Rothenfels. "I don't see why we shouldn't go!"

"But it is Madame's desire that we do not," said Marie, who was a law-abiding little soul.

"I don't care," retorted naughty Jo. "I'm going! And I don't care who says what!"

The others gazed at her in awe-stricken silence—all except Margia. *She* flashed a funny little look at the recalcitrant one. Joey flushed pink.

"I mean it," she said defiantly.

"It won't be running away, will it?" queried Margia.

"No; of course not. We're only going for a short while —just to see what it's like—then we'll come back and own up."

"But—will not Madame be very angry?" asked Marie doubtfully.

Up went Jo's head. "Of course, if you're *afraid*!" she said scornfully.

Marie was; but she had her fair share of pride, so she

retorted, "I have *not* fear! But Madame will be very angry, and she will also be hurt, and that I do not like!"

If Jo's tongue had been all right, the chances are that the last part of Marie's final remark might have carried weight. Instead of yielding, she merely snapped, "Don't come, then! We can manage without you!" Then she faced on to the others. "Any more funks here?"

"But I am *not* a funk." Marie was nearly in tears. "I will come with you, Joey, *of course!*"

The "of course" slightly mollified Jo, and, as the others all agreed without further argument, she calmed down considerably.

"Right! Then we'll fix up our plans and go. It can't do any harm just to be on the ice for an hour or so; and we'll own up the minute we get back, so it'll be straight enough."

It *was* straight—up to a point. What Joey wouldn't and the others didn't see was that it wasn't straight right through. It was all very well to say it was a "sporting" thing to do—this was one of Jo's arguments—but they all felt more or less uncomfortable about it.

Meanwhile Madge, having given her commands, imagined that there was no further need to worry, and plunged whole-heartedly into the term's work. The English and German of the school showed a tremendous all-round improvement; but the French of some of the juniors was appalling. Also, at the request of several parents, she had decided to have Italian classes for the seniors. The Chalet School must of necessity specialise in languages, and Miss Bettany had decided that it should have an excellent showing in them.

To these classes Jo, Paula, Marie, and Margia were admitted, although they were two years younger than most of the seniors. The Gräfin von Rothenfels had specially asked that Paula might join them, and had also mentioned that Frau von Eschenau would wish Marie to learn; while Jo and Margia both knew a certain amount already, and would profit by the regular work.

There were time-tables to arrange and rearrange; new stationery and one or two new text-books to give out; one or two kitchen details to see to; and the games to settle. It was hardly surprising that during all the bustle of the first week the mutiny of certain middles should be overlooked.

A fresh fall of snow on the Friday made it impossible for the girls to go out; so when games time came round, the big class-room was cleared, pretty Miss Durrant came over from Le Petit Chalet, where she had been teaching the juniors how to make raffia baskets with beautiful designs of chequers and triangles, and the girls worked off their superfluous energy in "Picking Up Sticks", "Jenny Pluck Pears", "Mage on a Cree", "Butterfly", and other country-dances. Then, when they were all sitting round the wall, breathless and laughing, Mademoiselle played a tune none of them had ever heard before, and Miss Durrant danced for them a morris-jig, which drove them all wild with delight.

"Oh, what is it?" cried Joey, her rebellion forgotten for the moment. "What *is* it, Miss Durrant? It's simply lovely —the jolliest thing I've ever seen!"

Miss Durrant, who was flushed and panting with the exercise, laughed at her enthusiasm. "It's one of the morris-jigs—you people are going to start morris this term —'Jockie to the Fair' it's called."

"It's simply top—er—*glorious*!" proclaimed Joey. "I just *love* it. When can we begin?"

"Jigs? Oh, I'd advise you to learn the steps first," said Miss Durrant demurely. "You surely don't want to start on jigs straight-away?"

"I don't care what we start on so long as we start on something," declared Joey. "Will you teach us the step today?"

Miss Durrant shook her head. "No. You've all been working fairly hard, and morris isn't easy. You must be fresh to do it well. We'll learn a new country-dance, though, and you shall begin your morris tomorrow morning. Form into sets of eight. I'm going to teach you 'Oaken Leaves'."

They ran to do her bidding, and were soon busily learning "Oaken Leaves", with its pretty figures, which was quite new to them. Joey, deeply enthralled by the work, forgot all about her plans for Saturday, and danced hard, all her zest showing in her face. If other people had been contented to let things be, the chances are that she would have forgotten all about the carnival till it was too late to make arrangements. Unfortunately, Simone was rather bored by the dancing, and before going upstairs to change from their tunics, she pulled Joey into a quiet corner and said eagerly, "And for tomorrow, Jo! Where do we meet, and when?"

"Oh, bother tomorrow! I'd forgotten all about it," replied Jo, frowning.

Simone had not been particularly keen on the escapade. However, once she had screwed up her courage sufficiently to enable her to agree to doing it, she did not wish to give up the idea. A wicked little imp inspired her to make the one remark that would bring Joey up to the scratch.

"Have you, then, fear?" she asked.

That settled it. The blood rushed to Jo's face in a crimson tide. "No," she said shortly. "I'll tell you about arrangements before we go to bed tonight." Then she turned and ran off, all the joy and zest gone from her face, and only a heavy frown on her brow. Madge met her, and stopped her to ask what was the matter.

"Jo! What's wrong with you, child? Has anything happened?"

"I'm all right," mumbled Joey, scarlet to the tips of her ears.

Madge concluded that she had quarrelled with one of her friends, and let her go. She could hardly push the question any further at the moment; and next day a letter arrived from her twin-brother, which put everything else out of her head; for Dick had written to tell her that he was engaged to his chief's youngest girl, and that they hoped to be married very soon. There was a note from the lady herself, which showed her to be a jolly, rather school-girlish, person, who evidently took life as a huge joke. She sent her love to her two sisters-to-be, and added that she enclosed some snapshots of herself, so that they could see what she was like. On the outside of the note was scrawled, "Can't find the beastly things. Sending them later." Madge giggled over this, and decided that Miss Mollie Avery was the right person for Dick to marry. She meant to tell Joey about it, but that young woman studiously avoided her, and then Marie contrived to upset a kettle of boiling water over herself, and was rather badly scalded. By the time things were righted, and poor weeping Marie was lying in bed with her own small sister to look after her while Eigen assisted Miss Bettany to do his sister's work in the kitchen, the entire school was playing net-ball, and Joey, at Centre, was unget-at-able.

In the afternoon she and the rest of the middles vanished into the shed, where Rufus, now a handsome fellow, with fine head and great massive body, spent the day with his mother. The Head had said that the girls were not to go outside of the fence today, and, unfortunately, this meant depriving the dogs of their usual walk, so she was glad to hear the sounds of romping that came from the big shed. Marie's accident made a good deal of difference, and Miss Bettany was kept busy till after the girls had had their coffee. As they came out of the *Speisesaal* to go and change for the evening, she contrived to catch Jo, and draw her into the sudy. "Jo, I've had a letter from India," she began.

"When?" demanded Jo.

"This morning, of course—— My dear Joey, what *is* the matter?"

Jo faced on her. "You've had a letter from Dick all day, and never told me about it till *now*!" she gasped.

"But, Joey baba, I've had no time!"

Jo made no answer. She simply stood there, very white, and with angry eyes. Madge looked at her, amazed.

"Why, Joey! What *is* the matter with you? Aren't you well?"

"I'm all right. Don't *fuss*, Madge."

Madge began to get angry now. "You ungrateful child! You don't deserve that anyone should fuss over you!" Then, as the memory of the tremendous news she had just received came to her, she softened. "Joey, don't be so cross with me; I am awfully sorry it's got delayed—the more so because of the wonderful news I have for you. What do you think? Dick is engaged!"

"What as?"

"Engaged to be married. We shall have a new sister before long."

"Rats! I don't believe you!" returned Joey rudely.

Madge was dumbfounded. She simply could not understand this attitude. She never once dreamed of connecting it with her refusal to allow the girls to go to the carnival, and she could not think that it was the result of not giving Joey the letter sooner.

"Joey! Do you realise how rude you are being?" she said quietly. "I have told you that I am sorry that I didn't show you the letter sooner. I see you are very angry with me, but I couldn't help it. Here is the letter; will you take it away and read it for yourself, please? And I don't want to see you until you have come to your senses."

Joey almost snatched the letter from her, and left the room. She *was* cross about not having had it sooner, but the principal trouble was the deep sense of shame she had. She had often been tiresome before this; but she had always been straight. What made it worse was the fact that she was dragging other people into it. She took the letter upstairs and tucked it into her drawer; she didn't feel like reading it just now.

When she got downstairs she found that the others had nearly finished their coffee, and through the unshuttered windows came flickering light from the bonfires which were being lighted. Snatches of music drifted across to them from the lake, accompanied by an increasing chatter of voices as the revellers began to turn up in full force. The carnival was beginning.

Miss Bettany had arranged that the girls were to go upstairs to the dormitories that overlooked the lake, and watch the fun from the windows; so, after *Kaffee*, the girls streamed upstairs, while Eigen closed the shutters of the downstairs windows. This was the chance of the naughty middles. They slipped into the dark cloak-room, and hid among the coats while the others settled themselves in the darkened dormitories. The staff went with the school; Marie was in bed; and Eigen had permission to go to the carnival for two hours.

It seemed ages to the six, standing as motionless as possible in the little cloak-room, before silence settled down on the lower part of the house, though, as a matter of fact, it was barely half-an-hour. When, finally, they felt safe, they closed the cloak-room door very quietly, and switched on the light. Then they dressed as quickly as possible in woollen jerseys, big coats, thick boots, woolly caps and scarves and gloves; lifted their skates carefully lest the jingling should betray them, and stole along the passage and out of the side-door, which had been made for the convenience of the day-girls. It was not till they were outside that they realised just how difficult it was going to be to get down to the lake without being seen.

"What *shall* we do?" asked Margia. "If they see us they'll come after us, and we shall have all the fuss for nothing."

Joey, however, was a resourceful young person. "Go round the back," she said. "Then we can cut across the cricket-ground, and climb over the fence, and go down by the side."

It was the only thing to do. They crept along, keeping well in the shadow of the house until they reached the cricket-field, across which they fled at full speed till they came to the fence. This had to be climbed, but they were all active enough, and even Simone, with a good "boost," was got over it in safety. When they were all at the other side they looked at each other. The excitement was doing its work. Even Joey had forgotten her conscience pains, and they caught hands and ran gaily down to the edge of the lake, where they sat down to put on their skates.

Joey got to her feet. Then she looked round. It was a wild picturesque scene. Overhead was a stormy sky, with a young moon gazing down on the white-clad mountains, remote and silent, even now. Against the snow the pine-woods stood out in black masses, and the ice-bound lake lay like a pool of midnight in its sparkling frame. Great bonfires flared up to the distant stars, casting a lurid light on the snow, and linkmen glided about the lake carrying flaming torches. Already the Seespitz end was crowded with figures, but just where they were it was quiet. On the frosty air the music from the great Tzigane band, playing like possessed creatures near one of the bonfires, came clearly to them. It was a wonderful picture.

The six little girls kept pretty close together. Frieda, Marie, Margia, and Paula were excellent skaters for their age, and Joey, during her fortnight's holiday, had learnt to be fairly safe, though she was by no means as good as she thought she was. Simone was wobbly to the last degree, but Frieda and Marie took her between them, and Paula caught Joey's hands, and they enjoyed themselves enormously for the first half-hour or so.

Then Paula took Marie's place with Simone, and Marie, anxious to prove her skill, began cutting a figure of eight on the ice. Joey watched her with keen interest—so keen, in fact, that she paid little heed to where she was going, encountered the dead branch of a tree which some one had flung on the ice, staggered, tried to recover her balance, and fell headlong, her hands above her head, directly in the path of a skater who was coming along at full speed!

He was going too quickly to swerve, and to the horrified children it seemed as though he must go clear across Joey's fingers. They set up a wild shriek, and as for Joey, she fainted, just as the skater flung himself wildly to one side and fell with a crash on top of her.

It was at this moment that Miss Bettany, hunting through the cloak-room, discovered that her missing pupils had vanished, and dashed upstairs to her room to scramble into her outdoor garments and snatch up her skates before she hurried out to reclaim them.

To say that Madge was angry, is to put it very mildly. She was *furious*. It was bad enough that the other children should have gone; but that her own sister should have set her at defiance like this was unbearable. She shut the door firmly behind her and hastened down to the lake.

A little cavalcade met her as she opened the gate. First came Simone, crying heart-brokenly with Frieda trying to comfort her; then came Marie and Paula, both crying too; lastly, Margia walked sobbing beside a tall man, who carried in his arms a limp burden that lay very still.

Madge said afterwards that she felt her heart stop beating as she saw them. Then she sprang forward. "Joey!" she said.

The stranger spoke in a reassuring tone. "She's only fainted—and she'll be a bit stunned too. I expect she's badly bruised, but that will be all. Let me carry her to the house for you."

The voice was vaguely familiar, but Madge could only think of Joey.

"Bring her in," she said, and led the way up to the Chalet and into the study, where she switched on the light. The stranger laid Joey on the couch, and as he did so she opened her eyes.

"Hullo," she said. "I say! Aren't you the man who helped us in that train accident last term?"

Before anyone could reply, Simone had flung herself down by the couch. "Joey—Joey!" she sobbed.

Then Joey remembered. "My fingers!" she gasped. "Oh, are they still on?" She tried to move, but the action was agony, and she screamed.

"There! Steady!" said the man, who had been stripping off his coat and scarf. "You'll be black and blue all over, I expect. Your fingers are all there; I fell on you instead." Then he turned to Madge. "I'm a doctor—James Russell's my name; you may remember me. If you will permit me, I will examine her."

Madge gave thankful permission, and while Miss Maynard, who had joined them by this time, removed the other children, she helped him to undress Joey and examine her. It was as he had said. Jo was badly bruised. In addition, she had sprained her ankle when she fell, but there was no serious damage.

When things had all been explained, Dr. Russell looked down at his small patient—now safely in bed—with a smile. "You've punished yourself," he said. "You won't be able to move comfortably for a week or more, and that sprain will keep you in bed for longer than that. Oh, I'm not going to rub it in; but you've asked for trouble—and you've got it!"

Then he said, "Good-night," and left her.

Madge came back presently, to find a thoroughly peni-
tent Jo awaiting her. "Joey!" she said.

"I'm a *beast*!" declared Jo. "I'm awfully sorry, Madge;
and it was my fault. Don't blame the others, please!"

Madge—fresh from an interview with Simone, who had
declared it to be *her* fault because she had taunted Joey
with being afraid; and another from the other four, who
had insisted that it was *theirs* for not opposing Joey's plan
more firmly—nearly smiled. She just stopped herself in
time.

"I'm not going to say anything about it," she said
gravely. "I know you are sorry, and won't do it again, so
we'll leave it at that. Now I'm going to give you some hot
milk, and read you Dick's letter, and then you must go
to sleep."

"Shake," said Joey, moving her right arm gingerly.

Madge took the bandaged hand in hers, and then, bending down, kissed her small sister as final token of
forgiveness.

"I *hate* ice carnivals!" said Jo viciously; "and you're a
dear."

CHAPTER NINETEEN

Jo Writes an "Elsie" Book

DR. RUSSELL had been quite right when he said that Jo
had made her own punishment. She had! For more than a
week she was stiff and aching from her bruises and her
sprained ankle, while any movement was a sheer agony
for the first two or three days. Like most excitable children,
she developed a temperature very easily, and during those
first nights she was quite light-headed, which might have
alarmed her sister seriously had she not been accustomed
to Jo. Then, when the worst of the bruises began to heal,
and the throbbing in her ankle grew less, the young rebel
became decidedly bored with life.

Very little had been said to any of them about the ice carnival affair. Bernhilda, it is true, had scolded Frieda roundly, and Wanda had followed her example with Marie and Paula; but the Head had merely informed them that their behaviour had showed that they were unworthy of the trust she had given them, and said that, for the present at any rate, they were to be treated like the juniors and always have someone in authority with them.

This hurt; and the five left the study, weeping bitterly. Miss Bettany had said very little, but what she said was impressive, and they all wished that they had never heard of such things as ice carnivals.

As for Joey, the leader in it all, there was, of course, no need to watch her. She was tied to her bed; the other girls were not allowed to visit her except at very long intervals, and she was thoroughly bored.

"I wish there were some fresh books to read!" she sighed one day.

The doctor happened to be with her at the time. "Find it dull?" he asked.

"Duller than dull! I wouldn't mind so much if I'd only something to read; but I haven't! I've read all the books in the library, and I'm tired of them. Dr. Jem, can't *you* lend me something?"

Dr. Jem—he had told her to call him this—chuckled. "As a matter of fact, I can," he said. "Ever read the Elsie books?"

"No; but I've often heard of them," replied Jo. "Aren't they about an awfully good little girl; and aren't there dozens of them?"

"But how in the world do *you* know anything about the Elsie books?" demanded Madge, who was sitting beside Joey.

"I picked 'em up cheap in an all-sorts shop," explained the doctor. "There are six or seven, I believe. I'd heard one of my aunts talking about them once, and lamenting the loss of her copies, so I thought she'd appreciate them. Anyway, I'll fetch them along sometime. At least they'll be fresh."

"Jolly!" said Jo. "It is decent of you, Dr. Jem."

He was as good as his word. During the afternoon Marie trotted up the stairs with a parcel of books which she gave the delighted Jo, who spread them all out on the bed in front of her and feasted her eyes on them. There were six of them—*Elsie Dinsmore, Elsie's Holidays, Elsie's Girlhood, Elsie's Womanhood, Elsie's Motherhood*, and *Elsie's Children*. Madge, coming upstairs an hour later, found her fathoms deep in the first, and felt thankful.

For the rest of the week Joey revelled in the deeply pious atmosphere of "Elsie" and her companions. The wild adventures with the Ku Klux Klan awoke a desire in her to know more about American history, and she nearly drove Madge crazy with her questions.

At length the sorely-tried sister struck, and vowed she would answer no more. "Read up your history if you want to know!" she cried.

"Well, get me some more books, then, please," replied Joey. "I'd like one all about the War of Independence, and the Pilgrim Fathers, and the Civil War. Oh, and an atlas to find the places! Where's Fort Sumter, and why did its fall start the war? And——"

Madge flew before the storm, and Joey was left with a half-finished question on her tongue; but presently Frieda trotted in with two or three books of general history, and a big atlas. "Madame sends these," she announced. "Do you require anything else, Joey? for I will bring it."

Joey considered. "Yes; you can bring me some paper—reams of it; and some blotchy—oh, and my fountain-pen. D'you mind, Frieda? You *are* a sport!"

Frieda brought her what she wanted, and when Miss Bettany came up in the afternoon she found Joey propped up against her pillows, and a pile of sheets, covered with her irregular writing, on the bed beside her.

"Well," said the elder girl, "what are you busy with now?"

Joey raised an excited face to hers. "Oh, Madge, I'm writing an Elsie book!"

"What! Morals, texts, and all?" inquired Madge, choking back a laugh—she had glanced through one of the books, and knew their type.

"No-o-o!" said Jo reluctantly. "I don't know enough texts."

"I see! How much have you done, Joey?"

"Just the first three chapters," replied Joey. "I'm calling it *Elsie's Boys*, and it's all about the boys—Eddie, and Harold, and Herbert."

"Don't start writing again. It's getting too dark to see, and you'll strain your eyes if you go on."

"Well, can't I have the light on, then?" pleaded Joey.

Madge shook her head. "No; not yet. Lie still and rest. You'll overtire yourself if you don't, and then you won't be able to get up tomorrow."

"Get up? Am I going to get up? Oh, how *gorgeous*!"

"Dr. Russell is coming to carry you down to my study in the morning, and you are to lie on the couch there. Herr Anserl, who will be here for the day, will bring you back here at the end of the afternoon."

"Mag—nificent!" pronounced Jo with a sigh. "I was getting *sick* of this room."

"It's your own fault you're here," replied Madge. "I'm *not* going to lecture now. You've had your punishment, and a fairly severe one. Past things are past. But I do want you to realise that it isn't playing the game to grumble at consequences." Then she changed the subject, and that was all Joey heard about her escapade.

The next day, as soon as Dr. Jem had left her, comfortably arranged on the couch, so that she could see out of the window into the garden, she demanded her "book" and went on with undiminished ardour.

As long as it was advisable to keep her quiet, Madge was thankful that she could employ herself so happily. But Monday of the next week found her back in the schoolroom, settled in an invalid chair, manufactured out of an ordinary one and some wood, so that she could keep her sprained ankle up. She was glad enough to be back with the others, but it was a fearful nuisance not to be able to go on with her writing. Every spare moment she had she devoted to it, and the pile of exercise paper containing the doings of the Travilla boys grew daily larger. Even so, however, she found it difficult to get on as quickly as she

337

would have liked. Then came doubts about it. It was sure to be full of mistakes. It was stupid.

At this juncture Madge unconsciously came to the rescue. "When are you going to let me see that story of yours?" she demanded one day. "Isn't it finished yet?"

"No—not exactly," faltered Joey.

Her sister looked at her amazedly. "May I see it, Joey?" she asked.

Joey mutely held out the bundle, and her sister gasped at its size. "Why, Jo, it's quite a book!" she cried.

Madge went off to her own den with the manuscript. It was some hours before she could get time to look at it.

Jo's writing was not her strong point, and parts of the "book" were almost illegible. Her punctuation was shaky, and her spelling frequently verged on the phonetic. But, for all that, the story was surprisingly good. The characters in it were *alive*, and the young authoress showed a decided gift for description. Dr. Jem, dropping in casually as he often did now, demanded that a chapter should be read to him. So, after some deliberation, Madge selected her chapter and began to read.

"Madge!" Joey stood before them. "*Oh!* How mean of you! How *could* you!"

Madge lifted amazed eyes to the flushed face above her. "Why, Jo——" she began.

The doctor stopped her. "Joey, it was *my* fault. I very much wanted to see what you had made of it, so I asked Miss Bettany to read it to me. I am the one for you to be angry with—but I hope you aren't going to be angry."

The flush died out of Jo's face; she looked at him in a puzzled way. "I don't see why you want to read it," she said slowly. "Madge is different—she's Madge! Why *did* you want to see it?"

"Because," said the doctor, "I had read your fairy-tale in the *Chaletian*. It was very pretty, Joey; but any ordinarily clever girl might have imagined it—though she would not have expressed it in quite your way; that, I grant you. This is a totally different thing, and I wanted to see how you would tackle it. Even the little I have heard has told me what I wanted to know. You can vary your style to suit your subject, and that is a very great thing in story-writing. It's early to prophesy—you are only, how old? Thirteen, is it?"

Joey nodded. She had never taken her eyes off his face once, and Madge was listening with the same tense eagerness.

The doctor looked at them. "You are very young, Joey; but I'm going to take it upon myself to prophesy after all. If you go on as you have begun, and work hard at grammar and literature, and all your other lessons, then, one day, you will write something really worth while."

Joey's eyes widened, and the slow colour flushed her face. "Do—do you really mean that?" she asked in a breathless sort of way. *"Really?"*

"Yes; I mean it. It will be hard work, Joey, and hard work all the time; but if you go on you will do it."

There was a little silence in the room. Then Jo, the undemonstrative, suddenly flung her arms round the doctor's neck, and gave him a vigorous hug. "Oh—oh! Dr. Jem! I love you!" she gasped.—"Madge, I *will* work—I'll be an angel of goodness at my lessons!" She released the doctor and collapsed into her sister's arms. "Madge!"

"You silly child!" Madge scolded her gently. "You mustn't get so excited, Joey baba.—Yes? Come in!" as a tap sounded at the door.

Gisela Marani appeared. "Excuse me, Madame, but Miss Maynard wished to know if Joey had told you that papa is here, as he has to hurry back, and would be glad to see you if you can spare him the time."

Madge looked at Jo speechlessly.

"I quite forgot!" said the future authoress.

CHAPTER TWENTY

Joey and Rufus to the Rescue

JANUARY had faded into February before Grizel returned
to school. She was a somewhat subdued Grizel, for her
grandmother had died only the week before she came back,
and the long days spent in the old lady's room had helped
to soften a certain hardness in her character.

She had also come back full of the Girl Guide movement. A company had been begun in the High School
which she and Joey and Rosalie had attended when living
in England, and most of the members of their old form
had joined. Grizel, always interested in anything new, had
learned all she could about the Guides, and she was very
keen for Madge to start one in the Chalet School.

Mr. Cochrane had bought his small daughter two of the
handbooks, *Girl Guiding*, and *Girl Guide Badges and
How to Win Them*, as well as half-a-dozen story-books on
the same subject, and she lent them all round among the
seniors and middles in her desire to make the others keen.
Many of the badges appealed to them. Living in a moun-
tainous district where ropes were in constant use, they saw
the value of learning the various knots. The making of fires
in the open, as well as the cooking and housewifery knowledge demanded for many of the tests, seemed matter-of-
course to girls whose mothers did a great deal of the house-
keeping and house-caring themselves. The Nursing tests
did not appeal to them quite so much; but the Arts and
Crafts they hailed with joy. Wanda wanted to take Artist's
Badge; Gisela felt a yearning for Basket-Worker's and
Embroiderer's; Joey plumped for Book-Lover and
Authoress.

The upshot of all this was that, finally, a deputation
waited on the Head in her study and begged that she would
let them start a Guide company.

Miss Bettany surveyed them consideringly. "Why?" she asked.

"It's such a fine thing, Madame," said Grizel eagerly. "It bucks you up and makes you smart!"

"Also, I like the idea of learning to do many useful things," added Gisela. "It appears to me that to be a Guide makes one also capable of much."

"And it will make for oneness," put in Juliet. "That is a big thing."

Miss Bettany nodded. "Yes, Juliet; you are right. A sense of unity is one of the biggest things in life. So is all-roundness and smartness. But the Guide movement seems to me to hold even more than that—it gives you a big outlook, and strengthens one's ideas of playing the game and being straight. And those are very big things indeed."

"Will you help us, then, Madame?" asked Grizel. "May we have a company?"

"Yes," replied the Head. "I had intended speaking to you about it before we broke up—which we do in three weeks' time—so it is only anticipating things a little. We cannot do anything much about it this term, I'm afraid. You must all work up for your Tenderfoot badge, and you can begin to learn Morse for your Second-Class. Next term we will begin in real earnest."

There was a little pause. Madge could see that the girls wanted to ask her something else, but that they felt shy about it. "What else?" she said, looking straight at Gisela.

"Will—will you be our captain, Madame?" said the head girl in response to the look. "We would wish it if you would."

Miss Bettany flushed with pleasure. "I should like to be your captain," she said quietly. "Joey and I are going home to England for these holidays, and I hope to be able to go to an instruction course for Guiders while we are there. It will be difficult for me to get training otherwise, I am afraid. By the way, Jo does not know of my arrangements. Will you please say nothing to her till I give you permission. I would not have told you, but, you see, you have rather forced my hand."

She smiled at them, and then dismissed them to go and tell the others that it was all right, and they were going to have their Guide company.

"But what about *us*?" demanded Amy Stevens. "*We* can't be Guides, 'cos we're not eleven yet."

"You can be Brownies—if Madame can get someone to be your Brown Owl," replied Grizel, finishing rather doubtfully.

"Probably Miss Maynard or Miss Durrant will do that," suggested Juliet.—"I say! It's half-past five and we ought to be at prep."

Silence presently reigned over the big school-room, where thirteen people sat struggling with algebra, and French essay, and history; with Juliet, the duty prefect, sitting with them, and striving to prove something complicated in conic sections. Joey Bettany, taking a peculiar attempt at a simultaneous equation up to her for explanation, thanked goodness that *she* hadn't such awful things to work out. She hated mathematics, and considered equations of all kinds an ingenious form of girl-torture.

Juliet, who *was* mathematically inclined, was rather horrified at the muddle Joey had made, and set to work painstakingly to help her to unravel it. Jo listened to her explanations with about half an ear, and then, having said she understood, went back to her seat, and proceeded to make confusion worse confounded, which resulted in her work being returned next day, so that she was kept in after *Mittagessen* to have an algebra lesson to herself while the others went out for a romp along the edge of the lake.

Before the younger Miss Bettany fully understood what she was supposed to have done, both she and Miss Maynard were hot and weary; and finally the pupil remarked that she loathed maths.

"Because you can't do them—or, rather, won't try," replied Miss Maynard scathingly. "Take your book back to your desk and work out that example and the next *correctly*."

Joey took her untidy exercise-book back to her desk, and flounced down on her chair with a scowl that said what she daren't speak aloud. Miss Maynard ignored her

342

little exhibition of temper, and went on with her corrections.

It was a glorious March day. Outside the sun was shining brightly, and a fresh wind was blowing the cobwebs away.

There was no hope of being let off; Joey knew that very well. She heaved a deep sigh and returned to x and y.

"Finished?" asked Miss Maynard, looking up for a moment.

"Not quite," said Joey truthfully.

"Hurry up, then! Ten minutes steady work will do it!"

Jo heaved another sigh, and then suddenly gave up the struggle, and went at it. Twenty minutes later she was racing along the lake-path like a mad thing, her coat flying open, and her hair tossing wildly in the wind. Grizel joined her just opposite the Kronprinz Karl, where already there were signs of activity in preparation for the coming season.

"O-o-oh! Isn't it a *gorgeous* day!" Joey gazed round her rapturously. "I loved the winter here; but it's been deadly dull since the snow melted. I must say I think thaws are the most boring things imaginable. Let's join the others over there, shall we?"

They walked along towards the little rivulet which acted as the outlet for the mountain streams. In the summer it was rarely more than a trickle of clear water bubbling over the pebbly bed. There was nothing of the trickle about it today. The snows on the lower slopes of the mountains were melting rapidly, and a perfect torrent of grey, rushing water fought its way between the narrow banks to the lake, whence the ice had melted for the most part, though blocks of it still floated here and there.

"If that river rises much more, it'll flood," said Grizel, as they stood watching it for a moment. "Look at those alders, Joey. They're nearly washed out!"

"Not quite, though! Madge says they root pretty firmly," replied Jo. "I s'pose they *have* to or they wouldn't be able to grow by the sides of rivers. What a noise the water makes, doesn't it?"

"Come on! Let's cross," said Grizel. "Miss Durrant must be talking of something awfully jolly, to judge by the

343

row they're all making! Let's go and see what it is." They hurried down the path to the light plank bridge which crossed the stream. Grizel danced over without a thought, but Joey shut her eyes as she made the crossing.

"Why on earth——" gasped her friend. "Joey! Why do you do that?"

"The water makes me so giddy," explained Joey. "I love the *sound* of it; but I do loathe to see it rushing along like that. It makes me feel all queer and funny."

"Silly flop!" said Grizel, a little contempt flavouring her tone.

"I can't help it!" Joey flushed scarlet. "It always does! It looks so—so *cruel*; as though it didn't care for anybody or anything! Ow!" She concluded with a wild yell as Rufus leapt up against her. He was growing up into a handsome dog; very big, with enormous paws, and a fine head. Several pounds of excitable St. Bernard puppy flung against her proved too much for Jo, and she sat down violently on the wet grass, Rufus rolling madly beside her, frantic with joy.

"Get *up*, Joey!" began Grizel. Then she stopped as a scream of terror cut across her speech.

There was a splash. Then a little grunt from Joey, and the next minute she was tearing over the ground like a possessed creature, while Miss Durrant, who had seen what had occurred, raced after her.

The Robin and two or three of the other juniors had been playing together with the paper dolls which had been Simone's hobby during the previous term.

Robin had brought them out with her today, and had been playing with them quite happily on some big stones a little way on past the bridge. A sudden breeze had lifted one and drifted it slowly across the grass towards the water. The Robin had run to catch it, and had forgotten to look where she was going and fallen headlong into the icy torrent that was raging down to the lake.

It all happened so quickly that no one could reach her in time to save her, and it seemed as if she must be whirled down to the lake before any of them could prevent it. Mercifully, her coat caught for a moment on one of the alder-trees swept by the water, and this just gave Joey time to clamber down a little in front of her. Then the coat gave and she was swept onwards. The current drove her into the bushes where Jo was waiting, and, clinging to them with one hand, she stretched out and caught the baby's shoulder with the other. Then she set her teeth and held on.

The racing water was frightfully near, and she was sick and giddy, partly from terror, partly from watching that swirling torrent. But any idea of giving up was very far from her. She clung with might and main to the little shoulder and the bushes, wondering dully how long it would be before the alders would give under the strain and send them down with that wicked grey water that seemed to be coming higher and higher.

It seemed hours to Joey, though actually it was barely two minutes before there was a crash and a splash, and Miss Durrant was standing beside her, waist-deep in the water, and lifting the Robin with one arm comfortably round her, while with the other hand she too held on to the bushes, for the force of the snow-fed torrent nearly took her off her feet, strong, big woman as she was. "Hold on, Joey!" she said. "Here come the others! Hold on!"

Then Gisela and Bernhilda bent down from the bank, and between them took the unconscious Robin from the young mistress. Miss Durrant promptly transferred her support to Joey, who found things fast becoming misty and unreal to her. Then there came fresh help, as a huge tawny body plunged in, and Rufus caught his little mistress's skirt between his strong young teeth! It was an easy matter after that for Miss Durrant to scramble up the bank, still holding Joey with one hand, lest even Rufus's strength should prove unequal to the strain. After that the world grew black, and Joey never knew what happened next. Of Miss Durrant's lying down on her face and lifting her by degrees from the water, while Rufus tugged and scrambled up beside her; of the sudden appearance of Dr. Jem on the scene, and his picking her up and racing back to the Chalet with her; of the stripping off of her wet clothes, and the plunging of her into a hot bath, she remembered nothing. She came back to the world with a hot stinging taste on her tongue—a nasty taste—and the rough hairy feeling of blankets next her skin.

"Hallo!" she remarked. "I say! What's up?"

"All right, old lady! Lie still," said Dr. Jem's voice. "Drink this like a good girl!"

Jo obediently swallowed it, and spluttered. "Ugh! What *filthy* stuff!" Then she remembered. "The Robin!" She gave a sharp cry.

"Quite safe," replied the doctor. "Snug in bed and fast asleep!"

"Sure?" Jo was growing drowsy.

"Certain. She's had a bit of a shock, of course, but she'll soon get over it. Now we're going to pack you off to bed. Come along."

Joey felt him lift her, but she was too sleepy to think of anything. Her head dropped on to his shoulder, and by the time he and an agitated Miss Maynard had her snugly tucked up in bed with hot bottles all round her she was lost to the world.

"She ought to be all right," murmured the doctor. "We've been so quick, I'm in hopes that she may even escape a cold."

"And the Robin?" queried Miss Maynard.

"She ought to do all right too. She struck her head as she fell, so she was a bit stunned and didn't take in the full horror of it. There *may* be a little concussion—I can't say yet! But otherwise, there's no need for alarm, I hope. You said Miss Bettany and Mademoiselle had had to go to Spärtz?"

Miss Maynard nodded. "They went to get some things we needed."

"I see. Well, I'll go and meet them and break the news gently. Don't leave these two alone—you can send up that sensible head girl of yours."

So it happened that half-an-hour later Madge Bettany and Mademoiselle la Pattre, climbing up the last bit of the mountain-path, were met with the story of the latest doings of the Chalet girls. They were horrified, but the doctor managed to calm their fears. He walked back with them before going off to the Post, where he had been staying ever since the night of the ice carnival, and, as he had predicted, neither Joey nor the Robin was much the worse for their adventure. Joey woke with a bad headache, the result of the neat brandy he had made her swallow to stave off a cold; and the Robin had a lump the size of a pigeon's egg on the top of her head, and was inclined to be miserable and fractious for a day or two, but otherwise they were both all right.

The girls were tremendously thrilled over having a heroine in the school; and Rufus was in a fair way to be spoilt for his share in the business.

The most discontented person in the school was Grizel. "It's too bad!" she moaned. "If only our Guide company had been formed, Joey would have been a Guide, and then she might have had the Silver Cross for saving life at the risk of her own. It's hard luck!"

CHAPTER TWENTY-ONE

An Unpleasant Problem

THANKS to the doctor's rapidity of treatment, and also to the treatment itself, nobody was much the worse for the ducking so far as bodily comfort went. But there was a certain amount of unpleasantness over it. For one thing, the juniors were forbidden ever to play near the brook again, no matter *who* was with them. For another, it was requested that, for the remainder of the term, walks should avoid that side of the valley, and should be taken either up to the Bärenbad Alpe or in the Seespitz direction.

Hitherto, no one had minded much where the walks went; but it only needed this prohibition to fill all the middles, at any rate, with a deep desire to go in the Geisalm direction. Even Frieda, the law-abiding, was overheard to say that she wished Madame had not made that rule. As for Grizel, she was nearly speechless with indignation. Nearly; but not quite. She managed to rake up enough breath from somewhere to voice her disgust. "It's too bad," she wailed. "The water from the dripping rock will be simply *shooting* down! I did want to see it in full swing!"

Thus reminded of the rock which overhung part of the way to Geisalm, and over which water trickled from a spring at the top on to the footpath, making it necessary to rush past at full speed—a proceeding not unattended by danger, since the path had broken away here, and the lake was deep at this point—everyone was seized with a deep desire to see what it would be like now. "I expect it's a regular waterfall," said Joey mournfully. "Oh, I *should* like to see it!"

"I also," put in Simone, who was standing at her elbow as usual. It was significant that no one suggested going to the Head and asking her to remove her embargo. They had learnt by this time that when Miss Bettany *said* "No," she *meant* "No."

"It's all your fault, Simone!" cried Margia unexpectedly. "Yes it is!" as Simone bristled up furiously. "If you'd never played with those idiotic paper dolls of yours, we wouldn't have had them! If you hadn't had them, you wouldn't have got tired of them. If you hadn't got tired of them, you wouldn't have given them—some of them, anyway—to the Robin. "If——"

"Oh, choke her off, somebody, do!" groaned Grizel. "It's worse than the house that Jack built!—Dry up, Margia, and give someone else a chance to talk! The amount you do, it's impossible to get a word in edgeways! Madame has said we're not to go there, so we *can't* go there, and that's an end of it! Now shut up and talk about something else!"

"Shut up yourself!" Margia was beginning heatedly, when Miss Bettany appeared on the scene.

"Grizel! Margia! Is that the way you talk when you are by yourselves? I think I had better send someone to sit with you children during your free time if that is the case. Clear away those books at once, and put this room tidy; it's more like a pig-sty than a form-room in a school!

348

And please don't let me hear *any* of you talking like little hooligans again!"

She walked off, leaving them all angry and rather afraid that she might carry out her threat and send them someone to sit with them while they played.

"It'll be Grizel's fault if we do," said Joey, who was feeling the effects of the spring weather, and was cross and out of sorts. She wandered over to the window and stared dismally out at the high fence of withes which cut off the view of the lake. There was little else to see, although in a week or a fortnight's time the ground would be green with the young grass.

"What are you staring at?" demanded Margia unamiably. "You might come and lend a hand instead of gawping out of the window like that at nothing."

" 'Gawping' is slang," pointed out Joey, somewhat priggishly, it must be confessed. "You're breaking the rules."

"You're so particular yourself!" fumed Margia, who felt that this was adding insult to injury, and resented it accordingly.

"You've *never* heard *me* say 'gawp'!" mentioned Joey self-righteously.

"I've heard you say a dozen worse things!" retorted Margia.—"Oh, *Simone!*"

For Simone had burst into tears. "You are so un—kind!" she sobbed. "Always it is me who must do the work—but always!"

"Oh, for goodness' sake, stop it!" groaned Jo.

Almost on the words the door opened, and Mademoiselle came in. "Simone, why do you then cr-r-r-y?" she asked dramatically.

"*Je n'en sais rien!*" sobbed Simone.

"In English, if you please."

Simone gulped noisily, and then wailed, "I do not know!"

"It's the spring," said Miss Durrant, who had been standing behind her, an interested spectator of all this. "She ought to have some sulphur or something, to cool her down a little."

At this lively prospect Simone literally howled, bringing

Miss Bettany to the spot. She gave the French child short shrift. "Off to bed with you!" she said. "A dose of salts will put you right.—Come here, you others. Joey, let me see your tongue."

Joey obligingly hung it out as far as it would go, and Margia followed her example. Miss Bettany promptly decided to dose them all round, and went off to superintend the mixing of a big jorum of sulphur, lemon juice, tartaric acid, and one or two other items. At seven o'clock the next morning she made the round of the dormitories, and saw to it herself that every girl took her dose.

The next day "Mrs. Squeers," as naughty Jo promptly christened her sister, appeared again with her medicine. All swallowed their doses in silence.

Work, that day, proceeded as usual. The only thing that was *not* usual was the behaviour of the dogs. Usually quite happy with their freedom of the enclosure and the long walk they always had with the girls in the afternoon, today they were restless and unhappy. Zita prowled up and down the fence nearest the Kronprinz Karl and the torrent, every now and then sitting back on her haunches and baying mournfully—an example faithfully imitated by her son, who yelped loudly.

"I can't think what has happened to those dogs," said Miss Bettany during the half-past ten break as she stood by the gate, talking to Miss Maynard and watching the girls, who were wandering about in twos and threes. "I never knew Zita to behave like this before!"

"You know the old idea that a dog howls at the approach of death?" said Miss Maynard.

"Marie has been wailing about it whenever we've met," replied Miss Bettany. "She's convinced that something awful is about to happen. But you aren't superstitious, surely?"

Miss Maynard laughed half-ashamedly. "I'm not, as a general rule. But there's certainly something wrong, and Zita knows it. Animals always sense coming disaster, I think—dogs and cats especially."

"She may be feeling unwell," suggested Madge. "Let's go and examine her."

350

They strolled across to where Zita stood with Rufus nuzzling against her, and Joey petting them both, the ever-faithful Simone beside her. She looked up as the two came near.

"I can't think *what's* the matter with Zita," she said seriously. "I've loved her and talked to her, and she only howls. Oh, do you think she's ill?"

"Let me see," said her sister, bending over the big dog.

Zita turned mournful eyes on her young mistress, then she lifted her nose to the sky and gave utterance to her long howl. Miss Bettany patted her head and felt her nose. "Poor old Zita! I wish you could tell us why you are so unhappy! What is it, my dear? Have you hurt your paw? Let me see."

Zita allowed them to examine her feet one by one, but there was nothing wrong there.

"Is she going to die?" asked Joey almost tearfully.

"Nonsense, Joey!" replied his sister sharply. "I don't know what can be the matter, but she's well enough in herself."

"Perhaps she wants a long walk," suggested Miss Maynard. "She seems terribly restless. Look at her!" For Zita was once more pacing along the fence.

Miss Bettany looked after the dog, and then glanced round. "I've a good mind to send the girls for their walk now, and let them have their lessons this afternoon. Look at that sky! There's a storm threatening in the near future."

Miss Maynard nodded. "You're quite right; there is! Isn't this Mr. Denny's afternoon, though? There won't be much time for lessons!"

"*Kaffee* can be half-an-hour later for once, and Mr. Denny has them in three classes, so we'll cut the middles' sewing, and they can have my history instead; I don't suppose *they* will object! There's the bell. Send Gisela round to the various forms to tell them to get ready, and ask Miss Durrant if she will take the middles and the seniors. Juliet and Gisela can take the juniors. They are to walk round the lake to Buchau and back.—The little ones

351

had better go no farther than Seespitz. This is very tiring weather."

"It's horribly oppressive," agreed Miss Maynard as she set off on her errand.

Needless to state, the girls were charmed at the idea, and ten minutes later were all ready. Then a queer thing happened. Joey went, as usual, to fetch the dogs. Rufus came eagerly enough, but Zita merely looked at her pathetically, and bayed again. She simply refused to stir from where she was.

"What a queer thing!" said Madge when she heard Joey's report. "I do hope she's all right. Leave her, Jo, if she won't come, but take Rufus."

However, when she saw the two long files of girls marching down to the gate, Zita reluctantly left her post and followed them, although she kept looking back at the three mistresses who were left behind.

"I simply don't understand it," said Miss Bettany. "Zita has never behaved like this before."

"It is the spring, perhaps," suggested Mademoiselle. "It is affecting the younger girls, and why not the dog too?"

"That must be it," agreed Madge. "Well, shall we go for a stroll in the other direction? We might go out of the pine-woods gate, and walk down by the river and along the lake-path home. What do you say?"

"I have much to do, *chérie*," said Mademoiselle. "If you will forgive me, I will stay behind and finish my work."

"You need a walk, really," said her Head. "However, if you want to work——"

"I ought to stay too," laughed Miss Maynard. "I have a pile of algebra books to correct. But they can come later on, and I'll come with you now."

They set off across the enclosure to the gate which opened on to the pasture, close by the pine-woods at the base of the slopes of the Bärenbad Alpe. There was no wind today, and the woods were very still. The only sound they could hear was the roaring of the torrent as it thundered down the valley to the lake.

"What a noise the water makes!" exclaimed Miss Maynard as they neared it.

A sudden turn in the road had brought them in full view of the stream, and a magnificent sight it was: the grey foaming water, tossing and boiling between its narrow rocky banks, fighting every inch of its way to the Tiernsee. It was a bare six inches below the summit of its banks, and it looked to Madge Bettany as if it must, ere long, overtop them and fling itself across the valley. She remembered it as it had looked on that hot day in the summer when they had gone dry-shod over the pebbles on their way to the Mondscheinspitze for her birthday picnic. She recalled, too, how Bernhilda had told her that three bridges had been swept away by the winter floods, so that now there was only a log across it. She glanced down to where she knew the log to be and felt a little wave of thankfulness to see it still there.

"Here's Herr Braun," said Miss Maynard suddenly.

Madge looked up, and saw the good-natured hotel-keeper coming to meet them. His face was very grave, and all the cheeriness seemed to have fled from it.

"*Grüss Gott, Fräulein,*" he said as he reached them.

"*Grüss Gott, Herr Braun,*" replied Madge; then she added, "the stream is very full, *nicht wahr?*"

"Too full, *mein Fräulein*, too full!" he said.

"How do you mean—too full?" asked Madge, paling slightly.

He explained. "As you can see, gracious lady, the banks are narrow. There is a great deal of snow still melting. That means that there is much water still to come down. If it should occur that the water was dammed higher up, then, when the dam broke—as assuredly it must—there would be little or no room for the flood to pass to the lake, and it would overflow and flood the valley."

"Has it happened before?" asked Miss Maynard.

"Twice within my recollection. Once, the village up yonder," he pointed up the valley, "was completely overwhelmed, and there were many lives lost. That is why all the houses are now built on the higher ground, while many are raised off the ground altogether. The other time it was not so serious, but still much of the valley was several inches under water for two days, and there were many goats drowned."

"And do you think there will be a flood now?" demanded Madge.

He shook his head. "*Der liebe Gott* knows, and He only. At least, *mein Fräulein,* you are safe, and the little ones; for the Chalet stands high. Nevertheless, if you will permit that I advise you, I would suggest that you take food with you tonight upstairs. If there should be a storm, it might chance that the water will rise high enough to make it unpleasant for you to eat in the lower rooms. It would soon drain away to the lake; but it is always well to be prepared." By this time, they had reached the Kronprinz Karl, and he bade them farewell, repeating his advice about the food. Then he left them and they walked home along the lake-path.

"What shall you do?" asked Miss Maynard of her Head.

"I wish I knew!" Miss Bettany looked worried. "If I thought there really would be a flood, as he suggests, I should take the girls to Seespitz, and ask them to take us at the Gasthof for the next few days until the water goes down. But I don't want to do that unless it is absolutely necessary." She paused; then, "What do you think yourself?" she asked.

Miss Maynard frowned. "I really don't know. It's fearfully difficult to decide."

Mademoiselle, tackled on the same subject, held the view that doubtless Herr Braun was exaggerating the danger. She also pointed out that the Kronprinz Karl lay much nearer the stream, and also that it lay at a lower level than the Chalet, and therefore might quite possibly be damaged by a flood while the school stood high and dry. The ringing of the bell for *Mittagessen* put an end to the discussion, and nothing more was said. After dinner, the afternoon's engagements were explained to the girls. The juniors would have their singing as usual at half-past one, while the middles had history, and the seniors mathematics. Then the middles would have their singing lesson, and the juniors would make up the French they had missed in the morning. It would then be the turn of the seniors for singing, and the middles and juniors would do English literature and German dictation respectively. Finally, all the school were to have half-an-hour's folk-songs at the end of the afternoon instead of the beginning. Then Miss Bettany made the announcement which set everyone gasping with surprise. "After we leave the table," she said, "everyone will go over to Le Petit Chalet. The juniors will bring their night things, brushes and combs, and washing paraphernalia, over here. The elder girls will bring the bedding, and we will make up your beds over here for once. Grace!"

She said grace, and then marshalled them out of the room, and saw them over to Le Petit Chalet, where the prefects took charge. Then she turned back to the *Speise-saal*, where the excited mistresses awaited her.

"So that is your solution of the problem?" cried Miss Maynard. "I congratulate you, Madame! It's quite the best you could have made!"

"But why? I don't understand," said Miss Durrant plaintively. "Is anything wrong that you are doing this?"

"Herr Braun is afraid the river may flood, and flood badly. I don't suppose we are in any real danger, but it's best to be on the safe side, and Le Petit Chalet lies lower than the Chalet itself; so I decided to bring the babies over here. Now come with me, all of you, and let us decide how we can best manage."

They went upstairs, and an exciting time followed while they pushed beds together and fitted in mattresses for the juniors. When half-past one came Miss Bettany and Miss Maynard went off to take their various classes, leaving Mademoiselle and Miss Durrant to wrestle with the problem of fitting thirteen extra people into the upstairs rooms.

Downstairs, in the big class-room, "Plato" struggled with the excited juniors. He wondered vaguely why they were all so much upset; but he lived largely in a fairy world of his own, and as long as they did not sing out of tune he did not worry about them particularly. It was worse when the middles came, for Miss Bettany had felt it would be wiser to give them some explanation of the state of affairs, and they were deeply thrilled. They simply couldn't give their singing-master any attention, and, finally, even "Plato" the gentle was roused.

Flinging down his baton he clenched his fists and hammered on the music desk, effectually awaking their interest at once. "This is terrible!" he shouted. "Nay, more! It is blasphemous! You debase the divine Apollo! You wrong the celestial Euterpe! It is not to be borne!"

The middles looked at him with gasping surprise—not at his invocation of Apollo and Euterpe. They knew all that he could teach them about those divinities by this time. No: what startled them was his anger. During the whole of the two terms during which he had taken them for singing they had never once seen him in a temper, and had, indeed, decided that he didn't possess one. Now, with his eyes blazing, the colour coming and going in his cheeks, and his lips set in a thin, hard line, they suddenly realised that "Plato" was, for once, in a thorough-paced rage, and that they must be careful.

For a moment no one quite knew what to say. Then, suddenly, the decision was taken out of their hands. A vivid flash of lightning leapt across the sky, tearing the sullen greyness apart; there was an awful silence; then a terrific crash of thunder, and at the same moment the rain came.

CHAPTER TWENTY-TWO

The Flood

"PLATO'S" WILD OUTBURST had brought Miss Bettany from
her study. She never got any very clear idea of what had
happened to upset the master, for the suddenness and
awfulness of the storm brought "Plato" to his senses. He
was thoroughly ashamed of having lost his temper; and
when Miss Bettany, shouting to be heard above the noise
of the rain and the thunder, asked what had happened,
he stammered out something about "the little maidens are
excited—upset by the approach of the storm."

He got no further, for Simone flung herself on the young
head-mistress, crying hysterically, "Oh, is it the flood? Is
it the flood?"

Madge shook the child. "Stop crying *at once, Simone!*"
she thundered. And Simone promptly stopped.

"Plato" had heard the question in open-mouthed amazement. "But, Sweeting," he cried, "there will not be a flood
as in the days of Noah! There cannot be! Our dear Lord
has given us His promise!"

Madge's eyes dared the girls to laugh, while she explained rapidly what they feared. "Plato's" face was grave
when she had finished. "I must go at once, Madame. My
sister is at the hotel, and it stands even lower than the
Kronprinz Karl, for it lies in the little dip near the fence.
If, in truth, there is danger of the flood here, how much
more there!"

"Bring your sister here," suggested the young head-
mistress. "It will be safer, and, if there *should* be a flood,
we might need a man."

He bowed sweepingly to her. "You are kind, Madame.

357

We will come with pleasure. My dearest Sarah has a great dread of water, and she will be happier here with you. I go; I will return swiftly."

They saw him crossing the enclosure with great bounding steps before he was lost in the grey mist of rain that beat down as though the skies were attempting to swamp the earth.

Miss Bettany no longer doubted that the torrent would flood—it most certainly would. But she hoped that the fact of the Chalet being raised above the rest of that part of the valley would tell in its favour and save them. There was quite a deep dip between them and the river, and this would help to carry off some of the waters.

"Will the whole valley be flooded?" demanded Jo suddenly.

"No; I don't expect it for an instant. I think the river will overflow its banks a little, but I don't suppose it goes much farther than just the pasture round," replied Madge. —"Put those desks straight, girls. Take out all your books and carry them to the stationery cupboard. I don't suppose the flood will touch us, but we'll run no risks."

She hurried off to give the same commands to the other girls, and for the next hour they were busy packing away all spoilable things, while the mistresses, Marie, and Eigen provisioned the dormitories as if they expected a siege of weeks. If only it had once stopped raining, Madge would have rushed the girls along to Seespitz. But she dared not risk it in that awful downpour, and it continued all the afternoon and evening in a steady, relentless torrent.

"Plato" duly returned with his sister, who, rejoicing in the name of "Sarah", had been christened "Sally-go-round-the-moon" by naughty Jo—"Sally" for short. Sally was short, sturdy, and plain, with a pair of twinkling brown eyes, which went far to reconciling the girls to her lack of beauty. Usually she was most matter-of-fact and full of common-sense. But her brother's remark that she was terrified of water was no more than true. The twinkle had faded out of her eyes, and she was very white and shaking when she entered the Head's study.

"My dear, I can't thank you enough!" she jerked out.

"I am a perfect fool where anything in the nature of a flood or running water is concerned."

"But I question if there will be a flood," put in her brother. "The river appeared to me to be lower than it was. Mayhap the snow has ceased to melt, or the water has found another outlet."

"I hope so, indeed," said Madge absently.

She left her guests to themselves in the study and went off to superintend matters. Later on Miss Denny made herself useful by helping to put the juniors to bed; while her brother moved desks and heavy furniture, and carried loads of fuel upstairs in case it should be needed. By eleven o'clock at night everything was finished, and the girls were all safely in bed and sound asleep.

Before she went up to her own room, where Joey and the Robin were already tucked in, Miss Bettany opened the jalousies at the study window and looked out. The rain had ceased to fall, and the full-moon was struggling out from behind the ragged clouds that were chasing each other across the sky. The wind was rising, and howling in melancholy fashion among the black pine-woods at the back of the house. In the distance the steady roar of the torrent could be heard, and Madge noted that the sound seemed less than it had been early in the day. Clearly the river was falling, and therefore the danger was past. A heavy "pad-pad" of feet behind startled her as she leaned against the window looking out, and she turned swiftly, to find Zita beside her, looking at her with anxious eyes.

"How you startled me, Zita!" she said, with a little laugh at her own silliness. "Poor old thing! What is the matter with you? And where is Rufus?"

Zita whined softly. Her dog instinct had sensed coming danger, and she was doing her best to warn her young mistress.

Madge closed the jalousies again, glanced round the room to see that everything was right, and then went out, switching off the light, and followed by Zita, who kept closely to her. The Head bolted the front door and locked it safely. Mademoiselle had made the round of the form-rooms earlier in the evening, and made sure that all the

windows were shut so Miss Bettany left them alone, and
went to the kitchen to take Zita to her own quarters. At
the door she paused. She didn't think there was any likeli-
hood of a flood now; still, perhaps, the two dogs would
be happier on one of the upper landings. She went into the
kitchen, called Rufus, who was curled up in a huge woolly
ball, and went upstairs, accompanied by both animals. In
her own room Joey and Robin lay together in her bed profoundly asleep. Anxious not to wake them, Madge began
to undress by moonlight. It was a glorious night after the
storm. The clouds were vanishing, and the dark lake reflected the light of the moon in its tumbled waters. Madge
opened the window and leaned out, revelling in the beauty
that lay around her. Suddenly the expression of her face
changed as a dull, thundering sound came to her. Louder
and louder it grew. The dogs outside began to bay loudly;
there were startled cries from the wakening girls. But
Madge Bettany paid no heed to these. Her eyes were turned
towards the valley where, coming with a swift, relentless
sweep, a wall of water, fully six feet high, raced across the
pasturage to the lake.

In a flash she realised what had happened. The torrent
had been choked somewhere up in the mountains. This
accounted for the river's falling. Then the barrier, whatever
it was, had given way, and the great mass of the water had
been literally hurled down to the valley below.

Even as the thought passed through her mind the wall
broke around the Kronprinz Karl, which for a few moments
was smothered in the foam. Then it raced, lower, but still
horrible to watch, right across the valley to the Chalet.

There was a minor crash as it encountered the six-foot
fence. But it was not to be expected that anything so light
should prove a barrier, and the next second it broke round
them, and the Chalet groaned and shuddered under the
force of the blow. It all happened so quickly, that to
Madge it seemed as if no time had elapsed between the
moment when she had first seen that horrible grey, white-
crested wall of water rushing down the valley and the
moment when it broke against the school. The horror of it
stunned her for a moment.

Then a voice from the bed roused her:

"The foot had scarcely time to flee
Before it brake against the knee,
And all the world was in the sea.

"It *is* the flood, isn't it? I say! *That* was a whanger!"

"Stay where you are, Joey," cried his sister as she hurriedly pulled her dressing-gown round her. "I'm going down to the others.—It's all right, Robin, darling!" as the baby turned a scared white face to hers. "Joey will stay with you, and I will come back soon." Then she vanished, and the two little girls were left alone together.

Joey's first reaction was to tumble out of bed and race over to the window. She gasped at the sight she saw. All round there was nothing but water, which seemed to be becoming momentarily deeper. Already it was well up to the first sash of the ground-floor windows, and it seemed to be rising in surges.

After the first two or three washes there were no more waves; but it was quite alarming enough to see the water rising, creeping foot by foot up the side of the house. Joey could see the Kronprinz Karl, which, as it stood at a much lower level, was heavily awash to the first-floor windows. From downstairs came cries and sobs. Then there was the patter of feet as the girls climbed up to the next storey.

The door opened, and Madge came in. "Get up and dress," she said quietly. "Joey, you must help the Robin. I must go to Miss Denny."

"I wish Dr. Jem were here!" sighed Jo. "I can't think why he should be at Innsbruck just when we need him most!"

"Be quick, child," said her sister gently. "Help Robin, and dress yourself."

"But *don't* you wish he was here, Madge?" persisted Joey as she began to put on the Robin's stockings.

Madge blushed, and shook her head. "I must go," she said; and left them to dress.

When they were ready, Jo looked out of the window once more. The water was up to the top of the ground-floor windows, but, as far as she could tell, was not rising now. The trouble lay in the fact of the narrowness of the valley, and the unusual fullness of the lake. It would drain off by way of the Tiern; but it looked like being a fairly long business.

"*What* a mess things will be in downstairs!" observed Jo. "I should think the place will be about knee-deep in mud. It'll take weeks to clean!"

Zita, who was near her, pushed a big sable head under her arm in search of petting. The dog knew that things were not right, and she was frightened. Joey stood pulling her ears absently, while the Robin hugged Rufus, who had followed his mother into the room. Here Miss Bettany found them, when she came along later to bring them some hot cocoa and biscuits, and to see that all was well with them.

"I'm sending Juliet up with Simone and Frieda," said the Head. "You are to stay here until I send for you. The others are quite safe with Miss Maynard and Miss Durrant to look after them, and Mademoiselle is taking care of Miss Denny, who isn't well. There isn't room for everyone in the other rooms, so I want you to stay here. I shall be in and out all the time, and you are quite safe. They will be bringing the boats along presently; and then you shall all go over to Seespitz until the waters go down again."

"And *that* won't be long," remarked Joey, who was hanging out of the window once more. "I b'lieve it's going down already. Look, Madge!"

Madge came and looked. "I believe you are right, Joey," she said. "It would drain away fairly quickly, of course; and the wind will help it."

"What about Le Petit Chalet?" asked Joey.

"Well, it isn't on the same level, of course, and it's a much lower house; but I don't think it has really suffered much more than this," replied Madge. "Now I must go."

"*Must* we stay here?" pleaded Joey, catching at her sister's arm.

"Let me go, Joey! Yes; of course you must!"

Madge went off to send up Juliet with the other two, and to help Mademoiselle to calm the fears of the more excitable of the girls. One or two of them were completely hysterical, and it was to prevent the impressionable children from seeing this that she kept them away from the others. Vanna di Ricci and Luigia di Ferrara in particular were very bad. Both were highly-strung excitable girls, and they had completely lost control. As far as possible, they had been isolated from the others, and were in Miss Maynard's little room with Bernhilda the placid, and Gisela, strong and calm, with them. The others were crowded into the big green dormitory and the little blue one, so that they were all on the top floor or the second one.

As the Head went upstairs to send Juliet with the other two down to her room, she was confronted by "Plato". "Pardon, Madame," he said with his old-world courtesy, "will you permit that I offer a suggestion?"

"Yes, of course," replied Madge. "What is it?"

"It is that our little damsels should sing," he replied. "Music acts as a soporific to disordered nerves; song is a drug to calm fears. Let us gather on the stairs, and all carol gaily."

Madge agreed that his idea was a good one.

There was a little silence when the singing was finished and Miss Bettany came out of the blue dormitory. "The water is falling," she said quietly. "I think it would be as well for you all to go and lie down. The danger is past, we hope; and you are all very tired. But, before we go, let us thank God, Who has kept us safe in the midst of so many and great dangers." She dropped on her knees as she spoke, and the girls followed her example. There was no thought of differences of creed in that moment as the school followed her through the General Thanksgiving and the well-known "Our Father". The Fatherhood of God came very near many of the elder girls then.

They were all so worn-out with excitement and loss of sleep that even the discomfort of their unusually close quarters could not worry them. When Madge went the round half-an-hour later, it was to find nearly everyone asleep already. Gisela was waking, and thrilled to the few words of thanks and praise her head-mistress bestowed on her. But the only other girl awake was Joey, who was cuddling the Robin, so soundly asleep that she scarcely moved when Miss Bettany gently lifted her out of the other child's arms and laid her down on the pillow.

"I couldn't help it, Madge," said Joey. "She's so wee—and I wanted something to hold; *badly*, I did!"

"I know!" Madge sat down beside her. "It's all right now, Joey." She took the hot sticky little paw Jo thrust at her in her cool grasp. "Go to sleep, Joey baba. All's well now!"

"You won't leave us?" pleaded Jo. "You'll stay with us now?"

"No. Don't worry, darling; I won't leave you."

Joey's eyes were growing heavy. Her long lashes fell on to her cheeks. "Madge, dearest," she murmured drowsily, "oh, I *do* so love you! I hope—I—hope—Dr. Jem——"

There was no more. She was asleep.

CHAPTER TWENTY-THREE

Joey's Bath

FOR LONG HOURS the Chalet School lay sleeping. They were all worn out with excitement and want of sleep during the early hours of the night, and most of the other inhabitants of the valley were up and out and hard at work before one of the girls stirred.

Joey was the first to open her eyes. For a moment she wondered where the yellow cubicle curtains had vanished, and why the Robin was snuggled down beside her. Then she remembered. With a low exclamation she scrambled out of bed and ran to the window, which stood wide to the sun and the breezes, and poked out a ruffled head. It was a curious scene of desolation which lay before her eyes. The ground immediately round the Chalet was clear of water; but there was a thick layer of grey mud all over it In the dip beyond there was a small pond, and the Kronprinz Karl was still surrounded, while the lake was tossing madly under the whip of the north-west wind upon its swollen waters. All around, wherever the ground was low, water was standing, and bushes and trees rose from lakes and pools all over. A haystack which had been swept down by the flood was entangled in some wild barberry bushes; and as for the six-foot fence, it was a thing of the past. Here and there a stake rose forlornly from the ground; but the withes were scattered all over, and it was quite obvious that the work must be done over again.

Jo had just taken this all in, when a little stir from the couch brought her in, and she turned round to find that her sister was looking at her with startled eyes. "Hello!" she said gaily. "It's gone down."

"What has? Where?" asked Madge foggily, for she was only half-awake.

"The water, silly! Mean to say you've forgotten about it? You can't be well!"

Madge sat up, fully awake by now. "No; I haven't forgotten, of course. Only I was so sleepy. Gone down, has it? That's a blessing!"

"Not everywhere," said Jo, who was hanging out of the window once more. "The hollow is swimming still, and it's all round the Kronprinz Karl, but we're clear. There's oceans of mud everywhere, though."

Madge threw back the bed-clothes, and got out of bed. "Let me see, Joey. What a mess! I wonder what the downstairs rooms are like."

"Awful, I should think. Are we going to get up now?"

"Yes. It must be fearfully late! Just look at the sun! I wonder Marie isn't about. Where are the dogs?"

"Outside, I suppose," replied Jo. "I say, what an adventure we've had!"

"More of an adventure than I like, thank you!" retorted Madge. "I hope to goodness we're going to have a little peace after this. We've done nothing but have excitements ever since we came to Austria. I don't want any more adventures for a long time to come!"

Jo considered her sister with her head on one side. Her remark appeared to have nothing to do with the subject. "I wonder when Dr. Jem will get up from Innsbruck," she observed.

Madge turned to the mirror, and began to brush her pretty hair with much vigour, and without saying one word.

"He's sure to dash up when he hears," pursued Jo.

"Do talk quietly, Joey!" exclaimed Madge. "You'll wake up the Robin, and I want her to have her sleep out, but she won't if you go on yelling at the top of your voice like that."

Jo moderated her voice, but she was far too excited to stop talking. Madge was dressed and downstairs before she had begun to brush the thick mop of her hair; and sundry sounds told that the other members of the Chalet School were waking up.

The damage done *in* the school was not very extensive. The rooms were muddy, of course, and far too damp to be used for two or three days. One or two books which had been overlooked in the hurried clearing-up of the night before could never be the same again; and one or two of the chairs stood in need of repair.

Miss Bettany collected all this information, and then turned to the rest of the staff. "What do you think?" she asked. "This is the twelfth of March, and we break up on April the second—that's exactly three weeks. Shall I break up now, and bring the girls back earlier? Or shall we just carry on as best we can until the proper date?"

"Oh, carry on, I should think," said Miss Maynard. "For today, of course, we can't do much. The rooms must be cleared and dried first. But it's Thursday, luckily. I should let the juniors have lessons in one of the big dormitories, and the middles in the other. The seniors might help to sweep the mud out of doors. Then Marie and Eigen can scrub the floors and get the stoves on. Set all the doors and windows open, and I should imagine the place will be comparatively dry by tomorrow. Then, if we can manage again tomorrow, we shall have the week-end, and everything ought to be all right again by that time. If you can start Marie straight away after breakfast, I'll clear away the breakfast things and wash up. I don't teach the first period, luckily!"

"Then," added Mademoiselle, "I will attend to the cooking during the next period. I could not scrub a floor, I! But I can cook!"

"I'll clean furniture when I'm free," decided Miss Durrant. "I'm a dab at cleaning windows too," she added, laughing.

"And I'll do odd jobs," agreed the Head. "Well, at *this* rate, I see no reason for breaking up early. I must wire the parents that we are all quite safe, and then, I think, we might get to work."

The staff were very pleased with the arrangements, but the girls were *not*. They had looked forward to a thrilling time of spring-cleaning, and the news that the younger ones, at any rate, would have lessons as usual completely upset their calculations.

Meals and lessons were a good deal of a scramble that day. The seniors and the mistresses worked hard to get the place into something like order. Eigen and Marie produced brooms, and the seniors swept the grey mud out of doors, where the sun and the strong wind were already drying up the sodden earth as quickly as possible. Herr Pfeifen, the father of the two servants, came along to see if his children were quite safe, and to let them know that all was well at Wald Villa, their home. He insisted on lending a hand, with the result that soon Marie was hard at work, scrubbing the floors, while Eigen lit huge fires in all the stoves, and stoked them assiduously. Shortly after noon, Herr Braun came round from the Kronprinz Karl, to see how it fared with the school. The hotel was much worse off, for, standing at a lower level, and almost on the bank of the river, it had received the first fury of the torrent, and the wooden verandah had been badly smashed, while the water had covered the first two floors. "And I have just had all painted and polished!" he groaned. "Now it will all be to do over again, and the season is at hand!"

"Perhaps it will scrub clean," said Madge comfortingly. "How is Frau Braun?"

"She is working hard," he replied. "Ah well! The good

God sent the flood, and doubtless He had some great purpose behind it. We can only bow to His Will!" With which truly pious remark he said good-bye, and left them.

By the evening the Chalet was clean once more, and it was drying rapidly. Miss Bettany looked round, pleased with the result of her labours. "Tomorrow we must attend to Le Petit Chalet," she said. "It is smaller than this, of course; but, unfortunately, it lies in the hollow, and the flood washed higher. I see the water is draining away from the dips, so I suppose it will be clear by Monday. The Seespitz path is fairly dry now, and I am going for a walk up there. If anyone likes to get into thick shoes, and coat and tammy, she can come with me."

There was a shout of joy, for the girls had been indoors all day, and were longing to get outside. The next moment the air was full of confused shouts and exclamations as they all fled to get ready. Ten minutes later, the whole thirty odd of them were walking demurely down to the path which had been cleared of mud earlier in the day, and the four mistresses came behind them.

Once they were past the white-painted fence, which showed by a mark half-way up where the water had reached, they broke rank, and the juniors ran, laughing, and chasing each other gaily up the lake road, while the middles wandered along in clumps, and the seniors, talking very seriously, paraded along by the edge of the lake. The staff, with one eye on the younger girls in case of accident, were busily discussing the next term's arrangements. There would be a good deal to see to, for Miss Bettany had several new pupils in prospect, and one of her reasons for going home to England for the holidays was to engage another mistress and a matron. "I shall get an English mistress," she said. "Now that we are growing so quickly, I really need more time, and as long as I have to teach all the English subjects to the seniors, and history and literature to the middles, I simply can't *make* the time!"

"We shall be very big next term?" queried Mademoiselle.

"Between forty and fifty, at least. It is quite possible that we shall be more, because we may get a few day-girls from the summer visitors. Of course the Maranis, the Mensches, and one or two others cease to be boarders; and next term is the last for Gisela and Bernhilda. Still, we are doing very well. We need a matron too. We've managed quite well, so far; but it will be far better to have someone— Good heavens! What's that?" as a splash and several shrieks rang out simultaneously. With one accord the staff threw its dignity to the winds and tore down the road, to find Amy Stevens, the Robin, and Simone Lecoutier scrambling out of the ditch at the side of the road. It was full of water and mud, and anything more disgraceful than the three dripping objects that Gisela, Bernhilda and Juliet hauled forth on to the road it would have been hard to discover.

"Girls!" gasped Miss Bettany. "What *were* you doing? Back to school at once, you three.—Miss Maynard, will you take them, please? Hot baths, hot drinks, and bed at once.—Joey, come back on to the path! How on earth did you get there?"

She might well ask! The ditch which lay between the roadway and the mountain slope at this point was, normally, two feet wide at the most. Since the night before it had increased to four feet in width, and its waters washed up against a steep bank covered with young heather and curly fronds of bracken. How Jo had managed to get across without falling in was a mystery. How she was going to get back seemed likely to prove another.

Jo evidently thought so herself. "I can't!" she said agitatedly. "It was a fearful scrum to get here. I can't get back, 'cos it's too steep."

Miss Bettany measured the distance with her eye. "You'll have to jump," she said. "Come down as far as you can, and then jump hard so that you clear the ditch. I'll catch you."

"No, don't! *Please* don't!" begged Joey. "Honest Injun, I'd rather you didn't! I can jump it all right—*really* I can!"

"I'm afraid you may hurt yourself," began her sister, but Jo waved her aside.

"I won't! I truly won't! Please let me alone!"

Realising that the child was working herself up to a

violent pitch of excitement, Madge yielded, much against her better judgment, and stood back, motioning the others to do the same. They obeyed at once, and stood watching a rather frantic Jo, who crept down as far as she dared, and then cautiously straightened herself. "I'm coming!" she cried, as she braced herself for the spring. "One—two —three—*O-o-ow!*" As she finished counting, she gave a mighty leap downwards. She cleared the ditch; she cleared the path—it was narrow just here—she went clean over, into the lake, and, with a terrific splash that quite outdid anything the others had accomplished in that line, she vanished under the water.

She was at the surface again in a second, and was swimming frantically for the bank. As a general rule, the water was not shoulder-deep here; but, then, you couldn't go by general rules today, as Miss Maynard remarked later when she heard the full story. Miss Bettany was leaning over and catching her wrists as she clawed at the bank. Miss Durrant joined her, and between them they lifted Jo out just as Dr. Jem appeared on the scene and took in the situation at a glance. "Hurry her home," he cried, not attempting to greet anyone. "Don't let her stand for a moment! Here, I'll take one side. Miss Durrant and Mademoiselle will look after the girls—and you, Miss Bettany, grab this awful infant with me. Now then, young lady, just buckle your stumps a bit!"

It was, of course, the end of the walk. Jo was raced home as hard as they could go, and obliged to share the fate of the other three. Mademoiselle, certain that the lake-path was charged with accidents today, and convinced in her own mind that it was tempting Providence to go any farther along it, marshalled the girls into "croc," and, with Miss Durrant at the head and herself at the tail, marched them back to school, uttering exclamations and ejaculations.

"Just as though she were a sky-rocket!" said Grizel. And was promptly embroiled in an attempt to explain to Luigia di Ferrara just wherein the likeness lay.

"What on earth made you do that?" demanded Dr. Jem of Joey later on when she was safely tucked up in bed.

"Hadn't you had enough of water for once in your life without pitching into it like that?"

"Well, I never *meant* to do it," argued Jo. "It was Madge's fault, really."

"My fault! How was it *my* fault?" demanded her sister indignantly. "It was your own stupidity! If you'd let me catch you as I wanted——"

"We'd both have gone in," Joey finished for her. "My weight would have sent you flying! O-o-oh! Wouldn't it have been priceless! You wouldn't have looked very dignified, my dear, pitching into the lake with me on top of you!"

Madge shrugged her shoulders. Then she laughed. "That's true for you, Joey, my child! But I don't for one moment believe your weight could upset me to *that* extent."

"I was jumping," Jo reminded her. "I jumped for all I was worth."

"I rather think you did!" laughed the doctor. "Well, 'All's well that ends well'; and it's high time you were off to sleep. You four must all stay in bed tomorrow till I have seen you. I don't, for an instant, expect there will be anything wrong with you, but it's just as well to be careful! Now, go to sleep. If you are very good, I may have something to tell you in the morning!"

"Oh, what?" Joey started up in bed.

He promptly laid her flat again, and tucked the clothes firmly round her. "You don't hear till the morning; and only *then* if you've been good.—Miss Bettany, you shall report to me."

"I think you're mean!" grumbled Jo as she settled down. "Oh, all right, I'm *going* to sleep! Good-night!"

"Good-night," replied the doctor. "Pleasant dreams!"

But Jo was buried in oblivion, and gave him no reply.

CHAPTER TWENTY-FOUR

Joey's Future Career is Settled

As MIGHT have been expected, the first person to wake that next morning was Joey. It was barely six o'clock when she stirred, opened her eyes to their fullest extent, and then sat up, wide awake. As Le Petit Chalet was far from fit for them to be in it, the juniors were still sleeping over in the Chalet, and were likely to remain there for two or three nights longer, so sleeping arrangements were, as Grizel had remarked the night before, rather on the crowded side. Joey stretched herself luxuriously, and then glanced down at the Robin, who lay in the profoundest slumber, her dark curls all rumpled, her lovely little face flushed with sleep. "Darling!" murmured the elder child. "I hope we can keep her for ages! It's just like having a wee sister of my own! She is a pet!" It was not in Jo Bettany, however, to spend time over thoughts like these. She had a horror of anything approaching sentimentality, and, except when she was well off her guard, never voiced her affection for other people. Now she slipped cautiously out of bed, and hunted for her dressing-gown and bedroom slippers. She wriggled into them with an eye on the couch where her elder sister lay sleeping as peacefully as the baby, and then, catching up her towels and her clothes, made for the bathroom. Ten minutes later she returned, dressed as far as her knickers, and proceeded to give her golliwog mop a good hard brushing till it shone glossily. Then she got into her gym top and tunic, caught up her slippers from beside the bed, and tiptoed cautiously from

372

the room, leaving the other two blissfully unconscious of her disobedience to Dr. Jem's orders of the night before.

Downstairs Marie was moving about already, intent on getting most of the day's work finished, so that she might go over to Le Petit Chalet and help to set it to rights. Eigen was busily stoking the stoves in the form-rooms and Miss Bettany's study, with Rufus accompanying him— apparently to see that he did his work properly. Marie looked up from her rolls with a cheerful, *"Grüss Gott,"* as Joey dashed into the kitchen demanding something to eat; but Eigen was far too busy to pay attention to anyone.

Marie rose to the occasion with a roll and some cheese, and Joey wandered forth into the fresh spring air, munching happily. She was wildly curious about Dr. Jem's remarks of the night before, and spent her time in wondering what it was he had to tell her. Of his hint that she should hear only if she had been good—which, she supposed, meant if she had obeyed his orders—she took no notice. As a matter of fact she had forgotten it, and she only remembered when she went in to seek a coat, as the morning air was sharp. "Goodness!" she gasped; and collapsed on to the lowest stair where she had been standing. Then, "Oh, but he *couldn't* be such a mean! He just wouldn't!"

A little doubt as to whether the doctor would really keep his word crept into her mind. Finally, she put her coat away again, took off her slippers, and stole upstairs in her stockinged feet. A minute later, Madge was rudely awakened from a thrilling dream by a scarlet-faced Jo shaking her.

"Made! Madge! Wake up, do!"

Madge sat up in bed, pushing back her hair from a startled face. "Joey, what is it? Are you ill?" She stretched out her hand and felt Joey's.

"Oh *no*!" said Jo promptly, as if she and illness of any kind were utter strangers. "I'm not ill in the least! Only I got up, after Dr. Jem said I wasn't to until he came, and now perhaps he won't tell me what he said he would!"

"Hush-sh-sh!" warned Madge, glancing across at the bed where the Robin was sleeping. "Don't wake Robin! Here, sit down on the edge here! You are an idiot, you know, Joey. You seem all right; but I do think you might have remembered!"

"I'll go back to bed if you like," suggested Joey in very subdued tones.

Madge considered the idea for a moment. "No; I don't think you need this time, as you are fully dressed. You certainly *look* as though there was nothing wrong with you!"

"I've just eaten a roll and cheese," said Jo, as if this were a guarantee of her all-rightness.

The elder girl relaxed, and bit her lips to stop herself from laughing. "You really are *awful*, Joey baba! All right! I'll tell the doctor I said you might."

"Madge! You gem!" Joey hugged her sister vigorously. "Then he will tell me what he was going to tell me! I do wonder what it is!"

"Well, it's no use asking me, for I haven't the least idea. He hasn't said a word to me about it," declared Madge as she threw back the *plumeau* and got out of bed.

"Reach my slippers over, Joey, there's a good child. Thanks!" She put them on, and then went across to the bed and bent over the Robin. News from Russia was very scarce, and Madge could not forget the pretty Polish mother who had died in decline. She was almost more careful of her youngest pupil than she was of her delicate sister. Luckily, the Robin was sleeping healthily, and they had been very quick in getting her home.

"She's all right, isn't she?" queried Jo.

"Yes; I think so. Now you can trot. I'm going to dress; then I'm going round to see the others. Put on your big coat if you want to go out. Tell Marie I shall be down presently, will you?"

Jo nodded, and left the room. Going downstairs she started whistling the Nonesuch air, and was promptly caught by Miss Maynard, and fined. Whistling was forbidden in school, and Jo had simply asked for trouble, as the mistress reminded her in somewhat caustic language.

Jo had nothing to say for herself, and listened meekly to Miss Maynard's strictures on her behaviour, shooting away downstairs as soon as she was free, and giving

Madge's message very briefly to Marie, before calling to Rufus and Zita to follow her out of doors.

Through the gaps where the fence had been she could see the Kronprinz Karl, the Post, the Zeidler, and the other hotels. The little valley was full of people working to repair the damage done by the flood. Already workmen were busy rebuilding the verandah of the Kronprinz Karl. The Villa Adalbert was receiving a fresh coat of paint. And along the banks of the stream were men busily engaged in deepening the bed.

Jo was so interested in what was going on that she paid no attention to footsteps behind her, and was considerably startled when a strong arm swung her round and she found herself facing Dr. Jem.

"Now then, young woman," he said sternly, "what did I say about bed?"

"Madge said I might——" began Joey. Then she stopped. She knew, better than anyone else, that if she had not been up and dressed before her sister woke up she would have been kept in bed until the doctor's arrival. Jo was nothing if not honest. "I mean—I was up, and she said I might stay up," she finished.

Dr. Jem scowled at her portentously. "Mutiny in the ranks, eh? Why can't you be obedient, you scaramouche? How do *you* know you're not sickening for something awful?"

"Like—like thrush?" said Jo unexpectedly.

"Well—er—no; not quite that. Still, that's not the point."

"I know it isn't! I forgot, you see. I *did* offer to go back."

"A lot of use that will be now! Let's have a look at you."

Joey promptly put out her tongue and offered him her wrist. He laughed.

"You monkey! Well! There's nothing wrong with you so far as I can see. All right! Passed with a clean bill of health!"

"Oh! Then *will* you tell me what you said you would last night?" pleaded Jo, clinging to his arm. "I'm *aching* to know!"

375

"I'm coming in to see your sister about ten o'clock," he replied. "I'll tell you then."

"But I'll be having lessons then—geometry," protested Jo.

"Then you can come out of your class for once," he replied. "I want to tell you when your sister is there——"

"Madge is up now. Oh, *do* come *now* and tell us!" Jo put forth all her coaxing powers into both voice and face as she spoke, but he was adamant.

"It can wait till ten o'clock. I mean what I say, kiddy," he added gravely. "It won't do you any harm to wait. Now I must go. Tell your sister from me to keep the other infants in bed till I come, and you keep out of draughts." He was hurrying off, when he suddenly turned and called the child to him. "Joey! Come here, please! Don't you have a singing-lesson today?"

"Yes! Why?" demanded Joey, staring at him wide-eyed.

"Mr. Denny is ill," explained the doctor. "I am just going to him."

"Oh, *poor* 'Plato'! D'you want me to tell Madge for you?"

"Yes, please. Will you say that I am afraid he will be ill for a while. And, look here, just keep it to yourself for a bit!"

"All right," nodded Jo. "I'll tell Madge, but no one else."

"Good girl!" he said. "You'll get your reward all right —at ten o'clock!"

This time he really did depart, and Joey was left to return to the house, where she encountered her sister, who asked where she had been.

"'Plato's' ill," said Jo in reply.

"Do you mean you have been to the Adalbert?" demanded Madge.

"No; I met Dr. Jem, and he told me to tell you. Oh, and he's coming to see you and me at ten o'clock. He's going to tell me then!"

"Joey! Talk sense!" cried her sister in exasperated tones. "Tell you *what*?"

"What he said he would. The others are to stay in bed, by the way, till he comes. I say, Madge, I think 'Plato' must be awfully bad. The doctor said he'd be ill for a while. Will that mean no singing-lessons?"

"I don't know." Madge looked worried. "Don't say anything to the others, Jo. Mr. Denny is not strong, you know."

"He behaved like a brick the other night," replied Joey. "No; I shan't say anything—Dr. Jem told me not to. Is breakfast nearly ready?"

During breakfast it was noticeable that Joey Bettany was unusually quiet.

This state of affairs lasted right through the bed-making period, and when Frieda asked her to come for a run by the lake before school she was startled by the answer she received, "Sorry, but I can't. Too busy!"

"But you do nothing!" protested Frieda.

"I'm doing a lot; I'm thinking," replied Jo with dignity.

"Mind you don't hurt your brain, then!" jeered Grizel, who was passing and had heard.

Jo said promptly, "All right, Frieda; I'll come after all, I think. Race you there!" And she set off at top speed, followed by Frieda, who was waking up, and was a very different person from the shy junior who had come to the Chalet School three terms before, although she still was much quieter than many of the others.

Rufus, who had been ambling along beside his young mistress, uttered a wild yelp and flung himself after her. They tore madly down the path, nearly fell over a group of the prefects who were busily discussing the examinations, which lay only a week ahead, and wound up their wild career by collapsing in a heap at Miss Durrant's feet.

"Get up!" she said severely when she had recovered her breath. "Get up *at once*, both of you! —Frieda, I am surprised at you! —Jo, what does this behaviour mean? Take that dog back to his proper place, and please don't race about in that mad way again!"

They got meekly to their feet, and Jo, calling Rufus to order—he was rolling wildly in the grass—led him off to his own quarters. Then, as the first bell rang just then, she made her way to the form-room to get her books out for the first lesson.

It is to be feared that very little sense was to be got out of the younger Miss Bettany during that period. She listened blandly to Miss Durrant on the subject of similes and metaphors, and when invited to show how much she had learnt by explaining what a simile was, absently murmured something about "a cake eaten in Lent in Yorkshire"—an answer that created quite a sensation.

Miss Durrant was righteously indignant, but much of what she had to say passed harmlessly over Jo's head, for at that moment she caught sight of the doctor walking up the path, and was at once lost to the world. Fifteen minutes later Maria Marani came to ask if Joey Bettany might please go to Madame in the study. Joey scarcely waited for permission to go.

She scampered down the passage, and literally fell into the study. The doctor was there, with Miss Bettany sitting opposite him, her eyes bright, and her cheeks vivid with excitement. As her little sister came in she held out a hand to her. "Come here, Joey baba! I am proud of you!"

Jo went to her sister's side. "Proud of me? Why, Madge!"

"Listen to what Dr. Russell has to say to you," replied Madge, slipping her arm round the slender waist.

Joey turned big black eyes, gleaming with excitement, on the doctor.

"Do you remember writing your 'Elsie' book, Joey?" he asked.

Joey nodded dumbly. She couldn't speak.

"Someone showed me your story in the *Chaletian*," he went on. "I liked it. It is good, you know, Joey. You have told the tale simply and freshly, and your people live, which is a big thing. I heard of a competition for children. Ten pounds was offered as a prize for the best short story written by a boy or girl under eighteen. There was a second prize of five pounds, and another of one pound. I thought your little tale might have a chance, so I copied it out and sent it. Yesterday I had a letter from the judges—a registered letter. Here it is!"

He handed it over, and Jo took it with hands which literally trembled. It was addressed to but she had no time for that at present. She tore it open, and a typewritten note with a crackly piece of paper wrapped in it fell out. Madge picked it up for her, and Joey unfolded it. For a moment the printing danced before her eyes. Then the words settled themselves, and she was able to read it.

There was a long silence. Then she turned to her sister. "Madge! They—they've given me the second prize! The five pounds prize is mine! Here it is!"

She held the five-pound note out to her sister. Not knowing what else to do, Madge took it, and then pulled the child down to her level. "Joey baba! I'm so glad!"

Then Jo disgraced herself for once in her life. Burying her head on her sister's shoulder she burst into tears, and cried as she had not done for ages. Madge held her close, petting and soothing her, till the outburst was over.

Then Jo suddenly sat up. Her eyes were swollen and red, and so was her nose, but this in no way detracted from her sudden sense of importance. "This settles it," she announced, with a hiccough. "I'm going to start in right now and be AN AUTHORESS!"

CHAPTER TWENTY-FIVE

The End of Term

"Good-bye, Wanda; good-bye, Marie! Sure you've got everything? Good-bye, Paula! I hope you will all have very happy holidays."

"*Auf wiedersehen, Madame!* We wish you the same! We'll send you post-cards from Prague, if we may."

"Please do! Good-bye, Thrya and Inga! Enjoy yourselves in Cologne! Ready, Margia? Good-bye, then! Remember me to your mother."

The last of the "early" people scrambled into the little mountain-train, which was running once more. They waved their hands excitedly out of the windows; there was a puff and a jerk; they were off!

Madge Bettany, standing on the path with her small sister and the Robin, waved to them, and then turned back with a sigh of relief.

"Let's get back to *Frühstück*," observed Joey, tucking her arm through her sister's. "I'm panting with hunger!"

"You look it," laughed Madge. "All right; come along. —Tired, Robin?"

The Robin shook her curly head. "No, t'ank you! But I *s'ould* like some milk!"

"You shall have it when we get back. Marie is sure to have it ready, because the Mensches, the Maranis, and the Steinbrückes are going by the next train; and Miss Durrant is taking Evadne, Juliet, Grizel, and Rosalie to Euhrbach by the ten o'clock bus."

"We *shall* be empty!" sighed Jo.

"Yes; but only till midday. Then we and Miss Maynard go off in the Paris-Wien express, and we shall be in England on Saturday."

"Why didn't Mademoiselle wait and go with us?" asked Joey.

"Because Signora di Ricci wanted Vanna home as soon as possible, and she had to change at Innsbruck. It was easier for all the Italian girls to go together, and for Mademoiselle to take the French girls and look after them all."

"I see," said Jo thoughtfully. "And Miss Maynard is at Spärtz to put the early people on to the proper trains, I suppose?"

Madge nodded. "Yes. Now you know all about it."

"Yes, I know *that*; and I know we're going to stay with Miss Maynard in the New Forest, which is gorgeous! But isn't there something else?"

"How do you mean—something else?"

"I don't know. Only there's a sat-on sort of feeling, as if something *thrilling* were going to happen!"

"In a way you're right. I hope to go to the big Guiders' Camp to train for a week while we are in England."

"When?" demanded Joey excitedly. "Oh, Madge! *Are* we starting Guides for certain sure next term?"

"We are, indeed! As for when, I think it's the second week of the holidays. You and Robin will be with the Maynards by yourselves. You know we are going to London to stay with the aunts for the first week, don't you?"

"Yes; and I jolly well wish we weren't!"

"Hush, Jo! You are not to say things like that! They want us; and we couldn't possibly be in England and not go to see them! They would never forgive us if we did that!"

"Well, I know it's jolly decent of them, and all that; but they bore me!" declared Jo. "They will talk about taking care; and say I'm delicate; and fuss, *fuss*, FUSS till I want to shy things round!"

Miss Bettany laughed. "Poor old thing! What an awful state of mind! However, you needn't worry! I don't think they'll fuss over you this time! The Tyrol has certainly made a big difference to you. You don't look like the same girl!"

"I know I'm fatter! And I've grown heaps! That frock I had this time last year won't go near me! Well, what do we do after London?"

"You two go down to Winchester on the Monday, where Miss Maynard will meet you and take you to her home. I shall come the following Monday. We leave England on the twenty-fifth, and get back here about the twenty-ninth. School begins on May the second. Now you know all our holiday plans, and I hope you're both satisfied."

"Razzer!" said the Robin emphatically.

But Jo looked doubtful. Madge shot a glance at her. There *was* more to tell, but she felt that she would rather keep it until they were by themselves, and she could explain things thoroughly. However, they reached the school just then, and there was no time for more, for Marie was ringing for *Frühstück*, and they had to hurry to get to the table in time.

It was a festive meal. All rules were in abeyance, and the people left chattered all at once, and in a wild mingling of English and German, which made the Chalet *Speisesaal* sound more like the monkey-house at the Zoo than anything else. When it was over, there was a scramble to finish up the oddments and see to the locking-up of cupboards. The Chalet was to be closed for three weeks, during which Marie and Eigen would be at home, taking Rufus with them. Zita had gone back to her owners, who had been almost hysterically grateful to Miss Bettany for her care of the great dog during the winter.

Herr Braun had undertaken to keep an eye on the place, and also to have the new fence put up while Miss Bettany was away. He had one or two schemes of his own, which related to the rolling of the cricket-pitches and the tennis-courts, the planting of a flower-garden, and so on. Of these, however, he said nothing as yet.

Nine o'clock brought Herr Mensch up to Briesau to escort the Innsbruck girls back to their own city, and to offer Miss Bettany a basket of little cakes from Frau Marani and his wife, "to be eaten on the journey, *mein Kind*. And here is chocolate for *die Mädchen* from *Grossmütter*."

When he had gone off with his charges, Miss Durrant was taken down to the steamer with hers. They were to catch the bus at Scholastika, and go by it to the nearest town, just over the border, into Germany. Then they would take train to Euhrbach, in the Black Forest. It was a roundabout journey, but all the people concerned had plumped for it, declaring that would be far more fun than going *viâ* Innsbruck and Munich.

At last the Bettanys and the Robin were alone; and, as they walked slowly round the lake to Seespitz to catch the mountain-train to Spärtz, Madge told her news to the two little girls.

"Do you remember how ill poor Mr. Denny has been?" she began.

"Yes," said Joey soberly. "But he's better now."

"Yes; he is better now," agreed her sister. "Dr. Jem says that so long as he remains up here in the mountain air he will be fairly all right. But he is to go still higher. Do you remember the day we climbed the Sonnencheinspitze last summer?"

"*I* wasn't zere," said the Robin reproachfully.

Madge smiled at her. "No; I know you weren't. But Joey remembers."

"Rather!" said that young lady. "Is he going up there?"

"Yes. They are building a huge place—a sanatorium—up there in the little village on the Sonnalpe, and Dr. Jem is going to take charge of it. He won't live there: he's going to have a chalet built above the village, where he will live."

"Coo! Won't he be lonely?" queried Jo with interest.

A little smile edged Madge's lips. "At first he may. But it won't be for long. You see, he's going to be married."

Joey stood stock-still in the middle of the path. "*Married!* Who to? Oh! How absolutely *rotten* of him!"

"Joey!" Madge fairly gasped.

"Well, it is! Oh, he *is* a mean! I just hate him!" And Joey turned and walked on, frowning heavily.

"Joey!" Madge's voice was sharp with dismay. "Why, I thought you liked him so much!"

"I *did*! I don't now! I think he's a pig! I'll never speak to him again!"

"But, Joey, why?" Madge was so much upset that she forgot to scold Jo for unparliamentary language.

"To go and get *married*! To a beastly stranger!"

The elder girl's face relaxed. "*Oh!* But—but—it *isn't* a stranger, Joey dear!"

Jo looked up sharply. Then the slow colour flushed her face. "Madge!"

"Yes, Joey!" Madge's eyes were starry, and she looked lovely as she smiled at her little sister. "You won't hate him, Joey dear, when he is—your brother!"

Joey's answer was to fling her arms round her sister, nearly upsetting the pair of them into the lake, and hug her vehemently. "Oh, Madge! Really, truly? Oh, I *am* so glad! I've wanted it for ages! He's such a dear—nearly nice enough for you! "

The whistle of the engine interrupted them then, and they had to tear across to the train, and only just got in in time. There were very few passengers, and no one but themselves in their carriage, so Madge finished her story on the way down.

"We shan't be married for a year at least, Joey. Probably it will be two years. I want to see the school well begun, and he has to establish his sanatorium. And I'm young yet; so I shall be Head of the Chalet School for some time yet. When we are married, you and the Robin will live with us till you have homes of your own; for, Robin, your father is leaving Russia, and coming to be Jem's secretary up here. Isn't that splendid?"

The Robin snuggled closer. "I am so glad, Tante Marguerite! And *Monsieur le docteur*, he will be my Oncle Zem, *n'est-ce pas*? And Papa and Zoë, too?—Zoë, you shall call my papa 'Oncle,' too! Oh, it will be nice! "

"Nice! " Joey repeated her words rapturously. "It'll be gorgeous!—Oh, Madge, it's just the very nicest and splendidest of all our adventures! "

Madge looked down at the slender ring on her left hand, where a sapphire glowed in the sunshine, blue as the waters of the Tiernsee under summer skies, and smiled softly to herself. "I think so, too! " she said.

THE END